SINNER'S GAME

TERINA ADAMS

To the one who champions my silent wars, nurses my wounds and sets me on my feet again.

CHAPTER 1

"Powerful factions rule this city. Just remember that. Don't go taking unnecessary risks. Keep y'self to y'self, learn what ya can, and return. Y'hear me?" Auntie Bea yelled from the kitchen.

"Got it," I yelled back.

"And don't talk to anyone. Guaranteed most won't be human. I better add some angelica to the mix." She grunted and huffed as she moved around the kitchen, retrieving what she needed to add to the foul concoction she expected me to either wear, gargle, swallow, or burn. Most of what she gave me rarely worked because Aunt Bea was a rummy. Plus, her understanding of herbal magick sucked.

She grew agitated in the days leading up to a retrieval, forcing me to sift through her gathered information a few times over, ticking off the details from a checklist of must-dos, meticulously penned on pieces of paper then left to sprawl haphazardly across the table—Auntie Bea had yet to go digital despite being adept at internet searches. Tonight was purely a reconnoiter: scope out the playing field and learn the contenders in the game. But the way Auntie Bea was acting, you'd think tonight was the retrieval. She'd never been this wound. This artifact must have particular importance. Why else would she be on the verge of pinging off the walls of our cramped, crappy apartment? Of course, any artifact of particular importance attracted powerful and dangerous people.

Her back was to me when I entered the kitchen. The loose skin at the back of her arms jiggled in rhythm to the clink of the pestle on the side of the mortar as she vigorously blended the herbs.

"It smells awful. What have you put in it this time?" I asked from over her shoulder, then blinked a couple of times to clear the swirl of her cigarette smoke from my eyes.

"That's dinner. Give it a stir, will ya?"

"I'm not hungry." I never was, pre-event.

She did a double take at me. "Ya not going like that?"

I glanced down at my leather jacket and denims, looking for rips or stains. "They're clean."

"Smithson and Row. Look it up," she grunted, jerking her head toward the table and her phone. A line of ash broke away from the tip of the cigarette hanging from the corner of her mouth and disintegrated to the floor. "You won't make it through the door looking like that."

I pulled my phone from my back pocket and turned to lean against the chipped melamine cupboard. The side strip was peeling off and caught on the zipper of my back pocket. The rental was a dive, but Auntie Bea had paid the bond and signed the paperwork before I'd even seen the place. "Who said I was going through the front door?"

"Forget it, girlie. Ya ain't getting in unless it's through the front door. Don't play cute. Not tonight. This ain't no back-alley deal. You're not talking rich old men out of their prized possessions or fooling young wealthy men out of money." Her grinding grew more vigorous as she spoke. A thin film of sweat had broken out on her forehead and beaded in the corner of her nose.

She dropped the pestle in the bowl with a tink and spun to face me. A jab of her finger in my direction flung more ash from her cigarette. "We're talking seriously dangerous people. Fucking powerful people."

"Hmm...I see your point." I dismissed her scaremongering and stared at the page opening on my phone. Slowly, because we had sketchy internet in Dim Bazaar. "It's very ritzy."

"The best auction house on both sides of the equator, in West Tuzet, which means fucking rich." She stabbed her cigarette back inside her mouth but continued to talk around it. "Millions...billions of dollars pass through its door every year."

"And how exactly do you propose I do this? It won't be easy to break into."

"Oh, blessed mother." She flung her arms into the air, taking a deep drag of her cigarette, flaring the tip a brilliant red. "Use ya head, girl. Alcatraz is a playground compared to what will be there tonight. I don't want ya causing a shit storm. You need to look like one of them potted plants they got all over the corridors." Her smokey exhale flowed around the words as she pointed at the image on my phone.

"Since when has an artifact been so valuable?"

"Since the skull surfaced."

"Skull?"

"It's made of stone."

"And the skull is special because...?" Typical Auntie Bea. She left the most important bits of information 'til last, sometimes withholding them altogether. Given most of the artifacts she'd hunted until now were little more than party trick trinkets, it mattered little what their magical properties were.

"What does it matter?"

"I'm about to enter a room full of powerful and deadly people, more than half of them likely not human, so I think that earns me extra intel."

Her eyes narrowed as she glared at me through her trail of smoke. The glare continued for minutes. I folded my arms across my chest and slumped back against the cupboard, ready to do this all night.

One grunt, and she snatched her cigarette out of her mouth and headed for the table. Another grunt eased her down into the closest seat, the stub of her cigarette disappearing into the dregs of her lukewarm coffee. It hissed as it went out, sending up a final swirl of smoke.

Years of herbal tinctures, odd concoctions, and spells, from magical and non-magical people alike, had failed. Nothing halted the slow but steady increase in her weight, which had, according to her, nothing to do with her diet of alcohol and excessive dairy consumption.

She shoved the coffee cup away, exposing a coffee ring left on the table. None of the furniture was ours, which meant everything would need a good scrub to remove the residue of Auntie Bea when our rental term ended. Cup out the way, she sifted through the loose paper sprawled across the table. I slid into the plastic chair beside her and waited until she found what she was looking for.

Gathering background was her part of the job. She was too old and too...generously proportioned to be of much use on the active side of the job. Besides, there were too many debt collectors after her head for her to wander out much these days.

Auntie Bea had a gambling problem. I didn't want to be traveling around the country with my aunt acquiring magical artifacts, but she was a disaster at looking after herself. And to be honest, I'd grown used to the easy cash this line of work provided. Better than getting up every morning and heading to a dead-end job that sucked all joy from your life. We split the proceeds from the sales of the magical artifacts. After four years, I'd grown a nice stash for my future, but it was fast dwindling because various debt collectors turned up in the early hours of the morning. My money got us to Davenport. Bea's money—in accordance with our deal—paid for our accommodation, which was the reason we found ourselves in this dump in Dim Bazaar, the seediest part of the city.

Mugshots passed before my eyes. She grew increasingly agitated. I snatched up a sheet of paper. A man in his fifties with receded hairline, bulldog cheeks, and a mustache trimmed into a neat line above his top lip looked back.

"Mr Hugo Mendale. CEO of Yarra Industries. Dabbles in the

property market and imports luxury boats. Net worth ...seven hundred and forty-six million. Human?"

Auntie Bea stopped her search and pointed to a bullet point toward the bottom of the dossier. Alongside species, she'd written: human.

"Where's your map of Davenport?"

"Why?"

"I want to see where Spard Cross is."

"Why?"

"It's where Mr Hugo Mendale lives. It's likely the ritziest district. I bet his house doesn't constantly smell of Korean takeout."

"Never mind that." She snapped another piece of paper on top of Mr Mendale, stabbing at the image of a bright blue skull.

"That's what a man worth seven-hundred something million dollars is hoping to buy?"

"You haven't reached the seriously rich ones yet."

"Are you going to tell me what's special about the skull?" I lifted the Smithson and Row pamphlet to have a closer read.

"It's a seeker."

I glanced across at her. "A what?"

"It finds things."

"You're joking."

Auntie Bea's expression remained pencil ruled.

"That's all? I expected invincibility, enhanced magical powers, immortality."

"The most powerful paranormals already have those abilities."

"True. What's the point in living forever if you keep losing your socks and underwear?"

"What if ya wish to find oil or gold? Or any rich, untapped deposit anywhere in the world? What if ya wish to hunt down your greatest enemy, who has the means of becoming a ghost? What if ya wish to find really powerful artifacts?"

"That's why you want it so bad."

"Good by peanuts. We'd make serious money. Hello Spard Cross. Better still, hello world."

"According to this, it's an Aztec artifact."

"They dunno what they're fucking on about. No one knows its true origins. Only what it can do."

Auntie Bea stretched across the table and dragged a tattered file toward her. Photocopied images pulled from various grimoires were stuffed inside, and some of them flew free when she wrenched the file open. This was Auntie Bea's own grimoire, comprised of photocopies of pages she'd gathered in secret with the help of myself and some sympathetic witches. Being a rummy with no real magical talent, the coven denied Auntie Bea entrance to their library. Worst still, they'd banished her from the coven.

Stealing knowledge from a wide source, Auntie Bea had gathered an extensive collection of interesting spells, most of which never worked for her, and a definitive list of magical artifacts, which she used to finance our lives. It had been three years since she got the mad idea of tracking down all the magical artifacts in her file. Three years of being on the road. Three years she didn't have to live with the humiliation of being a witch shunned from her coven.

She flicked through the pages of the file, scattering loose sheets. "It's in here somewhere."

"Don't worry about it. I'm not interested in all the details. Nor am I interested in reading all of this." I pushed sheets of paper away.

Auntie Bea slammed her file closed, then reached for her cigarette packet. If only she'd listen to my nagging and stop her disgusting habit. She usually smoked outside, on my insistence, but she'd been jittery since arriving in Davenport—more jittery than usual—and this dive of an apartment had no balcony. I'd relented for tonight, given her anxious energy, and granted her pardon to chain smoke her way through the two packets she'd had me pick up this afternoon, along with the bottle of gin. But after tonight, that was it. She'd have to make her way down the stairs to the street to have a smoke, and that might be enough to dissuade her from having so many.

After lighting the smoke and drawing in a long drag, she was ready to lecture me. Cigarette caught between her scissored fingers, stabbing them my way, she said, "Listen. There's only one way to play a sinner's game. And that's to win. Which means ya must know everything ya can about your opponents."

She took another long drag before reaching for her gin and glass. This game was in Bea's blood. As much as she stressed and worried over each job, when she held that artifact in her hand, her face glowed. Adding to that glow was the thrill she gained by forcing people with more magical ability than herself to squabble amongst themselves as they haggled to be the successful bidder.

The shot disappeared in one gulp, washing the smoke from her cigarette down her throat. "Let's run over the plan?"

"I'm to imitate a pot plant."

"Don't make eye contact. Don't talk to anyone. Don't even scratch your fucking nose. I'm not fucking paying for it. There'll be plenty bidding, plenty more watching those that bid, and plenty more again just waiting for the auction to end, so they can get their hands on what's not theirs by force. Once you know who ends up with it, you leave, come straight home, and tell me who it is."

"Then we send one of my little pals in."

Auntie Bea nodded and stared at the wall, absent-mindedly scratching the side of her chin before taking another drag. "I'll bet my ass many others will be making their plans to steal it. We've gotta move fast, but not so fast as we don't stay smart. We have one opportunity. Whoever wins it will lock that one away, making it impossible to retrieve."

"Why don't I take it tonight? I could—"

"Nah way." She shook her head. "Nah way. It's too dangerous."

The pounding at our door silenced her.

"Are we expecting anyone?"

"Shh," she hissed. She leaned close. "Stay quiet. They'll think we're not home."

"They probably heard us talking just now."

To punctuate my point, more pounding hammered the door. The sort of pounding that meant business.

"Auntie Bea," I growled in frustration, still keeping my voice low. "One week. That's all it's been." What mess had she got herself into now? She may be a rummy, but Auntie Bea had a magical gift for ticking off powerful people.

"I ain't done nothing."

"I'm going to answer the door."

She grabbed my arm, manacling her fingers until it hurt. "Don't you dare. We'll hide in the bedroom. They'll go away soon enough."

And with that, the door blew off its hinges, spiraling into the faux-leather couch. It felt like the noise blew out my eardrums. Auntie Bea shrieked, dragging me down with her as she dived under the table, our chairs clattering to the floor with us. I didn't think she could move that fast.

Two thuggish men stood in the now open doorway. One had ginger hair, a beard that reached down over his rounded belly, and skin so pale it was almost translucent. The other was dark-skinned, half the height of his friend, and at least one hundred pounds lighter.

Ginger moved through the door first, squeezing out his pal. Big, booted feet ate up the short distance in our cramped, crappy apartment. The skinny guy caught up, coming to stand at the side of his pal. "Which one of yous is Bea Jennings?"

"The fat, old bitch under the table," said the fat ginger haired guy.

"Get up," the skinny guy barked.

"We're here for a chat," said his pal. I got a waft of fried onion rings as he righted one of the downed chairs and straddled it, his ass hanging over the sides.

I helped Auntie Bea up as best I could, but she was a large woman. While she huffed and heaved, ginger helped himself to the gin, pouring half a glass and downing it in one long gulp. The sleeve of his leather jacket inched up his arm to reveal the runic symbol of the devourer tattooed on the inside of his right wrist.

Apostles of Eternal Night. Diviners of the darkest arts.

"I'll have something sorted real soon," Auntie Bea said, with little conviction in her voice, straining to get on her feet. I righted her chair and helped ease her back onto it.

"Whatever you're after—"

"Shut it, kid."

I was taken aback by being called a kid more than anything else. I had dealt with a long list of men chasing after debts Auntie Bea struggled to pay. After a while, you learned how to speak their lingo. But the debt collectors that usually came to our door were human. Based on the way they opened the door and the tattoo on ginger's wrist, these guys were anything but human.

Auntie Bea grabbed my hand and pulled me down onto the chair next to her. Pressing her lips together, she gave a gentle shake of her head. Shut the freaking hell up it said.

"See, the boss wants his payment now. Real soon is not now, is it? And we were told we weren't to leave, unless we left with cash or your ears." Ginger's eyes strayed to me, wandering from my legs in my tight denims up my body. They got lost at my chest before skipping up to my face. "We might take this piece of ass to sweeten the boss's mood. She may get a little damaged on the way, but the boss ain't gonna know how she started out, now is he?"

"We've got something big." I dived across the table, scattering papers as I frantically searched for the pamphlet, avoiding looking at Auntie Bea. "See this?" I shoved the pamphlet toward ginger, who snatched it out of my hand. The skinny guy moved in to read over his shoulder, or rather look. I doubted he could read.

"That piece of shit?" skinny said.

I half-stood, so I could lean over enough to point at the image of the blue skull. "That there is valuable beyond measure to people in the know."

"How's a fucking skull worth shit?" ginger said.

Not only were these guys likely illiterate, but both knew little about magical artifacts. Dumb muscle. The dumb muscle was usually kept out of sacred arts, the more powerful magic. Regardless, they had more magical tricks available to them than Auntie Bea or I. My innate magic extended only to influencing animals. It was enough to elevate me from being a rummy, but it wasn't a match for warlock power.

"That piece of shit is why all the powerful paranormals of Davenport will be at Smithson and Row tonight."

"What does that mean for us?" ginger asked.

"Just think what your boss will say if you bring him the skull."

They looked between them. "If it's that important, the boss will be there," skinny said.

"We've as good as got it." In my periphery, I saw Bea jerk, but I ignored her. "Your boss will miss out, but not if you let us retrieve it for you."

"You got something special inside that skinny little body of yours? 'Cause I don't see nothing that's gonna make me believe what you're saying," ginger said.

"A few men have underestimated me. The ones alive know better now." Talking like this was something I learned from my dealings with the many debt collectors who'd come before. It was all BS, but spoken with conviction, you could make anyone believe it.

Ginger death-stared at me until it was beyond comfortable. I stayed with him, matching his eye lock with equal intensity. That's what you had to do with these sorts of people. Thank god he wasn't from a pack, or he'd hear the mad rhythm of my heart.

Ginger burst out laughing, arching his head back to release a bellow that made his belly shake like Jello. As quick as he started, he stopped. "You have twenty-four hours to bring us the skull."

What? Hell. "I need more time."

"If you've as good as got it, you shouldn't need more time."

"Give me four days."

"Whadda ya reckon?" Ginger asked skinny.

"Four days. Then we take some souvenirs. First the fat bitch. And then you."

"Fair," I said.

The two wasted time eyeballing us some more to make sure we understood the threat and the depth of their commitment before crunching over the remains of the door as they left.

"The Apostles. What're you doing getting mixed up with them?"

"I didn't know they were involved."

I launched from my seat. Pacing was a better idea to cool the steam. "We just arrived. How can you already be causing trouble?"

"I ain't done nothing here. It was back in Snowton. They must have put a tracker on me. That concealment spell didn't work."

I was about to say nothing ever worked for her, but Auntie Bea was understandably sensitive about her lack of significant ability. "It's the Apostles, Auntie Bea, a little spell won't cut it. I can't believe you left without settling your debt."

"I couldn't pay. Alright."

"You should've told me. I would've sorted it out." Like I always did.

"Not this time, Laz."

"How much did you lose?"

She waved her hand dismissively. With the back of her other hand, she wiped at her nose, then sniffled. "Just forget it. We need to focus on the skull, now that you've handed it over to the fucking warlock high priest."

"I would've thought you'd welcome keeping your ears."

Auntie Bea dived for her packet of cigarettes, tapping one out with trembling fingers. The last cigarette slipped from the packet and fell to the floor. "Curse them fucking Apostles." She threw the empty packet across the table and collapsed forward, her face buried in her palms.

"I'll go change into something more appropriate for Smithson and Row, while you compile a list of the deadlier paranormals expected there tonight. The ones you think I should keep my distance from."

"What's the point? We've lost the skull. No way can we keep it from the Apostles now."

"It will keep us alive."

She sat up, wiping her eyes. "You're right. Where's my phone?" On finding it, buried under her paperwork, she glanced at the screen. "If you dress quick, we'll have enough time to go to church."

"Really?" I pressed my lips together before I could say anymore.

Every city we passed through, every time, rejection. But still she tried. But I guess everyone needed a home, somewhere they felt welcomed by their own. Poor Auntie Bea was an outcast, ostracized for something that wasn't her fault.

"We'll need all the divine help we can get," she said.

One week we'd been here, and I no longer smelled the exotic spies of the Korean food wafting up the stairwell and into our apartment. The fragrance permeated into the walls and gaudy brown carpet in the bedrooms so that I could close my eyes while eating a bacon sandwich at the kitchen table and believe it was Korean barbecue beef or mandoo.

Auntie Bea found the stairwell an epic journey that could only be done in stages. The two flights of stairs left her feeling like she'd completed the ironman championships. The single bulb, with its dull yellow glow, flickered a few times on our descent, threatening to blink out all together, which may not have been a bad thing. At least we'd be spared seeing the questionable stains smeared along the wall like the bloody hands prints of a dying man.

I was almost at the bottom when Chong Hyun-woo burst out of the Korean store, skipped the last two steps and collided with me, sending me backward in my lace-up high-heeled sandals onto my butt. Thank the mother I'd changed into a black V-necked jumpsuit and not the silk wrap mini dress, which would've flashed my knickers by now.

"Larnie, so sorry." He reached for my hand and gently pulled me up.

Chong Hyun-woo's family immigrated here with little money when Chong Hyun-woo was ten. Along with the help of the local charity center, their ethic of working hard bought them this building. They rented the space upstairs to help pay the land tax and turned the shop down below into a Korean grocery store and restaurant.

"I was coming up to see you."

"Were you?" I smoothed my braided updo before I could stop myself. Chong Hyun-woo was a really sweet guy. With his gorgeous golden skin, he was easy on the eye, not to mention around my age, single, and obviously interested. It had been like...forever since I dated a guy. It's kind of hard to do when you're always on the move. Even harder when you're not entirely human.

"My parents saw two men that looked like members of the Turono gang heading up to your apartment, then they heard a loud noise, like a mini explosion. They were too scared to go and see. But they saw the men leave. I would've come sooner to check on you, but I was out on a delivery."

"We're fine. As you can see. Who's the Turono gang?"

He smiled his perfect white teeth, which looked brilliant white set against his golden skin and black hair. "Yeah, sorry. I forget you're not from around here. Turono owe Dim Bazaar. I probably don't need to say anymore."

"It wasn't them. But our front door came off its hinges. Your parents must've heard when it hit the floor."

"I'll come take a look."

"Not now." I placed my hand on his left pec to stall him—noting the honed muscle under my palm—as he made to head upstairs. The dossiers Auntie Bea decided weren't important enough to bring with us, she'd left scattered on the table, along with her photocopied grimoire. She was not normally so careless, but the Apostles had given her adrenaline fever. Life-threatening situations had a habit of doing that.

Chong Hyun-woo stalled, one foot on the step above, and turned his dark eyes to me. In his expression I could've said we were more than acquaintances or neighbors, that the night held a promise both of us were eager to explore.

Oh, mother, I was eager to explore it…with him.

The heavy thuds and huffs of Auntie Bea descending behind me scrubbed the moment. I withdrew my hand as he glanced down at my clothes, the understanding glinting in his eyes. "You're on your way out."

A redundant statement, made awkwardly obvious by the fact we'd met him coming down the stairs.

"What about your door? You're going out without locking it?"

"Your parents are diligent at neighborhood watch. We have somewhere important to be. It can't wait."

"Yeah, sure. I'll fix your door first thing tomorrow."

"Thanks, Chong Hyun-woo."

"Just call me Hyun-woo."

"Okay."

We stared at each other for seconds longer than searched for other places to look while Auntie Bea grunted and cursed her way to the bottom of the stairs. "Chong Hyun-woo," she panted.

He bowed. "Ee-mo." I had introduced her by her full name, Beatrice Jennings, but out of respect he used the title Aunt.

"When's that lift going in?"

He laughed nervously, never sure whether she was joking because she only ever used one tone, harsh.

"We're outta here," Auntie Bea snapped, cutting off any further chatter.

"Sorry." I shrugged at him. "But we'll see you tomorrow."

"What's happening tomorrow?"

"Hyun-woo is going to fix the door that fell off its hinges."

"And the hinges. Too cheap or really old," she snapped again, then grabbed my elbow and pulled me to the exit.

The Chong's Korean restaurant and store were on the corner of the entrance to Chinatown, demarcated by a red-bannered archway and two stone dragons atop large stone plinths. Outside Chinatown markets, the streets of Dim Bazaar were a bustle at night, more so than during the day. Hawkers hassled pedestrians, selling everything from cheap watches to a hit of crack or tickets to a variety of peep shows, depending on your kink, at the many sex shops lining the street. The shops closed at night, boarding their windows for protection. If it wasn't for the sex shops and street food vendors with their food carts lit up with a festoon of small lights that turned the carts into insect magnets, Dim Bazaar would resemble a black hole.

A bus pulled up at the nearest stop, forcing Auntie Bea into a shuffling run, wheezing and huffing the four or so meters to the stop. I fared little better in my high heels. They were impractical, but it wasn't often I got to wear shoes like these, so I had to make the most of it.

The bus driver pulled away before we'd found our seats and Auntie Bea dominoed into me. I barely remained standing, sliding into the closest seat to the rear door before I hit the floor.

Once seated beside me, Auntie Bea said, "watch that boy."

I looked over my shoulder, expecting to see a beady eyed kid ready to steal off with someone's wallet.

"Chong Hyun-woo," Auntie Bea said with a heavy sigh.

"Don't be stupid."

"You're being stupid. This ain't his world."

"It's more his world than ours. We're the new arrivals."

"Ya know what I mean. Don't drag the kid into our shit mess."

"It's nothing."

"Bullshit, it's nothing. His eyes gobbled ya up back there."

"No, they didn't." *Did they?*

"Don't open the door, Laz. He'll blindly step through. Then what ya gonna do? We don't have time for regret."

"I was being polite. You ought to try it sometime."

She snorted. "I don't have time for polite." Out of habit, she reached into the pocket of her housedress, the one that looked like a sack and curled her lip when she failed to find her cigarettes.

"You can't smoke on public transport, anyway."

"Bloody shit rules. I'd hang it out the window."

"I gather you know where we're going."

"Pend South is two districts over." She dove into her satchel and pulled out the stack of dossiers, dumping them in my lap. "Go over those during the ride."

She'd reduced the scatter of papers from the table to a mere ten. On the top was a striking-looking man, despite his age of sixty-three. Mega-wealthy didn't come close to describing the amount of digits that came after the first numbers. He was more a Carlo or a Conrad than a Bernard, which reminded me of a cartoon I loved as a child.

"Watch him. He'll be top of the list. With more money than most combined. If ya split him open, rather than guts, ya'd find cash spewing out. He's a munsib."

"So he knows the true value of the skull."

"And will likely win the auction."

Munsib were humans. And some of them knew about the other side of life. Usually the wealthiest, because certain players in the paranormal community made a habit of enlisting them for nefarious means. Bernard Preston was a recruit most would want backing their plans.

"Who's protecting him?"

"That's never easy to find. My guess is the Order of Sotiria."

The nephilim. Only males were born, and they spent their life preaching the gospel of their god out of blood loyalty to their bound masters, but never did they put said preaching into practice. With their angelic fathers bound for eternity, there was no one around to pull their reins. Their business networks spread across the globe like a spider's web, infiltrating into the filth of humanity. Most of their wealth came from trafficking of every sort: stolen antiquities, modern art, arms, drugs, and women. Mostly women, because the nephilim inherited the curse of their fathers, to crave the daughters of man for eternity. It was their own sort of hell on earth because their lust would never be satiated. And while that may sound like a heaven on earth for most men, their lust burned through them like hellfire, making even the act of sex a torment, but still they hunger for more.

"They want it. He'll hand it to them the moment he leaves the room."

"Why don't they do it themselves?"

"They want to remain faceless. That way there'll be no trouble for them."

The nephilim were not angels in deeds and strength. Their angelic power was diluted through the human bond, which meant they weren't the most powerful paranormals around. Another reason they liked to recruit wealthy munsib to do a lot of their messy work. With angelic fathers, they were forever flagellating themselves for their chosen path while furthering their dark endeavors.

I lowered the stack of papers to my lap and stared out the window. What mess were we getting into? This was way above any job I'd done before. Normally, the artifacts I retrieved were too insignificant to mean much to powerful paranormals, which left me to steal from munsibs ignorant of the power encapsulated within the ancient trinket they held in their hands. Auntie Bea then pawned them to paranormals too far down the rankings to be of any real danger to us. She was looking straight ahead when I glanced her way. My dearest rummy, Auntie Bea, the only family I knew. I wouldn't tell her the plan sucked so bad we were going to get ourselves dismembered, because if we didn't win we were going to be dismembered. We had to be the ones to win.

We'd left the graffitied, dingy streets of the poor quarters behind and moved into classier neighborhoods. Like we'd crossed a divide, the streets widened. Ample lighting haloed down from lampposts spaced evenly apart, revealing lush street scapes and trees lining the curb. Apartments jammed close together morphed into houses with expansive lawns and a garage.

The bus made a left turn into Mewchamp street, according to the signpost. The great expanse of darkness on my side of the bus turned out to be an unlit parkland, stretching for blocks. Auntie Bea signaled our stop.

"Here?"

"Come on. The asshole's likely to drive off while my foot's still on the bottom step."

I followed as she shuffled to the rear door and off. The red taillights glowed bright like hell beasts in the night as the bus pulled away. No traffic crawled the street, no dogs barked, no sounds of noise from any of the houses. The place reeked of desolation.

"Where's the church?"

"There." Auntie Bea pointed toward the end of the parkland.

The bus disappeared around the corner at the end of the street, leaving us in the dark, except for two old-fashioned lanterns hanging either side of the arched entrance to the gothic stone church. Their golden light lit the angry faces of the two gargoyles sitting above them. The back of the church was nestled behind the park's dense shrubbery. As we neared, the shrubs receded, revealing soft flickering lights inside, tarnished a deep red from the vaulted stained glass window.

Those paranormals who practiced magic gathered in churches or temples and worshipped their gods or goddesses as a way to enhance their magic. To be honest, given I'd had little to do with the church, I found it hard to believe the gods or goddess had much influence over the paranormal world, but I was in the minority. Even Auntie Bea desperately clung to the hope our Dark Mother would rescue her from her rummy plight one day.

But there was one breed of magic wielder who kept clear of any church and didn't seem to suffer magically for doing so. Sorcerers—loners, rarely seen. Auntie Bea believes there are few born or still alive. No one in our coven—for the short time we had stayed within the coven after my initiation—had ever meet one.

Auntie Bea stopped at the bottom step. "Right. Ya ready?" She took a deep breath, pressing a hand to her stomach.

"You really want to do this?"

"We need all the help we can muster."

"I have my protection bag of goodies." I tapped my purse and the magical blend Auntie Bea had mixed earlier and gave to me in a pouch.

She frowned at my purse, knowing too well the pouch would do nothing for me. "So, we'll go up." She looked up the stairs to the entrance.

We stayed at the bottom on the street.

"I can handle the job just fine without any extra help." I hated seeing her feeling so small.

"No. Everything must be perfect."

"Okay, Auntie Bea." I waited for her to find her courage. The auction was going to start before we made it through the church doors.

"Right. We'll do it." She exhaled.

While I didn't always understand her need to punish herself like this, I would stand by her. I held out my hand. "We'll go together."

She made a dismissive noise and waved my hand away. "We're wasting time." Given the light was poor, Auntie Bea climbed with care.

There were always those in need of sanctuary or spiritual guidance, and so the church doors remained opened twenty-four seven. But not just to anyone. Wards were placed to keep the unbelievers out, particularly curious munsib who may have decided the church looked interesting enough to warrant a look inside. They would suddenly forget why they had climbed the stairs. At least that's how they did it at the church back home. But it had been a long time since I set foot inside. Maybe the practices had changed.

Halfway to the top of the steps and a low growl reverberated through the air. The guardian of the entrance appeared, a massive black dog with deep yellow eyes. Positioned in front of the door, her white fangs glistened in the lamplight. A drop of saliva dripped from her gums to the stone at her feet.

There was a time, before my initiation into the coven, before I knew I was a witch, when I would get terrible, frightening visions so vivid I found it hard to distinguish reality from what was in my head. Luckily, those visions had disappeared after my dakeu. Perhaps because I now lived those visions most days.

"She won't let me in," Auntie Bea said with a slight quiver to her voice.

"We'll see about that."

Auntie Bea stopped midway up, fearful of antagonizing the guardian, who had been known to rip a limb or two from unwelcome visitors—witches included. I finished my ascent and stepped forward, extending my hand for her to sniff, approaching her as if she were a happy Labrador, reaching out with my mind until my awareness skimmed the border of hers. Her mind was a sealed gate, but I tapped my awareness along her hard mental borders, looking for a way in. That's when I felt a sudden spear lance through my mind.

"Arh, mother," I groaned and stumbled backward, clutching my head.

"I told you she wouldn't."

"Just give me a moment."

"She'll fry ya brain."

Ignoring Auntie Bea, I tentatively reached out my mind again, this time, stopping short of spidering my awareness across her mental barrack, and hovering just shy of the gate. The heat of her power radiated out across my awareness, threatening, as Auntie Bea said, to fry my brain.

One foot in front of the other, nice and slow, I approached her again. "Great guardian, we have come in worship of our Dark Mother." I opened my mind, peeled it back so that she could probe inside and see to the heart of my desire. I felt her awareness, her awesome power penetrate me, forcefully, in a demonstration of her might. I slid to my knees, brought down by the savagery with which she entered, clutching my head between my hands before it shattered into a dozen pieces. It hurt. It hurt so much, but if I did not give of myself, she would likely take a limb or three from Auntie Bea.

I collapsed on my hands, the pain of clenching my teeth stringing my neck muscles to taunt bows about to snap. Her awareness dived deep, violent, merciless, ripping apart every secret part of me. My instinct was to protect myself, fight back, snap my mind shut, but I did not. To resist her was death. She was in me now. All I could do was surrender to her, to the Dark Mother whose body she was borne from.

Her awareness left as suddenly as it had entered. That I was alive meant she was satisfied with what she found. I panted through the residing pain. When I raised my head, the guardian had gone, the door to the church slightly ajar.

"Thank her dark reverence, that worked," Auntie Bea said from beside me.

"Just." I groaned as she helped me to my feet. It was because of my connection with animals that the guardian could enter my mind.

The elders of the church, nor the high priestess, could dictate to our Dark Mother who could and could not worship her, something they had a habit of forgetting. The elders of the coven and the high priestess of the church may have excommunicated Auntie Bea, but the goddess would decide who she would welcome into her protection.

Auntie Bea's hand hovered on the heavy wooden door, an achingly long indecisive moment, before she pushed it open and stepped inside. Once I had entered, the door creaked closed behind me, latching into place with a heavy thunk. The smoke from the incense burning at either side of the nave bathed me in my favorite blend of protection herbs. The smell always felt like home to me, which was strange because I rarely entered the church, given Auntie Bea's excommunication.

Auntie Bea quick-footed her way down the nave to the altar, the fastest she'd moved in years, in a hurry to get this over with before anyone interceded, no doubt. My high heels clicked on the stone floor as I scurried after her, forcing her to spin at one point and glare at me.

"I can't help it."

"Take 'em off."

I rolled my eyes but did as she asked, only to feel a sudden presence behind me. I glanced over my shoulder and squeaked at the sight of the tall woman standing behind us. This was trouble. She was dressed in the customary black robe of the high priestess, wearing her ink-colored hair in a severe knot, which accentuated her deathly pale face, looking chiseled from marble, all hard lines and edges from her sharp pointed nose to her ridged cheekbones, jutting from her angular face. You could hang clothes off of those cheeks. Tall was an understatement. I'd lost a good few inches removing my shoes, letting the woman tower over me.

Her glass-blue eyes settled on me. "Welcome, daughter of our Dark Mother." Her eyes flicked like a whip to snare Auntie Bea in a cruel embrace. "Rummies are not welcome." The tone of her voice sliced through the silence. "I can smell her feebleness from here."

"The guardian welcomed her."

She looked down her pointed nose at me, the slight curl of her lip evident.

"Our Dark Mother accepts all disciples into her protection, regardless of their ability," I added.

The high priestess snatched my chin between her taloned fingers, sending prickles and tingles down my spine. Behind me, Auntie Bea let out a small gasp. "Do you question the authority of your high priestess?"

"No. But Auntie Bea's as much a witch as me. Her life is devoted to serving the Dark Mother. She's one of the most devout people I know."

Her eyes slitted. "You are new to Davenport. What brings you here?"

"Sightseeing."

Her lip curled. She likely sensed the lie. Fingers still grasping my chin, she turned my head from side to side as if she was searching for hickeys on my neck. When done, she returned my head to center but did not release her firm grip from my chin, digging the tips of her pointed nails into my flesh. "She's family?"

A frost settled over my organs just listening to her voice. I tried to nod within her hold.

"Your parents?"

"My mother's dead. I never knew my father." If only she'd release my face from her punishing grip.

Her eyes, like glass shards, continued to pierce through me, then they flared wide, but she kept whatever sudden surprise she'd gleaned to herself.

"We only wish to make an offering. Ask a boon of our Dark Mother," Auntie Bea stammered behind me.

The high priestess withdrew her hand, and I resisted the urge to rub my chin.

"A blood offering?"

"Yes, your dark eminence."

She inhaled, pulling herself to even taller heights. "Our Dark Mother welcomes the sacrifice." This time she purred. The smile she gave could rip a crack through the earth and bring hellfire through. But she had accepted Auntie Bea into the church, if only for now.

Auntie Bea remained where she was, her face a mask of disbelief. "Auntie Bea." I whispered, pushing her down the center of the nave. She staggered along still seized in surprise. Her steps faltered as we entered the sanctuary and stood before the altar. There, she collapsed to her knees, dragging me down with her so I dropped my heels and landed on my ass. Auntie Bea didn't notice, as she was busy prostrating herself. She was going to have a hard time getting herself off the floor.

"Dark Mother, Goddess Hekate, I'm your humble servant," she whispered to the stones.

She dipped her voice, so I barely made out her silent incantations. When done, she kissed the stone floor and began the arduous journey of getting to her feet. Behind the altar, the high priestess watched in silence, making no offer of help. The light from the black candles surrounding the stone offering vessel, shadowed the crevices on her face, painting a ghoulish mask of her features. The statue of our Dark Mother rose behind her, brandishing her flaming torch.

When, finally, Auntie Bea made it to her feet, with lots of help from me, she placed her palms flat on the stone altar and closed her eyes. I stared at the slight tremor in her hands as she attempted to gain strength from the solidity of the altar. A blood offering was both a blessing and a curse, and not a gift given lightly. The tension coiled my gut as I waited for Auntie Bea to take the final step.

Avoiding the icy glare from the high priestess, she picked up the offering blade and held her left hand over the vessel.

"Stop." The high priestess's cry sliced through the silence.

Auntie Bea faltered, the blade slipping from her grasp to clank in the offering vessel. She winced at the sound and making such a blunder.

"She will do it." The high priestess shifted her icy gaze to me.

"But...it's me whose asking for the boon."

"The girl, or no blood offering will be performed tonight."

A swirl of emotions spun through Auntie Bea's insipid gray eyes. Anxiousness, shame and sadness combined in a manic war for supremacy. To ask a boon of our Dark Mother came at a cost. Every blood offering was a binding to the goddess, a piece of soul taken, a slice of freedom lost. For the greedy few, desperate to feel the immense power temporarily infused with her gifts, it meant an eternity of servitude. Auntie Bea had kept me from them. I had no binds to the church. My soul was intact. Our dark mother could not claim a single piece of me. It was Auntie Bea's devotion that bound me to the Daughters of Our Dark Mother. I had not grown up enfolded in the church's unity because it had been Mom's wish I stay out of the church. I did not understand the psychological chains that kept many of the disciples bound to Hekate, regardless of the sacrifices made, just to feel the union of minds and the power bestowed.

The high priestess took the blade from the offering vessel and held it out to me. "Once the child makes the offering, the church will welcome you once more." She kept her eyes on me despite talking to Auntie Bea.

I looked at the blade and then Auntie Bea. Shame kept her eyes on the offered instrument. Everything she had wanted lay in the palm of the high priestess's hand—to be welcomed back into the fold of the church, to be anchored in belonging. My mother had wanted me separate from the church. It was a promise she'd demanded from Auntie Bea before she'd disappeared and then later found dead. Out of love for her sister, Auntie Bea had done all in her power to fulfill her promise, despite our coven's demands that I be brought before the altar, that I give my blood to the goddess.

Auntie Bea avoided my gaze, but I could see it in her eyes, the desperate need sparked by the high priestess's promise, though she continued to stare at the blade. She did not want to influence me, or force my decision, and that is why she looked everywhere but at me.

"I will do it." I mean, how bad can it be, really?

Auntie Beas's gaze snapped to me. "Ya don't have to."

"The girl has decided." The high priestess faced the hilt of the blade toward me.

"Let's get this over with," I said.

Holding my left hand over the vessel, I took the blade and made a small slit at the tip of my finger, grimacing at the instant sting. A trickle of blood oozed out and ran into my nail. I tipped my finger downward and a single drop hit the basin of the vessel. I made to draw my hand away, but the high priestess placed her hand over mine and turned my palm over. She took the blade and ran the tip down the center of my palm in one quick slice. I cried out and tried to withdraw my hand from her grip, but she tightened her hold, resisting my pull, turned my palm downward and squeezed to force the blood into the vessel. It dripped like a leaky faucet. I glared up at her, but her focus was on the blood in the bowl. Nothing but classic evil witch in that expression of hers.

Satisfied with the offering, she released my hand and set the bloody blade down beside the vessel.

"Will you at least give me a tissue or something for my wound?"

It was as though she didn't hear me. Her eyes stayed glued to the bottom of the vessel. I leaned in when I heard the hiss. My blood had coalesced into a pool at the base. Small bubbles formed at the edges of the pool. In seconds, it boiled in earnest. By the surprised expression on Auntie Bea's face, I would say this wasn't normal.

From the furious boil, a spark ignited, a brilliant blue flame that spiraled up to the vaulted ceiling. But before the blue flame made it all the way, it transformed into a black mist that splintered into tendrils, writhing around each other like snakes. The tangled knot spiraled in an arch over our heads, down into the statue of Hekate and disappeared as the high priestess arched her head back, arms splayed wide as if imbuing some great power.

Maybe it was time we got out of here. Seeming to read my mind, the high priestess snatched out her arm like a striking cobra and clawed hold of my wrist. I squeaked.

"Hold still," she snapped, then ran her finger down the line of the cut. Pain infused the gaping wound followed by the spike of a dozen needles piercing the raw flesh.

When she pulled her hand away, a red scar remained.

"A gift for your sacrifice," she said.

CHAPTER 3

Smithson and Row was an edifice of glass and iron, dwarfing the buildings on either side, outstripping all close by with its grandeur. West Tuzet district, abutting the city center, was the cultural precinct of Davenport. The plaza was a walker's haven of cobbled paths winding around neat, trimmed gardens and small stone bridges spanning carp-filled ponds. Lace curtains of creepers clung to building walls, providing nesting hollows for small black birds that chattered and chirped as they flittered around their tangled homes preparing to bed down for the night.

I stopped along the path, closing my eyes with my inhale, and opened my mind to the noisy feathered creatures. Their minds were a darting, jumbled mess of hasty decisions, flitting from thought to thought. With an animal mind such as this, it could take minutes or longer for me to calm the flow and slip into the stream of their thoughts to make it my own.

My influence over animals was my one fancy power, the only skill that stopped me from being classified a rummy. That, and my clumsy and minor ability to cast spells, a gift for all witches, except poor Auntie Bea and other rummy. Her spells ended up limp at best.

Auntie Bea said my ability was a gift from the goddess Diana, with her dominion over the animal and natural realm, so I had asked her why we didn't worship Diana instead, but she replied that the goddess Diana was already claimed by another coven, a rival apparently.

The sounds of clacking heels and laughter drew me from my peaceful communion with the birds. A flux of elegantly dressed people made their way in through the giant glass doors of Smithson and Row. I glanced down at my jumpsuit. Thank the mother I'd changed. Auntie Bea was right. No way would anyone let me in wearing denims and leather.

I searched my small purse for my invitation. What if the doorman saw through the ruse? It wasn't a genuine invitation, just a white strip of card with a few magical glyphs creating a glamour over the blank face. Whatever the doorman expected to see would display.

Beside the two men in white suits standing either side of the entrance, checking the invitations of everyone who entered, a dozen bodyguards stood amongst the throng. Smart black suits failed to disguise their positions as the security detail. Auntie Bea warned me security would not be human, but what sort of paranormal were they? Bernard Preston was patron of Smithson and Row, but so too were a line of other mega wealthy business executives.

The skull had come into the hands of the auction house via a private donor, with an invisible trail. Most likely a neutral party of moderate power, which would explain why no paranormal factions had claimed it so far. I had snorted at the idea of describing any paranormal as neutral in this sinner's game, but both of us were at a loss to explain why any paranormal or human who understood the true nature of what they owned would willingly part with such a valuable prize. Not knowing was a dangerous gamble in this game. Not knowing could get you bound for eternity to another's dark ambitions, or see you banished to one of the many realms beyond the veil of our own existence.

Another inhale, and I strode up to join the back of the queue. The doorman kept the line flowing, so in no time, I was presenting my card, with a silent prayer to our Dark Mother, who now owned a piece of my soul. She had better keep up her end of the bargain and watch over her newest recruit. Auntie Bea kept secret the hushed words she'd mumbled to the stone floor while she humbled herself in front of the altar. I didn't push her—the boons made between a witch and our Dark Mother were private affairs.

As I neared the front of the line, I kept a subtle eye on the security guy closet to the doorman. A broad man with sandy blond hair pulled back into a low ponytail. He had the unforgiving face of a top-level hunter, pack perhaps. If so, he'd use more than his eyes to sift through the crowd. Statued in place, he looked more marble, sculptured by an unforgiving hand, than a living presence.

Someone cleared their throat behind me, snapping me out of my trance. There was a gap in front of me. That horrible prickling you got when you felt sure someone was eyeballing you crawled all over my body. Don't look. No eye contact with anyone. Auntie Bea's rules, which I intended to keep. But the irritating niggle pecked at the front of my mind despite my strong desire for self-preservation.

At last, I reached the doorman and flashed my bewitched card with a flourish. I skimmed his nondescript features for the briefest moment, caught the nod of his head and plowed for the entrance. Before I disappeared inside, I dared a backward glance and collided with golden-brown eyes. The blond security guy tracked me with his gaze. My stomach reacted by buckling up into a twisted mess. It was like being zapped from a hundred vaults. His were the eyes I felt, still holding my trail. I turned my head away, forcing myself to keep a casual pace. Was it my hammering heart that ran his bells?

Inside, everyone was watching everyone else, and I found it impossible to pick the ones that formed a safety net between me and the deadly paranormals and those that were the deadly paranormals. I wasn't from Davenport, and no paranormal fit the television mold. Besides, Auntie Bea stayed true to mom's wishes, as much as she could, and kept me away from the darker side of life for as long as she could. I didn't grow up knowing about this stuff. I finally learned the truth at eighteen and was initiated into the coven and church by force. At first, I was drawn to understand my heritage, then the coven excommunicated Auntie Bea, and in protest, I excommunicated myself. Since then, we've existed on the fringe of paranormal life, dealing with small time dabblers and lowlifes, the paranormals with minor talent, existing like bottom dwellers in a deep pond.

I deviated left and headed for the ladies, needing a moment away from prying eyes to gather my equilibrium. It was a bit of a walk to reach the bathroom, and all the while, I felt sure that wolf's golden-brown eyes tracked my path. I'd met a pack member only once in my life, a chilling affair. They demanded strict obedience for their members, were hostile to outsiders, and punished without mercy.

The bathroom was no sanctuary, but at least I could drop my facade in private. What happened in the church rattled me. Until tonight, I was a blood offering virgin. Mom wanted me out of the church and away from this life. Auntie Bea couldn't or wouldn't give me a reason for why mom wanted me out of this life. But knowing that's what she wanted for me kept me away from the altar and the offering vessel. To feel the flux of power created by the Dark Mother's boon was not an urge I'd succumbed to, something only achieved by making the sacrifice. Tonight, the blood had been mine, but the prayer was not, which meant I'd gained nothing. I felt nothing. But something had happened in the church. Something that had pleased the high priestess very much.

I rested my hands on the sink and stared at myself in the oval mirror. It was still me in there, and only me. Why, Auntie Bea, why? What terrible sacrifice have I done for you? There were no answers in the mirror. I straightened.

Time the game began.

The auction had already started when I entered the auditorium. Most of the seats were taken, and I was forced to squeeze on the end of the back row, which was fine, as it gave me a good vantage point. I flicked through the catalogue to ensure I'd not missed the skull. Confident I hadn't, I settled back and watched the auction unfold. Everyone's eyes were on the items being auctioned, and I was free to peruse the auditorium, searching for any faces from Auntie Bea's dossiers, but sitting behind limited me to the backs of people's head.

The atmosphere was charged, the bidding high and fast, and soon, they placed the skull on the podium. A tension twisted the air. I held my breath, waiting for the first paddle to raise. When it did, it set off a tsunami. A strange ripple creeped along my skin, turning the beat of my heart into a quick-step. The auctioneer accepted the bids like a racetrack announcer, dragging my pulse with him. I strained to see who was raising their paddles, but a large guy in front of me blocked my view. I couldn't keep up with who was in the game, and had to force myself to stay in my seat and not leap up to see all the contenders. The moment felt like a dizzy rollercoaster ride with me flung out of my seat and hanging by my fingers.

When the auctioneer dropped his hammer down on the last call, I was out of my seat, propelled by anticipation. And I hadn't even seen who won the bid. I slunk to the side wall, pressing myself close to a large painting, as if that would conceal me.

Again, I got the annoying itchy tingles of someone checking me out. I caught a guy in my periphery, one painting down, then got an ache in my eyes straining to see him better without turning my head. No eye contact with anyone. My body still twanged from the predator out front. Instead, I focused on everyone in the room. Item fifteen was on the podium, but the atmosphere had changed. The charge, sparking me moments ago, fizzed to a trickle. A handful of people headed for the exit, giving me my first chance to see their faces. Leaving so soon after the skull was bought, these were my targets, but from my position at the rear, I had not seen who of them had won.

I shrunk further against the wall, wishing I could actually turn into a potted plant as a short, lean man headed my way. His face wasn't on any of the papers Auntie Bea had shoved my way. I ducked my head, finding something more interesting on the carpet as he passed by. When I raised my eyes, Bernard Preston strode toward me. Surprised at finding my number one quarry before my eyes, I turned, giving him my shoulder. Silly, really. He didn't know who I was, hadn't even looked my way.

I watched in my periphery as he pass me by, then followed his strides to the door. A giant of a man clipped on his heels, so broad he blotted out Preston walking in front. Nephilim. So they had made an appearance. Perhaps monitoring their dog.

The two men faded out the door, and golden-brown eyes intercepted my gaze. The menacing wolf, leaning against the wall, one painting down from me, the reason for my itch. There was nothing welcoming in his granite stare. The wolf likely ate children for breakfast and crushed rocks with his bare fists.

I needed to get out of here before he cornered me with questions. Eyes dipped, I pushed off the wall, holding my breath as I passed him by. Nice cologne. I had to give him that, the sort that made you think you were falling onto silken sheets in a log cabin with a roaring fire and a bottle of full-bodied red wine.

No furry paw struck my arm as I passed, so I increased my stride, eyeing the exit. Outside in the foyer, and my quarry had disappeared. How had he vanished so fast? A handful of distinguished-looking people loitered over glasses of champagne, but no giant or Preston. Perhaps the bathroom? I doubled back toward the mens' bathroom, passing a darkened passageway as I went.

A hand snaked around my waist and ripped me off my feet, dragging me into the passage, leaving my gasp behind. I was spun, pushed against the wall and trapped by a male body. In a snap, his hand dropped to my wrist, pinning it above my head as he leaned in to rest his elbow on the wall behind. His other hand slapped the wall on the other side of me, his body keeping me caged. Onyx eyes vacuumed me up. The smell of the wilds steamed my mind.

"Challenge accepted," his voice reverberated deep down to my nether regions.

Oh, dark mother, think. "Glad to hear, but not now...I'm busy."

Like a sleeping cat waking from a leisurely nap, his lips curled into a sensual yet entirely wicked smile that peeled the clothes from my body.

He huffed a laugh that came up from deep in his throat. "I don't wait."

I beat you don't. His cologne was doing bad things to my concentration—that and his proximity, suffocatingly, achingly, deliciously close. If I inhaled deep, my breasts would press into his chest. Get a grip, girl. "This time you'll have to, sorry. Somewhere else is calling me."

I inched down the wall, intent on slipping from his cage. But dammit, he still had my left wrist pinned to the wall above my head, something I remembered when his grip tightened.

"I didn't expect to see you here."

"Ditto."

He quirked an eyebrow, and the look was all sin. "Maybe you could let me in on your secret."

"Not unless you tattle first."

"I love it when you play these games."

"I love it when you're more transparent."

He leaned down further, bringing his eyes almost level with mine so I could benefit from the full wattage of charged sex appeal. "Don't tease me, El. You know what happens when you do."

Me, tease you. How about snuffing your pheromones? Give me a chance to think. Mistaken identity. Just great. Who was this El person? A mash up from his drunken gaze? Or perhaps he was high? There was no whiff of alcohol on his breath, and his eyes were clear. I blinked myself back from falling into the promise of debauched bliss. I cleared my throat. "So, which item did you bid on?"

"I don't bid. You should know that."

"I was just making small talk while my arm went to sleep."

He lifted his eyes to look at my arm, cranked over my head, then he dropped his eyes back down to my face. "It's punishment for not answering my question."

"Which was?"

"Why are you here?"

"I wanted the rush of a night time auction. Pretty intense, wouldn't you say?"

"They bore you."

"Not this time. You have to admit, the skull livened things up."

"Skull? I barely noticed." He drawled. "My attention was on something far more interesting, which wasn't at the front of the auditorium."

I was out of my depth in this conversation, not understanding what he was talking about or who he was. He didn't have the brash, feral nature of a pack member, the height of a nephilim, the shifty eyes of a warlock, the stink of a demon, or the unearthly angelic beauty of a fae. I couldn't think of any other paranormal powerful enough to bother turning up to the auction. He was roguishly handsome, leaking danger with every syllable uttered and every breath exhaled. The two a deadly mix that would have any woman with a pulse between her legs eager to roll over and beg for a bite.

Bite. Perhaps. Dear dark mother. I strained against the manacle of his grip. "You've mistaken me for someone else." All fun had drained from my voice.

He leaned in close, sniffed my neck. My breath hitched as my heart spasmed through a frantic whammy of opposing emotions. Deadly, deadly, deadly games he played. A jet of heat, so hot it seared ice cold through my veins. I shook my head. This was not sexy. Definitely not sexy. This was bad.

"Maybe." He pulled back enough to bring his mouth devilishly close to mine. "Unfortunately, I don't trust you."

I opened my mouth to reply and sucked up his breath instead, tasting the rich fruit of red wine. I don't trust you. My body was wired, all sexed up and burning, yet sparking out alerts and primed to fight. The hairs along my arms spiked, as if reaching across the void to touch him.

How did I get myself into this position? How did I allow myself to be made so vulnerable in front of a…? He sniffed my neck. Vampire? But was he? I couldn't be sure. Then again, I'd never been this close to one of those deadly creatures before.

As suddenly as he'd trapped me, he released my wrist and backed away. "You're in luck. I've got places to be. Perhaps we'll call this one a draw."

"If you say so." My mind twirled about without a central force to ground it, and so my voice sounded like it was floating on a rough sea.

"Until next time."

I swear I felt the tease of his eyes like a feather on my skin as they prowled over me.

"Try for something a little less appetizing next time."

And then he left me, creating a void. With him gone, the cold sunk in where the heat of his body had been. I huffed the heaviest breath, bending forward to balance my hands on my knees. "Close one, Laz."

I straightened but had to place a hand on the wall to steady myself, still feeling totally unmoored and suffering from the punishment of restraining my lust.

"Oh no. Preston." I hurried to the mouth of the passage, glancing left and right. More people had moved into the foyer, but no Preston. Maybe he'd lost the bid. That was why he headed out early. I couldn't say for sure. But according to Auntie Bea, if anyone would win, it was Preston. I'd made a mess of it all. On a game we so needed to win.

Dammit. I felt wrecked, torn apart by Mr Mysterious. I sought the bathroom before I braved catching a bus home, empty of any information that would save us.

There was a feral savagery in my eyes as I looked in the mirror. I looked like a woman driven to the peak and cruelly denied. Maybe I could hunt down Hyun-woo when I returned. But the way I felt at this moment, I would shred his clothes before we reached his bedroom.

I splashed handfuls of cold water on my face, then straightened, only to shriek at the sight that met me in the mirror. There was a woman standing behind me.

I inched around to face her and wondered if I had turned around at all, for it was like staring in the mirror.

CHAPTER 4

"Isn't this a surprise?" My lookalike purred as she sashayed toward me, which she did so much better than I ever could.

"Oh, my...god" I never used such a title in such a way. He wasn't my god. But saying dark mother would sound weird to anyone on the outside. And this woman was a complete unknown.

"Amazing, isn't it? Here's me blissfully thinking I was an original. I must say, I'm rather disappointed."

"This can't be true."

"I can assure you I'm real." She quirked her elbow toward me. "You can have a feel if you need to convince yourself."

Like a moron, I simply stared, slack-jawed. She was so like me, unbelievably like me, except sexier in her death heels and black minidress hugging her body like skin. Even our hair was the same color and thickness, only she wore hers down like a black mane.

"Elka," she said, holding out a hand with lacquered nails inches long and painted a fire red, like her lips. They matched her dark makeup, shadowing her green eyes. She was a vamp compared to my Suzy homemaker attempt at style.

"Larnie. You can call me Laz." The skin on her hand was silken smooth, a woman with nothing to do but bathe in lotions. "I'm sorry... I'm speechless."

"Back at you, sister."

The word sister sunk heavy inside my core. But how could we look identical if there was another explanation? "I can't believe that."

"What, that we're sisters? I'm adopted, so anything's possible." She ambled over and rested her backside against the sinks.

"For me it's not. I mean, my mom died, and I don't know my dad, but my aunt would've told me."

"It's a puzzle then, isn't it?"

Was she like me, living with one foot in this world and one in the darkness of paranormal life? If us looking identical was a whopper of a coincidence, I wasn't about to unleash the secret.

And Elka. As in El. So this was the woman Mr Lava Hot, possibly a vampire, thought he was talking to. If she was human, then she was in trouble messing with the likes of him.

"I had a run-in, moments ago, with a...guy, who thought I was you."

"Not surprising, given the circumstances."

"He was...tall, dark, black eyes—"

"Oh, yes," she purred and turned to the mirror, smoothing her dress down her body. "You must be talking about Jarro Peers." She leaned in toward the mirror and gently wiped some invisible thing she thought messed with her makeup. "Scorching, isn't he? Has the face of a man who would make a nun abandon her vows and worship the devil."

I couldn't help but check out her body. She looked like her skin had been stretched over honed muscles. Plenty of butt workouts went into sculpturing that ass, I'm sure. And her legs were longer than mine, though that could be because of her heels, which were higher than I'd ever dare wear. When you were busy stealing artifacts, making deals with paranormals, not to mention keeping the coven and church at a safe distance so they didn't consume your soul, who had time to workout?

"He's your boyfriend?"

She stopped fiddling with her face and shifted her eyes to me. "Why, do you fancy him?"

"I got the impression he was trouble. I stay away from trouble." Because there was already too much of it in my life.

"Oh, he's trouble all right, sweetie, but the sort of trouble you can't wait to get dirty in. You needn't worry about Jarro. He has particular taste."

As in anything with blood running through their veins. But what was she meaning here? That I was not up to Jarro's standards. I glanced down at my outfit. Maybe I wasn't the sexy she-devil like Elka, but I didn't look too bad. I loved this jumpsuit. It was the most sophisticated thing in my small wardrobe of clothes. Auntie Bea wasn't a role model for fashion and, given everything going on in our lives, I had no time to think about style.

"Commitment and I have never seen eye to eye." She pouted at her reflection, then turned around to face me. "Why settle for one? Jarro and I are of similar mind."

Was she a witch? I couldn't ask her outright, in case she wasn't.

"Did you come to the auction with your family?"

"My dad's the buyer. Mom couldn't care less about the trinkets he fills our home with. She doesn't understand why anyone would waste money on ancient junk. How about you?"

"I came on my own. I'm interested in antiquities."

"Why haven't I seen you before now?" Elka pulled a small metallic box from her purse, unclipping the clasp.

"We're new to Davenport."

"Want one?" She offered the small box to me, revealing a stash of small, white pills.

I shook my head. "No, thanks." My life was already too weird and dangerous. I wasn't going to mess myself up taking drugs.

"They don't mess with your head."

"Then why bother taking them?"

She smiled the smile of the she-devil, the sort of smile a man would fight the hell-beast to win and dry-swallowed the pill in her hand. "Because they mess with other body parts." She shimmied her shoulders. "I'm off to a party. You want to come, newfound sister of mine?" She dipped her head and eyed me through her lash extensions, playing the sexy coy game that was lost on me.

She looked like me, but Elka was an entirely different species. She was the vixen, confidently wielding power against men. Hell, maybe women as well. Who knew these days. After Mr Lava Hot she was twisting my mind into origami. I had a sister. I think I had a sister. That was impossible. Why had Auntie Bea not said anything? Did she even know?

Elka pushed off the sink and turned back to the mirror to fluff her hair. Her eyes wandered to mine, then she looked over her shoulder, dipping her gaze down my body. "Cute outfit. Sexy but chic." She spun and clicked over to me. She stood an inch taller because of her heels. "The hairdo is nice too—kind of naughty school mistress. But I think you should go wild." She unfastened the clasps I had used to hold my updo in place and ran her hands through my hair to shake it out as it tumbled down my back. I stayed mesmerized by her confidence, allowing her to tweak my appearance to her satisfaction.

Once done, she moved aside and turned to face the mirror, wrapped her arm over my shoulder and pulled me close to her side. "There. Now no one can tell us apart."

"How are you so calm about this? I'm freaking out."

"You're sweet. I think I'm going to like you."

"Do your adoptive parents know anything about your biological family?"

She pulled lipstick from her purse and sashayed up to the sink for a closer look. "Not really. I never bothered to ask too many questions." She leaned over as she applied another coat on her already perfect lips.

"We should exchange numbers." Should we? What if she wasn't like me...in that way? But she would have to be. Unless... Which parent did we share? Mom was a witch, I knew that. But I couldn't say if my dad had any ability or not, since he was a mysterious blank Auntie Bea could tell me nothing about.

"I wouldn't have let you go unless I had your number. This is crazy fun. I want to know everything about you," she purred.

I searched my purse for my phone. "What's your last name?"

"Preston."

I fumbled my phone out of my purse but dropped it onto the tiled floor. Elka crouched quicker than I managed and scooped it up. The screen lit up, and she stared at the image of me and Auntie Bea. "This that aunt you live with?"

"Her name's Beatrice. I call her Auntie Bea."

"She looks...nice."

I took the phone from her hands, feeling a sour ache in my gut. Despite filling her sentences with more swear words than were in the dictionary, drinking like a homeless drunk, smoking more than a factory, having no sense of fashion, and fitting maxi size, she was my family.

She brought me up, shielded me as much as she could from the coven and the Daughters of our Dark Mother. They had bullied her into handing me over when I was a baby, saying a rummy had no right to care for a child of the Dark Mother. But Auntie Bea wouldn't let me go because she loved me. I was the only piece of her sister she had left; her sister, the one person who gave her love unconditionally.

"It doesn't matter. I'll help you from now on."

"With what?"

She moved in front of me and fussed with my hair. "You're twenty-two, right? The same as me. Save updos for your fifties. The look you're after is sex kitten, not muffin lady."

"Was your dad successful tonight?"

She stopped mid-fluff, her eyes slipping to mine, and quirked a perfectly plucked eyebrow. "Do you have a thing for my dad?"

"What? That's disgusting. My thing is antiquities. I was curious who won the skull."

She dropped her hands, one falling to her hip. "Only impotent old men are interested in skulls."

"I'm an amateur archaeologist."

She rolled her eyes, "Jesus. I blame that aunt of yours. You sure you don't want to come to the party?" She cocked her head to the side and flicked some of my hair away from my chin.

"Is Jarro going to be there?" I should warn her about him.

She rolled her tongue on the inside of her cheek. "A friendly warning, sister. Jarro's not someone you can handle."

"I was worried about you."

She laughed, mirthlessly.

"I got the sense he was dangerous. Maybe you should find someone else to play with."

"But that's no fun. The thoroughly dangerous ones make life a thrilling ride. Without men like him, I might as well take up the veil."

She pulled her phone from her pocket and looked at the screen. "I have to go. But we need to exchange numbers."

I gave her mine, and she texted me back.

"So, I'll message you. We must catch up. We've got a lot to talk about," she said.

"For sure."

"Just stay away from skulls and impotent old men's interests in the meantime."

I tried a smile. "Sure."

And then she left, clicking with catlike grace out of the bathroom. I headed for the basin, collapsing my hands on the porcelain, and stared into the mirror. What the actual hell had just gone on? How could I have a twin? Auntie Bea mentioned nothing. Why was she not with us? And how was I going to tell Auntie Bea that I lost the skull?

I let my head sink and stared at the plug. I had to fix this mess. The Apostles weren't going to magically leave us alone, and I needed to know how it was I had a twin and only just found out about her. I needed to know if she was a witch.

CHAPTER 5

Auntie Bea had downed a few while I was at the auction—an entire bottle of gin. The one I had bought today. Normally I refused to feed her habit by buying her alcohol, but she'd been particularly stressed about the auction, so I'd relented.

Never again.

She found the top of the table easier to look at than my face. "I never thought this would happen."

I slapped my hands to my sides and paced our small kitchen. "I had hoped you would say Elka's looking like me was a coincidence. Not that you knew and kept it from me all this time."

"She's Preston's daughter?"

"That doesn't matter. What matters is you've lied to me about my sister all these years."

"I've never said a word about her."

"Which is just as bad as lying."

She banged her elbows on the table and cupped her head in her hands. "Ya giving me a headache."

"You'll have a lot worse by the time we've finished talking. Why did you leave her, Auntie Bea? Why did you take me and leave her?"

She shook her head, which remained buried in her hands. "I need a drink."

"Too bad you've drunk the lot. And you won't be able to tell me anymore if you did."

"Laz, I can't talk about this right now. How 'bout in the morning."

"I won't be able to sleep."

"I could mix you some herbs, add a spell or two."

"No. I may not wake up again." She pulled herself out of her hands and stared at me, her expression like I had slapped her.

I tried never to rub Auntie Bea's rummy issues in her face. I never criticized her lack of wicca skills and pretended most of the magic she practiced made a difference.

"Sorry, it's—"

She waved my lame apology away. "I know I'm a sham."

"But you know it's not your fault, right?" I could carry on with the ruse, disagree with her, say she was no worse than half the witches in the coven. But for once, we were getting real. "It makes no difference to me what you can and can't do or what they call you. No one else fought to keep me. They gave you no support. You did it all on your own."

They only allowed her to stay in the coven and a member of the church, so they could keep a watchful eye on me. Once I was eighteen and old enough to make my decision, take my own vows and make my own sacrifices to the Dark Mother, they decided Auntie Bea was no longer useful. Sensing my attachment to her, they didn't excommunicate her right away. No, that was once they thought I had accepted the church without hesitation. Filled with their own prejudice, they couldn't believe anyone would love a rummy.

She shrugged. "What does it matter now? The Apostles will fix my problem."

I stormed over and slid down into the chair beside her, seized her hand and drew it across the table to me. "You listen to me, the Apostles aren't touching either of us. I will get the skull. Preston has it. I'm sure of it. And now I have a way in."

"You gonna let Preston know about ya?"

"Elka and I look identical. Maybe identical enough Preston won't know if we swapped lives, long enough for me to get the skull."

"Are you fucking insane? What do you know about living a rich life? What do you know about life in Davenport? Her life? Preston and his wife? How do you expect to fool a mom and dad into believing you're their daughter? Parents know their kids, stuff you couldn't hope to mimic. I should never 'ave brought us here."

"Too late now to worry about that. Preston has the skull and... well, there's no better way to steal the skull than when you're trusted enough to move freely through Preston's house. Auntie Bea, we have little choice. The Apostles won't back out of their promise. We have three days. How else do you expect us to succeed in three days?"

Auntie Bea threw up her hands and fell back in her chair. She closed her eyes as she shook her head. Never had I seen her admit defeat quite like this. I should question the sanity of my thoughts, but with the Apostles' looming deadline we were left with few options and even fewer ideas. Besides, if I was quick, I'd be in and out of Elka's house before anyone in the Preston family noticed. All I had to do was convince Elka of the plan. Somehow I felt she'd find it a big game.

"Yar mom knew she was gonna die."

"What?" Auntie Bea had always told me Mom died in an accident.

She slicked back her hair and let her hands flop onto her lap. "Keeping your sister a secret ain't the only lies I've been telling ya. I reckon ya mom was murdered."

"Reckon?" The word echoed around the room like a lost child wailing for her mom.

"She was running from your dad. That's why she gave me yous two. She told me to put you both up for adoption. When I argued with her, she said yous wouldn't be safe if I kept you in the family. She thought ya needed to be buried in the munsib world."

"Who was my dad?"

"I dunno. She never told me. And that's the truth. I saw little of ya mom when she met ya dad. He sucked her in, made her give up the church and her coven. She did it for him. So when she turned up that day, I was surprised. Overjoyed to see her again. She stayed one night to be with yous before she left. And then she made me promise. It was to save her girls."

"But you never gave me up."

"I couldn't. I just couldn't. I needed something of ya mom. I just couldn't."

"So you never knew who adopted Elka."

"Nah, never. I made sure I didn't. Just in case someone was watching, ya know. And I kept you hidden. I never told the church about Elka, neither. I never told them nothing. When you got older and no one came, I thought about looking for ya sister, but...I never did. Thought she'd be better off. Turns out I was right."

"I'm not so sure about that. She acted like a spoilt brat. Yeah, terrible for me to say, I know."

"That's what happens when ya rich. Wouldn't mind acting like a spoilt brat meself."

"So my dad was not a nice man."

"In the end, ya mom feared him. She was scared of what he would do to yous two, I guess. Like I said, she wouldn't say nothing to me. I tried to get her talking, but she said not knowing would save me."

I sat with a heavy sigh. It was not every day you learned your dad was a psychopathic asshole. "He was paranormal then?"

"To scare a witch? Yeah, I'd say so."

"That means Elka's a witch. I didn't want to ask, just in case."

"Who knows what coven she's joined."

"She must've found it hard growing up with human parents, knowing only the human side of this world, yet having these abilities."

"I could look into it. Find out what covens are in Davenport. Maybe she's with the Church of Living Light."

"I doubt it." The Church of Living Light was the Daughters of our Dark Mother's antithesis. We didn't divide ourselves between God and the devil, heaven and hell—that's what humans did. But if we did, then the Daughters of Our Dark Mother were more aligned with hell. We weren't evil, but sometimes, we walked the line. "We're going to catch up soon. I'll ask her. And I'll get this skull before the nephilim do."

Her smile was weak, but she took my hand. "Thank you."

"As if I'd let those assholes take your ears."

"I mean thank you for not hating me."

"As if I could. Not the woman who has been my mother for twenty-two years."

She let my hand go, finding other things to look at, and pushed up from the table. "Maybe a cuppa."

"Hmm." I half listened. "There was someone there tonight you missed in your dossiers."

"I'm sure there were loads. But I got the important ones."

"Not all. I think I came into contact with a vampire."

"Fucking bullshit, you what?"

"I'm not entirely sure." Given I had never met a vampire before. They were the most mysterious of all the paranormals, keeping to their own, staying in the shadows. Normally, they couldn't care less about the rest of us and our petty games.

"It's because of the skull. Ya didn't get near him or her, did ya?"

"How near are we talking?"

"It's safest to stay below their notice. Fucking hell. I never thought of them. I'll have to do some research. See how many of 'em there are in Davenport. Maybe I can find out where their hive is located. It's doubtful. Ya never find 'em if they don't want to be found."

"His name's Jarro Peers, and he's messed up with Elka. And if she's a witch, she likely knows what he is. That's why she warned me away from him. I thought she was doing it because she thought I was dowdy. Maybe she was protecting me."

"What are you talking about?

"I wonder how she knows?"

"Doesn't matter. You shouldn't see her."

"But she's our link to the skull."

"We'll leave town."

"Like you did before? The Apostles still found you."

"Laz, I don't want ya anywhere near vampires. They're dangerous and unpredictable. And that's saying something, given what I've dealt with in me life."

I tuned Auntie Bea out while I thought about the mysteries before me.

"Are you listening to me?"

"I'm not running. We leave now, and we'll be running forever. That's not a life. We sort this here. Besides, she's my sister. I don't feel a familial link at the moment, but I want to see her. I'll keep clear of her world and the people in it once I get the skull. And unless you have a better idea, the only way to do that, I fear, is to pretend I'm her. For a short while."

Auntie Bea came around and heaved herself down onto the chair again. "I don't like this. Ya mom wanted you protected. She wanted ya out of this dark world. She wanted a normal life for you."

"And that's another mystery I want solved. Why? What was so bad in her life that made her want you to give us up? I want to know who my dad was."

"Some things are best left a mystery. Ya live longer that way."

"Or maybe my past will come back to haunt me. Better I know what's there then get a shock if it happens."

"You go messing with this Elka chick and vampires, then something will come haunting you and it won't be ya past." Auntie Bea shook her head, knowing anything she said would not persuade me.

"You're gonna need help. I don't want to say this, but maybe ya should go back to the church and make another boon."

"No way."

"You've sacrificed once. The Dark Mother has a piece of ya now."

"One piece is all she's getting. I can do this without her help." I closed my eyes. "Blessed Dark Mother, sorry, but I very much want my soul to myself, all of it." Then I launched to my feet at the same time a knock came on the makeshift door Hyun-woo had erected in our absence.

"Don't answer it."

"And have it blown in again," I said as I headed over.

Hyun-woo stood in the passage. "Sorry, I didn't want to disturb, but I noticed your light still on."

"We were chatting."

"I was checking everything was all right."

"It will be."

He looked cute when his brow creased. "You're not scared without a door?"

"We're fine. There's little to steal."

We stood awkwardly glancing at each other and then looking away. "Tomorrow I can come early and fix the door."

"Sounds great."

Another awkward silence followed. I should put him out of his misery and say I was tired and wanted to go to bed, but I also didn't want to shut off any possibilities of getting to know him a little better. We weren't planning on hanging around once this was all over. It had never been our plan to make Davenport our home, so why bother developing a relationship with any guy. Perhaps it had something to do with Hyun-woo being normal and sweet and not about to curse me into oblivion.

I've had carnal relations with a warlock, fae and—I'm so not proud of this—demon. The latter was pretty hot, and I don't just mean where he lives when he's not menacing munsib on earth. All came with their problems, which made anything long-term out of the question.

Our secret life made handling humans a juggle of china plates. If you were hoping for a family life than witch life sucked. Just look at what happened to Mom.

If he knew the deal, then a short fling with a human wouldn't get messy, except if he was really nice, which would make it hard to say goodbye.

"Maybe we could go out sometime. It doesn't have to be fancy. Local, I was thinking. Just a drink and a chat," I said, stumbling my way through asking him out.

I'd seen him in a shirt and could confirm he had nice biceps.

"Sounds great. Not in Dim Bazaar. Maybe next district, Wolgod Quarter. I go to school there."

"Oh, you're studying?"

"Night school. I love history."

"A historian."

"Yes. It's a dream. My parents never wanted me to lose my life working in a shop. They want me to leave Dim Bazaar. Go live elsewhere. Once I earn enough, I can buy something big enough to move them out of here."

See? He's a nice, sweet, considerate, normal good-looking guy. "That's a noble dream. I know you will achieve it. Since you know Wolgod Quarter and I don't, maybe you can choose where we go."

"I'd like that. I'd like to take you there. Show you around."

I couldn't keep the stupid grin from spreading wide across my lips. Falling in lust was a great way to sweep some of your worries under the carpet. Temporary, I know, but whatever helped you survive sane.

"You're fine tonight?" He asked.

"Oh yeah, don't worry about us."

"Who ya gabbing with?" Auntie Bea yelled from inside.

Hyun-woo jerked, then stepped away from the door. "I'll come by tomorrow to fix the door."

"Sure."

"We can decide on a time—"

"Ya letting a draft in."

I rolled my eyes and Hyun-woo smiled. He glanced back once as he descended the stairs and I gave him a cutesy pie wave using only my fingers. While he wasn't looking, I admired his ass. His pants were a nice cut that molded perfectly to the contours of his cheeks. He must work out, or maybe it was just all that heavy work he did out the back of the shop, unloading supplies from delivery trucks that seem to arrive every day.

Hyun-woo disappeared inside the side door of the shop, and I was about to head back inside when I noticed a shadow move across the block of moonlight on the floor from the peephole window on the front door. Dim Bazaar was a busy place at night. Hundreds probably passed by the entrance door. But I could've sworn the shadow had been still a moment ago, like someone had peered inside and then moved away once Hyun-woo came to the bottom of the stairs.

Maybe it was my imagination. I had the creeps after being in one room with so many powerful paranormals. I spun on my heels and headed back into our apartment, fighting to close the makeshift door. Once shut, I headed across the apartment and inched the edge of the disgusting purple curtain at the kitchen window aside to sneak a peek. It looked onto the same street as the front door downstairs.

"Whatcha doing?" Auntie Bea said, coming out of her room.

"Just looking?"

"What did I tell ya about that kid?"

"I won't fall in love with him." But I wasn't really concentrating on what she said. I scanned the street below, but there were too many people to make anyone stand out.

"Ya listening?" She asked from beside me.

"No. Shh."

She wrenched the curtain out of my hand and peeled it right back so she could join me looking down at the street.

"I was trying not to draw attention to us."

"Who do ya think ya see?"

"I don't know. It could be nothing."

"Well, don't get ya knickers in a knot. And ya can't control who ya love."

"Can you drop it, Auntie Bea?"

"Conjure yaself a man doll, if ya must. The incantation is in me grimoire somewhere." She lost interest in looking out the window and headed for the table.

"I don't want sex advice from my aunt." And then I saw it. A dark shape, just outside the lights of a food cart. At first, I wasn't sure, but staring long enough I could make out the figure of a man, tall and broad, from the faint glow of the moonlight where it hit the building behind. He wasn't tall enough to be a nephilim, but taller than your average man nonetheless. And this was likely me being paranoid. I was in Dim Bazaar. Everyone hung out in the shadows. But then the figure disappeared. Like vanished. One moment he was there, and the next, the moonlight reclaimed the place he'd been standing. Humans couldn't do that.

CHAPTER 6

This is what it was like to be rich.

I stood on the paving, looking in through the decorative metal gates across an expanse of perfect lawn, to a house big enough to be considered a hotel. This was Spard Cross, the wealthiest district in Davenport, the district where my newly discovered sister and her adoptive family lived. This was their house, and I had not been invited.

Last night I had discovered I had a sister. Also, I lost the one thing that would save my auntie's ears, and the rest of her, and I could not wait for my sister to reply to my text and invite me around. I needed to get inside. Covertly. Because I wasn't ready to let her parents know there were two of us if my plan was to work. I'm sure Elka would also like to keep things secret from her parents given she now had a dowdy sister and an embarrassing aunt. Besides, I was too impatient to wait until she had agreed to my stupid plan.

And I didn't know how much I could reveal to Elka about the skull. She must know of its ability. Last night she'd pretended not to care, and I believed her act. That was a subterfuge. She was a witch. I was sure of it. Elka would be asking her own questions about me. And her dad was aligned with nephilim. At least Auntie Bea assumed as much, which meant maybe her dad knew about Elka being a witch. They both wanted the skull, and not because it was some antiquity that would look good on the mantelpiece and generate juicy conversation during fancy diner parties.

I could have it all wrong. Elka may not know anything about the skull, but there was one thing I knew for sure: she was street smart. She would likely do a better job than I in living life on the dark side of existence.

Auntie Bea didn't know I was here. I had snuck out while she snored her sore head away. I'd passed Hyun-woo coming up the stairs with tools in hand. We'd settled our date for the following evening in Wolgod Quarter, and I'd asked him to show me around his college. Any life that was normal attracted me, and so I was keen to hear about his future plans, walk around his campus, and pretend for a moment with him that this was me. I wasn't a kids and picket fence kind of woman, but neither was I any good at living the life I knew.

I flexed my fingers. Enough distraction. Time to get smart. And find a way in. Nighttime is the traditional time to break into a house, but that was so cliched it was laughable. Besides, I didn't need to be in her house in person to look around. I just needed an open window —of which I could see many from my vantage point out on the street —and a little bird would do the rest for me. But it was best I didn't stand out here on the street. Entering a creature's mind took all my concentration and made me vulnerable.

I walked to the end of their grand estate. The Preston property stretched half the block along the side street. Opposite them was another great mansion, this time tucked behind a brick wall, so that only the top stories of the house were visible. A pigeon perched on top of the gate. Halfway down the street was an alcove in the brick wall, perhaps for the postman to deliver the mail, but it was a good spot for me to hunker down while I allowed my mind to fly.

I dipped into the alcove, crouched in the corner and pressed my back into the cold, rough brick. I needed all the stability I could find for flight. Once settled, I opened the shutters of my mind and reached toward the pigeon. I sensed other, four-legged creatures close by, but of them, only the cat stood a chance of getting through the window, so the pigeon would have to do.

Birds were primitive, scatterbrained animals, whose mind strength was filled mostly with the difficulties of flight. When all their neurons and synapses weren't firing for balance, rotation, and speed, they were operating their acute eyesight, hunting for the smallest speck of food on the paving. A bird was easy to invade, queasy to operate, but had great three-hundred-and-sixty-degree vision.

It took a moment's blinking to move out of my current state of vision and into the bird's and a fraction of a moment to wield its mind into a central core way of thinking so I could manipulate its primary urges and force my own. Pigeons were particularly easy being half domesticated. They rarely fought my commands to fly through windows into enclosed spaces.

I pressed back harder into the brickwork as I sprung the urge to take flight into its mind. I was never a good flyer. It took a crash into a branch for me to realize the fine line between overpowering the bird with my control and leaving enough for the animal to do what it did best. Fly. After all, I had no idea how to operate all my appendages to make flight work.

The bird took off and banked hard left. I slapped my hand down on the paving beside me to counter my sway, and my stomach rolled a few times. We flew over the lawn, me resisting the need to force the bird around the shrub up ahead. It skimmed the side branches with a snap roll, and I jerked forward and heaved my guts, spreading my legs at the last second before I vomited on my thighs. The bird continued, and I was thrown back against the brick wall as it banked upward toward the top open window.

Everyone thinks flying like a bird would be great. It's not. I get motion sickness every time. I encouraged the pigeon to take a break on the windowsill while I wiped my face with the back of my trembling hand and inhaled deep to slow my breathing. My heart was hammering like I'd run a marathon.

Three-hundred-and-sixty vision was handy. I watched for any movement outside in the driveway and down to the gate while checking out the room. But to get a more accurate view it was better to turn the pigeon's head side on, giving me a detailed view of what was in front of it. Mahogany desk with a pen and a neat stack of papers, no computer, leather chairs with deep brown cushions, bookshelves to the ceiling, plush beige carpet. No computer ruled out an office. Perhaps a reading room. Or maybe these large houses had rooms that served no real purpose at all.

The door was open. Definitely a plus when you were controlling an animal with no opposable thumbs, or hands, for that matter. One crap later we were flitting across the room into the hall. Moving into a narrower space, my control slipped momentarily, the bird's agitated and flighty energy burst through, and the poor thing flew into the wall, fluttered hopelessly in confusion for a moment, and fell to the carpet. I eased back into control and allowed the poor creature to continue on foot, or talons. With any animal, fear contended with my ability to control them, and when flying, a bird's neurons fired at full throttle, and its heart pumped at max sped. In this heightened state, the slightest hitch of panic turned into an avalanche, near impossible to withhold or steer.

Muffled noises came from somewhere ahead. I quickened our pace and raced down the corridor, past expensive, abstract paintings and closed doors until the walls disappeared, opening into a vast stairwell. Below, the grand entrance, and voices rumbling deep inside another room. The bird spread its wings before I initiated the urge. Given the wide-open area, flying was a safe bet. Unfortunately, the bird had caught sight of the skylight, so instead of heading down to the tiling below, we went up and smashed into the sheet of glass at the top of the vaulted ceiling while releasing another crap. With a roiling stomach from the sharp dips and agitated fluttering, I squeezed my eyes shut, spiked my nails into my palm and gently soothed tighter control over the pigeon's mind. Being mid-air, and two stories high, I wasn't about to assume total control to force a landing.

My heart raced as fast as the bird's. Its frenetic need for freedom slowly crept into my mind such that I felt on the verge of leaping to my feet and rushing around the alcove in a state of panic. It took the pain of my nails in my palms to ground me enough I could smother the pigeon's fear and encourage it to get us down off the ceiling.

We skidded across the polished tiles on our talons, a few feathers following us down. Then it was time to walk again. The male voices came from the right, behind a closed door, which was a problem. We clicked over, checking out the circumference of the vast entrance foyer as we went. No sign of life, so far.

With the heavy thuds across the floor, I forced an immediate halt. Someone was moving about behind the door. But the bird's mind was not advanced enough for me to determine what direction they headed, around the room or toward us. Perhaps it was better we took flight and rested on the head of the large statue over by the wall opposite.

Too late, during my procrastination someone yanked the door open and stepped out of the room. The pigeon's own instincts took over and the thing gave one hard downbeat and left the ground but went little further. In an instant, our wings were pinioned to our sides, and we were held on our back, belly exposed.

The ground, the surrounds of the entrance on both sides of our head, the man in front, all were in view, and my mind spun in loops. I turned the pigeon's head side on and peered up into eyes of darkness, ink black, like a tunnel to purgatory. We were pinned in the large hand of Jarro Peers, wings stabled tight to our sides, and we couldn't even manage a wriggle.

He lifted us up, face height, pulled us close and looked in our eyes, and I felt like I was being swallowed by a vast nothingness.

"Well, that's a strange thing," came a man's deep voice from beside Jarro.

Preston, dressed in light colored casual slacks and polo shirt looking like he was heading out to his golf caddy. "Can't image how it got in, or what possessed it to enter in the first place." His vowels were clipped, his voice smooth.

Jarro quirked his left lip in the evilest smile that had ever tantalized my lady bits. "I think I can." All masculine vibes and subtle threat with the tone dropping to a soft rumble at the end of his sentence.

The pigeon saved me from slipping under, its mind flipping into hyper drive. I was zipped and zapped around in its brain as the poor thing prepared to die.

I'm sorry. But I couldn't stay inside. It was the best thing for the bird, the best thing for me. Somehow, that evil swine knew the pigeon hadn't arrived in Preston's entrance foyer under its own steam. I couldn't guess how, but if I pulled out now, perhaps he'd sense that, too, and let the poor bird free. Or maybe he'd eat it. I really couldn't say. No one knew vampires except their own kind.

I yanked my mind back, bricking up the enclosure I had developed to keep my mind and the animals around me separate. When I first discovered my talent, my mind seemed to stay prized open for any encounter. I was in and out of animals' heads until I lay near comatose, unable to work out where they stopped, and I began. Auntie Bea dug around in her photocopied compilation of grimoires until she found a useful practice I could adopt to strengthen my barriers and keep my mind intact. It worked just fine, but it still took moments after invading an animal's mind for me to feel normal again and remember I couldn't fly or the squashed, half-eaten bit of burger on the paving wasn't the best thing I'd ever smelt.

I palmed the paving beside me, kept my eyes closed, and inhaled the smell of exhaust fumes and daisies. My head swam, so I focused on the brick wall behind me, the solidity of its support, the cold as it seeped through my jacket. When I felt grounded enough, I opened my eyes and gently pushed to my feet.

This was bad. Bad, bad, bad. He had known. I could see it in those black eyes. Like prongs, I thought his glare would stab inside and pull me out, so he could dangle me in his maw. A tingle rushed over my bones. How? No one could do that. Maybe vampires could. Perhaps that was one of their super abilities the rest of us paranormals were clueless about. If he was a vampire. I didn't have proof of that. Besides, what was he doing there, if not hoping to beat the nephilim and win the skull?

This was a mess. I had to get home and tell Auntie Bea. See if she had managed further research on any resident vampires. I rushed out of the alcove onto the street and plowed into a solid wall of muscle. Hands gripped me around the waist before my mind had caught up.

"This is a surprise," came that low rumbled leisurely drawl that sounded like he'd just stretched out of bed.

"Oh...Jarro." And then my mind blanked.

"Changed your mind about the tennis." His gaze dipped, feathered across my middle region, dipped again down to my legs. I swear those eyes had fingers attached because my body felt all of it.

"More important things came up."

"Slumming it today."

What? My outfit wasn't designer, but denims, cord jacket, and trainers blended in anywhere. "I'm going for lunch in...Wolgod Quarter." Dark mother take my life now. "There's a cool cafe near the college."

His eyes forgot their wandering and settled on mine. They were better wandering, because looking at them sucked the rest of the street into oblivion. My dangerous, high-level predator warning beacon melted. My extremely lickable, and erotic-as-sin barometer exploded.

"Since when have you gone to Wolgod Quarter?"

"Since I discovered the cafe." I gave a gentle warning shove, the sort that says time for manhandling was up. He didn't take the hint. I'm not even sure he felt it, for his grip didn't change, his expression neither—gaze predatorily nailed on me, into me, like my skin was paper.

"What cafe?"

"The cute one opposite the campus."

His expression the perfect poker canvas. "I'm going to need a little more than that."

I blinked.

"I think I need to keep an eye on you. For your own good."

"I'm there with friends. It's a girls only thing."

"Your friends agreed to go to Wolgod Quarter?"

"We're trying new things."

Watching the slow smile creep across his face was like watching liquid chocolate poured into a mold. I had to swallow the saliva, resist sticking my tongue in the stream for a taste. This vamp was messing with my head. That was a fae trick, but maybe vamps had learned it. "Why were you at my place?"

"Is it unusual?"

I guess not. I had no idea what history these two shared. What was he doing here? Moments ago he was inside the mansion. And now, he was halfway down the street on my tail. Because he damn well knew, Laz. "I'm going to be late." I tried for another gentle shove and found myself pressed closer, invaded by smooth olive skin and warm minted breath. Only a short time ago I had vomited at my feet.

"You owe me, Elka."

"Later," I squeaked, trying to keep my breath to myself.

"Since when have I been patient?"

"A lot has happened of late. So, if you could remind me what I owe you."

He inched his face closer to mine, eyes sliding with sensual grace to my lips. The shadow of a roughish smile played a devilish tune with my nether regions. What was time? What needed doing, thinking? Did I even care? He was answering my request, hinting a promise. I felt it as a threat, to my clarity, sanity, judgement, hormones and peace of mind. D.E.A.D.L.Y. The absolute deadliest of the deadly; an enigmatic killer oozing sex appeal like a torrential downpour.

I pressed a finger to his lips; preservation instincts. Don't let those lips touch you, girl. "I think I can guess. Perhaps we can do this later, in private."

"It's never bothered you before." He spoke around my finger, warm, moist breath teasing the skin.

I didn't want to know these things about my sister. I didn't want to imagine the things they had done, the things he would be thinking about me right now, all the memories in his head of them together, believing I was Elka.

And the last thing I should be doing is wondering about the feel of his lips on mine; as seductive as the feel of his hand on my left hip, the other on my lower back, a finger slipping under the rim of my jeans. I should not be acutely aware of him, nor my body sparked alive as if I was sucking up volts like cordial.

"Are you going to answer me?"

"Yes...no...what?" He was talking? I needed to slap myself. Mix some fresh in with all those pheromones, dilute them down a bit. "I really need to go."

He set me back, and I teetered on the verge of falling into him. I blame the bird for upsetting my equilibrium. It usually took me a while to walk properly on two feet again.

"Soon." It was only one syllable, but he still made it sound like a delectable threat.

Because he didn't move, I turned and fled down the side street in the opposite direction from which I'd come, which meant I was going to have to follow maps on my phone to get back if I went too far. And I was not going to look back. Definitely not.

CHAPTER 7

Not only was Hyun-woo handsome, kind, thoughtful and rippling with a rack of muscles under his fitted shirt—I was sure, even though I had not seen under his shirt, but it fitted him well —he was also refreshingly uncomplicated and human, easy to talk to, and full of interesting tales. He gobbled up the bus journey to the next district of Wolgod Quarter with stories of life in his village, Daeseong-dong, which lay within the Korean demilitarized zone. His family had a good life but grew weary of the nightly curfew and head-count. His parents wanted more for him, which meant a better education than a tiny village could offer. This drove them to move farther south, and then ultimately, overseas.

After the disaster at Elka's I had run into Hyun-woo coming down the stairs after fixing our front door. I still felt a little funky after my time with Jarro, so on seeing Hyun-woo, I asked him to show me his campus this afternoon; I needed someone good and whole-some to fill my head and soothe the questions running around in my brain. Did Jarro know about Elka being a witch and did she know Jarro's secret? Given they lived on both the paranormal and munsib sides of life, surely they would have shared notes.

I hadn't wanted to be thrown into the middle of this disaster, but there was no backing out now. Not if I wanted that skull. Which meant I needed answers. I had messaged Elka on my way back from Spard Cross, but she'd failed to reply. I needed to warn her before Jarro tripped her up by mentioning our run in.

"Is everything all right?"

"Sure. Of course. It's an amazing place." I turned my head and pretended to find the campus of Santisima Pureza University amazing.

"Then why is there a crease in the middle of your forehead?"

"The sun. This is me squinting."

He glanced up at the cloudy sky. "You need to try harder than that." To ensure I wasn't offended, he playfully nudged my shoulder with his.

"Just thoughts you won't be interested in." What to say? "So why the yellow circle on the door?"

"It's a Korean thing."

"And all the red lettering in the center?"

"Another Korean thing."

Auntie Bea wasn't impressed when she saw it, using lots of colorful words to describe what she thought.

"Do all Koreans put that sort of thing on their doors?"

It had the look of magic. Real magic or not, I couldn't say. Munsibs loved their superstition, which made weeding out the real from the fabricated hard, especially when you weren't from that culture. And this was bad to own, but I knew little of magical practices outside of this country. Also, I wasn't a magical bloodhound, like some witches, who could smell the residual trace long after someone had performed magic.

"It's Korean shamanism. Yellow repeals evil spirits and red represents life and human emotions. In essence, blood and fire. It's my parents. They grew up steeped in the old ways. That's what happens when you spend most of your life in a small village with little outside influence. They insist on littering symbols all over the place." He rolled his eyes for effect. "You now have a protection symbol on your door. Not only from malevolent spirits, but also the living, with evil intent residing within their soul. It was Mom's idea." He sounded apologetic.

"That's sweet of her, but why does she think we need a protection symbol on our door?" Had Hyun-woo seen through our lies.

"The apartment is cheap, but the door didn't fall off its hinges by itself. I know, because I replaced it a few months ago, including the hinges. It got Mom worried. Especially with those men hanging around."

Whether it was just a picture on a door or a real protection symbol, I doubted it would keep the Apostles from entering if I failed to get hold of the skull. And if Auntie Bea wasn't a rummy with practically no magical gifts, even casting, and I only inheriting the gift of goddess Diana and not some smacking impressive abilities of my own, we'd not have to worry about the Apostles. Assholes could smell the weak.

"I know trouble is chasing you, Larnie."

Hyun-woo was not afraid to hold a level stare. Though polite, calm and unassuming, he was not afraid to tackle a difficult topic head on. "Laz. Only my school teachers and members of my...let's just say people I'm not overly fond of use Larnie."

"Okay, Laz, what sort of trouble are you and your Auntie in?"

"Auntie Bea loves poker. Sadly, she hasn't learned to stop when she's losing. It's caused trouble for us in the past."

He was still holding eye contact, which I found uncomfortable yet alluring. I'd never spent time with a guy who locked you in his gaze and held on like he were interested in every word you said. Problem was, most of what I'd said so far were lies.

"I didn't ask you here to talk about me."

"Isn't that what people do on first dates?"

Two conflicting feelings toyed with my equilibrium on hearing the word date. I'd spent a few hours with him and already I knew he was a keeper. But for some human woman who could offer him a stable, normal life. I had made a mistake asking him out. If I allowed him in, I would lose control of the depth of the mistake and destroy his innocence. People like the Apostles, my coven, the church, people like Jarro didn't care how many humans suffered, while they played their dirty games for dominance.

"Hyun-woo, I...I'm crap at first dates. I'm crap at relationships. And you should know, Auntie Bea and I aren't planning on staying long in Davenport. Once we've cleared our business up, we'll be moving on."

"You rented our apartment, so I figured you wouldn't be staying."

"This is fun. I've had a great time. But I'm not sure how many days I can spare to having a great time."

"Whatever you can spare, I'm happy to fill."

His eyes weren't capable of stripping me raw, but that didn't mean they weren't captivating.

"We're here, now. Perhaps you could show me some more of this gorgeous place."

Santisima Pureza University with all its pointed arches, spires, cavernous spaces, fancy windows, and whatnot, was a stunning place. According to the plaque on the lawn at the entrance, it was super old, dating back to the fifteen hundreds. I didn't know they built such amazing places back then. Classic gothic.

"Some gorgeous things have a darker side."

He left the sentence there, so I sneaked a sideways glance to find him looking at me. It was a significant look. The look someone gives you as they wait for the penny to drop.

Oh...he meant me, did he?

"Is that a lead-in to a gory story of the university's history?"

Was this Hyun-woo being flirtatious? If the metaphor in that statement was me, that would mean he thought me gorgeous. Blooming tingles messed with my concentration. No one had said that about me before. Tyros, my short-term lover demon, had used some descriptive adjectives to describe me, some of them ear scorchingly explicit, which suited what we wanted from each other, but he never used an endearing word like gorgeous.

"I have a few if you're interested."

"Aren't you the archeologist. Wait, they dig around at burial grounds and stuff. I meant anthropologist."

"Ancient history, actually. That's what I'm studying. And while the campus isn't ancient, it's got some stories to tell of interest to anyone who loves a ghost story."

"I love ghost stories, especially when they're gory."

"This one's better told at nighttime."

"Now this sounds like an interesting tale."

"A sad tale, actually. It was on this spot a terrible massacre took place between the native people of the region and aggressive invaders. It's your classic story of imperialism. A wealthier nation of people arriving to destroy what they see as an inferior, primitive way of life and occupying valuable fertile land." He leaned my way, conspiratorial like. "But if you dig a little deeper, you'll find some interesting texts that speak of magic." He raised his eye brows at me. "According to a different kind of legend to the academic version of events, the invaders were a people that wielded a magic far superior to the native people, who used a gentle form of earthbound magic."

"Earthbound, as in elemental?"

"You know your magic, I see."

"Fantasy worlds were my favorite as a child." I flashed him a cardboard smile.

"A lesser form of elemental magic. They used it to ensure fertility in all things, including themselves. It's why the invaders found the land so lush and bountiful."

"What were the names of these two tribes?"

"Neither tribes had a name. They had no written language. They passed their stories down through the generations. A lot of it came from the invaders, the biased tales, that is. But there were survivors of the massacre who lived to pass down their traditions through the generations long enough for snippets of it to be recorded in writing. It's all gone now, of course."

"If it was such a massacre, why aren't we taught about this in high school history?"

"Because most academics don't believe a word of it. There were excavations done on the site in the early eighteenth century and more about thirty years ago. All hoping to verify the ancient tales, but no one has found any evidence. There's no sign anyone was here that far back. It's now all myth."

"You're a historian in the making. What do you think?"

"My parents say the ground is angry. They say a hwanghae-do jinogwigut must be performed to guide the dead to paradise and ease their tormented spirits."

"They can't have liked you coming here."

"That's why I have this." He raised the short sleeve of his shirt to show me a tattoo of what looked like lines, boxes and funny squiggles inked in yellow. "My parents insisted. It was the only way I could pacify them."

"Yellow, for protection, right?"

"Yeah."

"Isn't it terrible that new arrivals would know more history about my country than I do? I've lived here all my life, and I did not know about this. How shocking is that?"

"You don't live in Davenport, and I'm sure half of Davenport doesn't even know this history. Probably half the kids at this campus don't know about it. I'm a history buff, remember."

"It pays to know our history." I murmured. Was any of this true? While I didn't believe every tale about magic, I didn't automatically dismiss them either. After all, I knew what lived amongst humanity, and a lot of the creatures lived very long lives. If there was truth to this story, did any of the paranormals inhabiting Davenport have ancestral roots here, either from the native people or the invaders?

"Have you seen any ghost activity here?" I tried to make it sound like I was treating it as a bedtime story.

"Nah. Liminal times are when spirits grow restless. Twelve midnight and twelve midday—the breaking of one day from the previous, creates the weakest link in the veil that separates our world from the beyond. That and the equinoxes, the exact moment when the sun dips below the horizon. There are others." He shrugged. "I grew up with suspicious parents. I couldn't even go to the toilet without performing some ritual of cleansing."

"You're joking, right?"

He laughed. It captured my attention. The way his smile carried on up into his eyes and bathed his face in warmth. When had I been around a guy who oozed both sex appeal and boy-next-door vibes? Oh, Hyun-woo, you are dangerous. The heart-severing kind of dangerous. And sometimes, that was the deadliest kind.

"How about you?" He asked.

"Oh, yes, we're steeped in rituals. Auntie Bea can't start the day without smoking half a pack of cigarettes. Says without them, her mojo is shite. That's also what the gin is for."

What I couldn't tell him was how close he was to the truth regarding spirits. Not that I knew a lot, because Auntie Bea and I kept away from anything to do with the spirit world. It required significant power and mind control to keep the divide between them and us intact. I'd witnessed a few summonings before we left the coven—emphasis on the witnessing. I'd never played a part. But that had been three years ago. It wasn't too uncommon for some superstitions to be built on facts, so it was no surprise his parents' beliefs weren't too far wrong.

"You're close to your aunt?"

"She's all I've got."

"My sister died six years ago. It's just my parents and me, now."

I stopped, facing him. "That must've been painful."

"My parents are still getting over it."

"And you?"

"We were close." He stared past me, sounding like he wasn't here beside me any longer, and I didn't want to interrupt the private moment with his memories by bumbling words and apologies. Then he blinked as if to orientate himself.

"I can understand why your mom wants you wearing protection charms." Not the smoothest way to fill awkward silences or move the conversation on from something as solemn as death.

He slipped his hands in his pockets and straightened his back with a stretch. Relaxing again, he looked over my head at the campus behind. I noticed the moment something caught his attention, saw the subtle shift in his expression, the intensity in his stare.

I glanced over my shoulder and saw a bunch of gothic buildings casting spiked shadows across the lawn. When I turned back, his eyes were back on me.

"Shall we get a drink somewhere?"

"Sounds good."

He took my hand and led me away from the campus. I was almost too busy concentrating on the warmth of his hand and how nice it felt wrapped around mine to bother looking one last time. Almost. Curiosity won out.

There was nothing there. Just arches, spires, and gargoyles. A lot of gargoyles. There'd probably been that many before, and I had never noticed. Given the tales he'd told earlier, I couldn't stop the small shiver, couldn't help but feel a moment of significance had flashed past, and I missed it.

CHAPTER 8

I came early and sat at the back of the cafe, facing the street, so I could see everyone entering and leaving. Elka was late, just as I expected. Her message was vague, and when I rang her back seconds later, relieved she had finally contacted me, her voice sounded equally vague. She was busy and would have to squeeze me in between a one-hour pilates session and her manicure, because we were sisters, she tacked on the end with false cheer. She would be late, I'd told myself after she promptly ended the call before I asked her if she'd spoken to Jarro yet.

The waitress passed my table numerous times, with a pad and pen the first time, then with a coffee pot the second time, hoping to entice me into ordering something so I could get a free cup of coffee. The coffee in Davenport tasted like diesel, so I wasn't tempted in the least. This time 'round, the server blocked my view of the door, coffee pot in hand.

"You lookin' to order?"

"When my friend arrives."

Her eyes roamed my face for lies, shifted to my clothes, the jacket and shirt all she could see while I was sitting, and shrugged her shoulders just as Elka appeared behind her, towering over her like a goddess of fine makeup application.

"Hey, hon, sooooooo sorry I'm late." She inched around the server, who remained like a mannequin as Elka shimmered passed in her red jeggings, which are one up from sweatpants as far as I'm concerned, but she made them look like a high fashion with her strappy high heels and crop top. "Oops, sorry." She cooed at the server, pouting her plum-colored lips like the false apology it was, and slid on the seat opposite me, dragging her bags of shopping with her. "Benedicts." She explained, waving her shopping bags, then settling them beside her. "They announced their latest winter range. You can't expect me to wait at the end of the queue. Charles understands my needs."

"Charles?"

"The saint." She grabbed a menu from the center holder and absentmindedly flicked through it. She suggested this place, so likely knew everything on the menu. Flickering her gaze to mine, she added. "My best friend and holy purveyor of the most gorgeous fashion this side of the equator. But for out-of-towners, such as yourself, you may call him Sir Charles Benedicts."

I nodded, unmoved by the theatrics. I had more important things to worry about than high fashion and the menu. I had a few days left to retrieve the skull before the Apostles arrived back on our door. Somehow I had to convince Elka to help me. How I did that without telling her everything was the big mystery. Unless she knew the sort of tale I would tell.

"Have you seen Jarro?"

She threw the menu down, delicately rested her elbows on the table so she could entwine her fingers and flashed her perfect smile. "That is the second time you have asked about that man."

"You got my message, right?"

"I was curious about that." She rested her chin in the cradle of her thumb and finger. Every move she made was like a camera pose. I expected flashing bulbs at any moment. "I don't remember giving you my address."

"You're Bernard Preston's daughter. I didn't have to hunt very hard."

The waitress appeared with pen and pad, minus the coffee. "You gonna order?"

Elka turned on her with a dazzling movie star smiled that flashed gleaming white teeth so perfect they looked like molds. "I'll have a freshly squeezed juice of chard, cucumber and barley grass, with a dash of turmeric, and a pinch of pepper."

"We don't do those." The waitress didn't even blink.

"I didn't think so," Elka breathed.

"I'll have a hot chocolate, regular milk."

"Hon, your hips. At least have oat milk." Elka glanced at the waitress. "Minus the marshmallows."

"Is that it?" The waitress's tone said she wasn't having a good day.

"Scram, we have secrets to discuss." Rudeness plus, and Elka added to that by moving closer to the table and staring at me like the waitress wasn't even there.

Knowing her cue, the waitress disappeared, probably to head out back and spit in my cup.

"You've never been here before, have you?"

Of course she hadn't. Cheap, cracked vinyl on the seats, chipped laminate on the corners of the tables and a discolored line on the linoleum floors where many thousands of feet had trod. "There's less risk of you being spotted here. That's why we're here, isn't it?"

"You hunted me down. Why?" She flipped the interrogation back on to me.

"Maybe it has something to do with the fact we're sisters."

"Possibly half."

Did she just say that? "Since when are twins half-sisters?"

She smiled. It would've been beautiful, if it didn't look so condescending. "I'm overwhelmed, really I am. But I think it's best kept a secret. Have you told your aunt?" She didn't want daddy knowing, didn't want a sister muscling in on her happy life.

"Of course. I wanted to know why she didn't tell me."

"They write tragedies from family wounds."

Best to ignore her constant lapses into incivility. "And you obviously never told your family?"

"I have a much better idea than telling my family about you. You can be my dirty little secret."

"I'm involved in too many secrets. I'm not excited about entering another."

She huddled over, rubbing her palms together. "You are juicy. Who would've guessed? Someone as plain as yourself. But you have my genes."

"Or you have mine." Now we sounded like sisters. Maybe it wasn't such a bad thing we got separated at birth. She huffed a laugh as she reached over and grabbed all her bags of shopping, each with Benedicts embossed in gold on the side, and heaved them over the table to me. "Take these."

"I'm sure no one's going to steal them while I'm here."

"No, silly, they're yours. I hope they'll fit. I bought a size bigger than I normally do."

The bags crinkled and scrunched as they tumbled to the floor; I missed all of them in my shock. "What're you talking about?"

"This won't work if you're dressed like that."

"Can you break down, in English, what you're trying to say."

"You and I are going to swap places."

Did she just say that? The whole thing about sisters thinking alike was true and eery. "You want me to be you?"

""It's the best fun you'll ever have. Father and mother know so little about me, you'll pull it off, no problem. You'll have to find some ingenious explanation for the weight gain, but I get the feeling you're good at talking yourself out of tight situations."

"This is ridiculous, and exactly the thing I was going to suggest we do."

"You were? Why are you acting so uppity then?"

"I'm not acting uppity." Pathetic thing was, now she'd suggested the swap ahead of me, I was backpedaling. "There's certain things you have to know about my aunt."

The waitress sloshed my hot chocolate over into the saucer as she placed it down in front of me and left.

"She'll never know."

"Oh yes, she will. Besides, why would you want to pretend to be poor? You've got everything."

"Life is a challenge. Until you have everything. Then it's just life."

"You could try taking more drugs." That was mean of me.

"Ouch. So you do have teeth. I was wondering if the mouse knew how to bite."

"My life's not a game."

"I'm deadly serious."

What if she got her mitts all over Hyun-woo? This was your idea, too. I wanted this swap, but Elka was dynamic and sexy. I could see her and Auntie Bea getting along. And Hyun-woo...well, he was a guy. What guy could resist someone like Elka? *He's not yours to fight for.*

"It's not forever. We could try it out for a month, say."

"I don't have a month. Auntie Bea and I are leaving town soon, just as soon as we've finished some business."

"I could help with that."

"You don't know what sort of work we do."

"I'm smart and learn quick."

"Not this sort of work."

"My, my, you are the enigma." She placed both hands on the table, palms flat, and slid them forward as she leaned over. Any minute now she'd offer me an apple, the temptress in the garden of Eden. "I'm totally intrigued now," Her words were like syrup.

I sat back in my seat, maintaining distance between us before she practically slithered herself across the table.

"Mysteries and secrets, an enticing mix. Do you journal by any chance?"

A whiplash change of topic. "No."

"Pity. I'd love to read it while I'm at yours. So I could get into that head of yours, loosen up some of those corset strings, strip that chastity belt."

I clenched my teeth and bit back a snarky retort.

"I'll give you twenty-four hours to think about it."

I didn't know Elka, but I was fast believing she lived life with agendas and schemes, every promise conditional, every word a twisted truth. She'd fit in well with the hierarchy governing the church. Not that she'd make a very devout disciple. I guess that was something we had in common

"There must be something you would like. After all, you did hunt me down."

My skin crawled under her expression. Blessed mother, she was a viper.

"The skull." No more games.

"Glad you've decided to play."

"I'm not playing. It's very important I get the skull."

"That old piece of junk."

"Which your dad handed over half his bank account to acquire."

She rolled her eyes. "Oh please, honey, he's much wealthier than that."

"It's a matter of life and death that I get the skull."

"And you know how to get it."

This was it. We hovered on the edge of the big reveal. She knew I knew, and I knew she knew. All that was left was to say it.

"If you are me, all you have to do is walk right into my house and take it for yourself."

"You're encouraging me to steal from your father just so you can have your fun and play being poor for a month."

"I'm helping my sister. Blood is thicker than water. Isn't that what they say?"

"Stop pretending, Elka." I couldn't do it anymore. The charades were mashing up my guts. I was about to throw up.

She heaved a delicate breath. "You know what? I genuinely like you. Every so often you flex a claw or two. It's so much more exciting than that dull Pollyanna complex you have going on."

"Just tell me."

She rolled her head slowly, like she was reenacting a stretch from her pilates class. When done, she eyed me for long seconds, then dipped her gaze to my now lukewarm hot chocolate. Within a short time, steam rose from off the brown liquid. Soon it was bubbling. I inhaled, glaring up at her.

"Is that words enough for you?"

She had more magic than I did. Everyone thought the gift of goddess Diana was a significant ability, but I was waiting to believe them. Who cared if you could follow a cat slink around the house while sitting outside. I had minimal spell-casting ability, which was real magic. So far, I'd only succeeded with minor party tricks. Bubbling coffee wasn't much more advanced, but she'd performed the spell in seconds, without twitching a mouth muscle, which meant she'd advanced to mental casting. Maybe she'd sucked up all my magic in the womb.

"I'm suffocated. I live in a house of munsibs."

"You know that word."

"I have to practice the arcane arts in secret." She went on like she hadn't heard me, probably because I had interrupted her moaning time.

"If you know what munsib means, then you can't be cut off from you heritage. Are you a member of the church?"

"Oh god, no, why would I do that?"

"Because no witch may practice outside the church."

"It's a good thing the church doesn't know about me then. Isn't it?"

But of course the church wouldn't know about her. They never marked her at birth like they did me because Auntie Bea had taken me and left her. The mark alerted the church to my ascension. Elka missed all of that, safely tucked away as she was in the orphanage.

"How do you know how to cast without a teacher or grimoire?"

"I'm surrounded by teachers." She did a twirl with her pointer fingers into the air to sweep in the whole of Davenport. "If you know where to look."

"Such as?"

"The Apostles of Eternal Night."

If my bottom jaw wasn't hinged to the top, it would be on the floor. "You're messing with them?"

"Honey, I'm messing with them all right."

"They're misogynistic assholes."

"Who know their magic."

"But they treat any witch stupid enough to join their church like dogs."

"I don't join churches. Besides, they're men. And all men are easy to tame once you know the one thing they want."

"You've been sleeping your way through the Apostles."

"Some of them are hot."

"So I don't embarrass you, I'll try not to vomit."

She arched her head back in a graceful, movie star pose and laughed a musical tone. "You obviously haven't tried them."

Seeing my hard stare, she straightened, her expression growing sulky. "Only three. Alright? I'm not so silly to get involved with any more. And I've never stepped foot inside their church. I'm not okay being chained to an altar. Don't worry, I know what goes on in their dungeons. I meet them when they're out drinking. There's a bar in Lower Boddock. That's where they like to hang out. It makes them easy pickings."

Who was I to judge? I had an affair with a demon.

"Where's Lower Boddock from here?"

"The other side of the city. But north of Daughters of the Dark Mother. They wouldn't want to be too close together. Sparrow Swift is the district between the two, occupied by the Church of Living

Light. I dallied there for a while, tried to convince them I was willing to convert, but couldn't quite pull off the piety act. They're too puritanical for my liking, Too many rules, even worse than the Dark Mother."

"I need a map marked with the locations of the strongholds for the most powerful factions. That way I don't accidentally stumble into anyone I'd rather not meet."

Elka swiped a paper hand towel from the dispenser in the center of the table. With a pen from her bag, she sketched me a rough mud map of the city's layout and drew in the locations of each paranormal faction's headquarters.

"Wait. The Apostles of Eternal Night are in Wolgod Quarter?" I said the moment I saw her scribble their name underneath the district name.

"Yeah so?"

"So is Santisima Pureza University."

"And?"

"I know someone who goes there."

"I thought you'd never been to Davenport."

"He's the son of our landlords."

"Is he cute?"

"No." I shouldn't feel so defensive. "What else is there?" I leaned further over the small paper hand towel.

"The Order of Sotiria are north of you."

"What does that say?" I asked, pointing at the district. Her writing was nothing but scrawl.

"Snin Cross."

She then scribbled a dark area at the top, the district of Upper West Shard and the same at the bottom, Lower West Nidin.

"Why the dark patches north and south of the city?"

"The Cantonia rule the south. The Vehan the nnorth. Go to either on pain of death. Both districts extend farther north and south than Davenport City, encompassing the forest and farming lands on both sides."

Vampires. The stories of their ancient feud was folklore in any paranormal circle.

"And to the far east is the Sojourn Lands. The pack HQ. Their range covers the deep forest to the east. The Fae folk claim all the lands of course, but between the pack to the east and the vampires to the north and south they are squeezed into the west district of Glimin Grove."

I stared at the patchwork map, outlining the regions I would have to stay away from. Preservation had taught Auntie Bea and I to keep clear of the top paranormal factions since we had little between us in the way of power. Most other cities weren't so infested with the top ranks of the paranormal community. Paranormal factions located themselves in one region of the country or the other, creating natural boundaries between themselves and others because few got along peacefully for too long, especially vampires and the pack. And the Vehan and Cantonia residing in the same city was impossible to understand. The Brothers of Redentore were never within the same city as the Church of Living Light. They preferred to stay clear of anyone so they could carry out their disgusting habits in peace.

"Why are there so many paranormal factions in Davenport? There's practically no place on this map that isn't claimed by someone powerful."

Elka slammed her hand down on the map, making me jump. "You don't know?"

"Obviously."

She moved her hand and circled the heart of the city a couple of times with big messy loops. And I noticed it. No one had claimed the very center of the city as their own.

"Why has no one claimed that part?"

"It's the nexus. No one can without causing total annihilation."

Of all the surprises Davenport had held since I arrived, that was not one of them, and yet it was the biggest freaking revelation anyone could drop. "Why did Auntie Bea not tell me?"

"Because she probably didn't think you'd come. Besides, I can't believe you don't know the location of every nexus."

"Auntie Bea and I stay away from trouble as much as we can, which means staying out of the paranormal community as much as possible. I know there's one in Chile and one in Russia."

"And Australia, and here."

The nexus were places of immense power. Living close by was like sitting on a nuclear power station, just waiting for the reactor to malfunction. "So that's why Davenport's of full of top level paranormals."

"The nexus attracts them like moths. Luckily all the factions are smart enough to understand that few would survive such devastation, otherwise someone would've been stupid enough to make a grab for the nexus by now. And since the different factions never trust each other, no one has been able to form an alliance and push the advantage. They sneak around each other, spy on each other, goad each other, but no one has come up with a smart enough plan yet to ensure they are the winners."

Elka gathered up the map, folded it, and handed it to me. "This is my gift to you, in exchange for your agreement with our deal."

I placed my hand on the map. "Thanks. But I was going to agree anyhow."

She kept hold of the other end of the hand towel. "With one proviso."

"And that is?"

"Stay away from Jarro Peers. He's Vehan."

"I know."

"Smart little girl."

"You sound like you know more about the paranormal world than me, but one thing I do know is vampires care for no one but themselves."

"That's the whole paranormal world, sugar. Everyone hates everyone. But two feuding hives within the same city spells big trouble. It's why they're on opposite ends of the city. They couldn't get any farther apart while still in the same city. And of course, neither one is going to tuck their tails and leave the nexus open to the other hive to exploit. They're caught here, like every other faction. But they clash a lot. Those clashes will build, and one day the clashes will be war. Don't get caught on a side. You'd best be out of Davenport by then."

"What about you? Would you hang around in Davenport if it looks like it would go that far?"

"This is my home. But I also like the idea of seeing the world. Who knows, maybe I'll have other plans by then."

There was that Elka agenda again. "Maybe we should catch up again before we do the switch? You need to run some house rules by me. Fill me in on do's and don'ts in your house hold."

"Sure, sugar. This is exciting. Sister's working on a secret together."

"Hmm." It was all I could say.

CHAPTER 9

When I crept out around nine this morning for the diner to catch up with Elka, Auntie Bea was still in bed. Nothing unusual there. Throughout the morning, I'd expected a text from her wanting to know where I was. But nothing.

On coming home, I headed for her room, thinking I'd find her snoring under the covers. The bed clothes lay in disarray over the floor. Since she wasn't here, the disarray became sinister rather than Auntie Bea's house proud style. Because the apartment was so small and lacked a lot of furniture, it took minutes to satisfy myself there were no signs of struggle. Not even Hyun-woo's newly hung door looked tampered with.

Maybe she took advantage of the high priestess's chilling welcome back into the fold of the church. Though I would not expect her to head off on her own without touching base with me, given she didn't know where I was.

I pulled my phone and tried her number one more time. The tone rang five times before switching to voice mail, and I left my third message. It felt like someone had pulled a heavy blanket over my shoulders, dragging them to the floor. I took the cover off my phone and pulled out the map of Davenport, unfolded it, and placed it on the table, running my hand over the creases to flatten them out as best I could. Wolgard Quarter was a couple of bus rides away. That's where I would find the Apostles of Eternal Night, and Auntie Bea, hopefully. The heavy blanket fell to my soul.

I replaced the map inside the jacket of my phone, grabbed my jacket, which I'd slung over the back of the kitchen chair when I had arrived, and headed for the door. While slipping the key in the lock, I noticed a discoloration on the red lettering at the center of the circle. I leaned in close, my hand hovering inches from a faded, coppery splat that looked like someone had hurled a paintbrush at the door and tried to remove the stain. The backdrop of yellow overlaid with red script blended the color perfectly, so it wasn't readily noticeable to someone dashing inside.

Feeling a prickly tickle on my palm, it was like someone had siphoned my blood away. I snatched my hand back. Only a few gifted witches felt residue from magic, like the ice queen Agatha, the high priestess who initiated me into our coven. I was not one of them.

The scenario played out in my head. The Apostles came, breaking our bargain by arriving ahead of time, hoping to replicate their entrance. Except the door remained intact, with barely a mark on it. No mistaking it though, the feeling on my palm came from magic, and Aunt Bea had disappeared. I wasn't sure what I could do against the Apostles of Eternal Night, but I couldn't sit back and let anything happen to Auntie Bea.

I bounded down the stairs and collided with Hyun-woo coming out the side door of the shop. On reflex, he snapped out his arms to catch me, his hands landing on my hips as I collided with his chest.

"Laz, sorry." His hands remained on my hips a beat longer than a stranger would allow. "You all right?" Those dark brown eyes searched mine.

What was it, my expression, or some vibe I exuded that let slip my agitation? "Sure. Sorry, I need to go."

He released me from his grip, but not his eyes. His attention drilled into me, a demanding intensity in his gaze.

"I've really got to go, sorry."

He stayed me with a sweep of his arm, blocking my path. "Not like you are."

Maybe it was living in Dim Bazaar with its shady characters, and the Turono gang menacing the shopkeepers, maybe it was life in the demilitarized zone in Korea. Whatever it was, Hyun-woo seemed attuned to my poorly guarded distress.

"Hyun-woo, please. I really need to go."

"Something's wrong, Laz. You can tell me."

If only I could. My eyes flicked between his as my mouth filled with words I wanted to say. Blessed dark mother, I'd bleed into that vessel for the privilege of keeping Hyun-woo by my side. He was good and caring and too human to be caught up in the dark world, as much as he was playing the protector right now. It suited him. Made him cute and sexy. But I needed to protect him.

"Mom saw your aunt leave with some men."

I closed my eyes, my pulse sucking me along on its flow.

"Are we talking the same men who turned up the other night? The same ones who took out the door?" He was way too acute for his own safety.

"Not sure. Could be some of her gambling buddies. But I've got to go."

"I'll come with you."

"What? No. You don't need to. I'm meeting—"

He stepped close, placed a hand over my lips. "Don't waste your breath with a lie."

At the press of his finger on my lips, a thread of goodness swamped my mind, body and soul. I'd savor this feeling a bit more, savor him a bit more if not for everything else in my life spilling out of control. "Hyun-woo, you can't. It's... You don't want lies, so I can't finish my sentence." The cheap tiled floor was easier to look at than his face. "Our lives are complicated. And right now they have taken a dive into the pit." Finding the courage to glance up at him, I found his smooth brow heavily ridged and thought about magically smoothing it away with a run of my finger, like a magnetic board. But I didn't have that sort of magic. "There's nothing you can do. It's something we need to sort out."

"You're in danger."

"Nah." I tried for causal, smacking him gently on the chest.

He stilled my hand with his, keeping it cocooned between the warmth of his chest and his palm. "I told you not to waste your breath with lies. I'm not as helpless as you seem to think."

In this you are. "I don't think you're helpless. But this is a—"

"You don't get it. I have a savior complex. I can't let someone face their demons alone if I believe I can assist."

Blessed mother, he was so sweet. I wanted him to be my savior, or at least ride beside me into battle. But I couldn't let him do that, nor could I tell him why.

"Just give me a moment. Then we'll go together." He ducked back inside the shop.

I gave him two seconds' count, darted for the front door, and out into the street. This was for his own good. He'd be ticked, no doubt, but no way would I have two lives on my conscience. Already, I felt responsible for Auntie Bea's predicament. Which was stupid. After all, she was the gambler, but I'd wasted time being sucked in by Mr Lava Hot and then dallying with Elka, instead of getting straight to the point.

I sprinted down the main street of Dim Bazaar, dodging the foot traffic on the pavement. During the day, the place was a flurry, a different sort of flurry from the nights. Passing under the stone arch demarcating Chinatown from the rest of Dim Bazaar, I cast a look over my shoulders, half expecting to see Hyun-woo sprinting up behind me. He looked like the kind of guy to run marathons at a jog and still cross the finish line first. I, on the other hand, gasped and puffed my way across the line of Chinatown.

A handful of people waited at the bus stop. Hyun-woo would guess I came here, so I legged past it, heading for the bus stop a block down the road. Maybe that was too close as well, but walking all the way to Wolgod Quarter would waste valuable time.

The streets felt concealing enough with throngs of pedestrians hurrying about their business. I tucked myself in the back of the queue and cast a glance the way I'd come. Would he bother to chase me at all? Back in the hall, he'd seemed intent on helping me. Those eyes spoke of bullheaded determination, a man uneasily swayed, rebuffed, or spooked. But Hyun-woo didn't understand the dark creatures that could spook a munsib.

We all shuffled onto the bus, me feeling like I wanted to elbow everyone out the way and whip the driver into a speeding frenzy. The choked traffic forced us to sit curbside until there was a clearing. Once free, the traffic sucked us into the midday jam, and it took us at least ten minutes to reach the end of the street, short as it was. I should've run. In the meantime, I pulled the cover from my phone and released the map. Elka had marked the Apostles of Eternal Night in capital letters, under which she wrote the street name Wylie Close. That was all she gave, all she had room to write on the small square of paper towel. I typed it into maps on my phone and pinged our location, then hit the mute button when a female voice began directing me on the route I had to take. Zooming the screen out, I followed the blue line to the Apostles' door, which was not the way the bus headed. I'd have to get off in seven blocks before the bus turned north and away from Wolgod Quarter.

While placing the map back inside its secret compartment, my phone rang. Only Auntie Bea had my number. I flipped it over to see a number I didn't recognize. Unable to make my fingers work, I stared at the screen while listening to it ring. Who had my number?

"Hello." One more ring and it would've shunted the call to voice mail.

"Get off at the next stop." A clipped male voice demanded.

"Who is this?" I asked, glancing around. Whoever it was could see me.

"Do as I say."

"Give one good reason."

"Bea Jennings."

Reason enough. "I had two more days to get the skull."

"Do you think I care? Make sure you get off at the next stop."

Keeping the phone to my ear, I rose from my seat and headed for the door while signaling my intention to get off. The bus was packed, mostly men. Some on their phones. A handful looked shady, possibly Apostles, but none looked at me. This had to mean they'd planted someone outside my apartment, watching every move I made. Thank our mother Hyun-woo hadn't come with me. That would put him in their sights.

As the bus slowed at the stop, I cast a glance over my shoulder to the people getting off with me. Two women and four men—one was more a boy than a man with a few sprigs of bum fluff sprouting on his chin. Didn't mean he wasn't one of them. They all started as boys. But no one looked at me. No one seemed to care.

"Head left until you reach Henderson. It's a men's shoes shop. On the right of the store is an alley."

"You want me to head into an alley?"

The voice didn't belong to one of the Apostles who turned up the other night to threaten us.

"Smart bitch. Now, do as I say."

"I need proof you haven't hurt Auntie Bea."

"Maybe you're not so smart. You're in no position to make demands."

"Give me a good reason not to smite your ass the moment I see you."

A huff. "I'm gonna enjoy this game."

I clenched my phone and waited.

"We think you lack incentive."

"And leading me into an alley is incentive?"

"No. But it will give me some fun. Once we're done, I'll take you to church."

"I don't follow your religion."

"But you were in a hurry to get there, not so long ago."

"And I'm still in a hurry, so I think I'd rather head there, myself."

"One call. That's all it would take."

"What would your high priest think of you tarnishing the goods?"

"I am the high priest."

I swallowed my saliva wrong and broke out into a fit of coughing.

"Sweet, confused child." His voice slipped a notch, morphed into a tone that creeped talons over my shoulder. I heard him inhale like he was breathing into my ear. "You are on the wrong path, heading the wrong way. I love to collect lost lambs and guide them to the darkness."

I ended the call and spun, expecting to see him behind me. My phone rang again, the same number.

"Don't tempt me." The voice lost its cool, low burn, sharpening to a blade. "You know what to do."

"I've made a blood sacrifice, Hekate has granted me a boon." Lies were going to get me killed, but this was my only, and wildly pathetic, way out. High freaking priest. Auntie Bea, if we survive this, I'm going to kill you.

"Then let us play."

"I've got better things to waste this boon on."

"Look around you. Take one good, long look."

The way he voiced the command, I obeyed with little thought.

"Such an ignorant, feeble species. Munsib. With no idea who walks amongst them. Why is it we hide from them, conduct our worship like we are ashamed? Like we are the lesser species."

I felt like I had hyperthermia.

"Are you willing to be their end?"

My body temperature dropped lower. "What are you saying?" My cheek bone smarted from the pressure of my phone pressed into my cheek.

"It would be nothing for me to do it."

"You wouldn't." I swallowed my heart back down.

"It would be my pleasure."

"I'll go to the alley."

"Of course you will."

I ended the call before I threw my phone to the paving to avoid the infectious sting of his malice. The men's shoe shop was too close. I'd never be able to think up a plan in that time. My feet took me there, even though my mind screamed for me to back away. High priest! There was no outsmarting, no outdoing the dark arts of a high priest, unless you were a witch gifted with tricks of her own who'd studiously studied wicca, but I was not that witch. Escaping into the mind of an animal would leave my body vulnerable.

I wasn't a daughter from the Church of Living Light. I wasn't a good girl. I slipped up countless times and dabbled with things I shouldn't, but I wasn't evil. Munsib were innocent. They didn't deserve to die all for the enjoyment of the Apostles' high priest.

"Blessed, Dark Mother. Stay by your daughter's side. Grant me your dark power." I whispered the words. "And I promise to make another blood sacrifice." It couldn't hurt to make the promise.

By the time I finished making my promise, I had reached Henderson with no idea what to do. Neither did I feel any special zing or sudden influx of power from the Dark Mother.

I slowed, feeling like I was heading into a gun battle. Pedestrians bumped past me as I stood at the mouth of the alley, peering down into a narrow, dingy passageway, shielded from the sun by the high, bricked buildings either side. It looked the perfect place for crime, felt as warm as a fridge, and smelled like a toilet.

A vacuum swallowed the street noise a few paces into the alley. The crunch of my shoes echoed off the bricks, sounding like there was a group of us. Not a group, just one more. His steps were distinct from mine, heavier, slower, prowling.

I inched around to face the Apostle, surprised to see him dressed in a suit with polished shoes. A neat mustache and goatee flung him straight out of a smoke-filled jazz den from the forties. Small creases at the corners of his eyes, but otherwise flawless skin, made me guess at late thirties.

He spread his hands at his sides. "No tricks."

"Tell me why the high priest of the Apostles would follow me."

"Straight to the point, I like that." He folded his hands behind his back and paced toward me, stopping when I took a step back. "I want you. But not for the reasons you may think."

Rape was on my mind, so that was a relief.

"There is something you will do for me."

"I said I would get you the skull."

"The fabled skull." He raised an eyebrow in acknowledgement of the gift the skull would be to the Apostles. "Yes, it's something I very much want. But I think you may be useful for another reason."

"The skull is all you'll get from me."

"And what about your Auntie Bea? Do you think she enjoys her accommodation?"

"She better not be in one of your dungeons."

His smile looked like it hurt him. "The dungeons are for more agreeable pursuits. And I'm afraid your aunt doesn't fit the criteria. She's, shall we say, ensconced in a more suitable place where she can't do herself harm."

"You mean chained to a wall."

He huffed a silent laugh. "You are quite an amusing thing. It's been some time since I've had the pleasure of dealing with such an uncouth woman."

"Tell me what you want from me." Before my skin crawled right off my body.

"It's something that will come to pass in good time, and is of little importance discussing."

"Then why did you lure me here?"

"When I said I needed you, I meant I needed you within my keeping until the right time."

I stepped back. "You'll bring war upon the Apostles if you dare."

"Do not think me ignorant of your standing with your church. The Daughters of Our Dark Mother would not even know you were missing."

"We've made our blood sacrifices. The high priestess has welcomed us in."

"You don't think your high priestess has her own agenda. You haven't wondered why she would accept a rummy?"

I faulted.

"Yes, that's right. I know your aunt is no better than the munsib. She has the stench of humanity all over her. It's you the high priestess wants. Unfortunately, she let you slip away...into my welcoming arms."

He knew too much about our situation, so either he had done things to Auntie Bea to gain the information, or he'd been snooping deeper than we'd thought.

"It's no use," was his response as I darted a look over my shoulder down the alley behind. It was a long way to the other end. I was doubtful I would make it that far without him using magic to bind me. And once I reached the street, then what? He was an Apostle, and their high priest, so I wouldn't dare push him too far, but I doubted he would do the terrible things he threatened on the munsib. If there was one thing the paranormal world agreed upon, that was the necessity of keeping our world a secret to the greater part of humanity. Some paranormals broke the rules occasionally, recruiting munsib for favors, but under pain of a life spent flailed in hell if the secret was ever released. There were a lot more munsib, for starters. They were also flighty and prone to react in negative ways when faced with things outside their scope of understanding, such as pressing buttons to release enormous weapons.

"I think you would agree it's best we get this over with, before some poor unfortunate munsib disrupts us."

"There are people who will look for me." Lame threat.

"You needn't worry about them. They won't find you."

I backed up as he paced toward me, feeling like an ant about to be stepped on. Then it happened so swiftly it was like I blinked and the world changed. The high priest went down to his hands and knees with a groan, his head lolling like someone about to be sick.

"Hyun-woo. What are you doing?" I shrieked.

He tossed the metal pole in his hand and leaped over the high priest. On touching down, he grabbed my hand and dragged me off down the alley. I tried to keep pace, but he was too much for me. Sensing this, he slowed a fraction. "Go as fast as you can."

"You shouldn't be here," I got out between gasps.

"Neither should you." And he squeezed my hand harder.

The wall beside us exploded, sending fragments of brickwork thundering down on us. Hyun-woo pulled me close, throwing his arm up over my head as the best shield he could provide while we sprinted. I dared a look over my shoulder to see the high priest staggering to his feet. He was likely dazed, that being the reason for his shoddy spell-casting.

"He's getting up." If he got to his feet and could still see straight, we'd be in trouble.

Hyun-woo released my hand and halted. "Keep going," he shouted at me and turned to face the high priest.

"Are you crazy?"

But he wasn't listening. Instead, he stood still, his hands clasped before him, head bent, eyes closed like he was in prayer.

"Hyun-woo," I called, but kept my voice soft, my hands at my sides, for there was something about the way he stood that surged a tingle through my body. I'd cast a few spells myself, and seen countless others performed. Using magic of any sort started similar to this. It took mind control to touch that buried deep within and concentration to wield it with intent.

Over the top of the building bounded the two dragon statues from the pillars at the entrance to Chinatown. They bounded down the wall like it was flat ground and they weren't made of stone. Their heavy feet hammered into the brickwork with a thunderous roar, punching holes and raining chips down on top of the high priest.

"Come on." Hyun-woo grabbed my hand, spun me and sprinted to the exit. The last I saw, before we whipped around the corner, was the leap of the first dragon as it reached the Apostle.

Out of the alley, Hyun-woo kept our punishing pace, sprinting for the nearly departing bus across the street. Thankfully, the bus driver slammed on the breaks after Hyun-woo pounded his fist on the door and we leaped aboard.

In our seat, I stared at Hyun-woo in silence. He took his time meeting my eyes, instead looking behind us as we drove away, pretending to check for any signs of the high priest making it out of the alley. When, finally, there was nothing left for him to look at, he glanced across at me.

I raised my eyebrows in question.

"I knew you were in trouble."

"I got that part when you manhandled me back at the apartment."

"Did you feel I was manhandling you? I'm sorry. I was worried for you. I didn't want you leaving alone."

"Forget it. I was being sarcastic. It's not what I want to hear."

"I'm a baksu."

"Which is?"

"I'm a shaman. As is my mom. It's not normally inherited down the male line, but lucky me." He shrugged.

"How long have you known?"

"Since the Apostles turned up at your door."

"You knew who they were?"

"I've been in this city long enough."

"So the symbol on the door is real."

"I'm sorry it didn't save your Auntie."

"It did. Kind of. I found the residual of magic on the door. I think they tried to enter like they did last time, but didn't succeed. Perhaps they knocked after that or lured her out some other way. But, thanks for saving me. Were they the dragons from Chinatown?"

"They were the spirits of Chinatown manifested. Do you know much about shaman magic?"

I shook my head, embarrassed to admit so.

"Shaman magic comes through the spirit realm. We don't have magic as such, only that which we conjure through the spirits."

"So you can bring spirits through the veil?"

"Guide is a better word. It's a dangerous craft. Powerful spirits are often malevolent. They'll fight your control in order to break the bonds. It takes a strong mind to contain them. I invoked the best I could at short notice. They aren't exceptionally powerful, as I didn't have time to ward my mind against serious attack from anything stronger." He closed his eyes, and a serenity settled on his face. "It was quick. The high priest is powerful. The spirits have returned across the veil. It was enough time to get us here."

I sat back and pressed my fingers over my eyes.

"I'm sorry, Laz, for your aunt. Do you know why they wanted her?"

"She's bait. To ensure I bring them the skull. But it also seems the high priest wants me for something."

"Do you know why?"

"The high priest wasn't forthcoming. It makes no sense. I'm not much of a witch. You've got more magic in you than my aunt and I combined."

"Mom and I can ward Chinatown. The spirits of the long dead will repel them. You will be safe there."

"That's sweet, Hyun-woo, but I can't stay there. They won't kill her while she is useful to them. I need to rescue her."

"How will you do that? You can't turn yourself over to the Apostles of Eternal Night. Whatever they want you to do will be bad."

"For such an insignificant magical artifact, that damn skull's proving a headache. I need to get it back. It's the only leverage I can use. He wants it. He may just want it more than me."

I needed Elka's help. She knew the Apostles intimately.

CHAPTER 10

I was cleaning. Scrubbing areas that hadn't seen a cloth in a week, but should've seen one on day one after Auntie Bea had blasted through. This was not a great time to be cleaning, and I wasn't doing it as a way of dealing with nervous energy.

Elka was coming to our apartment. Once Hyun-woo and I had returned from Wolgod Quarter, he'd done his baksu thing and summoned the spirits of the long dead to protect Chinatown. Hyun-woo said only the long dead would have the strength to withstand the Apostles. I really should've paid more attention during my early initiation and visited the library more. There was just too much of the paranormal I was unfamiliar with.

As a shaman, most of Hyun-woo's life involved dealing with spirits, benevolent or otherwise. According to him, spirits weren't good or evil. He preferred to see distinctions in their level of wounding. Within the jug-eum-ui jug-eum-ui, or the death realm, the dead drifted to natural dwelling places depending on their longevity within the realm. They weren't strong divides like the ones in the living world between the paranormal species, but more places of commonality that the dead naturally drifted toward. The olae jugeossda or the dwelling of the long dead was of particular importance when it came harnessing strong power.

Time didn't heal all wounds in the death realm. It tore them open, compounded the torment, bled them from the spirit until they drowned within their silent pain. By then they no longer felt the ache, just the fury, and that's what made them menacing. What made them powerful was time spent within the death realm, breathing in what surrounded them. And it wasn't air. It was energy, energy seeping through from the living realm that came from the relentless cycle of death, sentient or not. That energy weeped through the veil to form the primordial soup of the jug-eum-ui jug-eum-ui.

Ensconced with the protective charms of the long dead, I made my plans to free Auntie Bea. It involved the skull and Elka, and little else. Hyun-woo insisted on playing his part, but I wasn't keen on involving him. I didn't want any problems between him and the Apostles, after all, this was his home. But he fought me hard on that one.

"What about your family? You need to think of them," I had argued.

"You don't know my mom," he had replied.

The tiny little woman who bowed and smiled humbly when she accosted me in the stairwell with a bowl of kimchi was a powerful mudang. It was her control that brought the long dead forth to protect Chinatown, her control that would keep them from breaking free of their binds to terrorize the living realm.

To reassure me, Hyun-woo had taken me to entrance of Chinatown within an hour after our return from Wolgod Quarter. Atop the stone pillars, the dragon gargoyles had returned. And they were not alone. Dragon gargoyles appeared atop the buildings lining the street, nestled up high on the street lamps, on brick walls at the front of shops, tucked in the darkest recesses where the sunlight struggled to reach. Stone eyes watched and waited for their moment. Chinatown was now a fort.

It had been six hours since I discovered Auntie Bea missing. Six hours of me running through all the terrible things they could've done to her. The Daughters of Our Dark Mother weren't known for piety, but for the most part they stayed clear of the darkest arts. The Apostles knew no limits. As well as a lot of other factions.

Once I had scrubbed and ordered the apartment, I showered and then stood in front of my clothes—hanging over the back of a chair because the apartment didn't contain an actual wardrobe—deciding what to wear. Which was ridiculous. Amid everything that was happening, I fretted over dressing for Elka. She'd made me feel small the last time we'd met, small and fat. The Benedicts bags she'd forced on me sat in the corner untouched. And there they would stay was my first thought when I got home. Then that was all forgotten when I noticed Auntie Bea missing.

"Stop being so stupid," I'd berated myself after changing my outfit three times. There was so much more to worry about.

And now I paced the floor of our small kitchen because Elka was late, and I was beginning to believe that was her usual modus operandi.

When the knock came, I couldn't open the door quick enough, thinking I should've checked before flinging it wide to determine who it was first.

"Quaint," Elka said, "in the slums of Calcutta kind of way."

I grabbed her hand and yanked her inside. "Just get in here."

She stumbled in, emitting a girlish squeak and teetering on her heels as she staggered forward. "You missed me?"

"More like I need something from you."

Her eyes stalked my outfit for fashion faux pas. Simple skinnys, a sweatshirt and bare feet. Not the height of style, but comfortable. She, on the other hand, had decided a figure-clutching, siren red vinyl jumpsuit with a scandalous V-neck was just the style for Dim Bazaar.

"Twenty times I thought someone would mug me from the bus stop to here."

"If you had been less flamboyant. You know, maybe a different color outfit? You could've ditched the huge gold sequined bag for something smaller."

"Hon, wherever you go, you never know who you'll meet, such as that hot piece of ass downstairs. How often does he make the trip up here to sweep the cobwebs out of your—"

"Hyun-woo's not a part of this."

I'd warned him about Elka.

Her eyes lit up. "Oooh...how Last Samurai."

"Hyun-woo's Korean, not Japanese."

"Same diff." She strolled around the room trailing her sickly sweet perfume, glancing at the few scraps of furniture, keeping her hands shoulder high, like she thought she'd get germs if she touched something.

"This is where you want to live for one month."

"Who said I'd be here for the whole time? But after seeing your Korean friend downstairs, maybe it would be worth sticking around for longer than I planned." Her eyes fell on my outfit again. "Why aren't you wearing any of the outfits I bought you?"

"Things have changed since I spoke to you this morning."

"I do love a mystery, the more devious the better."

Plucking up the courage, she gracefully sat on one of the two single-seater couches in our lounge slash kitchen, keeping her hands off the armrest.

"Then you'll love this tale. The Apostles have Auntie Bea."

"Not the sort of woman I would have pegged them chasing. They like them young, buxom, and unwilling. I guess she satisfied the latter."

"She's ransom for my good behavior."

She quirked a perfect eyebrow. "My dear sister, you are a delicious mix of morality and sin. One week, and the Apostles already want your hide. What have you done?"

"Nothing that I understand. Auntie Bea and I came here chasing the skull. You know the value of it, don't you?"

She leisurely arched her head back to lean it against the couch, staring at the ceiling, and jerked forward, glancing over her shoulder, when she remembered the back of the couch could be hazardous to her health. "Not that thing again. It's a seeker, and everyone wants to get their hands on it, blah, blah, blah. It's old and smelly and probably carrying a disease. Whose head did it belong to, anyway?"

"It's made of stone." But she already knew that.

"What does all this have to do with the Apostles?"

"Auntie Bea has a gambling problem."

"Why am I not surprised?"

"And unbeknownst to her, she ended up indebted to the Apostles. They want their cash, which we don't have, so I offered them the skull."

"You devil."

"Only, your dad has the skull."

"And all you have to do is become me."

"But now, the Apostles want more."

She shook her head. "I can't believe we're related. I'd disown you in a blink if my acquaintances knew you existed."

I frowned at her.

She sighed and sat forward. "They're men, for one. And close to the top of the food chain. Since when has anyone close to the top not craved to stand at the top...Alone? Of course they're going to want more than was originally agreed."

"I've kept out of their way."

"Whatever." She dismissed my remark with a wave of her hand. "Were they specific?"

"What do you think?"

"This has made you feisty. It's a good look. And the only way you'll survive this place."

"I don't know what they want, and if I did, I wouldn't be hiding out in Chinatown hoping a costume change will be my ticket to success."

"Yes, I noticed the proliferation of dragons around the place. Whose responsible for those?"

Elka knew more about magic than I did. She likely knew a heck of a lot more than I did about the paranormal world in general. Not a hard achievement. At least she didn't know about Hyun-woo and his mother. Why did I feel protective of them? Of course I knew why. Elka was a predator. With her botoxed ass, glossy flowing locks, and bountiful cleavage—spilling like Niagara—she was a top predator.

"I'm not sure exactly. They appeared after the Apostles turned up."

"So who placed the protection charm on your door?"

Dammit. She was too good. I shrugged. "That's a mystery too."

She gave me another of her quirked eyebrows. "Is that so?"

"We don't need to worry about that. I'm willing to trade places with you."

"Of course."

"Temporarily."

"We'll see."

"And I need your help."

"You've got all my clothes, an unlimited credit card, a mansion— what more could you want?"

"How do I outsmart the Apostles?"

She blinked at me, then affected a Marylin Monroe laugh. "You're joking, right?" I just stared at her.

"You fuck the high priest."

"I'm serious, Elka."

"What makes you think I'm not?"

"Because not everything in this world is achieved through sex."

"You sure about that?"

"You're too cunning to believe that."

She relaxed back, then leaned forward once again because of the stained couch. "Alright Miss Marple, I'll tell you how to outsmart the Apostles. You don't."

"Come on. You're telling me after all your shagging that's all you learned?" Ouch, that was a mean thing to say, but I was tired of this circus. Only our Dark Mother knew what Auntie Bea was suffering.

Elka stood. "I see. You prefer to go it alone."

"I'm sorry, Elka." I stood with her.

She waved my apology away as she headed for the door, me on her heels. "That was rude of me. I'm sorry."

Once there, she spun to face me. "Just remember, Laz, witches exist in covens for a reason."

"But you're not in a coven."

"I don't practice. Not now. I stay off the path. Munsib life isn't so bad, you know, especially when you have the credit cards to a wonderful existence."

"You're lying. Otherwise you wouldn't be casting, let alone through thoughts alone."

"You know. I think you could get annoying."

"Thanks. I take that as a compliment."

"I wouldn't go against the Apostles. Not the whole church. I've used them enough to learn what I needed to learn and didn't push it beyond that. You need to know when to get out, otherwise you'll find yourself in quicksand. It's noble of you to want to save your aunt, but you'll never succeed on your own. You'll need a coven. But you won't find one willing to help because no faction in this city is prepared to take the step that will tip the balance to war. Not for an old lady."

"I need that skull."

"It's all yours. As is my life."

A knock at the door made us both jump. Elka opened it before I could warn her not to.

"Hyun-woo," Elka gushed, grabbing his hand.

He glanced from her to me and then back to her again. A pitchfork stabbed and tore at my stomach just watching his eyes flash over her body. I couldn't blame him. He was a healthy, young guy, and to his credit, there had been a struggle before his testosterone won out. Standing next to her, I felt like the corpse flower to her rose.

"This is my sister, Elka." A redundant thing to say.

"Hyun-woo can work that part out for himself. I'm sure. Oh, my," she purred, turning his hand over and running her fingers over his palm. "You are built for strong work. What's your specialty?"

"I've centered my practice on all specialities. At the moment I'm perfecting Hapkido."

I flicked a look between the two of them. What the heck?

"I do like a man that keeps himself in shape." To prove her point, she finger walked up his arm to his bicep. My hand was on the verge of slapping hers away when she glanced sideways at me. What emotion was behind that smile? Not a harmless girl-next-door smile at all, but was it a challenge or a warning? I took it as both. And I discovered one important fact at that moment. Elka may become an enemy.

"Sorry I can't stay and get more acquainted. I've got places to be. But I'll be seeing more of you soon." She gently, seductively brushed her finger under Hyun-woo's chin, held his gaze for an indecent amount of time, and then looked at me. "Tonight. Give me a text. I'll be waiting." Then she sashayed her way down the stairs, turning her hips into a pendulum swing of hypnosis with her heels clicking out the beat. And Hyun-woo fell for it, getting caught up in the porn, which was what her jumpsuit was. Not something anyone sensible would wear to Dim Bazaar...wear anywhere.

"Hi," I said to bring Hyun-woo back to earth.

"Laz...yeah. Hi." He blinked. "That was your sister. Wow." He flared his eyes. "You two look so much alike."

That's not what's got your head all twisted up. "It happens with identical twins. You should look it up." I turned and headed back into the apartment, not slamming the front door shut, but not bothering to hold it open until he came inside.

"I wanted to see how you were doing."

I half turned. "Did you see Elka arrive?" *Is that why you came up?*

"No. I was in the fridge."

I studied his face for lies.

"You look alike, but you're very different." *And which do you prefer?*

"Maybe we're not."

He glanced down at my jeans and sweatshirt. "It's not just your clothes."

"We're swapping places."

"What do you mean?"

"Elka's coming here to live, and I'm going to her mansion."

His normally smooth brow became the ripples from a stone tossed into a pond. "Why would you do that?"

"I need to get the skull."

"You can't. You won't get away with it. You won't fit in." He gestured to my clothes.

"Because I'm not vixen enough."

"Yeah. No, I... Laz, you're—"

"The high priest wants the skull, which means I need the skull. It's the only way to get out of this mess."

"I don't think it's safe."

"Nothing's safe, Hyun-woo. You should know that by now."

I ducked my head with a sigh. That was cruel of me. None of this was Hyun-woo's fault. Not even his drooling. No guy with a pulse could resist such a temptation, especially when she practically mounted him in the hall.

"If they really want to, at some point, the Apostles will break through the spirit defenses."

"At least let me find out why the high priest wants you. Mom's working on a protection charm for you. But it takes time. She needs to consult with her spirits to ensure she formulates the right wording."

"That's really sweet of her. But I don't have time. Every minute, she's suffering." I strode past him for my room, but he grabbed my elbow, stalling me.

"You don't have to do this alone."

"See, that's the thing. I do."

CHAPTER 11

"That's it?" Elka said as we stood in the alcove across from her mansion, where I had sat while I directed the pigeon in through her top window. The streetlight shone a cone of light across the paving, the perimeter of which stopped just shy of where we stood, leaving us in shadows, including her face.

"I thought I was wearing your wardrobe?"

"Yes, but I thought you'd bring a few personals."

"I have. They're in here." I slid the pack from my back.

Luckily her expression remained a mystery to me. She'd changed again, for the third time today, into clothes that were more my style, skinnys and a sweatshirt, but the sweatshirt was branded, and her large bag would draw attention, as would the hoop earrings, exposed now she'd pulled her hair back into a simple high ponytail.

I too had changed, into gold, high-waisted, slit, wide leg pants and a black lace top. The black strappy high heels were going to cause me trouble, but I would have to get used to them, since I had yet to see Elka wear anything below ten inches. My face didn't look like my own, now it hid behind a generous layer of makeup, and neither were the chain earrings me. Actually, none of me looked like me.

"This is for you." She handed me a credit card.

I stepped forward and held it under the halo of light and read the name Elka Preston.

"What are you going to do for money?"

"Don't you worry about that. And you'll also need this."

She handed me another card, which I inspected under the light and found it was a license.

"I can't drive."

"It's an automatic. You point it in the direction you want to go and hit the gas. Besides, you may need it for ID."

"I don't plan on going anywhere that requires ID. This is only until I get the skull, and then we switch back."

"Sure, hon."

The way she said it made my spine curl up on itself.

"Maybe you could give me some idea of where I could look first."

"To be honest with you, I don't know. I never bother myself with all that stuff. It's likely in his office. There's a safe behind a hidden panel. The panels behind the nude."

"Do you know the combination?"

"You think I know the combination of my father's safe, where he keeps all his personal and valuable things?"

"Yes."

She huffed like it was a major imposition. "Fifty-six, twenty-two, eight, seven, forty-nine."

I scrambled in my pack for my phone. No way would I remember the numbers. "Can you say them again," I asked once I had notes opened on my phone.

"How much of the paranormal world does your father understand?" I asked once done.

"I wouldn't know. It's not something he's going to share with his munsib daughter."

"Why haven't you told him the truth about yourself?"

"I'm afraid he'll use it to his advantage."

"You don't have a good opinion of your father."

"Money does things to a person."

She was probably right. Since Auntie Bea and I had never experienced that level of comfort in our lives, I couldn't claim to be an expert.

But she must have been curious how much he knew. And it was important I also understood how seeped he was in the paranormal if I was to be successful. "But he at least knows about the nephilim? One accompanied him to the auction."

"Bernard Preston is a cunning and manipulative man. He didn't get so rich by allowing others to play him. I think even the nephilim respect his shrewd ability to stay ahead when surrounded by a world of paranormals. Besides, he owns a good portion of a club called Distinctions. It's run by a respectable businessman by the name of Alfred Wilks, aka nephilim. On the surface, it looks like a gentleman's lounge, cigars, whiskey, and politics. I got friendly with a waitress from the club one night when Dad brought her over to work a charity function Mom and Dad organized for Eskimos in Peru, and she said it's about as gentlemanly as a cage fight."

"There's no Eskimos in Peru."

"Yeah, well, that's as legit as the charity was. The girl was from some country with too many consonants to make the name pronounceable, so what does that tell you?"

"Gentlemen's prostitution. What about your mom? She has to know something."

"Mom only knows gala diners, balls, the latest fashion, and the rules of tennis. If I moved out, it would take her weeks before she realized."

"So that's one person I don't have to worry about."

"Dad neither. He expects a cheek peck before he departs in the morning, if you're around, but other than that, he won't know what or where you are most of the time. Mom loathes contact of any sort. She's got a phobia about germs and love. It explains why they adopted me, and why Dad lives at Distinctions."

And I thought Auntie Bea and I had it bad with our squatter existence. I was still smarting over the incident today with Hyun-woo, but right now I felt sorry for my sister.

"How often does your dad bring paranormals into his home?"

"Don't worry, it's only the nephilim he's in bed with. They do the most lucrative deals."

"What about Jarro Peers? The vampire." *You and him seem cozy.*

"Jarro Peers." She rolled his name off her tongue like she was imagining doing other things with her tongue on him. "He's a lot more than that. It's best you keep your distance from him."

"I've tried, but he has a nasty habit of turning up."

I couldn't read her face, but the surrounding air frosted up. Now she knows what it feels like, perhaps she'll go easy on the charm around guys who weren't hers to pour all over.

"Just stay away. That's all I can say."

"What is he to your father?" *What's he to you?*

"I don't know. And that's the truth. Neither will tell me."

"I thought vampires loathed contact with everyone not a vampire."

"Then you know little about them. They're just better at concealing themselves. But they're more influential in this city than most people realize. Except my dad. And that's why he tries to get all buddy, buddy with the hive's leader."

"Jarro is their leader?"

"They've got their own thing going on with the Cantonia. Davenport is vibrating with the rumblings of war between the two hives. Dad can sense it. He's got a nose for opportunity. And he's picked a side already, the Vehan."

Blessed dark mother, what had Auntie Bea and I stumbled into?

"What do you mean when you said Jarro's more than a vampire?"

"I don't know. I can't say. But there's a reason he's obtained the throne of Vehan over vampires older, and by rights, more powerful than him."

"He seems pretty friendly with you."

A dog barked close by in the time it took her to reply.

"We have an understanding."

"It doesn't matter. I don't plan to be there long enough to run into him. I'll message you the moment I have the skull."

"You don't need to be in such a rush."

"I'm not abandoning my old life."

She rubbed my arm. "Relax, hon. Nothing's going to happen. Who knows, you may enjoy it." After everything that had happened between us, I found it impossible to accept her assurance. I couldn't shake the feeling she had an agenda. But what would moving to the slums do for her?

"Perhaps it's time we said our goodbyes," she said, sounding eager to be off.

Did I really want to do this? Did I have any choice? "It's best you stay in Chinatown under the Chong's protection." As much as I hated saying that, knowing how easily Hyun-woo had folded under her charm, I hated the idea of her being hurt more. It's something I would feel for anyone, not because there were any feelings of sister-hood between us.

"Don't you worry about me," she said, moving into the light.

It's when I noticed she also had little on her but her bling bag, but I didn't bother to point that out. She probably planned to buy herself a whole new wardrobe. I shouldn't worry about Elka. This was her city.

Was this the moment we hugged and wished each other luck? So far she'd given me no impression she like to cuddle unless they led in to something else. Elka saved me the worry by leaving. For the first time since meeting her, she didn't clip clop as she walked away; hard to do in Vans.

Okay, this was it. I rolled my shoulders, left the secrecy of the alcove. and headed across the street, taking it slow on the lethal heels. By the time I turned the corner and walked to the gate, my feet were killing me. I punched the code into the call box and waited for the gate to open.

There was a good deal of driveway to hike down, and in the end, I gave up and shed the heels. I was also losing my nerve, so by the time I reached the front door I was ready to message Elka and tell her the deal was off. All I had to do was imagine Auntie Bea chained up somewhere, half starved and beaten to keep me on track.

I'd played this game before. Cheating people out of magical artifacts was what Auntie Bea and I did for a living, so I shouldn't be so nervous. But this time round the stakes were higher—a valuable artifact, a billionaire, a city full of paranormals, Apostles on my ass, and Auntie's life in my hands. Not a lot to make a girl feel comfortable.

A noise from my left made my neck hairs bristle. I turned my head to look along the porch, seeing columned shadows cast by the pillars. The shadows stretched up the walls and in through the bay windows and French doors. I counted four rooms, one occupied, as the light was still on. Was this the office? I tried to map a floor plan in my head from Elka's brief description and from my time as a pigeon—an impossible task because animals never thought in terms of left or right.

What did the noise remind me of? It had been a flash, not long enough for my brain to associate it with anything I knew. There was nothing there, as far as I could see, and the light had a curious draw. If this was the office...

Rather than head in, I left my shoes by the door and detoured down the porch. Unlike the room before it, this room had French doors and one was open, and the hem of a white sheer curtain wafted in the soft breeze.

I slowed, inched my head forward, until I peered inside. Not an office, but a bedroom. The covers were half pulled back like someone had just climbed out of bed. Clothes were slung over the gunmetal grey chaise lounge, and a book lay on the side table. There were no other signs it was occupied, which made it look like a hotel room rather than a bedroom in someone's home.

I looked behind me, then down onto the lawn, but the light from the room shaded everything outside its perimeter, making it impossible to see anything clearly. Why was the door open? And where was the person who had tossed down the covers? Elka had not mentioned a relative staying.

I was about to turn and leave.

"Anything of interest catch your eye?"

I shouldn't have jumped. Not in front of him. "I was wondering why the doors were open."

It took all my reserve not to turn around. Standing so close behind me, if I did, we'd be too close. Jarro had a habit of materializing when he wasn't wanted. This was part of a vampire's arsenal, something that made them deadly foes. You couldn't track them and never knew when one was lurking near. They moved like ghosts, shifting through the shadows until their attack, and by then, it was too late.

"Are you hoping for an invitation?"

I could feel the heat of his body radiating along the contours of mine, like Reiki healing hands, only this feeling was the opposite of healing. Along with his body heat, his cologne invaded my private sanctuary of tranquility, arousing alluring thoughts of rolling on sheepskin rugs, smoking embers, and mulled wine.

"I've had a busy day. I was hoping for my bed." Alone...I mean alone.

"Turn around." It was as though he'd uttered a wickedly indecent proposal voiced with a tone reserved for sex dens and deviant masters.

As much as it thrilled along my skin like a delicate feather brush, I was not his to command.

I took a step forward, clearing some space between us, and inched around, but was not prepared for the sight of Jarro in relaxed mode, shirt buttons undone to halfway down his waist, inviting fingers to slip inside.

My senses zinged to overload, which signaled it was time to scram. But his presence here rose a lot of questions. He was the candle to my moth-like curiosity. Walk, Laz, just walk. This was his room. Why was he here? For the skull? Highly likely. Though it had been days since the auction. If he wanted it he'd have it by now.

"How far have you gotten with my father?" Every word I uttered was dangerous.

"I'm at the beginning." He took a sip from his tumbler, which I hadn't noticed until now. "Do you want one?"

"Not so close to bedtime." Oops. I'd said something more Laz-like than Elka-like, judging by his expression. "How much longer do you expect to stay here?" He needed to leave. Preferably tonight. How could I do this with a vamp in the house?

"As long as it takes." He took a step toward me, and dammit to hell, I took a step back, feeling like a wild thing about to be corralled. The narrowing of his eyes as he took a sip of his drink said I was doing everything wrong.

"But you already knew that."

"I had to make sure."

Jarro filled my space, forcing me to look up at him or meet his chest. His proximity spasmed my heart, and his intoxicating cologne mingled scent, giddied my head. I felt like an emotional punching bag. Never should I allow myself to be this close, this vulnerable to a dangerous predator. It scared the bejeebers out of me. My survival warning reached defcon one. At the same time my hormones were gushing like a burst dam, flicking the switch on my body to full blast.

"Are you that keen to be rid of me?"

Breathe. "I've got a lot on my mind."

He ran a hand over my brow as if smoothing creases. My mind followed every inch of that touch. "You need to alleviate that."

"I'll run a hot bath."

He leaned in close. "You hate baths." Expelling his whisky laced breath over my face. I could get drunk on both.

"I'll make an exception."

"You always welcomed distractions."

"This time, I'll use headphones."

He huffed a laugh and breathed more whisky breath. I inhaled it deep.

"You've become like a mouse, scurrying out of my grasp. I find it refreshingly addictive."

"I like to challenge."

"Just as long as you surrender soon, El, because I'm getting hungry."

Oh, dark mother, the sin on those lips.

"Maybe you had better go inside before it's too late," he breathed.

"Sound advice. If you don't mind, I'll just duck through your room."

He slipped a hand into his pocket. "Sure."

I backed up a step; never turn your back on a predator. Who was I kidding? I wanted to stencil the sight of him careless and raw into my brain.

Before I tripped over the threshold, I turned, only for his hand to snap out and latch onto my arm. "That's not my room."

"Oh." I jerked to a halt.

Glancing over my shoulder, I said, "whose is it?"

"Your fiancée's."

CHAPTER 12

Could things get worse or this situation become any more impossible? How was I going to pull this off? I was on the verge of gouging track marks in my rug with all my pacing. There was only one way out for me. I needed to steal the skull tonight.

I marched over and swiped my phone off my bed. Once on the right screen, I jabbed my message out, letting autocorrect clean it up.

You better reptile a star.

Or make it worse. I sat on my bed and hate-stared at the screen. Surprisingly, the three little jiggling dots appeared immediately.

You never asked.

How can I ask something I don't know?

Drug him. It's all there in my cupboard.

I swiped the screen away and scrolled through until I found her number.

The moment she answered, I yelled at my phone, "drug your fiancée?"

"He's a munsib. A pompous ass, though harmless. But if you want to climb into bed with him, be my guest."

"I can't believe you kept that from me."

"He won't get in your way, and if he does, you can drug him."

"How often have you done that?"

"Whenever we supposedly have sex. He's too embarrassed to admit he doesn't remember if we've done it or not. But don't worry. It doesn't happen often. And not when he's at our house. Dad's old school. He won't let us share a room. Thinks I'm still a virgin. And Frederick is scared my dad will zip the purse strings closed or call off the marriage, so he won't push anything while he's under Dad's roof."

"I thought you didn't do commitment."

"Do you think this is my choice? Dad's a controlling man. And powerful. He's only a munsib, but he has some powerful paranormals as friends. If I don't do what he says, he'd hand me to the nephilim. Let them display me in Distinction until I comply with his orders. Our family and Frederick's family are rivals. Him and I are the alliance."

"Is this why you're desperate to swap?"

"My life's more complicated than that. Look, you don't have to worry about Frederick. He's easy to handle. If you're opposed to drugging him, just tell him you want the wedding night to be special."

"How can I pretend to be you? He'll know something's different." Like Jarro did.

"Trust me, he won't. Just keep him talking about himself. It's his favorite topic. I've volunteered little about myself, and he's never asked."

"So you've never slept with him?"

"Once. I was curious. It was a limp affair. I faked my orgasm to end it."

Bet she didn't fake her orgasm with Jarro. I felt this horrible sickly feeling in my stomach just thinking about it, which could only be one thing. Jealousy.

"I've got to go. Remember, keep him talking about himself and you'll be fine." There was a noise in the background.

"Is everything all right?"

"Sure. I gotta go get ready for my date."

"You're going on a date."

"Hyun-woo asked me."

I could barely get the words out. "That was quick."

"He's a shaman, you know?"

"He wasted little time telling you that."

"Oh, he didn't. I sensed it the first moment we met. It wasn't hard to know who was responsible for all the dragons around Chinatown or the symbol on your door."

I hated how she made me feel like a rummy.

"The place hums with magic. And it's all coming from your apartment block."

Great. Don't tell me my sister can sniff magic as well.

"We have a lot to discuss."

Just as long as discussions were all she had in mind. But I had no say over what Hyun-woo could or could not do. If he fell for her sex appeal, then I would have to swallow it.

"What about Jarro? How am I to get around him?"

"You really need to stop thinking about him. He's not anyone you can handle."

"I don't want to handle him. I'd rather not see him again. He keeps getting in my way."

"If he's in your way, it's because you're placing yourself there."

"It's not my fault he's staying here."

"He's not."

"I ran into him moments ago."

"You're lying. This is about Hyun-woo, isn't it?"

"No. I'm not lying."

"I know you are, because Jarro has no reason to be there. He'd never stay overnight. Don't you know anything about vampires?"

"He was definitely here the other day when I came to see you."

"He and Dad were finishing some business. It's one of the few times he's been to our house. That's settled, and so there's no other reason for him to be there. He tolerates my father because of their secret business dealings, but like I say, that's over. He'll give my family little attention anymore."

She was lying. She had to be. Jarro did not act like a man willing to withdraw his attention from Elka. I had seen Jarro tonight. I'd felt him, smelled him, breathed him in.

Ridiculous as it may be, she was jealous. It was the only sense I could make out of what she said. Elka didn't want me near her quarry. Me, of all people. She was right in saying he was too much for me to handle, and he wouldn't be interested in me if he knew the real me. As hot as he was, I didn't want to have anything to do with him. I'd survived so far by staying out of the attention of the powerful paranormals. I wasn't about to change that.

"Does he know you're a witch?"

"What do you think?"

"I really want to know."

"Never reveal your ace card to the enemy."

"You think he's the enemy?" I thought she was crazy about him.

"Everyone's the enemy. You can fuck 'em, but don't weaken your-self in front of them."

"I'm going to take the skull tonight."

"Whatever, I've got to go." She sounded distracted. Perhaps Hyun-woo had arrived.

"I'm going to want my life back once I get the skull."

Too late. She'd ended the call.

I threw my phone onto the bed and fell backward beside it. There was too much in all of this I didn't understand. I had no idea what was true or false in everything Elka said. No way could she be right about Jarro ignoring her. Not with the way he acted around me, thinking I was her. The guy was bleeding testosterone every time we got close. He wanted her, was starved for her. This was a man who'd tasted forbidden fruit and would deny himself the taste of any other fruit again. Was she lying in saying he rarely came to their house and would never stay the night? That made little sense. If it were true, what was he doing here looking super comfortable with his shirt unbuttoned and whisky in hand?

Elka thought everyone was her enemy, including me. I heard it in her voice. Understandable when you lived such a life as this, with a father willing to feed you to the nephilim for disobedience. I felt sorry for her. I didn't know what it was like to feel as though you'd never been loved by at least one person.

I may feel sorry for her, but it didn't stop me believing she could well be right; we could be enemies. I needed to finish this. Get the skull and get Auntie Bea back. Then we needed to get out of this city and leave all this trouble behind.

I headed for what had to be Elka's wardrobe, two floor to ceiling mirror doors which slid aside to reveal the biggest wardrobe I had ever seen. Triggered by the opening of the doors, shelf lights flickered on displaying row after row of neatly folded clothes. Racks of glitzy clothes hung straight in front with slim shelves on either side, full of shoes. I tried some drawers, out of interest, and found accessories. Who needed that many bags? I could set up house in here and live happily for weeks before I felt cramped.

I bypassed all the fancy stuff and headed for what looked like the casual clothes shelf. It took some sorting through, making a mess of the folding, before I found a simple pair of jeans and sweatshirt, both designer labeled. With relief, I abandoned the sandals for a pair of flat runners.

Feeling comfortable again, I slipped my phone into my back pocket and headed out into the hall. It wasn't late, but the place was deserted. I tip-toed down the hall even though the faded charcoal carpet muffled every step I made.

I held my breath and peered down over the bannister onto the high gloss floor before descending. The place was quieter than a morgue. Elka's fiancée slept in a downstair room. Why was he staying here? And why was he not hunting Elka down, hoping for company before bed? And where was her mother? If not for meeting Jarro outside, I'd think the place was deserted. And where was he?

This was like some setup. Everyone was in hiding somewhere waiting to spring once I entered Bernard's office.

Get a grip. If I kept up with this, I'd lose my nerve. And I couldn't afford that.

I jogged down the stairs, halting every few to listen. Nothing. I finished the rest, orienting myself at the bottom, eyeing the statue of Venus by the wall; I think it was Venus. My map from the pigeon's brain meant Bernard's office was the door across the other side of the room.

At the door, I pressed my ear close, breath held, and listened. Silence from within. I tried the handle and found it unlocked.

I slipped into the darkness of the room, closing the door behind me with a soft click and felt along the wall for the light switch.

The room looked like an executive suite, austere, masculine and unappealing. Lots of leather, dark wood, large tables, and no-nonsense couches that gave you no enticement to fall asleep. The nude Elka spoke of hung on the left wall, and not behind the commanding desk like in any good heist movie.

To the left of the large French doors was a large bird cage covered in a blanket. A caged bird. I hated Bernard on the spot. But there was no time to think about that.

The soft soles of Elka's runners squeaked across the floor. With the silence, the sound seemed to bounce off the walls and come back at me in stereo.

The picture wasn't large, but tricky for one person to pull off the wall. It was wide enough only the tips of my fingers wrapped around the edges, so when I lifted it from the hook the thing toppled sideways. I performed an awkward balancing act and managed to get it on the floor without destroying the frame.

Behind the painting was a small panel the size of a safe. I pressed it inward and heard a soft click. The panel swung outward a few inches. Target acquired.

Crazily, I stalled for a few, mad, dashing heart beats. This was it. Soon, I would have the means of rescuing Auntie Bea. We'd ditch the Apostles and get out of this place, not before stopping by the church to see if the high priestess had a way of ridding Auntie Bea of magical trackers. Then we'd bury ourselves so deep we'd be close to losing ourselves.

The clicks rang around the room, so I held my breath as if that would help keep down the noise. It was tempting to rush it, but going past the right number by mistake would null my attempt and then I would have to start again. I dialed the final numbers and exhaled at the sound of the clunk as the bolt slid back when I pulled on the handle. The cord of muscles down my neck and along my shoulders unraveled like a striking snake. Thank the dark mother Elka had not lied about the combination.

I'd been intent on getting into Elka's house, on reaching Bernard's office, opening the safe, on this very moment, knowing it was my only hope. So when I opened the door and saw nothing resembling a skull, I could do nothing but stare while a wave washed through me, drowning my hope. I had to bite my lip to stop myself from shrieking out in horror.

Why had I not contemplated the possibility? Elka had not specified it would be here. I'd assumed. I'd grabbed hold of the idea because stealing it from his safe was an obtainable goal. This was an easily searchable place, unlike a safe deposit box at a bank. And I couldn't even begin to factor the nephilim into this.

I'd been staring in the safe, mind flying wild in desperation, so it took me moments to notice the piece of paper placed on top of everything else. Written in permanent marker, large black letters said,

Come and get it.

If you dare

J

I slammed the safe door shut. Too loud. The picture proved worse than difficult to replace. The tears banked, and I just about threw the stupid nude at the far wall.

I cursed myself some more during the time it took me to hang the picture, and it didn't make me feel any better. Finally it was up, slanted but up. I fiddled useless moments trying to right it but gave up.

I abandoned it and sprinted for the door. There was no one in the entrance foyer. I ducked out, clicking the door closed behind me and then sprinted across to the stairs.

Elka had to come home. The skull wasn't here, and I wasn't staying around to smooch with her fiancée.

The front door opened as I took the first step. In walked Bernard Preston, looking smart in a black suit and followed close behind by a younger man who reminded me of a beetle. Dark-framed glasses like bulbous eyes, narrow shoulders that swelled out into a round torso then dipped back into bowed legs.

"Sweetheart. Still up?" Bernard said.

"Darling." The beetle guy said, holding his arms out as he approached me. "How are you feeling now?"

"Slightly better." I allowed him to enfold me in his embrace. So this was Elka's Frederick. No surprise she ran. "Did you enjoy yourselves?"

"Not nearly as much as if you'd been there."

I rested my head on his shoulder and caught Jarro walking through the door, his shirt buttoned up, a bow tie neatly in place, eyes hammering into me like a nail gun. He closed the front door, leaned back on it, and slipped his hands into the pockets of his suit pants. My palm itched to slap his face. If only he didn't look so bedroom-ready.

Who was the note for? Not Elka, surely. As far as he was concerned, she was a munsib, which meant she'd know nothing about the properties of the skull. The nephilim, perhaps.

I buried my head into Frederick's shoulder. Anything to get away from Jarro's laser stare.

The vamps had the skull. How could I expect to retrieve it?

I disentangled myself from Frederick's embrace. "I don't feel too great." And that was the truth. Being in the same room as Jarro, feeling his eyes stalk me, missing puzzle pieces, I wanted to throw up. I was screwed. Auntie Bea was screwed worse. How would I rescue her from the Apostles, get us both free of this city? My reality had blown the top right off the Richter scale.

"You look a little pale. I'll come up and tuck you in."

"Don't bother." I snapped, which sounded rude. "You probably want to finish the night with a whisky."

I glanced to Jarro and found he'd remained causally slouched against the door, ghosting into the background, despite being a black hole sucking in all my light.

"We've already downed enough whisky to open a shop," Frederick said and chuckled at his own joke.

"I'm up for one more round," Bernard said. He turned to Jarro. "Mr Peers, shall we continue our discussion?"

Jarro pushed off the door like a panther stretching before a hunt. "With pleasure."

His phone chirped in his pocket, and we all stopped and stared at him while he pulled it out to answer. The mussed bedspread aura disappeared in a blink, replaced by a suppressed savagery. In that heartbeat, my mind blew clear of all the sexual energy turning my thoughts about him pornographic, and my body chilled to minus eighty degrees. Lethal hunter replaced porn boy.

He ended the call so fast I'm sure the caller said one word, if he or she were lucky. "Another time."

"That saves me from a hangover," Bernard said.

The room unfroze in seconds, Bernard and Frederick dismissing his sudden withdrawal out the front door. As for me, a tremor shook through my body as it switched to scream alert.

I rested my hand flat on Frederick's chest, feeling no suggestion of muscle definition underneath his shirt. Bernard was a cruel man if he expected Elka to be satisfied with a man like Frederick.

"Stay. Finish your conversation. I just want to sleep."

"I relent. If that's your wish." He sandwiched my hand underneath his, his other arm snaked around my waist. "But not without a goodnight kiss."

"Really, it's not—"

Too late—his mouth found mine. His tongue speared out, jabbing at my pressed lips for a way in. I relented, to get this over with, opening a little, but that's all he wanted. Wet, sloppy, greedy, and rough, and my nether regions shriveled to a husk. I gagged on his tongue and convulsed backward, breaking us apart, resisting the urge to wipe my mouth.

"Go, keep my dad company." I pushed him away, turned, and quick-stepped it to the stairs.

Halfway up the stairs, I slowed and looked down as Bernard and Frederick retired to another room across the entrance foyer. I remained in place until I heard the door close, spun, and sprinted back down the stairs, and crashed into the office door because I missed pulling the handle down enough to open it in my haste.

Inside, I dared not bother with the light, instead using the half moon to get my across to the birdcage. The blanket caught on the side of the cage as I tried to yank it off, causing the bird inside to squawk.

"Shh. You're all right, buddy."

It was a giant colorful parrot from some exotic location.

I had to slow my own chaotic thoughts and heart rate before I could reach out with the filaments of my mind to penetrate its bird brain, soothing its flighty reaction, so I could ease my hand into the cage and peel it off its perch.

"You're going to do something really important for me." I stroked its brilliant plumage. "You're going to hunt me a vampire."

CHAPTER 13

Such a bad mistake. The poor parrot didn't know how to fly. We were on the lawn of the mansion, walking around in circles. Three times I encouraged it to flap its wings, but its breast muscles weren't strong enough to lift it off the ground. And I was wasting my opportunity. Maybe I had lost it already. Parrots weren't bloodhounds. Jarro would be long gone.

The parrot's mind was a dizzy mess. Knowing only the walls of his cage, the outside world was information overload. I withdrew from his mind as I gathered myself off Elka's bedroom floor and sprinted out the door, tripping over my feet because I'd not given myself time to orient back into my body.

I slowed, long enough to satisfy myself Bernard and Frederick were nowhere to be seen, sprinted down the stairs, and out the front door. On seeing the parrot marching across the lawn, I nudged into his mind to calm his frenetic steps and headed over.

"You'll be safer in the house. But I don't have time to put you back in your cage." Bernard would just have to speculate over how he got out.

With the parrot wandering and crapping on the high polished tiles, I shut the front door and sprinted down the driveway. There was Elka's car, but I didn't know where she kept it, which one it was, or any of the road rules. I'd have to take the bus.

I didn't stop my sprint until I reached the same place I'd caught the bus last time I was here snooping. By then I was wheezing for breath. With impeccable timing on my behalf, bus lights swung around the corner halfway along Elka's streets, heading my way.

It was near empty, and I found myself a place opposite the doors and pulled my phone from my pocket. After retrieving the map from the back of my phone case, I raced my finger around the paper towel, searching out Pend South and the church of Daughters of Our Dark Mother. It was on the opposite side of the city from Spard Cross, which was going to take me an age to reach via public transport, but I had no other way.

Involving outside help was risky business, especially someone as chilling and aloof as the high priestess, but if anyone could scry with success it would be her. I didn't want her knowing my business, but right now, letting Jarro walk free was a worse crime than revealing my target. Hopefully, the high priestess didn't have some skin in this sinner's game that seemed to involve every paranormal faction in Davenport.

While the bus wove down darkened streets, I entered Mewchamp street into maps on my phone, then determined when I would have to abort this bus for another. I then found the bus timetables for Davenport and with some messing around and cursing, I mentally sketched a rough route using two different buses to get me as near to Mewchamp as I could.

My rough path passed me through the center of Davenport to the heart of the central business district, and according to Elka, the heart of the nexus. And this bus took me right there, a direct route to the central bus terminal. Only a few paranormals would have the power to pinpoint the exact location of the nexus. Those without that ability would closely monitor those who did.

I watched the dimly lit streets of the districts give way to bright lights, neon flashing signs and the busy hustle of a city alive at night.

Central Davenport buzzed with a charge of chaotic eagerness. Shoppers' fever electrified every street. Crowds pulsed around popular bars, clubs and trendy retail shops, the munsib jostling and jiving on the waves of the energetic beat of the nexus.

I disembarked at the main platform and spun in circles, trying to check my bearings. According to the digital timetable, I needed the three-zero-six to Pend South, departing from platform nine. There were no platform numbers as far as I could see, just a bustling groove of people. Drill music pounded out from a group, lost in black tattoos and smoke, sitting on a bench by a vending machine and a large leafy plant. The pedestrians flowed in an arc around them as they hurried on by.

I weaved through the crowd, looking for platform signage, and ran into an old woman dressed in tartan. She spoke with ferocity in a language lost on me. I bent and retrieved the paper she'd been holding, handing it back and ducked out as she said some more rough words, or maybe that was just the sound of her language.

I continued on through the crowd until I felt prickles along my back. I glanced over my shoulder to see a guy from the drill music huddle following behind. Maybe he'd not been a part of that group, but he matched them. Unbuttoned black vest, naked chest, tattoos around his nipples, forking down his sculptured pecs. There were more tattoos on his bald head and below his bottom lip. If anything, they enhanced his look, but the guy screamed murderous insanity. I didn't need that type on my tail right now. And why was he on my tail? It had taken me split seconds to pass that bunch, seconds enough to make me a blur in anyone's consciousness.

I didn't want to think of the reason he would find me interesting. But of course, it wouldn't leave my mind and accelerated my heart until I was diving through the crowd like I had fire licking at my heels.

Goblin. My first thought had been fae. Dark fae, but this one had the look of goblin more. Any munsib society antagonist, gang member, or street rebel would choose certain sigils supposedly associated with evil as tattoos. But munsib sigils were mostly interesting pictures with no significant meaning or power. The tattoos this guy had circling his nipples and running down his pecs were dark wards. Placing them close to his heart meant he'd imbued the essence of multiple animals to strengthen the potency of his abilities. It was old magic, originating from powerful dark fae from a millennium ago.

Goblins were the resurrected spirits of dark fae, given form by imbuing the life force of animals. Their resultant form became a grotesque distortion of the living animal, but like all fae, they retained the ability to glamour their appearance. Their magic had its limits, pushing them down the magical food chain. But dark warded goblins were not to be messed with.

I'd had a nasty run-in with a goblin before I was initiated into the coven. It left me scared and heavily prejudiced against the earth intuits. And I attracted goblins because of my affinity with animals, something they loathed. The lesser ones I could wage a mental war upon, seeking the animal within. If I focused enough, I could usually gain the upper hand, inflicting commands they fought to obey. I'd never met a dark warded goblin. Given their age, their minds were better fortressed. However, they had formed themselves around multiple animals, which should mean I had multiple chances of leaching control.

I didn't want a confrontation. Not here, but it would be tricky to drop this guy given goblins seemed to sniff me out; it had something to do with my gift from goddess Diana.

While ducking through the crowd, I spied a number, black on silver, beside a stairwell. At last I'd found the platform numbers.

I doubted the dark warded goblin would do anything nefarious while surrounded by so many munsib; they may be evil, but they weren't dumb. I had to hope so, which meant as long as I stayed surrounded by munsib, he'd keep his distance. That should get me to church. If I was lucky.

I scurried along further, casting an eye over my shoulder to see he was still in pursuit, clearing a path amongst the crowd by virtue of his menacing look. Neither was he too worried about making his presence known to me, or his stalking.

I bee-lined for the opposite side of the station, burying myself deep by bending down to keep my head below the average persons' height, and picked up my pace.

The stairwell was approaching. Another quick look behind, and I'd separated us. It was temporary, but hopefully it would give me a chance to slip down the stairwell, leaving him to double back and engage his sniffer dog to relocate me. I could only hope the bus would arrive before then.

On platform nine, I found six people. Six people was not a wall of protection. Domestic terrorism could explain the death of six people. No sigh so far, but I was by no means free of him.

There was no sign of the bus. I fumbled for my phone, all the while casting fleeting glances back to the stairwell. No drill rapper coming down the stairs. Yet.

The digital sign overhead counted down the minutes before bus departure. Two. How good was the dark warded goblin's nose? Would he detect where I was within two minutes?

I couldn't look at the stairwell. The niggle was too great. It would only sink my organs. But I had to know, had to be prepared.

The bus lights came into view as it loomed forward out from under the depot tunnel. Come on. I willed it to speed.

I glanced over my shoulder. He was there. Lolling down the stairs like he had all the time in the world. I swung away, stared ahead at platform ten with its crowd. Hiding amongst munsib only put them at risk.

Things could be worse. He could be a warlock, demon, fae, pack, or vamp. The Order of Sotiria dared not sacrifice too many lives or suffer the wrath of their masters, and the Brothers of the Redentore were more low key, more interested in luring the few into their sick world than causing mass destruction. All the same, a dark warded was a handful.

The bus stopped in front. The dark warded came up beside me.

He was audacious enough to stand close, filling my space with his ganja reek. My eyeballs hurt with the strain of trying to look sideways without moving my head. I had to swallow my heart back down into its cavity before I spewed it onto the paving.

Then I felt the tingle sparkling through my legs, rising up into my torso. By the time it had gotten that far, it had become an irritant. Like the itch from poison ivy, it spread along my stomach and rushed up my throat. I clenched my teeth, hands fisted as I forced a block. The dark warded was trying to break through, gain control of my mind, but in a roundabout way.

Goblins were super animals, imbued with the magic of animal spirit power. Their capabilities went beyond barking, purring, loving cheese or whatever habit their totem animal carried. They could also influence animals, as I could. Which led them to think they could influence me. And if they could influence a witch, they could gain access to the coven, the church, and in their wildest dreams, a witch's magic.

My barrier worked, the itching progressed no farther. The dark warded grunted beside me, raised a hand and slammed his fist into the palm of his other hand.

I jumped on the end of the line, following the six munsib on board with the dark warded breathing down my neck. He'd abandoned his attempt to slip inside my mind, but that was not the end of his attack.

On board, he sat behind me. When the bus pulled away, he sat forward and hung his arms over my seat so they appeared in my periphery either side of me.

"I'm on your trail, witch."

I said nothing. I kept my concentration trained inward, surveying for any slow creep of strangeness, tingle, prickle, stab, compression, anything that would mean another attempt at invading my mind.

He breathed ganja-laced breath my way as he spoke into my ear. "Do you surrender?"

"I've got my own games you wouldn't want me to play."

"I do love a bitch with claws."

Though spoken into my ear, the words drifted over me. They were nothing but bait. I ignored them as I tunneled my focus. The mind of a goblin was a multitudinous mess. Layered with fae life, a magnitude of years, evil deeds, and animal instincts gone feral, twisted through a labyrinth of sin. Finding control was a journey into the realms of insanity. And then I came up against a wall, high, wide, and no cracks to break through. A spearing agony pierced through the center of my skull. He yanked my head back by my ponytail, arching my head against the rim of the seat, and I let out a cry.

"Don't even try."

I breathed through the pain at the back of my head and the residual in my brain from coming up against his wards. Now I knew my success at penetrating the mind of a dark warded goblin.

"Hey, how about you leave the lady alone?"

A tall, lean man with a long face stood beside our seats. "I don't want any trouble, and I don't think the lady does either. Let's just finish the ride peacefully."

It must've taken courage to come over and say something. The munsib didn't know who he was dealing with, but the goblin looked like serious gang trouble, enough to make anyone turn their heads and pretend not to see.

"It's fine. Go back to your seat," I said. He needed to get out of the goblin's face.

"Did you hear that, Mr? This is our business. The lady enjoys a little fun."

The guy glanced at me, questioning my sanity. I nodded at him, tried for a warming smile.

Looking unsure, hesitant to leave, he turned, but stayed where he was. Then he turned back to face us. "You lot mess with this city. You make it a terrible and unsafe place to live."

Both I and the dark warded stared at him for moments. The atmosphere in the bus thinned, making breathing difficult. I shook my head, a silent warning. The grip on my hair loosened. Behind me, it sounded like the dark warded was getting to his feet.

The munsib backed away. I spun to see the goblin had stood. With his hip at my eye level, I saw the hilt of the small blade poking out the back of his denims.

"It's trouble you want, I see."

"You can calm down. Okay. I don't want that. I just... We're getting tired of the problems."

The dark warded looked around at the few other people on the bus. All eyes were on the action, but the tall guy had unwittingly dragged the rest of them into the argument, and they turned away.

"I don't see anyone else willing to fight for your cause."

"There's no fight. I'm not wanting to start a fight."

"Hey, what's going on down there?" yelled the driver.

The dark warded flashed a malicious smile, his lip curling up into a snarl. Perhaps there was dog in there somewhere.

"You all sit down, or I'll radio this in."

The tall guy suddenly collapsed to his knees, clutching at his head and screeching a sound like someone possessed.

As quick as he'd collapsed he clawed his way to his feet, baring his teeth and growling like a member of the pack.

A lady two seats up screamed and leaped over her seat, scrambling as far away as she could.

"Jesus Christ, man, cool the fuck down," a guy said from the seat across the aisle. He too had leapt to his feet, flicking glances to the safety of the seats further up front.

"Sit down, or you're off the bus," yelled the driver. His only view and understanding of what was unfolding came from intermittent glances in his review mirror.

The tall guy was off the ground, ripping at his hair, tearing at his clothes, gashing finger nails across his pale abdomen until it bled.

The dark warded's eyes filled with malicious glee.

The tall guy's frenzy seized. His head snapped toward me. Then he snarled. He actually snarled.

He launched. I propelled myself over the back of my seat. He caught a foot and yanked. My feet smashed into the seat, my leg being painfully yanked backward, my other leg already clear of the backrest.

The dark warded laughed, the sound a hollow evil that would lurk in my sleep.

Fueled with adrenaline, I went ballistic, kicking with such force it felt like I'd just dislocated my leg.

"What's going on down there?" the driver yelled.

There was a screech of tires and the bus swayed violently to the right, sending everyone tumbling my side of the aisle amid frantic cries, including the tall guy who lost his hold on my foot and smacked his head on the window.

Feeling the sudden freedom. I dragged my leg over the seat. I gritted my teeth through the pain, not sure if my leg would work as it should, but at that moment the bus veered violently again, teetered on a severe angle, during which I dove for the edge of the seat and manacled my grip.

The sudden crash to its side, and my head snapped back, but I'd kept my hold. There were more cries and screams, which meant people were still alive. Sparks flickered and flared as the bus continued on its side before coming to a sudden, shuddering stop with a deafening crunch of metal, which threw me forward and into the seat behind before I sank to the floor—now the side of the bus.

There was no sudden silence, but a world of tears and moans. I'd join in, but I had to take care of the dark warded first. I'd dropped the knife I'd swiped from the belt at his back, and I found it on the window between my legs.

On retrieving it, I used the edge of the seat to pull myself up with a whimper and peeked my head down the aisle. Two people up front had done the same. The dark warded was nowhere to be seen.

I pulled myself out further into the aisle and sat on the edge of the seat. Someone yanked me backward by my hair. I fell onto the rail of the seat behind, jarring a sharp agony up my back. This time, I did cry out.

His face loomed over head. "Enough playing. You're dead, witch."

"Not if you go first." It was an awkward angle, my ass dangling between the seats, my head cracked painfully on the rail behind. I hit him in the arm. He roared as it went in. Using his distraction, I struck again, this time focusing my aim, and got him straight through his right nipple, crippling the ward. The resistant pressure of the blade sinking in, the wet sound—I wanted to gag. A woman screamed behind me, a long eardrum-puncturing sound filled with a magnitude of horror. I had to ignore her, ignore what she would think of me.

The dark warded released me and staggered backward into the seat before sliding down onto the window with a loud crack of the glass pane.

I jumped down off the edge of the seat and bent over him, knife raised. His hands were at the wound, smothering the seeping blood. But it was not his blood that gushed through his fingers. It was the animals he'd imbued. The poor defenseless animals that had become his life support. I didn't want to continue, but he was not powerless enough. So I stabbed his left side through the middle of the ward, closing my eyes at the last.

More screams erupted from the front. Those who were able scurried off the bus. In the distance, sirens wailed.

I spared one glance down at the dark warded. If there was any way, I would've spared the animals within him. At least now he was no longer their master. With their deaths, his eyes grew dim. Soon he'd lose his glamour and revert to the grotesque mishap creature he was. Before the police or paramedics entered, he'd hopefully be nothing but grey ash. And I was not waiting around to make sure.

The sirens sounded closer. I wiped the knife clean and dropped it beside him. Already his skin had mottled and buckled into an inhuman shape. My fingerprints were all over the seats, so maybe it was pointless wiping the knife. But then, it looked as though there'd be no body, by the time emergency personnel found their way inside.

I leaped up onto the edge of the seat, climbed across to the opposite side of the aisle, using the pole at the back of that seat as an aid. I awkwardly shimmied myself out the open window. It wasn't large, but neither was I. Once out, I jumped over the side of the bus, groaning with the sudden jar of pain from my hip, and hobbled off into the darkness of the side street.

CHAPTER 14

The guardian appeared. No fangs this time, but no docile dog either, as her eyes tracked me up the steps to the church. I kept my eyes to the stone, striding up the steps like I meant business, ignoring the pain in my side. If you weren't confident to pass through those doors, then you weren't welcome. The church judged every action a witch did a trial of her worth. You had to earn your right to worship the Dark Mother, earn your right every single day. If you performed with timidity, the church would question your fit amongst them. The Daughters of our Dark Mother were not a warm, community-fostering, caring bunch.

Once at the top of the steps, I settled my eyes on the guardian. I matched her stare with the solemnity required. Confident but not antagonistic. She stayed still. The giant, ornately carved wooden door swung ajar as an invitation. Having previously sparred her will with mine, she received me as a suitable member of the church.

I slipped inside and sank into a vault of candlelight and silence. If this place was anything like our church back home, the high priestess kept a presence inside the church most hours. Her residence was somewhere deep in the bowels of the church and out of bounds to any but her most trusted. Hopefully that was the case here. I needed her help, even though she had appeared carved from granite with ice crystals for a heart, and likely as trustworthy as the devil, a high priestess was the only person likely able to track a vampire.

I inhaled the incense. Closed my eyes and drove the scent further down into my lungs. I needed the grounding and courage of a familiar smell before I attempted to do the unthinkable; enter the vampire's lair. Crazy, stupid idea, but Jarro had the skull. I needed that skull. But to sneak up on a vampire was a foolish idea, an impossible idea, a lethal idea. Perhaps we could negotiate. Maybe if I told the truth, reveal who I was and explained the problem with the Apostles, he'd let me borrow it. Help me, Dark Mother, to see the light.

Wishful thoughts done, I opened my eyes to discover the high priestess standing in front of me. She looked the same as she did the first time, same impenetrable hull, same shrewd, steely eyes.

"It is a pleasure to see you return." I would not have been shocked if she hissed at the end of her sentence. "You're injured?"

"It's minor. I need help."

"Another blood sacrifice. Our Dark Mother will be ever so pleased."

"I was hoping to skip the blood sacrifice and go straight to you."

She did a Morticia eyebrow arch. "Of course, my child. Please, come this way."

She turned into cotton candy and Mother Mary. Maybe it was because this time round she didn't have to contend with a rummy, like Auntie Bea, in her presence, darkening the floors of the church with her useless stain, as Agatha, the high priestess of our coven and church back home, would say.

I limped along behind her, down the aisle toward the nave. The light grew dim in the middle of the church, shrouding us in shadows, but glowed fiercely at the altar. To my surprise, at the crossing, the high priestess turned into the north transept, and then out through a door into a dark stone passage. Miniature crawlies scurried up and down my neck, down my spine to the belt at my jeans. The horrible feeling had me shivering for release. My muscles clenched, poised me on the verge of turning and bolting back into the candlelight.

Since my dakeu, a witch's soul-journey, which brought forth the wicca gifts she was—or wasn't—destined to receive and initiated a witch into the church, I had learned to never trust a high priestess. They were as power-hungry as any other paranormal, even to the point of leaching the skills and gifts off their initiates. A witch without a coven was vulnerable, but once in the coven, a witch could only trust a few. It was best not to make a mistake with whom you gave your trust.

The light that guided us came from windows cut high on the solid stone walls. The half moon skimmed across our heads to shine blocks of light along the opposite wall. Our footsteps were the drums that accompanied us along our journey. With no glass to keep the elements out, the wind swooped and rolled down the passage, driving a gentle breeze that tickled the sweat on my forehead and down my neck.

"Can I call you by your name?"

Not all high priestesses were obliging when it came to personal greetings.

"You may call me Elaine."

"I'm Larnie."

"Yes, I know."

The antagonism between high priestesses from differing churches meant it was unlikely she'd heard about me from Agatha, the high priestess of our former church. Nearing the end of the passage, which ran alongside the interior of the church, the high priestess swept her arms wide from her black robe and the doors in front clunked with the sound of heavy brass latches groaning their complaint at being disturbed.

Darkness swept out from inside, but with another flick of her arms, the interior slowly came to light from a dozen candelabras hanging low from the vast ceiling. Ribbed beams overhead were the perfect places for owls to hide, owls and bats and any manner of hungry creatures just waiting for the right morsel to come their way. A stone fireplace roared to life with a high heat that fanned across the room in seconds. A fur rug lay in front of the fire. I headed over, drawn by the disastrous possibility. The fur rug turned out to be a patchwork of furs stitched together to make it expansive enough to suit such a large space.

"This is real?"

"Of course."

"How many wolves went to making this up?"

"A dozen or so," she replied airily.

Each fur was larger than your average wolf, much larger. "You stripped pack skins."

"They don't need them when they're dead," was her flippant reply.

If any pack member knew about this, there would be war upon the Daughters of our Dark Mother. The paranormals would choose sides, and a war would ensure, one to destroy Davenport. It was the height of disrespect, a display of such contempt. I'd even go as far as to say it was evil. This differed none from patching human skin together to make a lampshade.

I stared at the rug, unable to bring myself to move any closer. The acid in my stomach swirled like a vortex, stirring bile up my throat.

"I hope it doesn't upset you." She appeared beside me, offering a glass of amber liquid. Brandy, by the smell of it. The firelight danced in her glass-blue eyes, making it appear as though she carried the flame inside.

"It's our little secret." She settled herself back in one of the leather chairs, crossed her legs and took a sip. "What help do you need?"

"It was more a favor, nothing big, but I think I can work it out for myself."

"Sit," she commanded. The doors behind me slammed closed. I jumped at the unexpected noise and sloshed some brandy, which landed with a splat at my feet.

"Please," she said with the hint of a smirk.

I slid down onto the nearest seat, which kept me at a distance from the skins. When I realized I'd hunched at the edge, feeling like a skittish colt about to bolt, I eased back further, using that time to soothe the savage beat of my heart and clear my racing thoughts. I couldn't be honest with her. Not a woman who skinned pack members and walked over them daily like they were nothing better than the dirt at her feet. I didn't trust the pack. I didn't much like them, like the rest of the paranormal world, but this was... I didn't have the words.

"I can sense your pain. I smell your blood."

I couldn't swallow.

"You're injured."

I didn't know I was bleeding. But what sort of witch smelt blood? The vampire or pack type. There was no such thing. "I had a few problems getting here."

"Indeed." She worked her eyebrows into another Morticia arch.

"There was an accident. Some crazy driver. I'm fine. Is there a library attached to the church? There was back home. I was hoping I could look something up."

"You can tell me about this...favor you wish to ask."

"It's nothing, really. I just wanted to read up on a few things."

"You will find me the perfect guide to any grimoire, but first I must know what it is you seek. If I am to point you in the right direction."

"I need to do some scrying."

When she smiled, her cheekbones turned to cliffs with sharp overhangs.

"You do not need a grimoire for that, my child. I can do that for you right now. It's a simple enough task."

"I would like to do it myself."

"Chasing an errant lover." It wasn't a question. Not with the condescension in her voice.

"I'm trying to find someone."

"You must get your words right, hold strong with your intention. That will not be easy for you, I sense." She placed her glass down on the small, round wood table beside her chair. The surface of the table showed stained rings of moisture stamped from countless glasses of brandy.

"If you wish to be accurate, then I suggest you relinquish your resistance and allow me to guide you."

"I think I can work it out."

She rose gracefully and moved away from the fire. The hem of her robe glittered in the firelight like a night sky as she glided away. Likely bling sown around the bottom, sequins or something. If so, I'd imagine that was her only nod to glamor.

Was I meant to follow her? I stood and placed my untouched brandy beside hers, about to follow her across the room, but she was already making her way back toward the fire from a private altar she kept along the far wall. It was a replica of the altar in the church minus the offering vessel. Instead, she'd placed a small statue of our Dark Mother. The facing figure of the trimorphis statue held a large ring painted black. The phase of the moon, the circle of life, I understood the symbolism. It was our Dark Mother's key to all things, from birth to death and beyond, but I'd never seen it represented as black.

"There is no need for you to stand. We will conduct the scrying before the fire."

I hadn't agreed, and neither had she listened. I stayed where I was as her robe brushed past me, heading for the low wood table in the center of the skins. Unable to watch her walk across them, I turned my head away.

She held out her hand, guiding me forward with a curl of her fingers. "I can't scry while you're standing over there."

I glanced at the rug. "I don't need it anymore."

She came toward me, moving without noise as she crossed the rug. "You have made your choice." Her hand manacled mine. She dragged me across to the fire. I resisted, but she'd caught me off guard with the first yank, tumbling me forward.

"Stop this." I jerked my hand back.

She folded her arms and looked at my feet. My gaze dropped to find I was already on the rug.

"There is no point in refusing, now. Sit."

"What's it to you?"

"Your Aunt's entrance to the church is conditional."

"We're not staying, so it doesn't matter." There goes my idea of having her scry for Auntie Bea and cutting out the middleman, namely Jarro. Although, something as valuable as the skull for leverage would be handy.

"Davenport does not let its people go as easily as that. A series of events have been set in motion. There is a stirring within the depth of the nexus. Ancient binds will be broken. We are heading for war."

"I didn't know." This was a trick. Had to be. "It's got nothing to do with Auntie Bea or I. We just want to finish our business and go."

"Where? No witch exists outside the bounds of the paranormal. Do you believe you can outrun colliding fates, that the munsib world will protect you?"

"All I wanted was a scrying." Not your hell and brimstone mumbo jumbo.

Her hand gripped onto my wrist, and she yanked me a few more steps forward. Ignoring my cry, she twisted my wrist in an attempt to make me drop to my knees. "With pleasure, my lamb."

I could punch her in the gut, but I'd likely discover she was made from lead and break my knuckles. I could spit in her face, if I didn't suspect, as high priestess, she would have more power than a coven put together. Acting against her would see my skin sewn as a decorative outer rim on the rug.

Once on my knees, she released her hold and lowered herself down beside me. "If I do what you want, you will give me something in return."

I should've guessed. Why would the high priestess of this church be any different from the church back home?

"I need to know what it is you want first." Like I had a choice.

"You will know in time."

"That's doesn't sound fair."

"Nothing in this world is fair. It's time you learned that. Now give me your hand."

"I've seen scrying done with water and a mirror." But she hadn't bothered with either, or anything else for that matter. Instead, the two of us kneeled by the low table on the backs of pack members brutally skinned.

"Primitive methods."

"Do you use fire?" We were kneeling in front of the fire.

She ignored my question. "Tell me who is it you are hoping to find."

Do I waste my deal with Elaine by telling her a lie? "A vampire."

She slowly turned her head from the fire to face me. Side on to the fire, her face became the half moon, shadow on one side, the other exposed by the glow of the firelight. I couldn't help think how accurately it depicted her. The shadow side of Elaine was somewhere I didn't want to delve.

"For one so young, there are many hidden paths within you." She took my hand and turned it up, exposing my palm to the flame light. "Many that needs to be explored. I can show you the way, but not the outcome," she said, as she doodled her finger over the creases and grooves.

"I just want to know where the vampire is."

"You play a dangerous game, Larnie. You stand little chance of succeeding."

"I know. But it's the only way to solve my problem."

"If you ask the wrong questions, you get the wrong answers."

"And you know the right questions. Is that what you're saying?"

She stopped her doodling and tilted her head up slightly to peer at me. "I am as curious about your journey as you are. I am merely the guide."

Then why force me into this? Why force me into your deal? No one in the paranormal world was merely curious about someone else.

You were either an enemy or you were of importance to their overall gain. "I'm not interested in knowing what's ahead. I like to be surprised."

"But we all can use a little helping hand."

She removed the finger that had traced the lines on my palm and disappeared it down beneath her robe. "Do not think you are strong enough to face the future alone. I will be by your side."

Most of what she said tonight confused me. She sounded prophetic, but in a hallucinogenic way. "Sure, whatever."

I caught the movement in the corner of my eye, a blur and then the sting. I cried out and tried to withdraw my hand and was forced to watch in horror as Elaine dragged a blade down the center of my palm, three inches long at least. "What the hell are you doing?"

She dropped the knife on the table, pressed her thumb along the side of the cut to ooze the blood. "Hold still," she hissed. Against me, she pressed harder, running her thumb back and forth to encourage as much flow as she could. "Stop fighting me, stupid girl. I'm giving you what you want."

"I never asked you to mutilate me."

"You want a vampire. I'll give you a vampire, but that sort of quarry needs accurate reads. You will only capture his trail through his greatest desire." An assumption on her behalf, but correct. I was chasing a male vampire.

I grimaced as she continued to milk the blood from my wound. "So what is this called?"

"Aimomancy. Blood scrying."

Satisfied with how much blood she'd forced out of me, she smeared a tacky mess across my palm, closed her eyes, and smoothed a hand over my palm, skimming across the top without touching my skin. My palm warmed. The sting turned to a tingle. Once done, she tilted my palm into the firelight, moving my hand in increments and leaning in close to get a better look. A spark and crackle occasionally punctured the silence as she read whatever was apparent in the bloody mess.

Suddenly she straightened and pulled what I thought was an old-fashioned doily from its ornamental place on the table and handed it to me. "Clean yourself."

With my hand finally released from her wicked grasp, the blood rushed back into my fingertips with a pins and needles feel. I wiped the smears, then pressed the doily firm over the cut. "What did you see?"

"Your failure."

"I thought you wanted to be my guide."

"When you choose to do what is sane."

I pulled the blood-soaked doily away to find the cut fast filled with blood again. "Do you at least have something to stop the bleeding?"

"It is your best way of attracting your vampire."

"I'm not looking to become diner."

"Then cease your search."

"If only it were that simple."

"You will fail, Larnie. That I can tell you. But I understand your need."

Wow, what?

She rose and glided away to the far side of the room. I was exhausted and not interested in seeing where she went or what she was doing. My hip had yet to stop throbbing. Only the pain was now eclipsed by the sting from the large cut on my hand. Jarro would be long gone, the skull out of my reach, Auntie Bea horribly tortured, Elka turning tricks with my boyfriend—not that Hyun-woo was my boyfriend.

Elaine returned with a small bronze bowl. She settled down beside me again and dabbed a cold paste over my cut that reeked of horse manure. "The blood will stop within minutes. It will be scabbed nicely by morning."

Finished with the stinking paste, she placed the bowl on the table, produced a pen, and scribbled something on a scrap of crumbled paper she'd pulled from a hidden pocket in her robe.

"You will find what you are looking for in Snin Cross. Look for a red sign with black lettering. The name is Darken Lounge."

"Is that a club?"

"I don't know what it is. It's what I see."

I couldn't believe she'd helped me in the end. With a price.

"Thanks."

She gave me a look. "You may put that in the fire."

It had looked antique, but covered in my blood, I guess it wasn't worth a cent. I headed around the table and tossed it into the fire. The moment it hit the flames, they whooshed upward in ferocity, turning a brilliant blue and spiraling up the chimney. I jumped back, tripped on the rug and fell onto my ass, causing my injured hip to complain.

I turned back to look at Elaine, but her eyes were on the blue light, her eyes aglow with something more than astonishment. I'd be safer if I jumped into the fire.

CHAPTER 15

It was late. Way too late to be chasing vampires around the city. But since I had the details of my prey on a sheet of paper in my back pocket, I had to do this.

What had that look on Jarro's face meant when he received the phone call? I saw nothing but the world's best poker face, except for the twitch of his jaw muscle. Subtle. Since I'd studied his face closely on a couple of occasions, I'd unwittingly memorized every curve.

The bus dropped me shy of Darken Lounge by a handful of blocks. I would use the walk to think up a plan, which could only involve staying the heck away from anything to do with vampires. Auntie Bea and I had successfully steered our lives clear of dangerous adversaries such as the vamps. As a consequence, we were still alive. But I was not a smart girl.

The next block along, I stumbled on a small pool hall called Snooker Blitz. I ducked inside, keeping my hands in my pockets to hide the blood smeared mess and bee-lined for the toilets. It was best to be clean of any traces of blood before I got too close to any vamps. The city was alive with beating hearts pulsing blood through warm, fleshy bodies, an endless distraction of delectable bites, but spilled blood would cut through the olfactory assault, dissolving other potential meals and singling me out.

Hands clean, clothes scoured for any accidental blood droplets and deemed clean, I was back out on the streets, following maps on my phone when my phone rang. It was Elka.

She didn't give me a chance to get a word in. "Where are you?"

Just like that, fired off the bow. My mind blanked for a fraction of a second, then raced a million miles. What do I admit? "Out."

"Your fiancée knows you're not in your room."

He must've come up after his whiskey with Bernard. "I thought you said he won't push anything while under your dad's roof. And he's not my fiancée." It was creepy, the way she referred to her life as mine.

"Doesn't mean he won't go looking for a goodnight smooch. So, where are you?"

"I'm after the skull. That's the whole point of this swap."

"That tells me nothing."

"Look, I can't talk. I'm getting close."

"Laz, stop," she yelled down the phone as my thumb hovered close to the red end call button.

"I have to go."

"Leave it. You won't get it."

"You directed me to your dad's safe, offering it up, remember? Now you don't want me chasing it."

"I guess you know dad doesn't have it anymore."

I stopped causing a drunk coming along behind me to crash into me because she didn't have the dexterity to avoid me in her state.

"'Ey, where'd you come from?" She slurred as we both tumbled forward. I juggled my phone as the guy she was with apologized and caught her before she hit the paving.

I shoved the phone to my ear. "You knew all along."

"What happened?"

"Answer me."

Her reply was a frustrated sigh, like I was an imbecile. And I was, because I had trusted her.

"Sure. It's not such a big deal. The skull's gone. It won't help you. End of story. Move on."

My fingers gripped my phone so tight if I was superman it would be splinters by now. Smashing it to my cheek, I accidentally ended the call and furiously jabbed through to her number to get her back.

"How could you do that? Why did you do that?"

"Chill, all right. You wanted the skull, and I wanted out of my life. Easy solution."

There were so many words I could say right now, but none of them would come out sane with the way I felt.

"I am not a part of your world to amuse you." It came out sounding squeezed through a thin straw. It was the best I could do. "You knew all along who had it."

"You do realize the Apostles are all over this place?"

"They got past the long dead?"

"They're not in Chinatown, but I can't get out. They've surrounded the place."

I folded my one free arm across my chest. "Doesn't feel good being in a cage, huh?"

"I've lived my life in a cage. I didn't break free to end up in a smaller one. This is your mess, you need to clean it up."

"I can't. Not yet."

"You better get your ass back here and sort this out."

"You're me, remember. You sort it out."

Her inhale was so strong I felt sure she'd suck me through the phone. Her exhale was one long tornado of wind. "Fine. I'll have to do things my way."

I didn't like the finality in her voice. Knowing her, she'd find a way to make her solution my problem.

"Leave Hyun-woo and his family out of it. It's got nothing to do with them."

"They're the only ones keeping Dim Bazaar in one piece. You

don't need to worry about the Chongs."

"What are you going to do?"

She kept the suspense by not replying. In the silence, I envisioned the ways she would find to set the Apostles on to me without giving her secret away.

"Are you going to back off the skull?"

"What's your problem with me and the skull?"

"I don't give a shit about the skull."

Of course, all she cared about was me getting close to the person who had the skull, and that concern had nothing to do with my safety.

"That depends on how you deal with the Apostles."

"Nothing overt. Don't worry, I'll keep our dirty little secret. But, perhaps, they already know. Did you think of that?"

She was right. I mean, the high priest would know of Elka Preston. Mystery was, why had he not said anything to me. "Okay. And I'll get creative on how to rescue Auntie Bea and give up any leverage I may have over the Apostles."

"This is fun. Sisters, trusting each other."

"Yeah, isn't it." I ended the call. Like hell I would give up on that skull. Just as she was not about to keep her end of the deal.

My phone led me across the street, turning left down the next. Up ahead a crowd spilled out onto the paving as a line formed for those eager to get in. Above the line of people was a red sign that read Darken Lounge.

Two bouncers stood either side of the door like ancient monoliths. The Order of Sotiria. According to Elka's map, Snin Cross was the heart of their territory. Their temple would be close by.

These two were zibuian, the deeply devout of the order's congregation. Their tattoos were zibu, or the language of the angels, and a means, they claimed, of communicating with their masters, gifted to them by the angels themselves. They saw their bondage to their masters as a gift.

The zibuian were good at extreme forms of punishment for their sins. And they did not restrict their punishment to each other. They took it upon themselves to punish any heathen who did not bow to their masters, particularly women, who in their eyes, sinned just by living, because the zibuian could not keep their hands to themselves. The zibuian were big, powerful nephilim with big, powerful appetites and a grudge to bear. And here was my ticket to jump the queue and get inside, because the zibuian, like any nephilim, were pawns to the wiles of women. As long as you kept out of their dens, out of their clutches, and ensured you never fulfilled their desires, they were puppets dancing to the tune of their insatiable libidos.

Shame about my clothes. They weren't anything sexy, but I loosened my ponytail and shook my hair free, then pulled it forward to tumble over my shoulder. I pressed my lips together a few times, because that's what they did in the movies to pump the lips with blood instead of a fresh coat of lipstick, and shucked my sweatshirt for an unimpressive T underneath.

Shoulders back, I approached the closet zibuian. "Hey." I tried for a sexy smile, then finished with a pout, which may have been way off the mark. To set the trap, I ran a finger up his bare arm, encircling one of the zibu. "These are pretty. Do they have any meaning?"

He took my fingers in his huge hand, the back of which had ugly, small scars, wounds from his martyrdom. These scars looked recent. The zibuian had a habit of suspending themselves by their palms to suffer the pain of crucifixion in order to prove their twisted zeal.

"Nothing you're allowed to touch."

I snorted a small laugh that was no reflection of the way I felt. His grip hurt, but I swallowed my grimace. "What am I allowed to touch?" I crawled my eyes up his chest, which I found hard to call bare, because of all the zibu covering his skin. He had a piece of his left ear missing. The zibuian got carried away with their devotion.

He lowered himself from his impressive height. "You want a piece of me, woman?"

"I'm very much a woman." I ran the tip of my tongue along my upper lip. His eyes flared as they followed the bait. "I think I could handle..." I wandered my eyes over his body. "All of you, after a drink or two."

Open sesame.

I stepped past him, but he grabbed my wrist and swung me close, so I crashed into his chest. His hand snapped up around my throat, a firm grip that sparked my pulse to triple speed. A small tingle rippled from underneath his grip before he released me.

"What was that for?" Asshole.

"Your collar." He sneered. "You're branded as mine."

Blessed dark mother. I touched my throat, but nothing felt different. What did he mean?

I scooted inside, away from his hungry, salacious glare. The sultry interior of shaded lights, cushioned floor seating, low tables, and bluesy jazz would've been my ideal place to hang out, if not for the zibuian at the door and the vamps inside.

On passing a huge brass pot with a spray of grasses painted gold and black, I stopped to check out my reflection. The lighting was too ambient, the brass not shiny enough, and I couldn't see much. Tucking myself behind the brass pot and grasses, I pulled my phone from my pocket and turned the photo app to reverse and had a good look at my neck. "Oh, hell." The zibuian had branded me all right. There were bands around my neck that really did look like a collar.

How stupid of me. But I'd never heard of them doing that before. Granted, I was no professor on the subject, and this was definitely not something I could've dreamed up. Was this the equivalent of the Apostles' tracker? Something else I had to deal with when I had time. Right now, I had a vampire to hunt without making myself the prey. Again.

Low lighting made it hard to pinpoint faces. Two steps down led you to the lounge. People were sitting cross-legged, sprawled, or with their backs to the wall. The place heaved with the vibe of a heroine den slash bedouin tent, with slow spirals of smoke. A thick cocktail of naturally-grown and manmade vices swirled through the air. The perfect place for seedy deals. And given this was a nephilim-run club, topless waitresses dressed in a thong with diamantes and chains hanging from their nipples clicked around the darkened room in high heels.

The heat from the cram of bodies suffocated me, so I slung the sweatshirt around my waist for want of a better place to hang it and headed into the den. Or around the rim, which was the platform above the lounge where people stood. Most were leaning over a black railing watching the jazz band, talking in groups, checking out the competition or possible bed partners for the night from those below.

I found myself a vantage point, squeezed in between two separate groups, and scanned the lounge. It took me awhile before I found Jarro, slouched against the wall at a table close by. Despite his intense concentration on the man beside him, he appeared at ease. My eyes were caught on the triangle of skin under his unbuttoned shirt. Why did he keep buttoning and unbuttoning his shirt? That was twice in one night.

It wasn't until a man knocked me sideways that I realized I had been staring way too long at Jarro's mouth as he spoke to his companion, and at the tantalizing promise of a glimpse of more chest every time he moved his hand to take a drink. I was sucking him up with my eyes, swallowing every morsel of him, and if not for the knock beside me, I would've stayed that way until dawn.

I pushed away from the railing. I needed to cool my jets and get serious. I'd been attacked by a dark warded, slashed by the high priestess, and branded by a zibuian without a plan for what would come next once I found Jarro. This better all be worth it.

When I looked down at Jarro's table, he'd disappeared. I gripped the railing, scanning the club until I spied him heading up the steps from the lounge, the man he'd been talking to beside him. There were four more men following along behind. Vampires for sure. And they were heading for the exit, past the zibuian.

I grabbed a waitress passing by. "Where's the emergency exit?"

"Left of stage, back of the main bar and end of the corridor to the toilets."

"Great, thanks."

There were too many people crowding the bar exit, even though it was the closest, as was the exit from the side of the stage, so I descended into the lounge, wove around the tables and cushions and up the steps on the other side.

The exit sign at the end of the corridor glowed in the dim light. Opening the door would likely trigger an alarm, maybe bringing a horde of zibuian after me. I needed to be fast.

To my surprise, nothing happened the moment I punched out into the alley at the back of Darken Lounge. I sprinted around the side of the club, but skidded to a stop and dived backward behind the shelter of the building after spying Jarro and his cohorts standing at the mouth of the alley. My luck was holding. Better he was there, than driving away in a car right now.

The hard smack of shoes and the crunch of gravel signaled people were heading my way. Apart from the exit, a one-way door, and a dumpster, scaling the ten-foot brick wall was my only option. Which really meant the dumpster was my only option.

I lifted the lid and climbed inside without bothering to look, slipping my way between bags of stinking yuck and wet, soggy disgusting things. I sank until I thought I would drown in whatever horrible waste was in here. The lid closed shut behind me, plunging me into semi-darkness, thanks to a small bow in the lid's lip. A rustle came from deep in the bags, once I settled on the bottom. Something was in here with me, a furry something on four legs that could prove useful.

By now, the vampires had reached the back of the club. Muffled voices penetrated the heavy metal of the dumpster. Nothing but garbled nonsense. I relaxed the walls around my mind, allowing a part of it to flow outward in search of my little furry helper. The rat's mind proved sharper than a bird's and easier to control, given he was eager to get away from me.

He scurried up the side of the dumpster and out through the bow in the lid. I tightened my control over his momentum, forcing him to stop before he scuttled away. This is where control over his simple little mind got tougher. All he wanted to do was escape, driven by his freight train heart-rate, but I needed him to spy on my target.

Jarro and the man he'd been with inside the club were arguing. The other four men surrounded them, forming a perimeter of no escape. The man pulled a piece of paper from his pocket and held it out to Jarro, who swiped it, read what it said, scrunched it up, and threw it away. He then lunged for the man, grabbing him by his shirt front and pulling him off his feet, until the guy was kneeling before him. Words never came through an animal's brain in a decipherable manner, but what played out in front of me needed no dictation.

I didn't like this guy's chances. Even through the small eyes of the rat, there was no mistaking the fury in Jarro's movements. Rage emanated as far as the dumpster, threatening to blow it sky high. They'd looked like partners in some nefarious business inside the club. Maybe they were, and this is what vamps did to partners when they passed their used-by date.

The rat itched to get going, his nose twitching for danger, his muscles bunched with the need to scurry. His angst transferred into my body, tensing my muscles. I felt on the verge of busting out of here and making a dash for the open end of the alley. I pumped my fists to remind myself this was the rat's feelings, not mine, and I was the puppeteer.

Things were tense up ahead. The guy was pleading. Jarro's voice had dropped, so I couldn't hear any of what he said, but he'd crouched and pressed his temple to the guy's like he hoped to drill it right through. When dangerous people spoke in calm, low voices, that's when you had to worry.

And then it happened. I had expected it would. My body quivered with the low vibration of horrified anticipation. Jarro struck. Latched on to the guy's throat. The guy, kicking and shrieking, was too much for me. I released the rat from his binds, and he scuttled away as fast as he could.

I buried myself in dumpster garbage, cradled my head in my elbows and waited for it all to be over.

CHAPTER 16

They cleaned up their mess.

When I climbed out of the dumpster, having heard silence for some time, there was nothing to show for what had gone on in the alley except a dark stain. I was not about to get any closer to investigate, until I remembered the paper Jarro had screwed up and tossed away. He'd tossed it away, so perhaps it wasn't important to him, but it may be of interest to me. At least give me some insight to what had happened here.

Really, I shouldn't get involved in vamp politics. This had nothing to do with my problems. It wouldn't rescue Auntie Bea, and it wouldn't get the two of us out of Davenport ASAP. But I was next to useless alongside the paranormals that lived in Davenport, and I couldn't come up with a better way of convincing the Apostles to let Auntie Bea go, unless I had the skull as leverage...or, and this was crazy, I persuaded Jarro to get her for me.

Stupid, crazy, insane idea. But what if I played up his desire for Elka? Spun some lie about Auntie Bea's importance to me—or rather Elka—and convinced him it would be worth his while to help me out with this one small task. She seemed adamant he wasn't interested in her anymore. A lovers' spat, perhaps, or a lie on her behalf to keep me away from him. Both were equally plausible. But if the way he acted was a guy not interested, then dark mother help her if he was hell bent on having her. Besides, what did it matter to me? As long as Auntie Bea and I were long gone, I didn't care what went down in this messed-up city. I wanted to see the city lights fade on the horizon as we bolted from this place.

I found the scrunched paper easy enough, but it wasn't nearly as exciting as I'd hoped. Fountain Row. That was it. A location? Street name? Meeting place? I stored that name away in my head and ditched the paper.

I needed to head back to Elka's. Even though I really wanted to return to Dim Bazaar, I'd have to continue the charade of being Elka for a while longer.

Nearly at the mouth of the alley, a bag of muscle stepped out from the front of Darken Lounge. The zibuian asshole who'd branded me. Dammit to all hell. I'd forgotten about this guy, the rings around my neck.

"I don't take too kindly to my possession walking away."

My hand involuntarily hugged my throat.

"That place was sure crowded. I needed some fresh air."

"Through the back door."

"There was no room to squeeze out the front."

"The night's built some tension." He cracked his neck. "Lucky for me, my man Altro has agreed to take my place. Which means I get to work out some of this tension before I'm called back on the job."

"Lucky you."

I flicked a look to the street. There was still a decent crowd trying to get into Darken Lounge. Would he dare cause a problem in front of them? Don't bring attention to the dark world. An unwritten rule all paranormals abided by, more or less. I could scream and kick up a fuss. It was hard to say how far the zibuian were prepared to go when it came to soothing their itch. While all nephilim were driven by testosterone overload, thanks to the curse of their masters, the zibuian were a couple of levels over the top with their hunger.

I gave him half my concentration. The other half went flying outward into the streets, scraping every corner, every alley, every hiding place for help. There were a myriad of helpers I could call upon, but I needed something much bigger than a mouse. A dirty, great big dog would cause a ruckus. Enough, perhaps, to aid my escape. And what about the bands around my neck? The magical tracker. Maybe I'd have to seek the high priestess's help again; best not think about what that would cost me.

The zibuian stomped closer, minus any of the grace of their angelic masters.

"Wait." I held up my hand, but he seized my wrist.

"You don't get to play and think you can turn me away." He jerked me close, crushing me against the rock wall that was his body. "What you want is never my concern."

"What about the people on the street? If I scream—"

His fingers gripped my cheeks like a vise. He tilted my head back to meet his face. "Try it. You won't like what happens."

I couldn't reply because his fingers were squishing my cheeks together painfully tight, and I probably looked like a fish gasping for air.

"Ditto." The male voice came from behind.

The zibuian turned around to see who'd spoken, still holding me in his painful grasp.

I never thought I would feel such relief on seeing Jarro. He slouched against a street sign, one hand in his pocket, looking superimposed from the pages of some hard-boiled fiction, that and a generous dose of James Bond. Yes, he was the greater danger of the two paranormals in front of me, and had also shown an interest in getting me into bed, but so far he'd not pushed.

"Keep out of my business," growled the zibuian.

He pushed off from the street sign and strolled toward us, keeping his black eyes on the zibuian. "Maybe I want it to be my business."

"This is a private matter. It's no business of yours."

"It is when it involves my interests." Jarro had yet to look at me.

"Look," the zibuian snapped, wrenching my head to the side to expose my neck.

"You should know better than exposing a woman's neck to me," Jarro drawled.

If I wasn't in such a painful predicament, granite fingers on the verge of punching through my cheeks, my body would likely react to his velvet tone. "You know what this means. I've branded the bitch mine."

"You think some pencil marks make her yours?"

The zibuian shoved me away and spun to face Jarro. Such was the force he used in his fury, I staggered backward into someone standing behind.

"You all right?" A male voice asked me, his arms snapping to my waist to help steady me, but I was concentrating on the other two men.

"I'd make way if I were you. Those bouncers are mean fuckers. You don't want to mess with them. That insane guy's got a death wish."

I moved from his steadying hold. "I know the insane guy."

The zibuian blocked Jarro with his massive frame. Despite Jarro being a big guy, none could compare to the nephilim.

The street had grown quiet. I glanced over my shoulder to see everyone in the line had turned to watch them.

"Sorry, but I don't like his chances," the guy beside me said.

"I wouldn't write him off."

As if I'd cursed his fate, the zibuian dropped to his knees in front of Jarro, for no apparent reason. None of the munsib would understand, but the tension in the zibuian's back spoke of more than tough words at work. While still on his knees, he buckled forward, one hand dropping to the pavement for support. His back muscles hunched and buckled like they were straining against a force.

Jarro took a step toward him. Towering over him, he said, "Don't cross onto my turf."

"Holy shit. Never thought I'd see that," the guy.

But I was already backing away, pressing through the crowd. Thank the dark mother, enough people loitered outside to make my disappearance easier. I barged through coiffured hairdos, hairspray, and a toxic blend of perfume, sending women in stretched tube-dresses tittering on their high heels, and receiving plenty of grouch words from the guys.

I burst through the crowd and ducked into the shadows of the building next door as I hurried to get away. I didn't even want to think about what happened back there. I had a of couple more build-ings to go before I reached the corner of the street. And I dared not look over my shoulder. Get some distance, Laz. My heart-rate gave my legs wings.

Just another two buildings to go and I'd be around the corner. I scurried along, hugging the shop fronts like a mouse. And then, finally, I was around the corner and into a deserted street, before I was backpedaling into the slip of space at the front door of the shop that offered a smidge of coverage. Even munsib women knew deserted streets were trouble.

I couldn't go back. And not because of the zibuian. Dammit. I punched my thighs with my fists. That crossed out my plan of using Jarro to free Auntie Bea. No way was I messing with him anymore. What the hell was that back there? What had Jarro used to get the zibuian to his knees? Blessed dark mother, what talent did that vamp possess? Vamps had teeth, ridiculously serious strength, speed, agility, hearing, smell and anything else that made them an apex predator, but never had I heard of one possessing magical talent. But there was no other explanation for what I'd seen.

"Okay. Plan, Laz. How to get out of this mess."

Every turn I made sunk me deeper into the black hole of Daven-port. I was losing track of the number of people who wanted my head.

Car lights swung around the corner. The car was so low to the ground its undercarriage was practically scraping along the asphalt. It swung in to the curb in front of me with a sudden but smooth curve. I pressed up against the glass shop door as the car door swung open.

I had to bend to see the driver inside, but I already knew who it was, and there was no point in gluing myself to the door and refusing the ride. The open door was invitation enough, as he didn't say a word.

Don't do this, Laz.

As if I could refuse. I slid down into the racing car seat, feeling cradled in place. The inside smelt of leather and the heady blend of balsam, cinnamon, and musk coming from my sexy lethal nemesis. The seats were decadently plush to match the oil black interior surfaces. Jarro swung away from the curb, leaving a noisy rumble of engine power in our wake.

"You didn't say thank you."

"Thank you." I was better off pretending I had no idea of the implications of what had happened. Elka said Jarro didn't know she was a witch. And for once, I believed her. "That was a little freaky. That bouncer got a little intense over some slight. It wasn't even me. I wasn't even in the club. He just jumped me as I was passing by."

I resisted the urge to slide my hand up and cover the bands around my neck. How to explain my understanding of these? Oh, dark mother, what a mess.

"The last I saw you, you were heading to bed."

"It's such a long story. You wouldn't be interested."

"We've got a drive."

Feeling his gaze creep all over me, I slowly turned my head and looked out the passenger window, closing my eyes as a way of escape. Bury me now. We were locked in a cat-and-mouse game. And I was not the cat.

What are you? The words were there, but they would never be said. Right now, it felt as though my supposed naïveté about the paranormal world was the only thing that kept his teeth, plus what extra funky mojo he had tucked within those firm abs, from my throat. And his shirt buttons were still undone.

"I got a call from a friend needing help."

"Do I need to go back for her?"

"Turns out she rescued herself. At least I didn't see her there. That bouncer got a little surly when I refused to pay. I told him I didn't want to stay. That I just had to check on a friend."

"But you weren't at the club."

Dammit. "I wasn't. I went to go in, but then she called to say don't bother. She was okay." What would he do if I leaped out the car window?

"It must have been some slight."

"I don't remember. He went all caveman and feral for no reason."

"Frederick will be worried."

"It's got nothing to do with Frederick. So what did you do to him back there?"

"Why did you run?"

"Are you kidding? A two-hundred-pound blockhead just vise gripped my cheeks. In my world, that means don't hang around to give him a second go."

He turned his face toward me, stared at me with those impenetrable eyes. I was being diced here, dissected like a lab rat.

"You didn't trust me to take care of him?" His voice should not slip over me like a silken sheet.

"I guess." Time out. This conversation had to stop because I couldn't keep it up.

"You're... I'm struggling to find the right word."

"Then don't. I'd rather not be offended."

He laughed, a low manly rumble that rippled through the air and into me like some soothing, melodious chant.

I pressed into the seat, resting back on the headrest. "I've got a headache. I think I'll shut my eyes for a moment."

This morning, I arrived home to find Auntie Bea missing. This morning! Two days ago, I attended the auction and meet Jarro and Elka for the first time. Two freaking days ago. How many people were after my hide now?

I rested my head facing him, with no intention of closing my eyes. Not completely. I cracked them open a smidge. Through my lashes, I found him staring at me. Would I ever not feel haunted by his gaze?

I sat up. "You never answered my question. What did you do to that guy to make him go down on his knees?"

How far was he willing to go?

"I used the right words."

"I used the right words. Like scream, and police, and jail for assault, but it didn't have the same effect."

"You don't know my words."

"Yeah, I do. Money."

"Touché."

I should have made him squirm. Though, I doubt Jarro knew how to squirm.

"Who were the other guys you were with?" I might as well see what he would let slip.

"I don't remember being with anyone when I met you on the street."

Shoot me. That was before, when he... "Sorry. I thought the guy who helped me up was with you. Oh wow, look. We're here." I exhaled.

Jarro turned into the driveway, slowing before the gate. I had my door open before the car came to a solid stop.

"Thanks for being there. And thanks for the lift. I'll see you later. Maybe." I was out the door, shutting it behind me like I could lock him inside.

Horror movie tingles crept up my back with the sound of the car door opening.

He kept the headlights on, obscuring himself with the bright lights when I looked over my shoulder. There wasn't even the crunch of his shoes on the asphalt, just his grip on my upper arm as he turned me around. So suddenly, his hand was at my throat as he pushed me back into the brick wall framing the gates. Back lit by the headlights, his face was a silhouette. Until he shifted in close, shielding me from the harsh glare and revealing his uncompromising expressing. "One of us is playing a game. Who do you think it is?"

"I only know board games."

"I thrive on the challenge."

"I—"

He tightened his grip. "For as long as it takes me to win."

"Sore loser, I see."

"As delectable as you might be, don't get in my way."

"You can remove your hand from my throat."

"First time's a warning."

"There won't be a second time." Because I'll smite your ass. The high priestess will show me how to smite your ass.

"Make sure of it."

He held my throat for breaths longer because he wouldn't do anything I demanded. But rather than set me free, he forced my head to the side. My pulse jackknifed with the feel of his breath along my neck, and it had nothing to do with feeling sexed up. He'd know because that was a vampire thing. He'd hear the hammering of my heart, the sloshing of my blood through my veins. Would that get him off in a sick vampire twisted way? Next came his inhale. If he dared to lick me, I'd embed my knee in his balls.

"You're dangerously close to assault. My father has cameras all over this place."

Slowly he relinquished me, backed away like he couldn't bear to turn around. But I missed his expression, missed seeing the open buttons on his shirt sneaking a taunting reveal of his chest, because of the headlights. Okay, maybe I'd been sexed up a little. Only a smidge, because he'd threatened me.

Jarro had just announced us as enemies playing the same game. How far into the game did we have to sink before one of us lost? He held all the cards, but I was a fighter.

As he faded behind the car lights, I had an injection of memory. I turned around and punched the code in, then went through the gate as he pulled away from the driveway. Inside the perimeter, I sprinted the rest of the way to the front door, then up the stairs to my room. Pressed against the door, I relieved my memory. A man pressing me against a pillar, made silhouette by the intense light behind. He'd threatened me, sniffed his way along my neck, licked me. My dakeu. Jarro was the mysterious man in my dakeu. A witch's dakeu was her own mental journey. It was impossible for him to have been there, not in the flesh. But I had come out of that adventure still feeling the cold at my back from the pillar and smelling his scent on my clothes.

In my dakeu, he'd labeled me a threat, promised to burn me in hell if I took what was his. Whatever that meant.

I pushed off front the wall and headed for the en suite bathroom. I was shattered beyond belief. At this point, the Apostles, the dark warded, the high priestess, the zibuian, all the paranormals that hoped to carve some skin from my bones was nothing compared to Jarro. A vamp with a shot of extra magic juice.

In the bathroom I stuttered to a standstill, staring at myself in the mirror. I pulled my shirt away from my neck. The zibuian branding had disappeared, and I could still feel the warmth from Jarro's hand at my throat.

At least that was one thing. He'd released me from my zibuian bind.

CHAPTER 17

I left early to dodge Frederick and Elka's father, blindly running forward, no plan, no idea what the heck I was supposed to do next. My options were...nil. The bus was packed at this time of morning. Who would've thought so many people would be in such a hurry to get to work. I stared out the window, trying to distance myself from everyone. Never had I felt so separate from the munsib world as I did at this moment. I felt sorry for all these innocent people. None of them knew the dangerous, unstable forces stirring alongside of them. It wouldn't take much to ignite a chain reaction that would blow this vibrate city apart.

Beside me sat a middle-aged man smelling of aftershave and citrus laundry powder with a small stain high on his tie. Briefcase on his lap, he flicked through some documents, lips moving along with his silent reading. Perhaps the most important thing in his day was a board meeting or presentation he'd have to give in front of a room full of people thinking of their dwindling bank balance or whether their spouses would somehow catch them out with their lovers. Maybe that wouldn't be such a bad life. Once upon a time I loathed the idea of being enslaved to a normal existence, where the only thing stressing you every day was meeting your mortgage repayments. Now, it seemed like a pretty good deal.

My stop came sooner than I was ready, and I had to excuse myself past the briefcase guy, upsetting his stacked papers, and hurried off the bus before the driver closed the doors.

There was no other way of entering Chinatown except through the entrance, which may or may not be heavily watched by the Apostles. Already I could see the stone pillars looming into view, the dragons on watchful guard at the highest points.

I hurried along the pavement, keeping alert to everyone around me. If they believed Elka was me, they had no reason to be watching people enter as much as watching those depart.

I picked up my pace to walk alongside a group of three young women, keeping my head bowed. "Are you heading for Chinatown?" I didn't care where they were heading, just that they provided a cover.

"No," the closest said.

"Where are you heading?"

"What's it to you?" said one of her friend.

"Just making conversation. It's a lovely day."

"Piss off," said the woman closest to me.

"I'm just being friendly. It's a lonely walk to work on my own otherwise, but you needn't worry, I won't bother you for much longer. I just need you to pretend my conversation is really interesting until.... Okay, thanks for the chat." I peeled away from them and raced for the entrance, not breathing until I passed the dragons. Sparing one look behind me, I saw no one standing beyond the entrance, looking frustrated and menacing. Maybe I hadn't needed the ruse.

I hurried down the main street toward Hyun-woo's restaurant and store. I didn't know what would come of me returning here, but I was out of options. The Apostles still had Auntie Bea, and Jarro had made it very clear what he'd do if I got in his way. The only thing I could think to do was surrender to the Apostles in exchange for Auntie Bea, but first I wanted to see if Hyun-woo or Elka could come up with a better plan than the one I'd disastrously executed.

"Laz."

I spun to the sound of Hyun-woo's voice. Seeing him standing in the middle of the street was a warm greeting home. I'd spent the last twenty-four hours surrounded by unfriendlies, trusting no one, fearful of some. Hyun-woo was the only person in this city on my side. Possibly Elka, but I wouldn't bet on it.

"I didn't think I'd see you so soon. I hoped I would but...did you get the skull?" Through that little hurried speech, his eyes never left my face. It was like he wanted to survey my features to imprint once again the few parts he'd forgotten.

"No. And I don't stand a chance of getting it. It's with the Vehan."

"Preston gave it to the Vehan? I thought he was a lapdog to the nephilim."

"I don't think he gave it to them. I think Jarro stole it."

"Do you mean the Vehan King?"

"It's weird they still use that title. It's so old-fashioned."

"To them it's not. They're old."

I shook my head, dismissing the banal matter. "I've run out of options. I've got nothing to bargain with. The Apostles will never return Auntie Bea out of the goodness of their hearts."

"We'll find another way."

The fact he said *we* stirred a warm feeling in my heart. Hyun-woo didn't need to involve himself in my mess, and the fact he did made me feel less alone. Truth was, I'd never been alone before. Auntie Bea and I had been a team. She was always there, no matter how much trouble she got herself into, how hopeless she was in all things magical, I'd never been alone.

I rested my hand on his arm. "Thanks, but I'm not sure how. In the last twenty-four hours I've had to dodge several pretty unpleasant situations. I feel like I'm in a glass tunnel. On all sides, there are dangers peering in, and I've got nowhere to hide. All I can do is keep running."

"Davenport will do that to you. You've got to know which regions you can enter and which you have to stay away from."

We were slowly heading back to his parent's restaurant.

"How did your sister die?" It just came out. "I'm sorry. If you don't want to answer that…"

"It's fine. The pain's not so raw anymore."

"Now I know how involved you are in the paranormal world, I was wondering if her death was normal."

"What's normal? I've known nothing else, so everything about this life is normal."

"I think of my life in two parts. There's the CC, and the LA. That's comfortably callow and lunatic asylum. I didn't find out about any of this until I was eighteen, when I first starting displaying talent. Before then, I was a normal teenage girl in my period of comfortably callow. Then hell rained down, and I entered the lunatic asylum."

"I would've liked to have known you as a normal teenage girl."

I savored his cheeky smile. "I was failing life as a normal teenager. And now I'm failing life as a witch."

"You're no longer protected by your coven, yet you're still alive and not a pawn in some powerful paranormal games. I'd say that's a pretty successful run."

"You got two things right. But I'm very much a pawn now. But I don't want to talk about that. What happened to your sister?"

He bowed his head, looked at his feet for a moment. I was about to say we didn't have to talk about it, when he finally spoke. "My sister turned to black shamanism. She turned her back on her ancestral spirits and meddled in the dark path. It consumed her. It's this city. The evil's like an infection. Once it's inside of you, you can't get rid of it. It twists you."

I stayed silent, allowing the story to unfold at his pace.

"She left us. We had no idea where she'd gone. For months, we looked everywhere, tried everything to find her, but she'd hidden herself so thoroughly. A part of her was ashamed at what she'd done. That's why she couldn't face my parents. My mother especially. But the shame was not enough to stop her."

"But you did find her?"

"She'd moved to Lower Boddock. She was mixed up with the Brothers of the Redentore."

"Dark mother, you're joking. The Brothers—" were a messed up lot. And that was saying something. "It was about a guy, wasn't it?"

"A part of it, yeah. But there had to have been more. I think she saw the possibility of greater power. Power beyond the reach of a shaman. We deal with spirits. That's where our strength lives. But there are some elements of the spiritual world we don't touch. It's dangerous energy. The realm of the long dead is one of those places. Only experienced and powerful shaman dare meddle with them. But we're not the only practitioners who tap into the spirit world. And some do so without care to what they will inadvertently unleash."

"Sometimes witches evoke spirits—"

"No. I'm talking about the Brothers."

"I thought they were too busy taking life to bother about messing with what comes after."

"There is a cult within the Brothers, the Living Dead, who partake in the dark art of jug-eunjaleul il-eukida, raising the dead."

"Necromancy."

"A spirit made flesh. It's a deadly thing. Spirit energy is too powerful a thing to be set free. But it's not just the dead that the Brothers hope to raise. They wish to cross the spirit void and into the realms beyond. No one knows what exists beyond the spirit void, but as shamans dealing with the spirit realm, we come close to catching glimpses."

"Let me guess. Nothing good."

Hyun-woo shook his head.

"Do you think they're succeeding?"

"The Brothers are not warlocks. They lack the skill or power. It doesn't stop them trying."

"How was your sister involved?"

"The idea of touching these other realms seduced her. As a gifted shaman, she skimmed the surface of that which exists beyond the spirit void. It enticed her to know more. It could've been anyone. I'm sure the Apostles are also trying their luck, but she met this Brother. He convinced her they were closer than anyone else to harnessing power beyond anyone's reach."

"How did she die?"

"She allowed herself to be sacrificed."

I gasped.

"I'm not sure if they convinced her of that, or if it was her own idea. The most powerful liminal time is at death. I believe she thought she would transcend beyond the spirit void and into the deeper realms at the most powerful liminal time."

"Did she?"

"She may have done, had mom and I not intervened. We imprisoned her within the realm of Sansin where her vengeful spirit can do no harm."

"That's awful, Hyun-woo."

"Mom still feels her betrayal. She hopes to soothe her spirit and reunite at the time of her own death. Only fate will show us. We try to keep an eye on the cult's practices, but it's not so easy. They're good at hiding. We know they have a place on Fountain Row—"

"Wait. Fountain Row. You know where that is?"

"Lower Boddock. The cemetery's there, and little else. We believe they have a place within the cemetery, a small stone church built centuries ago. We believe there's a crypt underneath. It's also likely the cult have made a tunnel that runs from their own catacomb at the Brothers of Redentore temple to this place."

"I have to go there."

"That's crazy. Why?"

"Because I saw a man killed by vampires. He was carrying a piece of paper with Fountain Row written across it."

"How... Laz, where were you to witness that?"

"It doesn't matter."

Hyun-woo's expression said it mattered very much to him.

"I followed a vampire."

"You did what?" He finger combed his hair.

"They have the skull. It was my only hope of getting Auntie Bea back. I felt...I still feel helpless. I couldn't just let it go."

"Where?"

"Darken Lounge in—"

"Snin Cross. The Order of Sotiria own Snin Cross. You have no idea—"

"I have plenty now."

"Did they know you were there?"

I faltered. "Not sure."

"Laz."

"They may have done."

He squeezed his forehead with his fingers. "Did the vampires know you were there?"

"Most likely."

"Who was it?"

"I don't know. I don't know any of the nephilim."

"I didn't mean the nephilim."

"I think it was Jarro."

"Jesus Christ, Laz."

"What does he care? I'm nothing to him."

"How did you know what was on the paper?"

"Does it matter?" When he hard stared at me, I elaborated. "I saw them discard the paper before they killed the guy, so I snuck over and had a look."

Hyun-woo continued with his frustrated gestures.

"They don't know I read the paper."

"Are you kidding? Honestly, Laz. You're not that stupid. I know you're not. No one witnesses the dealings of vampires and is allowed to live. Unless you have the eyes of a hawk and saw all of this from blocks away, they would've smelled you."

I had hoped hiding in a dumpster hid my smell. Jarro had been waiting for me at the mouth of the alley, which proved he'd known. But apart from threatening me, he'd let me walk away.

"He thought I was Elka."

"Who, Jarro? You spoke to him?"

Oops. I shouldn't have said that.

"Elka and him have a thing."

"They do?"

That should not stab a spear through my insides like it just did. Why would Hyun-woo say it like it meant something to him? "Looks like it saved my ass. He dropped me back at the mansion." I held my hands out. "See, no harm done."

Hyun-woo's eyes turned needle-like, pricking into me.

"I want to check out this place on Fountain Row."

"Because you're not in enough trouble yet."

"It's something to the vamps. They killed a guy for that information."

"Doesn't that tell you something about how dangerous it would be?"

"So is sitting around waiting for the paranormal world to erupt around you."

"I thought Auntie Bea was your priority."

"Unless you think I should hand myself over to the high priest as a swap, I suggest you tell me what you know about Fountain Row, the Brothers, and why it would have anything to do with the Vehan." I jabbed my hands on my hips, leaning toward him as a dare to say anything against me. I'd gotten worked up over that brief speech, but I meant ever word.

He visibly deflated. "If the Vehan are involved, then its got something to do with the Cantonia. They wouldn't bother themselves unless it was to do with their enemy. Though I'm not sure what the Brothers would have to do with it."

"And there's nothing else on Fountain Row?"

"Just the cemetery."

"It looks like I'll be paying my respects to the dead."

"Not alone."

"No, Hyun-woo. You can't come. You're right in saying this is dangerous."

"And what are you going to do? Even if you enlist the help of all the animals in Davenport, you're not safe. I do speak to the dead, you know. And they listen. There is more power in that cemetery for those that deal with the dead realm than anywhere else in Davenport."

"We have to be inconspicuous."

"Like you've managed so far."

I ducked my head and fought with a smile. He was so sweet to want to help, and I wanted him there. I wasn't a warrior. Neither did I think I was particularly brave, just desperate.

"I should also have a word with Elka."

"She's not here."

"But I thought she couldn't get out of Chinatown. Apostles and all."

"I thought she wouldn't dare risk it. But she did. Early this morning."

You went looking for her early this morning? Or maybe he rolled over to see her gone. *Don't think like that.*

"She left a note. That's how I know."

Did I just wear my jealousy on my face?

"She's smart. She'll be safe."

Unlike me, huh?

"You're not from around here. You don't know this city. And you also told me you and Auntie Bea stayed away from the powerful paranormals, so you're a tad naïve about how things really work."

Do shamans read minds?

"I've got a few things I need to do for my parents. And I want to consult with Mom, first."

That sounded like too much time wasted. Especially if he wanted me to accept something from his mom.

Hyun-woo took me by the upper arms. "Laz, please, be patient. I want you to accept what Mom gives you."

"Seriously. Do you read minds?"

"Not minds. Just your face. It's amazingly expressive."

"Great," I sighed.

"People with open faces are compassionate, loving and kind. They have great social intelligence, strive for honor, and seek justice. They also happen to be bullish, fail to think things through, and struggle to accept help."

"That's not me."

"They're very pig-headed."

"Excuse me."

"They also make great lovers."

I slammed my mouth shut and felt the first flush of heat rush up my neck and major spasms sink down into my nether regions.

CHAPTER 18

"There is no time now for the mark. You must take this, instead."

Hyun-woo's mother, Chin-Sun, handed me a bracelet she had made of knotted yellow fabric. Unrolling it showed a detailed chain of symbols written in red. She had spent the last few hours in deep meditation while she consulted her spirits as to the right symbols to use as protection against the darkness I may face.

Hyun-woo had brought me pot after pot of tea while I sat in the small lounge room of their home, tucked behind the shop. When Chin-Sun entered her deep trance, the atmosphere in the room warmed. I'd never felt so tranquil, so at peace with my world as I did drinking tea and imbuing the soothing vibes that spread through the room. This was nothing like my experience on joining the coven or entering the church. Shamanism was a balancing, healing discipline. Perhaps Auntie Bea and I should join the Church of Living Light. Maybe it would be more like this. Though I couldn't see Auntie Bea prostrating herself on the flagstones of the Living Light in humble obedience.

Chin-Sun tied the protection fabric to my wrist. "It will not come off easily."

"Thank you."

She took both my hands in hers. "You must do as Hyun-woo says. Lunaris Cemetery is not a place you want to be without a spirit-walker."

"A spirit-walker?"

She laughed, her smile breaking her face in two, it was that big and bountiful. She patted her chest, then gestured to Hyun-woo.

"You call shamans spirit-walkers?"

"It's Mom's nickname. She thinks it's more in keeping with modern trends. She also watches a lot of fantasy on all the streaming channels."

"I like it."

She squeezed my hands and laughed. Then her faced sobered. "But listen. Lunaris has long been abandoned. The living rarely go there any more. It's where the forsaken dead fester. They're restless and angry. The Living Dead have taken advantage of this, making it their home. They are a weak cult, but they have made the veil unstable. Their practices have also attracted dark spirits to the cemetery. Stay away during liminal times. And never go there without Hyun-woo."

"Got it." I glanced to Hyun-woo, who winked at me. "We should go."

Chin-Sun turned to her son "You are prepared?"

He nodded. "Come. We need to time this right."

"Thank you for what you've done," I said to Chin-Sun. She took my hands in hers, squeezed them while she nodded her head in acknowledgment. "May your auntie be safe."

"I'll make sure of that." The promise was hollow, but I had to give myself something.

Hyun-woo slowed once we reached the entrance to Chinatown. "The spirits will shadow us only so far before they stretch beyond the binds Mom has in place, which would be disastrous for everyone. When the dragons leave us, I will gather my own spirits, but be warned, I am not as strong as my mother."

"I have this, now." I held up my wrist.

"It's more easily breached by powerful magic compared with the risen spirits, but it's better than nothing."

"How about we go before you make me change my mind."

"I doubt you would change your mind, Laz. Not when it comes to your Ee-mo. You're too courageous."

"Sure you don't mean foolhardy?"

"I wanted to be polite."

We smiled stupid, childish grins at each other, until someone in the street yelled out, drawing us out of our private moment.

"Shall we?" Hyun-woo held out his hand.

I slipped mine inside of the warm fold of his palm and savored the feeling of having a friend beside me, someone willing to enter into battle alongside me. Hopefully it wouldn't come to that. But neither of us had any idea what we were headed toward.

The name Fountain Row could've meant nothing to Jarro. This could all be a waste of our time. I knew I was clutching desperately to anything that may prove a way to rescue Auntie Bea. And my heart was still set on that skull. The Apostles would do anything to own such a powerful gift, even give up their plans for me—whatever those plans may be—in order to possess it. Having the skull would solve everything.

Hyun-woo increased his pace, once we were outside of China-town. I glanced over my shoulder at the dragons on the entrance pillars to find they'd disappeared. Neither were they visible anywhere else.

"You will not see them," Hyun-woo said. "They move with the shadow of the spirits, but they are there."

"How long until we lose them?"

"They won't go beyond Wolgod Quarter."

"Why don't we head to central, and then up into Lower Boddock?"

"As I said, once we lose Mom's protection, I will have to drawn on my own spirits. Even though they're contained, I don't want to bring enlivened spirits that close to the nexus. I don't want to push my control that much."

"Got it. How long will it take us to reach Lower Boddock?"

"We'll have to change buses a few times. And end up on a meandering detour of the districts, but we should arrive by late afternoon."

"We miss one liminal time, but won't sunset also be a problem?"

Hyun-woo said nothing, instead flagged our bus down. Did he not hear me or did he deliberately not answer? Hyun-woo continued to say nothing for the rest of the bus ride. Sitting by the window, he kept his focus outside. When he finally turned around, he rested back into the bus seat, sank his head to his chest, and closed his eyes. We must've crossed over from Wolgod Quarter into Pend South, leaving his mom's protective spirits behind.

I felt the tingle of apprehension knowing he was consulting with his spirits and doing whatever else it was that spirit-walkers did to coax the spirits to this realm as protective guardians.

It took minutes before he opened his eyes and blinked. "This is our stop."

I shuffled off first, but Hyun-woo gently took my arm and slowed me, allowing him to move down the bus aisle first. Sweet, but surely he wasn't going to play the overprotective savior all through today.

"I'm not helpless, you know," I whispered once we stood at the doors waiting for the bus to pull in at the curb. He settled us behind another couple also wanting to exit.

Leaning in close, he said, "Helpless is someone sitting at home biting their nails not daring to do what you've done in the last forty-eight hours. You are far from helpless. But exiting the bus is a tricky time. Your attention is somewhat divided. There's a confused mix of people getting off and people wanting to get on. It's the perfect time to launch an assault. That's what I'd do."

"I have this, remember?" I held up my wrist.

"Yes, you do. But can't you give a guy a chance to be useful?"

I pouted for effect. "Just this once."

Hyun-woo politely waved the couple first, but tacked on close to their tails. Once off the bus, he hurried us along the paving, blending into the crowd.

"Where to, now?"

"We want the bus stop around the corner." He stilled, gasping an inhale, concaving forward.

"What?"

"They're here."

I almost gave myself whiplash looking around us.

"They haven't breached the protective wall. But now they know it's there, they will double their efforts, try some magic next time. Come, we're safer on the bus than in the street."

Hyun-woo broke into a run. Not easy to do with the crowds. At one point, I lost his hand when he doubled over again, this time clutching his stomach. No doubt they were getting nasty and employing magic to bust their way through the spirit defenses.

Hyun-woo righted himself and grabbed my hand again. We plowed our way through the crowd, gathering curses and foul looks as we went, until we burst around the corner and across the street.

The bus wasn't there. But there were plenty of people and even more pigeons. I'd never harnessed the minds of a multitude of animals all at once. But one pigeon would be of little use.

At the bus stop, Hyun-woo consulted the timetable. "We have five minu—" That's all he got to say before doubling over and blowing out his cheeks like he'd just been punched in the gut.

"Assholes. Where are they?" I took his arm and helped ease him upright again.

We gathered a few curious stares from the people at the back of the queue. The last lady in line shuffled forward like she hoped to avoid whatever infection we seemed to be carrying.

"The protection still holds. But they are doubling their attack."

Hyun-woo had not lowered his voice, and his remark was met with heavy frowns and disapproving glares from those that had heard. I stared back until they looked away. "Will it last?"

"We'll leave them behind, once we're on the bus. Don't think this is the end of it, though. I would say, from the pain, there's a few involved."

"Ouch, you're in pain?"

"It's not the first time," he said in a dismissive tone.

"Hyun-woo, you shouldn't have done. I don't want you to suffer."

"I'm a shaman, Laz. This is what we do. Protect the innocent. You can't honestly expect me to turn my back on someone needing help."

Hyun-woo's gaze shifted over my head. I spun, expecting to see the high priest or something equally as bad, but it was just the bus, finally arriving. Once on, we took seats close to the front, and I stared out the window this time, thinking I may see someone suspicious looking in the crowd, staring our way as the bus passed by. "How far does your protection wall extent?"

"A couple of blocks." He settled back into the seat, and once again, closed his eyes. Perhaps he needed to do maintenance on the protection wall, such as convince the spirits to stick around and not pack up and head back to the death realm.

His silent meditation lasted for most of the journey. It was like watching someone in peaceful slumber, leaving all their worries and stresses in the wakeful world. This had to mean the attacks on his defenses had ceased. Maybe we'd gone far enough, left the Apostle scum back in Wolgod Quarter.

When Hyun-woo opened his eyes, he met my happy smile. It felt like he'd gone away, not just mentally, and was now returning. That was the problem with relying on others. It was easy to become dependent on them; it was likely worse to feel alone.

"We need to get off soon."

"Everything all right?"

"The spirits are calm, but there is a growing presence. I can feel it lurking just outside the perimeter of my defenses. They have not given up."

"Dammit. They're like dogs. How are they keeping on our tail so closely?"

"I fear that's because of the spirits. Their essence is easy to track, if you know the right way to search. The Apostles are no strangers to the ways of the shaman."

"So why don't we bid your spirits goodbye?"

"It's likely not the only way they are tracking us. And without the spirits we are vulnerable to warlock magic. At least this defense gives us a chance."

"What happens when we reach Fountain Row? They aren't just going to go away."

"That's why we must get off at the next stop. We're in Sparrow Swift. Lower Boddock is the next district over. We need to get a few things before we get there. If we keep to the crowds, it will make it harder for them to do anything."

We clambered off and sprinted down the street before the bus had pulled away from the curb. When Hyun-woo swung left into a large department store, I was confused.

"You think we need a disguise?"

"Something a little more lethal."

I wasn't sure I liked the sound of that, but with the Apostles on our tail, anything that gave us the advantage was a bonus.

Hyun-woo scanned the shop layout on the information plaque beside the escalator. I couldn't make out what he was saying as he skimmed through the board, muttering to himself. Having found it, he leaped onto the escalator, me stumbling on behind because I wasn't half as fit as him. People weren't sticking to the left, so we excused our way through to the top.

Once there, he veered left and quick-stepped into the kitchen department. A sales lady in a super tight pencil skirt bee-lined toward us from behind a display of crockery, but I waved her off before she got too close.

"I hope there's a logical explanation," I said to his back as I hurried along behind him.

Then he stopped, forcing me to crash into him.

"There is," he said as he spun, a meat knife in his hand.

"You're joking, right?"

"We have an enclave of Apostles on our tail, who will eventually bust through my spirit defenses, and we're about to enter a graveyard full of restless, dark spirits close to a liminal time. Do you think I'm joking?"

"I'm not sure I can do this, Hyun-woo. The only thing I've knifed is a dark warded. He bled animal blood and disappeared into cinders and ash. Apostles bled their own blood."

"Whose blood do you want split?" Hyun-woo said as he looked behind me to see where the sales lady was before slipping a smaller vegetable knife down his jeans leg.

"This won't fit." I held my dirty great big meat knife.

He took it from me and slipped it down the other jeans leg.

"I hope you put those two in safely away from any important bits."

"I'd have you check if we weren't in such a hurry." He took my hand and veered me around the knife display, away from the sales lady before I thought of a comeback, because my head was all muddled up with how sexy cute the remark was. Talk about bad timing. That was the perfect lead in to another sort of conversation, but not something you had while you were on the run with dangerous weapons down your pants.

We'd left the kitchen display when Hyun-woo collapsed forward, grunting through gritted teeth. His jeans tightened over his thighs, revealing the outline of the knives for anyone passing by. Too many people glanced our way, too many had to skirt around him, blocking their path.

"We need to get on the bus," he said around a pant.

I took an arm and slung it over my shoulder. Given he was taller than me, it had no effect. He pulled his arm away. Instead, he took my hand again, and we moved to the escalator.

"They're still at a distance, I hope."

"The protection holds, but they're getting stronger." He continued to hold his stomach for the escalator ride down to ground floor. "When we get to Lunaris Cemetery, you need to follow my instructions."

"You won't do anything stupid?"

"No more stupid than stealing kitchen knives from a department store."

"Do you have experience using a knife?"

"I've had my share of experiences."

This was a side to Hyun-woo I didn't know. Gone was the serene shaman, replaced now by a fighter who knew his way around this paranormal maze.

Before easing down into his seat on the bus, Hyun-woo withdrew the knives. The seats opposite ours were vacant, so less prying eyes. When Hyun-woo handed me the smaller knife, I nodded. I was less likely to stab myself with something this size.

As the bus wove its way through Sparrow Swift, and at some point crossed the district line into Lower Boddock, the sunlight shone in golden sheets through the bus window. Long shadows stretched across the front lawns and out onto the road. The air chilled, and I felt ready to move. At some point I'd developed a slight tremor in one leg, like I was tapping out a rapid rhythm to some silent tune. The knife lay hidden up my sweatshirt, ready to fall out once I stood.

"Okay, Laz. This is us."

I followed Hyun-woo off the bus. The next district north from Lower Boddock was Upper West Shard, which spread out into farm-land and forest, but already, the roomy rural feel had permeated into this part of Lower Boddock. The houses were spread apart, allowing for a decent garden or even some trees. A dog came barking out from a veranda, baring its teeth, and I felt a stupid sense of release at seeing it, despite its unfriendly welcome. Animals had always done that to me, unraveled knots I often didn't know I carried.

"Now we walk. It's not far."

"Didn't your mom say we shouldn't be in Lunaris Cemetery at a liminal time?"

"It's the perfect time, actually."

"Are you going to tell me your plan, or do I have to adapt as it unfolds?" Hyun-woo kept a good pace. I was panting around my words.

"I hope you won't have to do anything. At least not with the knives. They're backup, in case things go wrong."

"Glad to hear they aren't our first defense. But I'm not sure what a knife is going to do against the Apostles."

"When we reach Lunaris Cemetery, I will lower my spiritual protection and release them back into the dead realm. It's not a good idea to bring spirits into a resting ground already inhabited by many determined to break free. This will make us vulnerable. The protection Mom provided will hold up for a while, but it was never meant to protect against an army."

"We're going to end up in a knife fight, aren't we?"

"Not if I can help it, but you must stay close beside me."

With our quick pace the houses disappeared to be replaced by trees and a long stretch of lonely road. To the left of me, through the shrubby, I spied a mausoleum. White stone, long washed an ugly gray, rose over the tops of the shrubs. A little farther on and we stopped at an asphalt road, pockmarked with potholes and crumbling on the edges around patches of rotted, sodden leaves. The words Lunaris Cemetery faded into the moss-covered sign.

The weak sunlight found gaps in the canopy to skim the tops of the white tombstones with a golden shaft of evening sun. Under the dense parts of the canopy, the cemetery was already shaded a gloomy blue. A creepy itch pricked along my arms onto my shoulders. "Do we go in?"

"Laz, I plan to touch the dead. You should know that."

"I thought the dead in this place were a nasty lot."

"It is our only hope against the Apostles."

"Can you keep control of the spirits here?"

"I have to."

I tapped his arm. "I'm sorry for dragging you here. We shouldn't have come. I didn't expect the Apostles would be so organized or persistent. It makes no sense."

"They must believe you have something special."

"I don't, trust me."

"Nothing that you know of. Yet."

"It's been four years since my ascension. And nothing remarkable has manifested. I'm not holding my breath."

"It could be something you can retrieve for them, beyond the skull."

"They're more powerful than me. There's nothing I could do they couldn't do deadlier."

Hyun-woo grimaced, his shoulders tensing up around his ears, but he held himself upright. His eyelids slowly lowered, like he was sinking into a hypnotic trance. I knew by now to stay quiet and patient for him to return, which he did after three breaths.

"We need to be farther inside the cemetery."

"Did you just lower your defenses?"

"And the forsaken dead are calling to me. Soon, the long dead will arrive. They sense a spirit-walker is amongst them. The sun is almost set. The Apostles should arrive just in time."

For what?

Down the treelined avenue, the gloom swallowed us. The canopy was so dense it formed a blanket. Either side, great edifices to loved ones long gone crumbled and decayed, like they too were dying. Between them, smaller graves sat unadorned, broken or missing. Our path forked, the two trails disappearing into the ever-increasing gloom.

"Which way?"

"This way." I was glad for Hyun-woo's hand. It was nice to be reminded someone living walked beside me.

"Are you sure? It all looks equally foreboding."

The weeds and grass had grown to hide the smaller gravestones, and would soon choke out the rest.

"Yes."

"Have you been here before?"

"No."

"Then how do you know where to go?"

"The dead are calling to me." He took the knife from its hiding place under his belt. "Keep this handy."

"I have my own." I held up the vegetable knife.

"They're both for you."

"But what are you going to use?"

"Don't worry about me."

"When people say that, it's time to worry."

"Come on. I want to make it to the crypt. And the Apostles have just arrived."

I spun to look down the way we'd come. "How do you know?"

"The dead told me."

Just great.

CHAPTER 19

The building rose out of the penetrating gloom. Its marble white gleamed with no aid from the sun or moon-light. A thick knot of creeper grew around the foundations like a skirt and up one side of the wall. But the creeper was mostly twigs and withered leaves. Trees hugged close, their branches bare of foliage, the trunks tortured into ropey twists and ugly gnarls. Their roots broke through the soil like thick tentacles spreading across the ground.

"Is this where the cult of the Living Dead have set up camp?"

"In the crypt below. To the north is the Brothers of the Redentore. Their temple borders Lunaris Cemetery."

"Do you think they know about the cult?"

"I'm sure they do. I doubt they care much about what some of their brotherhood choose to do in their spare time, if it doesn't effect their worship."

I glanced in the direction we'd come. With the sun gone, there were plenty of dark pockets to hide within. Dotted through the overgrowth, below the weeping canopy, reared the heads of tombs like the dead rising.

"To be honest, I'm not sure what to do now. I thought it would give us something. Why would that guy be carrying the name Fountain Row if there wasn't some significance to the Vehan?"

Hyun-woo paced a few meters, his hands on his hips. "If that's the case, it'll have something to do with the Vehan-Cantonia conflict. Definitely not a conflict we want to get involved in."

"I hope I didn't drag you into the middle of it all." I stood there with my two knives grabbed in either hand like a serial killer. If we weren't standing in the middle of an abandoned graveyard in the night, I would feel ridiculous.

"If the Living Dead are involved, then us spirit-walkers need to be involved. Mom and I have kept an eye on their activities since they first started. Messing with the dead, the divide that keeps our realms a part, is messing with the natural order. We were unaware vampires had become involved. So don't worry, Laz, I would've become involved, with or without your help."

"Thanks. It doesn't make me feel so bad. But what do we do, go inside?"

"We have a better chance of defending ourselves against the Apostles from within the crypt."

I released the walls of my mind, filtering my awareness out into the surroundings and touched on a multitude of creatures I could bend to my purpose. Not the best attack against magic wielders, but a cadre of swooping bats would slow anyone down.

Someone moved in front of a tombstone to the left of the path. "There." I stupidly pointed my vegetable knife in the movement's direction.

"They're all around us. It's time we went inside."

"Why are they hiding?" A group of them backed by magic, and two of us, backed by two kitchen knives. What did they know we didn't?

"They're wary."

"I find that hard to believe."

"They understand the power of this place for a spirit-walker." In the deep blue of almost night I saw Hyun-woo had closed his eyes.

The sun had passed the horizon, sinking us into a liminal time. "The long dead surround us, the forsaken dead are close behind," Hyun-woo said as he slowly emerged from his trance, then looked to the sky. "If it was a deviant moon I could light this place up with the dead."

"I've never heard that one."

"Shaman speak for the full moon. One of the most powerful liminal times. It lasts but an instant but in that moment the veil is so thin to be nonexistent."

"I thought the full moon lasted for days."

"Sure. What you see from earth. But the zenith, the true deviant moon, is gone in an instant."

I wanted to ask if it was safe to deal with the long dead at any liminal time, but who was I to argue.

"We must enter the crypt. I need to learn what it is the Living Dead have been doing here that Mom and I missed. The long dead will be our sentinels."

My mission had now become Hyun-woo's, for different reasons. He waved me toward the crypt, taking backward steps himself, always keeping his eyes forward to our enemy. Not that we could see them.

"How many long dead are here?" I felt the tickling creep of the heebie-jeebies rap along my spine. I cared little for things I couldn't see or sense, having little experience with ghosts. The Apostles became the second issue lurking in the dark, as I glanced around me, expecting to see apparitions ghosting around the crypt.

"Their rage is consuming. It makes for the perfect weapon."

That did nothing good for the speed of my pulse.

"As long as they know who the enemy is."

Moss covered the bottom step to the crypt, turning it into a slide. I wobbled, dancing the knives through the air as I struggled to stay standing. Hyun-woo grabbed my arm for balance and we both backed up the three steps.

"We'll have to fight, you know?" His voice was low, but strong, resolved to our fate.

"I figured as much." My knuckles were already aching from my grip on the knives.

"Blood will be spilt, Laz. You must be ready for that."

"I'd rather it be someone else's."

This was not me. I had lived in this dark world four years, but never had I faced something like this. Since turning our backs on the coven, we'd made a good life for ourselves keeping clear of places like Davenport. "Any quick pointers about using knives?" I cringed at the lack of confidence in my voice.

"Cut and thrust."

"That's it?"

"Hopefully, that's all you'll need."

I jerked off the pillar I'd accidentally bumped into and the meat knife clattered to the stone floor. The noise rang out in the silence like the clash of a cymbal played out of sync. Hyun-woo was quick to scoop it up and return to me.

"It's too early to throw them."

The joke didn't work. My heart stayed in my throat.

He pulled me backward toward the double doors of the crypt, then doubled over with a guttural cry, clutching both hands across his stomach.

"Hyun-woo."

"Get inside," he rasped between his clenched teeth.

Two knives gripped in one hand, I tried the door. "It won't open."

Hyun-woo buckled to his knees and growled out a sound like an animal. He emptied his lungs of the pain, howling out whatever it cost him to maintain the surrounding shield. I rushed to his side, but he jerked my hand off his elbow, shaking his head, then tipped his head back and roared to the night, to the cowards who hid in the shadows to launch their attack.

I couldn't do much, but a face full of bats was better than being useless. I flung my awareness outward, only for Hyun-woo to smack me in the leg with a sweep of his arm. "Go."

He staggered to his feet, bent double, a hand hugging his stomach, and backed up to the door. Eyes squeezed tight, he brought a fisted hand up to his face. For a few dashing beats of my heart, I waited, hovering on the verge of yelling at him to hurry alone, when he gasped and punched down on the brass serpent that served as a door handle. The door creaked wide into a black vault.

I hurried inside, half dragging Hyun-woo in behind me. "Lucky you had the right touch," I said as I slammed the inches thick door behind us and sunk us into darkness.

"No one can keep a spirit-walker from places of the dead."

I dared not move from where we stood in case I fell down some stairs or tripped over a sarcophagus.

Hyun-woo breathed deeply in the dark, slow, even breaths, like he was meditating again. From around his middle a small glowing ember fired, the seed of golden light that grew in intensity, casting our shadows off the marble wall like draping curtains.

"I thought you didn't do magic." I stared at the light emanating from the middle of his palm.

"We are within the boundaries of liminal time, allowing me to harness the power of the long dead. I am touching energy normally outside of my grasp. It's why I lowered the shield."

"Nothing of this sounds safe."

"Go down below." He nodded to the stairs, then turned his back on me.

"This is crazy."

"Now is not the time to be bullheaded. Please, just do as I ask."

I handed him the meat knife. "You need this."

"No, I don't."

Instead of taking the knife, he released the glow from the center of his palm and it floated up to the ceiling, bathing the mosaic roof of the small entrance in a glorious bowl of light, which then dripped down the walls like melting wax.

I turned back to Hyun-woo to see another light sparking within the cradle of his palms. It warped and rippled, taking form, expanding and shimmering into a glowing shaft that bowed and stretched out of his hold and into the shape of a blade.

"What is that?"

"A Turko-Mongol saber. I'm borrowing it." The glowing golden blade illuminated his smile.

"Who from?"

"Genghis Khan."

"You're borrowing weapons from a long dead warrior. Is that safe?"

"We're slipping from liminal time. Once it goes, I won't be able to imbue the long dead's energy. Unless you want to fight magic with kitchen utensils, I suggest you get down those stairs."

That's when the world erupted. The doors of the crypt blew off their hinges, and a gust of magical energy blasted through me. I teetered on the edge of the first step, lost my balance, and fell backward, throwing the kitchen knives, and tumbled down the stairs. Before I disappeared, I caught a fleeting view of Hyun-woo, unaffected by the blast, holding his ground, the saber poised to strike.

It was a painful ride down all fifty steps, or so it seemed, and I landed in a heap at the bottom, not sure I could move any of my body. Adrenaline came to the rescue. I turned over onto my back, raised up to sitting. The light Hyun-woo had drawn from the long dead still bobbed about on the ceiling upstairs, so I wasn't totally in the dark. Stuck in the stone walls surrounding me, skulls stared back with empty sockets, which I swore could see me. A large stone sarcophagus rested on a stone plinth in the centre of the crypt. The place smelt old and damp with the lingering whiff of incense or some herbal mixture. Whatever the Living Dead were doing, they wanted the blend of magic to make it happen, but the Brothers of the Redentore possessed no real magic. Instead they had to suck the small morsels of energy a human soul could deliver right out of a munsib's body, preferably when they were alive or within seconds of their death.

With the noise of fighting above, I forgot about my creepy

surroundings. Howls of pain, desperate shouts, and then, a rush of intense light that waved down into the crypt, scorching my face and singeing my eyes. I fell onto my back, flipped to my side and crawled away on my hands and knees toward the sarcophagus. Where were those damn knives?

There was another cry of pain, then the grunts and scuffs of someone tumbling down the stairs. I had yet to reach the sarcophagus but stopped and glanced over my shoulder as an Apostle bounced onto the stone floor. About a meter to the side of him, I spied the meat knife.

He moaned but didn't move. The Apostles knew Hyun-woo wasn't alone. The point of them being here was me.

I exhaled hard, then made a dash for the knife, as the guy rolled to his side, still groaning from his fall.

Our eyes met as I bent to retrieve the knife.

"You little bitch," he spat. Not injured at all. He moved quicker than I expected, diving forward and snatching a hold of my right leg as I swiped the knife off the floor.

Pulled off my feet, I fell hard, losing my breath. Despite the noise from upstairs, the clatter of the knife beside me echoed in full blast stereo off the skull decorated walls.

The Apostle dived for the knife while I gasped for the air now punched from my lungs. Seeing him with the meat knife clutched in his hand, I rolled to the side, thinking only of scrambling away, but he yanked my ponytail, snapping my head backward until I collapsed to the ground.

He wasted no time clambering on top of me. "This is what happens when you put up a fight," he said, leering over me, breathing his garlicky breath into my face. The long dead's light, shining over his shoulder, softened the ugliness of his face, dimmed the repulsiveness of his lecherous smile.

I had seconds before he pinned me with his body. I reared my knee with as much force as my adrenaline laced body could muster, straight into his groin. He stiffened with a grunt, back arched, his expression a painting of agony.

Even in agony, he fought me as I tried to push him away. He'd become a dead weight. "Witch," was all he managed to say as one hand clutched his nuts.

I shimmied and pushed my way out, while he collapsed forward, half on me. The hand with the knife fell sideways. He growled and manacled his fingers as I tried to wrench it out of his hand. A groan from him was my reward for punching down on his arm. At last, his grip loosened. I pulled the knife free and wrestled the rest of my body out from under him and stumbled to my feet, only to find them swiped from under me. By magic, this time.

Facing me, his cheek pressed into the stone, the glow from the light upstairs revealed all the crevices, creases, and lines of his triumphant sneer. "You're no match for me."

My fingers still gripped the hilt of the knife. Not bothering to argue, I lunged, plunging the knife into his chest, closer to his collar bone than his heart. The lack of resistance as it cleaved through his flesh flushed bile up my throat. I had to gag back another wave on drawing the blade out and seeing the blood gush onto the stones, a deep, rich, brown-red because of the long dead's light.

"You fucking bitch," he howled as he spasmed forward into the fetal position.

I crawled backward on my ass. The clang of the knife, gripped in my fist, followed me along the floor. I had to get out of here. Any minute, he would find the strength to launch another magical attack, if he didn't bleed out first.

My feet wouldn't obey. This wasn't like knifing a dark warded. Goblins were nothing more than the husks of animals puppeteered by the risen dark fae. Apostles were different.

Get it together. I clenched my teeth.

Before I made it up, Hyun-woo came racing down the stairs, minus the saber in his hands. The light above was also fading. "Are you all right?" He glanced at the Apostle, who was making feeble gurgle noises.

I nodded. "He's not. He might not make it. You lost your saber."

"Liminal time has passed. I can't draw on their power as my own anymore. The light will disappear as well."

"What happened to the rest?"

He inhaled. "Let's just get out of here."

Right. Don't ask questions. And don't think about what you've just done.

He grabbed my hand as I moved to pass, his fingers digging in too tight. He yanked me into him, snapping his hand up to grasp my chin, anchoring it in place. In the fading light, I saw the curl of his lip, the snarl ready to escape.

"Hyun-woo, what—"

He released me and stepped back, fists clenched and growling. "Sorry." He cradled his head. "Give me a moment."

"What's going on?" I took a tentative step toward him.

He held out his hand. "A moment...I need a moment."

He spun and punched the wall with a yell, then recoiled. "Argh." He shook his hand out before cradling it with his other hand. "Dammit. That hurt."

"And that was for?"

"It was the quickest way to shake him. It takes time to rid them, especially when they're as strong willed as him."

"Him?"

"Genghis Khan. I didn't just take his saber. I had to embody him. I do not know how to fight with one of those."

"You shouldn't have done that."

"It was our only hope. Don't tell Mom, or I won't hear the end of it. To tell you the truth, I was a little worried I wouldn't have the strength to control him. The guy was a god at fighting. Couldn't have done it without him. But you're right. It was dangerous. I'm not as strong as Mom. But he's gone." He swiped his good hand down over his face. "Yep, his gone."

The light disappeared, throwing us into the black of the crypt. I reached out in the darkness for him, found his arm and gently squeezed it. "Thanks."

"I was going to tell you most of the Apostles got away."

"I shouldn't care whether they lived, but—"

"It's what makes you one of the good guys."

"I'm sorry you missed your opportunity to see what's down here."

"Communing with the long dead here has given me a good idea of what's going on." With the weight in his voice, I could imagine it wasn't good.

Using the wall as a guide, I climbed the stairs. The half-moon had risen, shining a soft blue box of light through the doorway. One door hung from its hinges, the other was not to be seen, which would raise some questions.

Lunaris looked different in the moonlight, the neglect no longer visible. The cracked asphalt, caked with sodden leaves and soil, was now a smooth, black path disappearing under the black blanket of the canopy. Weeds and overgrown grass became a gray carpet. The night even hid the scars of the desecrated tombstones.

"We'll have to walk back to the bus stop," Hyun-woo said.

"Perhaps you can tell me how it went with the Apostles on the way."

He flung his hand out, barring me from going any further forward.

"Someone else is here."

"More Apostles?"

"No."

I turned to Hyun-woo when he said no more, to find his head bowed. I couldn't see his face, but knew he would be gathering his spirit shield. Next minute, he flew backward into the gaping entrance of the crypt, disappearing in the darkness.

"Hyun-woo." I retreated to the doorway, but heard the crunch of footsteps on the asphalt and spun. A man stood at the bottom of steps leading up to the crypt. The moonlight haloed the back of his head, casting his face in shadow. But I didn't need to see his face to know who he was.

"I warned you to stay out of my way." His voice failed to give me sexy tingles despite still exuding that bedroom ready timbre.

"Maybe you should stay out of mine." Asshole. What had he done to Hyun-woo?

"What business would Miss Preston have in a cemetery, with a man that is not her fiancé, alone, at night?"

"I'll tell you my secret if you tell me yours."

I couldn't see his face, nor could I read the quiet. The scrap of footsteps from inside the crypt told me Hyun-woo was all right, alive at least.

Seeming to read my mind, Jarro said, "Your lover is a little bruised, but unharmed. For now."

I inched toward the opening of the crypt, not daring to turn my back on Jarro. "We're not interested in what you want here. We'll just go."

"Maybe I have questions of my own."

"Jarro, please."

"What are you begging for, Elka?" He emphasized my sister's name, which hackled the hairs on my neck. It was a taunt. Did Jarro know about us?

Inside, Hyun-woo climbed the stairs. His steps sounded slow, agonized. He must've taken a hard tumble. When I no longer heard him coming, I turned to peer inside only to see some misty, vaporlike apparition wafting out of the interior darkness. It flowed forth like it was being sucked out into the night, too fast for me to duck out of the way. Instead, it flowed straight through me, drilling icicle tendrils down into my soul. I felt swept off my feet, dragged down a shaft that turned into a kaleidoscope of muted colors, my mind twisting and spinning loose from reality. A mishmash of shapes swam around my head. My throat felt stuffed full of cotton wool, and I choked on my breath. Then the voice, funneling down a tunnel. "Help me."

I swiveled on my ass, feeling blindly with my arms for the stone beneath me, the edge of the step I knew wasn't far away.

"Please, help me."

The voice. It niggled at the back of my mind, brought a distance memory out of hiding. Déjà vu anchored me into place. He'd called to me before. A long time ago. Before I was a witch. During my dakeu. Begging, begging for my help, to take something, to release him. I was the only one, he'd said.

It was Hyun-woo's cry that pulled the walls down of my altered reality and brought me back to Lunaris. I was on the edge of the step, about to tumble and land at Jarro's feet.

Hyun-woo. I swiveled on my ass. Hyun-woo was bent double, breathing heavy, his hands covering his chest, making pitiful wounded sounds. I turned to Jarro—both his arms were raised. In the darkness, he was a menacing black shape, no distinction to his features. But one thing was clear in his body language. He was gathering energy, calling up whatever wicked ability he possessed. I couldn't feel magic, but I didn't need to. The air was wild with fury, electrified with his intent.

I jumped to my feet, blocking his direct line to Hyun-woo.

"No," I shouted. "Don't." My voice softened to a plea as I held my arms out.

Time unwound, suspending us in a vacuum of silence, except for the staccato of my heart, punching a furious rhythm against my rib cage, the small wheezing grunts of Hyun-woo behind me as he fought through the pain of whatever Jarro had already dealt. We stood in the eye of a storm, a false calm that would last only moments before the chaos descended once more. It didn't matter that I faced certain death, that the might of what Jarro was about to release would likely disintegrate me to dust. It didn't matter.

Jarro lowered his hands, his body visibly relaxing. The taut strum of the atmosphere surrounding us unraveled. For the first time in minutes, I inhaled a lungful of air rather than sucking it through a paper straw.

"This is a surprise," Jarro said.

I slowly eased my stance, relaxed my arms. "Just let us go, Jarro."

"I have no interest in him. I'll let him go. You, on the other hand…"

Blessed mother, what did he mean? On my next breath, I found my lungs wouldn't work. Instead, I made silly whooping sounds as I tried to suck in air. Flecks of black appeared in front of my eyes, blotting out the already dark night. I staggered about, as my head felt like it was floating and a shadow filled the corners of my vision, rolling across like a wave. I hit the edge of the step, lost my balance, felt myself falling through space, thought vaguely about the pain that was about to come.

The pain never came. Firm arms caught me instead.

I should fight, but the blackness became absolute.

CHAPTER 20

The bed was soft. I was warm, cozily so. I rolled, pulling the heavy cover up to my neck, smelling vanilla and jasmine. Bliss. Not the astringent odor from that disgusting laundry powder dispensed at the laundromat around the corner from our apartment.

Why was I smelling vanilla and jasmine? I rolled onto my back again. A line of light ran along the floor as my only light. It gave me enough to see the faint outline of the expansive room, shapes of furniture, the rug beside the bed.

What the hell? I rolled up, losing the covers, and swung out of bed. I was halfway across the dark room, heading for the door, when my memory returned. "Hyun-woo," I whispered.

We were at Lunaris, kicked some Apostle ass, then faced Jarro on the steps outside. What had he done to me? I rubbed my chest, remembering how he'd stolen my breath. And not in a nice way. So where was I now? And where was Hyun-woo?

The door wasn't locked. Thank the dark mother. I inched my head around the doorjamb and found a long stretch of corridor, a gigantic, long stretch of wide corridor, like palace sized big. A hotel? A past century hotel with the stuffy trappings of yesteryear. Wall lights in archaic sconces—the brackets looking tortured into being and strangled by hardened wax—shone a warm, dull candlelight onto a thick woven rug, probably made from horsehair and hand stretched on a loom by a grizzled old woman.

One glance down eased the sudden thought I was in the nude or in some spinster baggy, high neck nightie. Given I woke to find myself in Wuthering Heights, anything was possible.

Where was Heathcliff, the dark, brooding ass who knocked me out and brought me here. Things could be worse. Jarro could've killed me as easily as he was about to kill Hyun-woo. For some reason, he hadn't. But why kidnap me?

I eased out of my room, my socks muffling any noise I made. Nice someone had taken off my shoes before tucking me in bed. Jarro? The thought was too weird. And made little sense.

There were enough doors on either side of the corridor to house a large party of guests. At one end, the half-moon glared through an arched window, its face cut up into small panes of glass. The question being: was it still the same night?

I headed in the other direction, keeping to the wall, not that there was anywhere I could duck and hide if someone came around the corner. At the end, I found another wide corridor, much the same, so making my way back to my room would be a case of eeny meeny miney mo.

I skimmed along the wall of the next corridor, then slowed with an awed gasp when it opened out into a massive staircase, cascading down to the floor below like Niagara. There were ribbed ceilings, suspended candelabras, stone everything, decorative stuff and fancy junk plucked straight out of some black-and-white movie reenactment of medieval royalty. All shrouded in dull, yellow, flickering light from the millions upon millions of candles and their stalactite wax. Definitely a creepy vampire den. Where were the vampires?

I slinked down the staircase, stopping periodically to listen for any movement in the house and whenever a board creaked under my feet.

The entrance was in front of me, the only obstacle an enormous expanse of stone floor with nothing to hide behind. Why bother to bring me here only to let me walk right out the front door the moment I woke up?

The cold of the stone penetrated through my socks the moment my feet hit the floor. The cold acted like a starting gun, propelling me across the great expanse until I collided with the door, fumbling with the large brass door handle. It wouldn't budge. Of course it wouldn't. It had been too easy.

There was only me and my thumping heart in the cold hall. And one partially opened door on the far side. A flickering light danced at the entrance. And now, I noticed the hint of smoke.

Go back to my room, explore each room hoping to find an open window or go see what or who was waiting inside? Not much of a choice.

I headed for the partially open door, probably heading into the jaws of hell, but by now I wanted to talk to someone, yell at someone, preferably. Just my luck, the room was empty. A fire crackled happily in a large hearth, framed by chunks of rough-hewn stone. The leather chairs were huddled around it, leaving a vacancy to the rest of the room, punctuated only by the bookcase walls and huge, detailed tapestries, which I couldn't make out because of the lack of decent lighting. Heavy curtains cut out the moonlight so the only glow came from the fire someone had bothered to build.

I should go, find other places to ransack for an escape, but the fire drew me like a moth, being the only sign of life inside the house.

First, I headed for the window, sifted through the heavy pleats and folds for the opening, then gave up and grabbed it from the edge. The window was at least four meters wide and twice again tall, which meant the thick curtain weighed a ton. Once I fought behind it, I discovered a locked bay window, looking over a vast stretch of lawn that faded into the night with a hint of trees beyond. No escape that way unless I broke the glass, which I had yet to cross off my plans.

I came out from behind the curtain and took a moment to think of the next thing I should do. There was a drink cabinet on the left side of the fireplace, backed against the wall. A shot of whiskey would be welcome. A bottle of whiskey would do better, but I needed my wits.

It was hard to read the labels this far from the firelight so I poured a glass of whatever was in my hands. A crack from the fire made me jump. Glass to my lips, a breath at my neck turned me to stone.

"It's rude to help yourself without asking."

I inched my head around to meet the dark eyes of a woman, the smooth pale skin of youth. Her raven black hair was left to tumble in wild waves over her shoulder. A floral-oriental scent caressed the skin just under my nose, had me tumbling backward into a bed of cushions surrounded by a drape of silken fabric embroidered with delicate swirls.

"I didn't realize anyone was here."

I stepped back to breathe in some air not tainted by her heady perfume and couldn't help noticing her black outfit, which appeared to be painted on.

She followed my step backward, keeping the distance between us intimate.

"Maybe I will make an allowance since you're the guest."

"I'm a guest?" As opposed to a prisoner. Good to know. Although I was sure her definition and my definition of guest would diverge.

"Do you like your room?"

I continued back, and she continued forward in a creepy, prowling way. Given she was a vampress—she could be nothing less in this place—her advance was definitely a prowl, as in a hunter's prowl.

"I haven't had a chance to look at it yet."

"I chose it for you. And I tucked you in."

Thank the dark mother, she left my clothes on. She was still advancing, and I was backpedaling.

"You looked so helpless in Jarro's arms. A poor innocent waif, as innocent as a lamb."

For the slaughter?

She glanced down at my socks, her lips sweeping into a seductive smile. "Jarro said you were anything but innocent. That I was not to be fooled by your apparent helplessness. He says you aren't to be trusted." She winked. "I think otherwise. Perhaps we'll become real good friends." She inhaled, allowing her eyelids to slowly close. "Smelling like that, you are going to be irresistible."

"Is there anyone else in the house at the moment?" Anyone who could be the intermediary between her hunger and my life.

She huffed a girlie sound. "Would it scare you to think it was just you and me?"

"Not if I'm a guest."

"Oh, we treat our guests real well."

I was still backpedaling, until I hit the seat behind, lost my balance when one socked foot slid forward, and fell back onto the leather couch, spilling my drink over the side onto the rugged floor.

Undeterred, the vixen vampress slid over the top of the couch. I continued to crawl backward as she snaked toward me, her black catsuit blending with the deep rust-colored leather. Soon, I hit the armrest on the other side, and she slithered up over me, pressing me into the leather. "You look positively scrumptious," she purred, then nuzzled her face into the nape of my neck before running her nose up my throat. "You smell totally divine."

That did terrible things to my pulse, flaring it wildly into a manic rhythm.

Like most vampires she was taller than me by a good few inches, and she turned to all legs when she snuggled up next to me, draping one leg over my waist and using a hand on my chest to pin me in place, her fingers splaying either side of my left breast. "Hmm," she breathed, laying her head down next to mine. "Couldn't you just stay like this forever?"

"I'll get a crick in my neck."

"And I'd massage it better." She trailed a finger up the center of my chest, inched the neck of my shirt down and ran her finger on the ridge of my collar bone from left to right. "You're not nervous, are you?"

"Only minorly."

Next, her finger wandered down between my breasts before she settled her hand over my heart. "Then why is your heart beating fast? It makes your blood swim through your veins." She brought her lips close to my ear and whispers. "Do you have any idea how good that sounds?"

"I'm getting a clear picture."

"Would you be offended if I had a taste?"

I tried to jerk off the couch, but the press of her hand on my heart increased. Her strength was such it felt like a ton of bricks, compressing my lungs along my spine. She moved, sliding herself down on top of me. "Don't be such a spoilsport." She simpered, then licked her lips.

"That's enough, Valree."

I would've jumped at the sudden sound of the male voice if I didn't have the weight of Valree holding me down.

"But that's not fair. I thought she was my present."

We both looked to the high-backed leather chair directly in front of the fire. Jarro gazed into the fire like he didn't know, or didn't care, we were there, a glass of some amber drink hovering at his lips.

"What were my instructions?"

She slid off of me, sashayed her way over to him and slinked onto his lap like a cat finding the perfect spot in the sun. He moved his drink away, enabling her to get comfortable before bringing the drink to his lips again. Valree snatched it from him and drained it in one go. In a snap of violence, he fisted her hair at the back of her head and dragged her lips down to his.

I wanted to look away, tried to look away, and failed totally. Instead, I became hypnotized. One kiss sound melded into another, along with her moans as she undulated her hips along his lap. My body vibrated to the tune, quivering down into my nether regions and flared a burn.

Jarro gave her the sort of kiss a man gave a woman when he wanted her to feel as dirty as sin, and Valree ate him up. With every moan and smoochy smoochy sound, I became a part of the fun, became the woman forced to take his kiss, the woman suffering his one hand possessively clasped at the back of her head to keep her in place, the other at her lower back, guiding her gyrations home. I crossed my legs. Oh dark mother, I was inexplicably, shockingly, embarrassingly aroused.

Jarro suddenly broke the kiss and turned to me, catching me unawares. I'd not been prepared for his eyes, not had a chance to clamp down on my emotions. Flushed high on arousal, I felt raw and open, naked to his gaze.

I snapped my head away and stared into the fire, glared at it until the flames turned to a blur, all the while, painfully aware of Valree making exaggerated wet smacking sounds as she feathered Jarro in kisses over his neck. At least, that's what it looked like in my periphery. I had to fight myself not to look again.

At one point I thought about leaving the amorous couple to it, but I doubted either of them would let me get too far. Then finally Jarro ended it. "Leave us now."

"Why don't I get to stay?"

"You're making our guest uncomfortable."

"I know how to soothe that."

"Valree," came his soft rumbled warning.

I sneaked a look in their direction to catch Valree folding her arms in a fake sulk. When she caught my eye, she blew me a kiss.

With snake-like ease, she smoothed off Jarro's lap, running her finger along his jaw as she passed by the side of his chair.

She stopped, glancing over her shoulder. "I'll see you soon." Then she disappeared out the door with only the crackle of the fire as noise to her departure. Vamps were mesmerizing, graceful creatures when they wanted to be.

I felt a little safer with only Jarro in the room, given he could've killed me many times over, but hadn't. Hopefully that reticence to finish me would carry through to my imprisonment. And I had the protection of the fabric around my wrist. I ran my hand over my sleeve to feel the welcoming knot of fabric only to find nothing there. They'd cut it off.

"Dad will wonder—"

"Cut the shit," he snapped, sending a prickle of unease down my veins.

"How long have you known?"

"Since the moment I smelt you at the auction."

And I'd played the stupid charade for all that time. Embarrassing. "Why did you play along?"

"You intrigue me." He rose and crossed to the drinks cabinet. He moved like a predator at leisure in his den. Dressed entirely in black, black hair, black eyes, olive skin, he was a man born of the night.

My eyes followed him against my will, watched as he filled two glass, then jerked my attention away when he returned. Staring into the fire, a glass appeared beside my face.

"If you'd like. Otherwise I'll finish both."

This close, he infected me with his rich, warm, sultry cologne, smelling good enough to peel the clothes from a woman's body.

I took the drink, sniffed the contents to burn my nostrils of his smell, and took a gulp. Not feeling settled enough, I drained the rest, then arched my head, stretching my neck as the heat of the whiskey burned down my throat and across my chest.

The second glass appeared in front of me.

"You look like you need it more than me."

I didn't take the offered drink. "What did you do to Hyun-woo?"

"You're not here to ask questions."

Jarro lowered into the seat beside me. Alarm bells clanged in my head as he eased back and slid his arm across the back of the couch, reaching dangerously close to me. I turned to petrified wood, flicking glimpses at his hand inches from me, then his profile. The firelight flicked and danced across his face, revealing soft curves and hard edges, creating interesting shadows. If I was a sculptor, I would spend a good deal of time fashioning his lips. Dammit, what was it with this vamp that I found alluring, despite him being an arrogant asshole and lethal?

"What's your relationship with Elka?"

"Please, just tell me about Hyun-woo. Is he all right?"

"What's he to you?"

"He's a friend."

"A friend." It was like he was testing the word for plausibility, swilling it around in his mouth like you would a new wine.

"He's helped me with a few problems I've faced."

"Problems?" He brought the glass up to his lips but stalled before taking a drink.

"This city's full of unfriendlies, in case you hadn't noticed. I've run into a few issues."

"I've noticed." He slowly shifted his eyes to me. "Your issues, that is. When you stick you nose where it's not meant to be, bad things happen."

"Thanks for the..." I touched my neck. "Well, let's just say it would've been inconvenient for me."

"I didn't do it for you." He settled back, rolled his neck from left to right, captivating me with the movement. I thought of a cat preparing itself to stretch out in front of the fire. "I won't tolerate trouble in my affairs. Especially trouble that pretends to be someone else and hides in dumpsters to spy on business she has no part in. Witches aren't welcome this far north of the nexus."

"Right now I couldn't get much further north of the nexus and still be in Davenport."

Jarro feathered his thumb across his bottom lip as his dark eyes explored my face. "I can't decide what it is about you that's so irritating."

"Well, don't worry, I know exactly what it is about you that's so arrogant."

He was across the couch before I took one breath, fisting my hair, pulling my head back against the couch, leaning over me so that I felt his body hard against one side of mine, sparking a tingle of adrenaline. Nothing about this hurt, not even the firm grip on my hair. That was the disturbing thing. If he'd made it hurt, I would rage with hatred. He wanted to scare me, pose a silent threat, but he did it with control, exerting just enough pressure to assert his warning, holding off from pain.

I hung poised in a lingering moment of tensity, dangling on the edge of a cliff, alert, every inch of my skin prickling alive and waiting. A wildness convulsed inside of me, spasming up through my chest so my insides quivered with anticipation. The jumble of emotions became a thorn bush of spikes, gouging me full of fear. And worse. So much worse...yearning.

"You're alive at my pleasure."

"Thanks," I squeaked.

"I could as easily decide you're too much of a problem."

"I've never been a problem in my life. I think Davenport is the real problem."

He inhaled deep, running his nose down my cheek, then relaxed his hold and settled himself back, still invading my personal space. "Valree likes you. She usually eats our guests before they can speak."

"I'm glad I've made a friend."

"Friend is too strong a word. I'll ensure she's restricted to a nibble or two if you become more obedient."

"Will you give me some answers, at least?"

"If it pleases me." He rose with perfect fluidity and grace. "For your own safety, I suggest you return to your room. By my will, that is your sanctum for now. Annoy me, and I'll withdraw my protection."

He held out his hand. I hesitated, unsure if he was being gentlemanly or if he would use it as a lure to another threat he planned. In the end, there was nothing else for me to do but take it. I tried my hardest to ignore how warm and firm it felt.

"I just want to know—"

He pressed a finger over my lips, and that shot another confusing, irritating zing through my insides.

"Don't test me."

I closed my eyes, steadying myself, then inched my head back, freeing my mouth from his enforced silence. "Hyun-woo? I need to know."

"Untouched."

"Thank you."

I left as quickly as I could manage without appearing to dart away like a disciplined child. I'd likely pressed his patience enough times tonight.

"Goodnight, Larnie."

I froze at the door, keeping my back to him. Was there no end to his reach? Then I scurried out.

CHAPTER 21

I t must have been the whiskey, because I actually slept. When I returned to my room, which hadn't been so hard to find, I thought I would lay on the covers and stare at the ceiling until the sun came up. The sun was up and I was under the covers and waking, feeling like I had slept for years. I blinked at the ceiling, and rolled to my side, facing the window.

"You snore."

I shrieked.

"It's a rather pleasant sound. Soft and melodious. It almost lulled me to sleep."

I tried to creep the covers up to my neck, but Valree lay on them. "How long have you been there?"

"Long enough to become drunk on your smell." She wriggled her shoulders and shimmied closer to me. "I'd love to get drunk on a lot more of you." She creeped her fingers over the covers toward me. "If you'd like. Just say the word, sugar. Jarro can't get angry if you invited me."

"I'd rather keep all my blood."

"Oh, it doesn't have to be blood."

She moved, looking like she was about to pin me down to the bed with her body like she did last night on the couch, so I scooted backward...and fell out of bed.

"Is that how it works? I get to decide to share myself or not."

She looked over the edge of the bed, giving me a seductive eyeballing as she smoothed her hand along the white sheet like she imagined it was my body.

"For as long as it takes Jarro to decide how useful you may be."

"And if I'm not useful?"

"Then he will withdraw his command you aren't to be touched, and you and me can have some fun." She poured herself off the bed and onto the floor. "I know how to make you feel good."

"I feel plenty good as it is, so I'll pass."

She ran a finger through the air, inches above my arm, trailing down to my fingers. "You have no idea what you're missing. Bloodletting during sex is amazing. Your orgasm will blow you apart. It will take hours to piece yourself back together."

She yearned to touch me, but kept her finger hovering above my arm, a symbolic gesture to my refusal. This was a very interesting discovery, one that made me feel a smidgeon safer. Unfortunately, the no-touching rule did not extend to Jarro, their king, who could do whatever the hell he pleased.

"Thanks for the heads up. I think I'm all done with orgasms at the moment." My stomach rumbled on cue, reminding me I'd not eaten since Chin-Sun fed me bowl after bowl of mandoo until I thought I would pop.

"You're hungry." Valree was on her feet with fluid grace. "Let me escort you to the kitchen."

That was one of my weird discoveries while searching the archives of our coven's library back when I was an initiate, before Auntie Bea and I turned our backs on the coven. Folklore convinced me vampires only drank blood, so it surprised me to see they ate food like the rest of humanity and paranormals, though they were big on red meat and consumed it raw. So when Jarro said Valree ate their guests, I had every reason to believe he meant it literally.

I still wore the clothes I'd arrived in. Not about to ask Valree if I could take a shower first, in case she insisted on sticking around to watch, I climbed to my feet and followed her out the door and down the corridor.

Today she wore a black mini top and a black skirt that stopped just below her knickers, showing off her ultra long legs. Super heels meant she towered over me.

"How many vampires live here?"

"If I tell you all our secrets, we would have to keep you here forever."

So glad she didn't say kill me. "I don't need exact numbers."

She laughed, tossing her mane back off her shoulders. "You are adorable. I can see why Jarro took you."

"Why did he take me?"

"He thinks you're a pest. Like a cockroach. Always turning up when you're not wanted."

"He said that?"

"Don't worry, sweetie. He rarely likes anyone."

"Could you tell me in a round-about way that won't seal my fate what his interests are with Bernard Preston?"

"Jarro mentioned you were an identical match to the Preston woman."

"Elka?"

"He had no trouble with her. But you. You've caused him trouble since the moment you arrived in this city."

"Were...him and Elka a thing?"

"Fucking, you mean. You can say the word, Sweetie. We're all grownups here. And no. Jarro doesn't mess with anyone outside the hive. He doesn't need to. There are enough women in the hive eager to satisfy his needs."

"Women only?"

She gave me a sly sideways glance. "Some of us have open tastes, like me. Some enjoy humans, like me, or other paranormals, like me. Jarro's straight up heterosexual, vamps only. That way he remains in control. Always. And he has a savage appetite. One to rival the zibuian."

That meant nothing to me. It really didn't. I didn't care, and neither would I ever imagine what Jarro looked like during one of his savage sexual frenzies. Besides, he didn't do women outside his hive. A good thing, too, because I would not be interested in his advances at all. He'd been teasing me all this time, pretending Elka and him were a thing when he knew all along I was not her.

"So what do he and Bernard have in common?"

We descended the stairs.

"You are trouble."

"I have a lot of questions."

"It's hive business."

"Is it something to do with the Cantonia? What about the Living Dead?"

"For an outsider, you know too many secrets about this city. That's a dangerous position to be in, when you're as helpless as a munsib."

"Who said I was helpless?"

"Where are your coven? Why haven't they come to rescue you? You haven't even tried to bust out of here. Any self-respecting paranormal would've done that by now."

So, I was a cockroach, pathetic as a munsib, but still good enough to eat.

"We parted ways with our coven." I couldn't see any harm in voicing what she had likely already guessed.

"We?"

"My Auntie and I."

"Isn't that adorable. The hive is family. Mess with one, and you mess with us all. I like that your aunt stuck by you."

She thought it was because of me we were out of the coven.

"The Apostles kidnapped her." Would I be able to win Valree's support in helping me deal with the Apostles? She seemed to like me. I mean, she hadn't eaten me yet.

"They usually like their women underaged."

"I don't know what their plans are, but I want to rescue her. She means a lot to me, being family and all. My only family."

"Oh, sweetie, that's tough, losing all your family. But you have your sister."

She wasn't bending as easily as I'd hoped. By now, we'd headed across the expansive entrance hall for a wide corridor behind the staircase. There were no lights back here, nor windows, only gray stone, dark wood doors and paneling. It surprised me there was any light in the place at all, given vamps had eyes like cats. Perhaps the candles were for my benefit.

Halfway down the corridor, Valree veered into a kitchen. Yet another enormous room, which would make any master chef fall dead with envy. This was the first time so far I'd seen a room brought out of medieval times with modern conveniences such as stainless steel bench tops, a sink with running water, electric oven and even a dishwasher.

"Welcome to our bloody banquet hall. Sit. I will see what's in the fridge. Do you drink coffee?"

"Interesting name for a kitchen." I headed for the long table in the center of the room, stretching a good ten meters. I didn't bother counting the chairs.

"I can't remember who named the kitchen. We named most of the rooms in the house. The ones we use. It's what happens when you live a long time."

"Why are you being so considerate?"

Buried in the oversized fridge, she surfaced to reply. "Perhaps I'm always like this."

"How often do you have guests?"

"More often than you'd think. In fact, tonight is a special occasion. We're having a party."

"For the hive?"

"It's for a lot of distinguished people."

"Munsib?" Only the ultra-wealthy and influential, as they would be the only ones capable of giving the vamps anything of worth. And only those who were made privy to the paranormal world.

"As if we'd allow other filth to cross into our domain."

"What's it for?"

"It helps to remind the munsib who are really in control of Davenport."

"I hope Bernard Preston is not on the list. You might have some explaining to do if he is."

"He's out of town at the moment, lucky for you."

"Shouldn't that be lucky for you?"

"It means you can come to the party. I've got just the outfit. It might be a little tight, since your tits and ass are bigger than mine, but that's only going to make your evening more enjoyable."

"Aren't you afraid I'll say something to one of the guest?"

"Honey, you can say all you want to the guests. They won't help you. That would mean going against Jarro."

I attempted to pull out one of the chairs but found it too heavy to do with one hand. After some struggle, I freed it a foot to find a cat curled up on a sheepskin mat. A living cat. A blood-filled, heart-pumping animal. "You have a cat."

"Boffin," Valree replied absentmindedly as she prepared me a coffee.

Boffin looked up at me through sleepy eyes. "Is he breakfast for someone?"

Valree clicked her way toward me with a steaming cup in one hand. She placed it on the table and scooped the tabby up from his bed. "We're not savages. Boffin's the hive cat." She rubbed her face in his neck fur. "I think it was Arnett who had his mother for a snack and discovered she had a litter of kittens to feed. Boffin was the only one to survive. He's good to have around. Helps us desensitize. When you spend your days smelling fresh blood, even if only animal, it helps strengthen your control.

But our appetite for blood is not as consuming as most believe. It's a ridiculously delicious delicacy, and it gives us strength, but we aren't so driven by it we lose all sense of decency." She placed the cat on the floor. It rubbed against her leg once, then sauntered off toward another chair.

She took two slow steps toward me. "I would like to sample you." She played with some loose strands of my hair. "Very much. But I would know when to stop. We kill when necessary, but most of the time, we leave enough blood in a person's veins. I mean what's the point in killing all the providers of your most treasured resource? Some are particularly tasty, and it's nice to have that source ready on tap."

"Glad to hear, but as I said, I'm not ready to share my blood with anyone."

"You might think differently tonight."

Maybe I didn't want to attend the party. "What happens at your parties?"

"Lots of fun. The munsib like their alcohol and drugs. They especially like their blood orgies."

Don't ask if you don't want to hear. Isn't that how the saying went?

"But you needn't worry. Jarro won't let anyone touch you. He may want you all to himself."

"I thought you said he only gets involved with women in your hive."

"I'm talking blood, honey, not sex."

"Do I get a choice?"

"No one ever refuses."

"There's always a first time."

She huffed. "We'll see. Your coffee's getting cold."

The coffee tasted good, the first good coffee I'd had since arriving in Davenport. I sipped while watching Valree move about the kitchen, preparing me breakfast, which was totally odd. Here I was, a prisoner in the Vehan's stronghold, surrounded by a hive of vampires, and one was making me breakfast. When she opened the fridge, I craned my neck to get a good look inside but didn't see jugs of blood cooling for a quick snack if needed.

Once done, Valree glided to the table and placed in front of me an enormous plate of eggs, beans, toast, and bacon. At least I think the charred remains of crispy strips were bacon.

Noting where my eyes stayed, Valree said, "You people have strange eating habits. I thought you'd appreciate knowing your animal was dead before eating it."

"Usually once it's cut up, I can guess the thing is long dead."

She did another of her sleek eyebrow raises and settled back in the chair, half facing me with her arm slung across the back. "I can see why Jarro finds you a puzzle that needs cracking."

"So I'm a cockroach and a puzzle."

"You're a lot of things to us. They're the two things most likely going to save your ass. Just be thankful Jarro doesn't deem you a threat, otherwise it would be your hide I'd be dishing up on the plate for the hive."

"I'm thankful. Don't worry. And I'm grateful for the breakfast, charred bacon and all."

"Vance got the bacon for you. We don't eat something as destroyed as that."

"Just for me? I'm privileged. And confused. I didn't expect a hive of vampires to care too much about their prisoners."

"Guest, sweetie. We kill our problems, we don't waste our time keeping them as prisoners."

"Then I'm glad not to be a problem."

She sat forward, slid her arm across the table and rested her chin in her hand. "Jarro thinks you're a big problem."

My hand stilled halfway to my mouth. "He does? So why am I being given bacon for breakfast?" I couldn't bring myself to joke about being fattened up. The tickely prickles spiked along my skin.

"You tell me."

"I'm a cockroach remember? An irritation, a puzzle."

"Oh, there's a lot of other things he's saying about you. And, yet, here you are, eating at our table. There are few people outside the hive we find useful, and none we like. If you fall into the former, you live, if you're in the latter and we cross paths, you die. You 're not useful, so therefore, we don't like you. But Jarro has given the order you're not to be touched. He even told Vance you needed bacon. He won't fuck you, and he can get blood anywhere. Yours is nothing special. So, sweetie, I can't work out what's going on between you."

I forced myself to take another bite so I didn't have to answer her. Our conversation told me one thing about Valree I would do well to remember. She was not my friend. As buddy buddy as she acted right now, making me coffee and breakfast, trying to seduce me into having sex with her, offering to dress me for tonight, she would just as happily kill me if Jarro gave the all clear. I was surprised by her apparent eagerness to be friends, but not surprised about this revelation. Everyone in the paranormal world was out for blood, both literally and metaphorically.

Disconcertingly, she continued to watch me eat until I had finished my breakfast. At one point I thought about lying and saying I was full just to get out from under her watchful gaze, the way her lips parted and her eyes smoldered as she followed each forkful to my mouth and then the glide of the morsel down my throat. I'm sure, while watching my body do its thing as I ate, she fantasized how lovely it would be to gnaw on my neck for a while.

"That was scrumptious," she purred as I lay my fork on the plate.

A male vampire entered the kitchen, tall and lithe. He'd yet to button his leaf-green shirt. The sides gaped wide as he sauntered to the table, pulled out a chair with ease and slouched down into it like he'd already had a big day. He'd tied his long copper hair into a messy low ponytail, which swept his handsome face clean of distraction. Though slim, he had an abdominal rack and mounded pecs dusted with a soft swirl of dark hair.

"Webster. Have you come to watch our guest have breakfast?"

Webster popped something from his hand into his mouth and chewed slowly as he eyed me. "This is the trouble Jarro brought into our home?" He leaned his head sideways and made an obvious show of checking the rest of me out. "Not sure why he bothered."

I'd certainly made an impression amongst the hive, none of it good.

"Some qualities are not apparent."

"If they're not apparent, they're not worth considering."

"Don't mind Webster, he's been out all night, and he's yet to have a feed."

He pulled himself forward in his seat. "I reckon I could do with a nice bit of fresh bloody meat."

At that moment, Boffin appeared and meowed once at Webster's feet, who leaned back, giving the cat space to jump on board. Watching me with dark brown eyes, he tickled the cat under the chin. Seeing him pet the cat gave me a smidge of courage. There was at least one living creature under their roof not turned to mince; and the rats I sensed scuttling through the thick walls. Though I'm sure vampires wouldn't stoop to sucking rat blood. Boffin didn't stay with Webster long before he jumped down off Webster's lap and sauntered out the door.

"I think that's enough teasing for now. Come, sweetie, Jarro instructed me to show you the limits of your range. Can't have you triggering a reason to deal with you."

"Can't have that." The skull was here somewhere.

I was almost out the door after Valree.

"Hey, witch girl," Webster said.

He didn't look to see if I'd stopped. I guess he smelled my presence.

"I'll be watching you," he said over his shoulder. "Every step of the way."

Okay, creepy vamp. Stay away from Webster.

I followed Valree from the bloody banquet hall, more than happy to discover they didn't expect me to clean my plate or the mess Valree had left and exalted to leave Webster behind. We headed back down the dark corridor I would not be returning to in a hurry alone, given how many doorways and shadowy places were back here.

"This is the corridor of the condemned," she cheerily informed me.

"Leading to the bloody banquet hall. Such nice names."

"Oh, you'll love the rest of the names in Wrathridge Manor."

We returned to the grand entrance hall.

"And this is the entrance of insanity."

"Figures."

She led me to the left of the staircase, shaving close to the room where we'd first met last night, passed that and on down another large corridor.

"We're now in the corridor of despair."

Halfway along, the wall on our left turned to glass, looking out over an atrium. The sun had yet to climb high enough to peek over the mansion walls and down into the indoor garden, but it looked spectacular, even shrouded in the deep blue of early morning. Lounging on a stone bench in the shape of a chaise lounge sat Boffin, on the lap of a yet another male vampire, whose head rested on a black cushion.

"That's Boffin's favorite, Maluc."

Maluc's arm covered most of his face, leaving a trail of thick, dreadlocked, sandy blond hair as my only way of singling him out. He wore denims and a close-fitting black turtleneck that contoured along the curves and ridges of his well-honed chest. As we passed, he removed his arm and lifted his head, settling his gaze on me. The only movement he'd made. The rest of the time, he acted like a Bernini sculpture.

"You like what you see?"

"The indoor garden is stunning."

Valree huffed. "Maluc had the hardest time with Jarro's

command. He's partial to witch blood. You'd be a decedent treat for him. But he's not known to spare anything for afters."

I snapped my eyes away but continued to feel his hungry gaze on my back as we passed by.

"I suggest you don't visit the loci of tranquility. As tempting as it may be. Maluc likes the sun. Don't make this any harder for him."

"Message understood."

"The gallery of the forgotten is up ahead. We rarely use that. Tonight's gathering will be in the desecrated library and will likely spill over into the room of defiled bliss. It's a low key whiskey and cigars affair."

"And the names of the rooms reflect the activities within?" Blood orgies had to mean sex and vampire feeding, simultaneously.

"You may enter the desecrated library by day if you want. It's at the front of the house, and you've already been in the room of defiled bliss."

We passed another shut door on our way to the gallery of the forgotten.

"Hell's choir is also on your list." She pointed to the next door on my left.

"You mean the room."

"It's the original music room."

The last door on my left differed from the others. It looked like a vault door. Huge metal beams criss-crossed over the front like a barrack to entry.

Valree turned, hearing me slow. "If you want to end your life now, be my guest."

"It looks like the entrance to a dungeon?"

"The dungeons of doom."

"I thought you didn't keep prisoners."

She sashayed back toward me, eating into my personal space. "You could take a look. If you're so terribly curious."

"What would you do if I did?"

She held her hands up and waved her fingers in air. "Not me, sugar. I can't touch you, remember?" She dipped her head, then slowly tilted it to face me in a seductive, teasing way. "But I know who will."

That's where the skull was kept. It had to be. Question was, how far was I willing to push to get it, what risks would I take?

CHAPTER 22

Valree had given me a red piece of material that smacked back against my body when I tried to stretch it away. It was a dress, supposedly, but to me it looked more like a tube of material with arm holes and a V plunge that reached as far as my naval. Not quite so far, but my cleavage would not stay contained. No way could I fit my bra underneath, and my nipples spiked outward like large tacks.

Valree burst into the room without warning. On instinct, I smothered my nipples with my palms, given Valree had tried enticing me to succumb to her ravenous desires, in both forms, sexual and edible, without me flashing my tits at her.

"My my, don't you look a treat."

She looked more the treat than me, if you were into women. Donning another of her catsuit outfits, with an equally plunging neckline, a loose metal chain around her waist and more lethal heels. She wore her hair in an artfully wild and messy way that would've taken a tank of hairspray to pull off.

"I can't wear this."

Even without platforms for shoes she'd towered behind me. I watched in the mirror as she snaked her arms around to my front, clasped her hands at my wrists and lowered them down to my sides. "That wasn't a good look."

Adding a scandalous edge, she cupped my breasts and jiggled them about a little to fatten the amount of skin poking out of the material. "That's an even better look."

I moved away from the mirror and her. "I'm not wearing this."

"It's fun."

"I'm not the entertainment tonight."

"You sure about that?"

My protest died on my tongue. "I am?"

"Everyone will believe you're Preston's daughter. Imagine what they'll think when they see not even wealth and influence keep family members out of our reach."

I was a warning. "Doesn't mean I have to go like this."

"No, but it will make Jarro furious."

It was official, Valree and Elka were related, not Elka and I. Both thrived on provoking.

"Besides, it's too late, now. Jarro doesn't tolerate tardiness."

She scooped to pick up my heels and dragged me across my room. Out in the corridor, she shoved the heels at me. "Quickly."

I complied, knowing any more delays, and I would see Valree's vampire side emerge. Being so pathetic in high heels, I scrambled after her quick pace, threatening to twist my heel on plenty of occasions, and I used the bannister on the way down the stairs so I didn't end up at the bottom on my ass.

Classical music strained out through the door to the library. A live band, by the sounds of it. How civil, for a bunch of bloodthirsty paranormals. As we drew nearer to the door, voices bubbled under the tune of the violin.

Valree cast me a couple of glances as she went, making me feel self-conscious, so I checked myself before she pushed open the door, noticing my breasts had worked their way further into the V, dramatizing my cleavage, after my rough ride down the stairs. At this rate, a nipple would soon peek around the edge of the fabric. After another of her periodic checks to ensure I was still behind her, I shoved my breasts back under the fabric and tried to make the two edges join in the middle, with no success.

Left hand slipping sideways inside my dress, trying to poke more breast away, Valree flung the door to the library open wide in a grand style entrance, which drew all eyes to us. I ripped my hand away and succeeded in releasing my left breast a few inches more for display. Right now, I could spin and march back up the stairs to my room, but Valree, seeming to know my mind, grabbed my hand and drew me into the throng of people, past swirls of cigar smoke and a heady mess of cologne and floral perfume. Massive chandeliers cast a warm, golden light over the crowd below, softening everyone's features.

I moved into a room full of black and white suits, a few coiffured women amongst them, impeccably dressed in ball gowns and elaborate braids or bun twists. And Valree had me dress like this. Eyes, from both the men and women, zeroed in on my cleavage. The women's gazes dipped soon after to skirt the rest of me, but the men's gazes seemed content to stay on my cleavage. Typical. I met a lot of them eye to eye, feeding them bad vibes so they knew what I thought of their lecherous looks.

Then a waitress teetered past wearing lace panties and nothing else, which set the tone for the night.

Normally I would feel uncomfortable holding Valree's hand, but I clung to it like she was my lifeline. I couldn't tell who were munsib influencers and who were members of the hive, but the way eyes ate me up, I'd say most here were lining me up for a bite. Valree drew her own share of attention, fugitive glances. By the way they darted their eyes away, I'd say she intimidated most. No surprises there. These people were familiar with hive parties. Maybe some had experienced some painful misfortune when gawking at her in the past. Me, on the other hand—it felt like Valree was parading me through the crowd as an appetizer for the night to come, letting everyone know this is what happened to their daughters if they crossed the hive.

I had no idea where Valree was heading until we parted a group of men like Moses, and I found myself over the other side of the room, close to the musicians and three men standing with their backs to a gigantic fireplace. Jarro stood between the two, dressed entirely in black. If not for the fire behind him, contrasting his black with an orange glimmer, he'd have disappeared into the scene. He turned, the moment we cleared the group, and nailed me with his stare. He never had a warm, smiling gaze, making it impossible to tell what his dark eyes were saying right now. Speaking a word to both men, he left them and headed over.

Yanking Valree by the elbow close to his side, he snarled, "Get her out of it."

"Come on, Jarro, baby. It suits her. Wouldn't you say?" She finger-walked her hand up his front to his chest.

Jarro seized her hand in his. They locked eyes, Valree not looking at all subdued by the steel he sliced her way.

"If that's the game you want to play." He slipped his jacket from his shoulders and threw it my way, not even looking at me to aim. "Put it on."

Gladly. I'd stitch it up my neck if I had thread. Once tucked inside his jacket, Jarro seemed finally able to look at me. "Don't take it off." There was nothing soft in the way he commanded me.

"Thanks."

He'd looked away the moment he'd uttered his command, but my thanks drew his attention back to me. He turned his body toward me, standing way too close and feeling way too imposing and stormy. No more praises for him tonight if he was going to act like that.

"You're here to stand in the room so everyone can see you. And that is all."

"What if someone talks to me?"

He took a step closer, making me crane up higher to meet his eyes. "You don't want to push me, Larnie."

"Usually I tell my friends to call me Laz, but since we're the opposite of friends, you can keep calling me Larnie."

He leaned down. "You have no idea how dangerous I can be."

"I have a good imagination. And you don't have to worry. I'm not interested in being involved in the charade you're playing with these people."

His eyes flickered back and forth on mine, then trailed down my face to my lips, trailed further down to my neck. They had to stop there unless he wanted to stare at the buttons on his jacket. Valree said he only bothered with women in the hive, but not always for drinking blood. He sure seemed to find my neck interesting.

Suddenly, he lifted his head and glanced around him like he was snapping out of a trance. Without another word, he turned his back on me and moved away to join a conversation with a group. I looked around to find Valree had deserted me to flirt up a storm with three men. She caught a passing waitress by the arm and whispered in her ear. The waitress nodded, then made a bee-line for me.

Once in front of me, she winked, holding her tray toward me. There were three cocktail glasses left. Not talking to anyone meant it would be a long night, so I might as well have a drink to pass the time.

The liquid was sweet, cool on the lips, and warming in my belly. I couldn't tell what sort of cocktail it was, but when I licked my lips, they tasted like caramel. Better have another sip. These were damn nice. Before I knew it, half the drink was gone, so I glanced around the room hoping to see a waitress with another. The glass was a whisper away from my lips when Jarro appeared like lightning, and smacked it out of my hands. I gasped as the glass smashed to the floor, spraying the remaining contents on the back of a man's pants.

Jarro snapped his head around to look at Valree. She smirked at him, turned her shoulder, and renewed her conversation.

Hands on hips, Jarro glared for a few heartbeats, the typical pose of someone trying to find some equilibrium. Finally, the taut bunch of his body and the vein pulsing on his neck subsided—he glanced down at me. "I suggest you take a seat by the fire." Bizarrely voiced with a hint of, I couldn't believe it, thoughtfulness.

The request sounded reasonable to me. I could avoid everyone by imitating a cushion. While I followed behind him, I thought about what led him to smack the glass out of my hand. Either he didn't want me drunk and making trouble, or the drink was drugged. I'd say by the smug smile on Valree's face, it was the latter. How much did I need to drink to feel the effects? Given Jarro instructed me to sit down, I'd say not very much. How dangerous was it to consume party drugs in a room full of vampires and sex-crazed billionaires? Maybe I should look for an exit.

Jarro's jacket was large enough it hid my legs and the dress when I folded them underneath me. I leaned into the headrest and felt nice and comfortable. Until a man came and joined me on the couch, bringing with him the smell of cigar and scotch. A James Bond looka-like in manner and dress. The stubble on his chin did wonders for his appeal and the tattoo creeping out from the neckline of his shirt, plus the gold stud in his left ear made him look mafia.

By the way he slid up next to me, destroying social etiquette with the distance he didn't leave between us, I would say he was a vampire. It seemed they didn't respect people's personal space. At least, Jarro and Valree didn't.

"Why are you here?" His grey eyes were like dirty icebergs.

"Jarro thought I should sit down."

"No. Why are you here?" There was nothing nice in his tone.

I had to navigate this guy with caution. He'd been here seconds and already I felt prickles from his glare, menace radiating from his body language.

"If I knew I'd do everything I could to reverse the situation."

"Why dangle Preston's daughter in front of this crowd?"

"Is that a rhetorical question?" Did he know who I was?

"Where'd you come from?"

I guess he did. "Elsewhere. We weren't planning on staying long, but things have slipped out of our control. My name's Larnie."

He looked at my hand, then my face, making no attempt to shake. "Santani. We can't afford Preston going to the Cantonia."

"Valree said no one here will say anything."

"And the king's willing to risk that?"

"Perhaps he wants to scare everyone here into staying away from the Cantonia by demonstrating his reach. Besides, Elka is in Davenport somewhere. She'll go home, eventually." And why was I pacifying this vamp's concerns?

He settled his iceberg eyes on me. In the end, the intensity grew too great and I turned away to stare into the fire.

"The likeness is uncanny."

"We're twins." I had to stop myself from eye rolling at my stupid response.

"How can you not know about each other?"

"We were separated at birth." If only he'd lose interest and leave.

"Now is a terrible time for our king to get distracted." His gaze shifted to the fire.

"Problems with the Cantonia?"

He slid a sideways glance at me.

"I'm not sure Jarro found anything useful at Lunaris Cemetery."

Shut up. This conversation only made him glare harder at me. But... "If I knew what he was after there, I could offer some information. I spent some time in the crypt." That was such a mouthful to say. And now I was all out of conversation.

He turned to me, sliding his knee up on the couch. "Perhaps you're what he was after."

Me. Nah. Really? I huffed a laugh. "Hardly. He attacked my friend and I, practically suffocated me." Then I giggled. For some reason.

"Outside the hive, Jarro bothers only with those useful to him. He had no time for your sister, and she's hotter than you. If he's sniffing after you, it's because he sees a potential he can use."

Not good. The last thing I wanted was for Jarro to find me interesting. Him using me was better than him desiring me. Safer and much better.

And...what were we talking about? Something to do with... Dark mother, it was too hard to think. And the fire was so nice.

My head felt heavy, so I relaxed it onto the headrest. The couch was super comfortable. And in front of the fire like this, I was heating up. In fact, I was getting hot, but cooling down would mean taking off Jarro's jacket, and I didn't want to do that.

I shuffled further into the couch, mesmerized by the flames, twisting and dancing, entwining like lovers, breaking apart or dying away, only for more to flare up in their place. This was gloriously cozy and dreamy. It was nice of Jarro to suggest I sit in front of the fire.

"Hey, witch girl."

Oh, that guy was still beside me. Whatever his name was again. How long had he been there?

"Hmm." I liked the vibration that played at the back of my throat when I made that sound. "Hmm." It kind of tickled.

"You ought to come with me."

That would mean getting up. "That's too much effort."

"Not with me it's not."

He was in front of me. At what point had he gotten off the couch? Arms wrapped around my waist and pulled me to my feet. They were muscular arms that stayed there once I was up, warm and snug and very nice.

There was a gentle tickle in my ear. "Come with me." A soft velvety command, too irresistible to refuse. His voice was like fingers soothing over my skin, tingling it alive.

"Anywhere." The words swam out of my mouth, suppling my body until it felt like elastic.

We walked through a golden room. There were sparks above, and deep, rich hues in front of my eyes. I was floating, not walking, floating like a butterfly, anchored only by the hands at my waist, powerful hands that kept me snug beside him; the kind guy who was guiding me. The world looked perfect, and so did all the faces turning toward me. Beautiful, friendly people, smiling at me, laughing because life was worth laughing at. I joined in, and my body felt like it would disappear into space, it was that buoyant.

We continued to move through a kaleidoscope of colors and fireworks of brilliancy. What a great place to be. Whoever suggested we come had a fantastic idea. I could just do this forever, float suspended in this sea of wonder and tranquility.

It looked like a door in front of us, but then it suddenly disappeared and everything changed. My sea of colors wasn't colors at all, but people. The room changed, the atmosphere different. The smokey haze and reverberant strains of the violin diminished into a treasure trove of jumbled people consuming every space, including the floor, so the rugged floor moved and rolled like a gentle sea. They slithered like snakes over each other, bare flesh basking in the golden light, arms and legs wriggling, writhing, bodies meshing, grinding, undulating to a sacred rhythm I was privileged to see. The chorus of their pleasure was a primal song no one would dare sing in the hallowed halls of the sainted Living Light. But I was a child of the Dark Mother and living in the dark was a boon from our mistress. I sucked the chorus down into my core to spread it like seed.

An untamed bounty unfurled inside of me like a giant flower splaying its petals to the sun, opening, releasing, unfolding. A firm pressure pressed into my back, and the sound I made in response rippled a caressing vibration down to my chest. Hands moved up to cup my throat, splayed fingers consuming every inch of my flesh. This was too good to experience in the light, so I closed my eyes, arching my head as I floated away, cocooned in a feeling of surreal bliss.

I felt the presence in front of me, not the weight of their being, but the aura of their body, my own reaching out to collide with possibility. Yearning pounded my body, frenetic, feral, pumping me alive, ripping at my flesh in the savagery of anticipation.

I opened my eyes, stared into the grey ice of his desire, those beautiful eyes, like the wilds of the arctic, a vast empty wilderness of danger. It was his hands at my throat, his hands tilting my neck up to the ceiling, making it hard for me to swallow. I'd not swallow again just to stare into his eyes. He lowered. I waited, hung on a thread.

"Give me the pleasure." He skimmed my face with his lips and bent further.

"I'll give you anything."

"Would you. Give me. This?" There was the soft wetness of his tongue at the nape of my neck. I unfurled further, swooned closer, but he disappeared.

"Anyone's but hers."

It was another man's voice. I forced my eyes open, sadistically pulled from my sensual world to find the mesmeric vacuum of Jarro's dark eyes. I wanted to dive deep, deep down inside, swim to the bottom and lather myself in all of him, bathe in the sweet toxicity of his musky cedar scent.

The evil man kept his hands in his pocket like he dared not touch my skin. My mind struggled to find equilibrium, find its way back to the ground. Jarro shot me off once more by lowering, lowering until the magical moment, the elation of heaven, the euphoria of hell, the first touch of his lips, like a feather. Splaying his hand at my neck, forcing my head back, so I could stare into his eyes. His lips moved across mine as he spoke the words. "You don't want this." They felt like the sensual stroke of a finger, and not on the lips of my mouth.

"Don't be cruel," I whispered back. My lips moving on his was an erotic dance I would happily die not to end.

"It's my nature." Teasing me with the brush of his mouth.

"Then show me how brutal you can be."

The pressure of his fingers at my throat tightened. "Don't ask unless you truly understand what you're asking for."

"I do—"

"This will never be safe for you."

"It's—"

"I will never be safe for you. Your night's over."

I floated, floated, floated in a pool of darkness.

CHAPTER 23

I remember most, but not every detail, just the important bits, like my need bleeding out of me from a gaping hole ripped through my side by whatever poison the vamps put into the drinks. I'd learned a valuable lesson. Don't trust Valree. Two valuable lessons. I was horny as hell for a certain someone and not to trust Valree. The first lesson would need some radical intervention, scratch the itch so to speak, the second would resolve itself once I got free of this place.

And get free I would. I was up in the air about how to make it happen, but it was my solemn mission. That, and stealing the skull. These vamps played games I couldn't win, blood was the primary commodity, and no one was getting any of mine.

Bloated dark clouds muddied the stones of the mansion an ugly steel blue, turned the lawn a dull deep green, sucked the hue from the forest so that it appeared lifeless and gray. I closed my eyes to blot it all out and found flashes of last night spun images and color through my head. It was a confusing jumble of faces, people, bodies, and more. Sex mixed with blood-letting, a blood orgy. That's what the wealthy of Davenport got up to. What about Bernard with his spinster wife? Did he surrender his neck as payment for the pleasure of dipping his wick?

And that bastard, Santani. He'd been the one to lead me into the room of defiled bliss. Despite Jarro's order to leave me alone, he'd been willing to take a drink. There was consent. He'd asked for it, and I'd willingly given it. Under a cloud of love poison, which was no consent at all. How far would he have gone?

I shook with a sudden shiver. I had always been vulnerable around the heavies of the paranormal world, but the vamps took me down to a new level of vulnerability, mostly because every action of theirs was intoxicating.

Witch lore stated that to allow a vamp your blood was to allow him or her into your soul. I wasn't sure of the truth about that. It sounded more like a folktale to keep witches from straying from the Dark Mother who claimed the devotion of her children, and the entirety of their souls. True or not, I was not about to fall victim to anyone. Already, I'd surrendered a smidge to the Dark Mother. The vamps weren't getting a single piece of this witch's soul.

I left the window and slunk out into the hall, still dressed in my clothes from days ago because I was not wearing that red dress. My playground was inside the mansion, according to Valree, except for the dungeons of doom, which I would find a way to explore. It was the only logical place to keep the skull. That, and Jarro's room, which was at the top of a tower, artfully named the tower of wrath, entranced by a door at the back of the mansion, but that part of this place had not been included in Valree's tour.

Poor Auntie Bea. She was still a prisoner, and I'd made one bungle after another in trying to rescue her. I needed that skull, and I needed out of here.

Once again, I found the place empty when I reached the bottom of the stairwell. The vamps were a private lot, even with each other, which was fortunate for me. I hurried across the floor, heading for the corridor that led to the gallery of the forgotten. My actual destination was the dungeons of doom. Not that I was stupid enough to contemplate heading down if I found the lock undone, but I wanted time to stand outside and work out a plan.

The loci of tranquility stood in my way. Maluc's favorite spot, Maluc the unfriendliest, if Valree was to be believed. I faltered, finding my steps awkwardly slow. It was impossible to creep up on a vampire. If he was there, how far would he hear me from the other side of a glass wall? I really needed to get better info on the true abilities of these guys if I wanted to avoid them in future.

I stayed pressed against the stone wall, held my breath, because that was going to stop my heart from beating, and inched my head around to peer inside. Not Maluc this time. Jarro sat on the bench, looking at his phone. For the first time since meeting him, he wore denim jeans and a white t-shirt, casually reclined on the black cushions like Adonis. His wet, black hair tumbled down to his chin in a mess tangle of waves.

What do I do? No way could I slink past and not go unnoticed. I couldn't think of a valid reason to be down this end of the corridor. I pressed back against the wall, feeling the cold and the sharp edges of the rough stone against my back.

Then came the knock on the glass, which made me jump. I peered around to find Jarro standing close to me, one hand resting on the glass wall. He raised his eyebrows in a 'well' gesture. Caught out. "Dammit," I whispered. Options. Disappear back to my room or go out there and glean as much information as I could. I chose the latter, not because I wanted to be in his presence, but if there was a chance to learn something about this place, where Jarro hid the skull, vampire lore, Davenport, you name it, I'd take it.

Without the sun, the temperature had cooled uncomfortably. The stone seat looked as inviting as a...stone seat, so I grabbed a cushion to sit on. "Since I can't go outside, I thought this would be a good place for some fresh air." Let's hope he wasn't a good lie detector.

"Any lingering effects from last night?"

As in, did I remember him talking to me with his lips feathered against mine? As if I would forget. I remembered everything I needed to remember, even the psychedelic coloring, but mostly the mess of bodies doing things to each other illegal in all states, I'm sure. And the blood-letting. Sex and feeding. Everyone seemed to enjoy it.

"What was the drug?"

"It's Valree speciality. She likes to spice things up for the guests, release their inhibitions. Not all are comfortable with the idea of sharing their blood."

"So lack of consent is not an issue for you guys?"

He looked at me like I'd asked him if the sun will rise tomorrow.

"At least Santani asked me."

"Do you think he would've stopped if you said no?"

Probably not. "I'd like to think so. I had no control over myself last night." I turned away so he wouldn't see the heat I felt inching its way up my throat. Begging him, both of them, to put their paws all over me, dark mother, the embarrassment.

"That's the point of the drug. Valree's faced her punishment for offering it to you. I've been too lenient with her of late. She had her instructions, and she disobeyed. I wanted everyone to see you, but not that much of you."

How much of me was he happy to see? "You've made me a pawn."

"A warning."

"So Valree and Santani were right."

"Do I have to punish Santani as well?"

"He said little. But you can punish him for possibly taking my blood while I wasn't in control of myself."

"Santani is one of my trusted."

"Why did he take me to the room of defiled bliss? Was that in your orders?"

"No. But I'd say he was trying to prove a point."

"To who?"

"Me."

"I don't get it."

"Don't expect me to tell you."

I wasn't going to get anywhere in any conversation with Jarro, but at least he was being civil, not dark and broody.

"I just want one answer from you. It's a simple thing."

He settled himself to face me, leaning against the armrest of the chaise lounge, one arm on the back of the stone seat, a plump black cushion at his back, his eyes holding me spellbound to the moment. He would know his effect on women, but I doubted he meant to flex it with me. I hoped he didn't guess where my mind rummaged every time I looked at him. Was it written on my face?

"And what question may that be?"

"Why did you bring me here? And don't tell me it's because you wanted to parade me as a warning in front of all the influential in Davenport. You had Elka eating out of your palm. It would've been easy to bring her here. Hell, she would've stripped naked last night and dive-bombed into the fun with no need for drugs."

"You're right. Last night was a secondary thought."

I waited. When he said no more, I copied what he'd done to me by the glass wall and raised my eyebrows, throwing a hand gesture in as well, as I doubted he'd be as easily lead.

"It doesn't serve my purpose to tell you."

"Have you thought about what Elka's dad will do when he realizes she's missing? I'm sure Frederick is going to notice."

"What munsib do is no concern of mine."

I sighed, shaking my head and looked up to the sky. It was like banging my head against a block of stone.

"Fine, can you at least tell me how long I have to stay here?"

"It's time you answered my questions."

"You haven't answered any of mine."

"That's not how this works."

I would get nowhere arguing. Like he had done to me, I squared myself and glared my thoughts about our conversation.

"Where are you parents?"

"I don't know."

"How long have you not known?" Said with a patience bordering on crumbling.

"They abandoned me at birth. Have you grilled Elka like this?"

"Elka's not a part of this conversation."

"She thinks you don't know her secret."

"I'm not interested in what Elka thinks."

"When did you know she was a witch?"

He snapped forward, making me jerk backward. Damn him. A muscle in his jaw twitched. "Who were your parents?"

"They abandoned me at birth. I don't know."

"Why did the Apostles take your Aunt?"

"Why ask me who my parents were if you know about my Aunt?"

He grabbed my wrist, pulled me closer to him. "You are playing a dangerous game, Larnie."

"Auntie Bea owed them money she doesn't have, and so we promised them the skull. It's why I was at the auction. We lost the skull, so she's ransom until I get it."

He let go of my wrist and reclined on the cushion, arm on the back of the chair again, only this time he assumed the perfect sculptor pose, giving me his profile, elbow bent, tapping his thumb to his bottom lip, deep in thought.

"Is Hyun-woo searching for me?"

Yeah, I shouldn't have said that. The slow turn of his head, the narrowing of his onyx eyes, told me so.

"I was hoping for some give and take. I just gave you something."

"You haven't begun to give me what I want."

Had this been last night, with my mind juiced up on sex drugs, I would've taken that as erotic lingo. In the new world of today, with my clear, sober head, those words blew in on a savage wind.

"So tell me and let's get this over with."

"Why were you at Lunaris?"

"I wanted to ask you that?"

He swept to his feet with grace and speed, giving me an eyeful of his perfectly fitted jeans. And barefoot. How had I missed his bare feet? Bare feet on a guy shouldn't be as enticing as they were. They led to thoughts of warm, mussy men just climbing out of bed.

"You're building your cage, but you're too foolish to realize," he said.

"I'm giving and open to people who earn my trust. You, I'll never trust."

"In that, you show intelligence."

He walked away, disappearing inside, leaving me in a void. I couldn't begin to make sense of his cryptic mumbo jumbo or untangle the complexity of him.

Dark mother, the dungeon. He'd be heading for the dungeon. It was just down the hall and that's the way he turned when he went inside.

I leaped off the seat and slipped into the corridor. The dungeon door. It was further down the corridor, and thanks to the loci of tranquility letting in plenty of light, dull as it may be today, I could see the slim crack, the slightest opening. He had gone inside.

I wouldn't be so stupid as to follow him down. I took seriously Valree's warning yesterday about entering the dungeons. Luckily, I did not need to go down in person to see what he was up to.

The only other door this far down the corridor of despair was the one that led to the gallery of the forgotten, a place on my could enter list. On tiptoe, I snuck past the dungeon door and down to the gallery. The heavy, wooden twin doors took muscle to open and groaned and creaked their old age with enough noise to wake the long dead. I grimaced at every inch gained until I could slip inside.

Only the light from the corridor, as poor as it was, gave the room any sort of lift from the dark and dreary. Thick curtains blocked the sunlight, and dead people's portraits lined the walls. The air carried the old stale smell of relics uncovered after centuries of being buried away.

I slid down the wall, bunching my knees to my chest and let my eyes close while releasing the restraints barricading my gift. The edges of my awareness streamed out around the mansion, seeking my fat, fluffy friend. I found many little creatures making home in the thick walls and deserted passages. Those were the closest to me, but of no use. Finally, after spreading my awareness to the far reaches, I found Boffin in peaceful slumber.

His brain was a slushy mess and difficult to rouse. The big guy was a lazy oaf, fed too many treats to bother about the rat problem. Several nudges later, I succeeded in rousing him. He stretched too long, yawned a couple of times, and then ambled along with the slow, sluggish brain of a sloth. It took much persuasion to get him into a trot, which felt lumbering and awkward because of his low-slung belly swishing from side to side as he went.

Unfortunately, I'd discovered him somewhere down the other end of the mansion and it took patience and many mental nudges to keep him heading my way and stop him from getting distracted by the next comfy place to sleep. House cats were useless. Give me a feral alley cat, instincts honed to self-preservation, any day.

The dungeon door was in front of me. Not far now, but Boffin slowed, his lazy mind deciding the dungeon wouldn't have the weak sunlight or plump cushions he needed. I had to exert a little more force to make him finish the final leg and stick his nose inside the slim crack. Together, we sniffed the air. I smelt dank and dusty tight spaces. Boffin backed up, until I overrode his own desires with my own. For this, I would have to flood Boffin with my commands and hijack his body, something I rarely did.

We inched in, until we felt the pressure of the door on our shoulders, and Boffin baulked and tried to back out, so I used a little more force. The doors were ridiculously heavy, so for a moment I worried he would be unable to get it open by pushing through, but it turned out his pudgy waist easily squished up when entering narrow spaces.

We smelt the stench of rats, but being the overfed cat he was, they didn't interfere with our soft, padded descent down the steep stone steps. Since when did mansions have dungeons? Since the vamps moved in, I guess.

The steps curved gently, with no light anywhere down here for guidance, but Boffin's eyes picked up all the necessary shapes.

Around the bend and we spied the dirt floor, smoothed from hundreds of years of treading feet. At the bottom of the stairs we found Jarro, back to us, hunched over a stone bench, head bowed. Motionless. Nothing nefarious in that, expect what may be on the bench in front of him.

We were about to pace forward when Boffin's keen ears picked up movement from behind us, sounding like a ruffle of bed clothes. It was now I got my first injection of kitty jitters as Boffin flicked his head, bunching up like he was ready to bound away. I inhaled, breathed the calm of my being into fat cat to ease him out of alert mode and back to facing Jarro. I almost had him under control again when Jarro paced toward us. Now it was my heart that hiccuped, but Jarro marched past us and up the stairs. Perfect timing. With him gone, I could get Boffin onto the stone bench and have a good look at what he'd hunched over.

I was wrenched to my feet by my upper arms from a rough handed grip. I flung back from Boffin's mind and stared into Jarro's face.

"Curiosity killed the cat," he snarled.

CHAPTER 24

"I t's in my nature," I said, as he dropped one arm and manhandled me to the door. "As cruelty's in yours, and I haven't blamed you for that."

He marched me out of the gallery of the forgotten without saying another word.

"I've stayed within the boundaries. You're really going to punish me for obeying you?"

In front of us, Boffin streaked out of the dungeon door like a monster was on his tail.

At the door, Jarro paused, and let me go. "I'm not punishing you. I'm giving you want you want."

"The skull?"

"A look inside."

I darted my gaze between both his eyes. Was this a trick? Most likely. Vampires didn't do things for anyone unless it benefited them.

Jarro did an exaggerated sweep of his hand, a witch at the ginger-bread house welcoming Hansel and Gretel inside. The frosting and candy were in the dark down the bottom of the stairs. All I had to do was find the courage to have a taste.

"I'm not a cat or a vampire. I need a little light."

"At you command." His face remained passive, no humor, no sarcasm, just cardboard, your typical serial killer expression.

I led, waiting for the shove at my back to push me down the stairs. Though that was a lame way for a vampire to kill someone. I used my hand along the rough wall, occasionally suffering a jab or two on my finger pads from a protruding stone edge. Following the curve, I came to the end as a small light grew from a tiny spark overhead. It reminded me of the light Hyun-woo had made when he drew on the long dead's energy, giving off the same gentle yellow glow that hid the poverty of the dungeon. Was this something Jarro could do?

I soon forgot all that when I saw the skull on the stone bench, the one thing I'd been chasing for what seemed eternity within reach yet so far out of my grasp it might as well be on Mars.

"Why did you bring me down here?"

Jarro strolled around me. "You went to the trouble of hijacking my cat just to sneak a look."

"You know I've been chasing the skull. Did you really expect me to sit around here twiddling my thumbs, waiting for the next party, so you could drug me and parade me around again?"

"Don't think I'm doing this for you."

"I'd never be so stupid as to think that."

He'd moved to the side of me by now. Turning my head to look at him, I remembered the ruffle of sheets Boffin and I had heard. Jarro's attention was on the skull, so I inched my head and shoulders further around behind us.

The light failed to penetrate that far back, but I made out an assortment of wood crates, an old stool and...

"Don't you want to go closer?" Jarro whispered, suddenly standing behind me, blocking my view.

Damn vampires and their speedy agility and grace. Interesting that he doesn't want me looking back there.

Since I may not get another chance, I stepped up to the stone bench and stared down at the unimpressive-looking skull. "Everything Auntie Bea and I have suffered. For this. It doesn't seem worth it."

The warmth of Jarro's breath tickled the hair on the top of my head, as to the warmth of his body, inches from touching my back.

"It was her idea to come to Davenport. She hoped it would rescue us from our current state of near poverty. But she failed to tell me everything. I doubt she even realized exactly what she was taking us into." I shook my head. "It was so stupid of her to think we'd succeed. I don't care about the skull. I just want Auntie Bea back."

"Finally, I hear the truth."

I couldn't look around, not with him so close to my back. Turning my head would place us at too intimate a distance. "You have what you want, Jarro. You don't need me. Just let me save my Aunt."

He placed his hands over mine and raised them up from my sides.

"That's the problem," he whispered as he drifted my hands toward the skull. "I don't have what I want." He held my hands suspended over the skull. "I'm far from what I want." Then he lowered them and placed them flat on the skull.

The moment was laced with intimacy, mood lighting, the two of us, whispered words, practically rubbing up against each other. But it was far from intimate.

I was being manipulated. Once again, a pawn. I pushed back into him, struggled against his hands, pressing mine down on the skull.

"Jarro," I growled.

He resisted my struggles with ease, his body sandwiching me in place.

I soon halted all attempts at breaking free when the skull warmed under my palms, too fast for my hands to be responsible. I relaxed against Jarro, consumed by the weird heating of the skull, the shimmering, flecked blue of its color, like a galaxy of stars were swirling on the cranium.

"What's happening?"

I got no reply, not that I wanted one. Jarro leaned down, bringing his head level beside mine, the hairs on our cheeks tickling each other. His attention was on the skull, reflected in the center of his iris.

A fine vibration started in my hands, a sparking and tingling, then a sudden burst of bright light, blinding in its intensity, followed by a great wave of energy. Like a punch in the gut, it forced me backward into Jarro, but my momentum swept him up and sent the two of us skittering backward.

I waited for the sudden impact when I hit the wall behind. That didn't happen, because I found myself cradled in Jarro's arms. Of course, he stayed on his feet like a cat flipping after being dropped from a height.

He set me down, his attention on our surroundings. I would've said thanks for catching me and saving me from the pain of a jarring fall, but the words shriveled in the awe of where we'd landed. Not the dungeon, which was the amazing thing.

Desolation. A wasteland. The atmosphere was a heavy weight pressing down on my shoulders, burdening my soul. Sepia colored the landscape of nothingness an oppressive ugly tint. In the distance, where the horizon met the ground, the tint deepened, forming what looked like a wall of dust. The air was like syrup, too thick to breathe with ease.

"Are we stuck in a waking dream?" I said.

"Not a dream."

"Did you know this would happen?"

Jarro ignored my question and walked away. Since there was nothing around here, he seemed to walk for the sake of moving. Not wanting to be left, I followed. "Shouldn't we grab the skull?"

"There's no point." He kept walking into the nothingness.

At least, it started as nothingness, until something emerged from the gloom. Pillars first, making themselves in front of our eyes. The pillars grew into a grand colonnade and turned into a magnificent temple looming out of the desert.

"I thought the skull was a seeker, not a portal through time," I said.

"Or other realms."

"Dark mother."

I caught up when Jarro stopped before the entrance. "What do you think, Larnie, do we go inside?"

"That's not a good idea. We should return to the skull. Get out of here before something happens, however we got here."

"I'm not sure we're really here."

"Okay, so this is a mental trip." Like my dakeu. "What is it you're seeking here?"

"The question is, what are you seeking? This is your doing."

It was my hands on the skull. "I know nothing about this place, so why would I be seeking anything here?"

"You don't know what you need to know. Not yet."

"That's possible. I never seem to know enough when it comes to the paranormal world and anything beyond."

"Perhaps what we need to learn will be inside."

"Jarro. I have a bad vibe about this place. I'm not sure we should be here."

To make my point, a horrible screech echoed through the air, rebounding off the pillars, making it impossible to tell where it came from. Given the sound, I'd say the creature was big, and there weren't too many places a large creature could hide, but there was no sign of it. Hopefully Jarro was right, and we weren't really here. But the last time someone had promised me it was only a mental trip, I ended up with the smell of man all down the front of me. And that man happened to be standing right next to me. Our surroundings were creepy, similar to my dakeu experience, but that had been four years ago, when I first became a witch. I couldn't remember how everything looked clearly enough to say this was a mirror image.

Jarro seized my arm. I turned to him, but only saw what appeared beyond him, hanging off the side of a pillar. "What is that?"

"An unfriendly."

The half lizard, half bird clung to the pillar using impressive talons. Its hooked beak looked a good fit for stabbing and tearing so it could peck out soft insides. While not massively big, it was sizable enough to cause real damage if given the chance.

"I've changed my mind about going inside," I said.

Jarro took my hand and led me toward the temple. Slowed by my cumbersome strides, nowhere near as agile and speedy as he could move, we weren't quick enough before another of the creatures landed on the top of the temple. Both screeched in unison, in a tone pitched just right for bursting eardrums.

The one on top took flight, swooped in a low arc down toward us. Jarro yanked me behind him with more force than perhaps he thought and sent me rolling in the dirt. A billow of dust clouded up around me, fogging my vision and getting up my nose. I inhaled a lungful, and practically coughed them up.

Ending my roll on my stomach, I lifted my head to see Jarro finishing the creature off, one wing already discarded yards away, leaving a trailing bloody mess, the other wing in his bunched fist. The creature lay lifeless at his feet.

He looked over his shoulder at me, then turned to face the other creature, still digging its talons into the pillar. A distant screech came from somewhere out there in the gloom.

"More," I breathed.

Jarro threw the wing in his hand away and marched back toward me. "You need to get inside." He yanked me off my feet, leaving an imprint of bloody fingers on my sweatshirt sleeve.

"I thought you said this was only in our heads."

"For once, I'm wrong." He pulled me forward.

"Wait." I withdrew my hand from his grasp.

"This is a horde attack. It's the blood they seek. I can't keep an eye on you and fight them off at the same time."

Behind him, the remaining creature joined in the growing crescendo of screeches from those approaching. They were intelligent, else why was the one that first arrived holding off after seeing Jarro decimate its partner?

"Let me try something."

"Beyond our realm, the rules could be different. They usually are. You might not be able to penetrate their minds."

"Shh," I hissed, closing my eyes and shredding aside the barrier I erected around my mind to keep every animal mind from invading mine. The filaments of my mind swept out across the desolation, encountering the creature closest to us first.

Expecting to butt up against a wall or some other magical barricade, I funneled through as easy as any animal back home. But the connections in this beast's mind were different. If I could compare, it was like a sound system with the off as on, the left as right and a whole jumble of extra wires in between that seemed to randomize off into unknown places.

I expanded my mind outward to meet the incoming horde. Then felt dizzied, twisted and spun in circles, trying to find a way into any logic I could understand while also navigating the unsteady sensation of flight. The obvious route to the vision loci was ass about. The controls for movement were buried underside, and wrapped around so much beating drive, my brain was close to combusting.

I staggered about on the silty dirt, clasping my head, trying to keep myself upright. This many minds, the velocity of their flight, the sudden swoops some of them made, I didn't stand a chance. My knees hit the ground first, buckling further forward until I was on my hands, convulsing, powerless against the violent retching.

My stomach spasmed once, and I emptied the bile in my stomach before an indomitable force of hunger racked my body. Like a fist through my heart, I felt punctured to bloody pieces. I was in, spearing their minds and down into the core of their instincts, unlimited by self-control.

"You lost your chance," Jarro growled, wrenching me to my feet and dragging me forward, but not out of my mental link.

The horde was closing in, and with the barrier down, my mind was a sponge. I sucked the force of their will inside, the magnitude of the horde's primal pulse.

I caved under the potency of their thirst, losing Jarro's hand to clutch at my temples. My mind warped and raged with a chorus of a thousand screeches, ripping my sanity apart. The closest came from me, a long, wretched wail, half full of confusion, half full of untamed desire.

"Larnie?"

I opened my eyes. Jarro stood in front of me, his hands and the smears on his clothes a bloody lure. An excruciating thirst muddied my clarity. I groaned, my eyelids fluttering closed as I thought of licking him clean. There was a small part of me, the woman, craving this. Mostly the bestial savagery belonged to the horde. In their minds, it became my desire.

I lunged for Jarro, fingers rigid in a maniacal claw, intent on gouging his throat, ripping his windpipe out and sucking it up like spaghetti. Too fast he countered my blow, spun me around with my arm pinned behind my back, his arm across my throat.

"Fight what you feel," he snarled through clenched teeth. "Fight it, Larnie, and gain control."

I screamed out my torment. Blood was all I was. All I wanted to know. Bound to Jarro's body, I bucked wild, struggled, growled my fury, only to find his hold tighten.

"Be their master," he hissed into my ear.

"Dark Mother," I wailed. "Jarro," I breathed through my anguish.

"Be. Their. Master."

I latched on to his words. Used them as the anchor to pull me through the maze of primal hunger so I could surface enough to enforce my will without losing connection.

They had arrived, the screeching now a deafening rhythm in my ears, the beat of leathery wings casting shadows across my face, the silty dust spiraling up into flight, but I had found my strength. Severing myself from the worst of their thirst, then coring into the labyrinth of their minds, I poured out my will. With as much strength as I could muster, I unleashed everything I had, felt it tap into the very essence of my being and drain me away. *You do not want to be here.*

The screeching was in my ears.

"You do not want to be here," I yelled. "Go. There is nothing for you here." I repeated it over and over until my throat burned.

Jarro's grip on my neck relaxed. I sagged into him, his arm around my middle the only thing keeping me up. All around us, the swoosh of downbeats from their powerful wings slowly diminished, the screeches too, as the horde departed. The receding noise left us in a strange vacuum of silence.

Jarro lowered to the ground, taking me with him. I collapsed in a folded heap, head dropping to my chest. My mind felt hollowed, my emotions picked clean like bones from a feast. He sat behind me, his body cradling mine so that I could feel his heart beating its rhythm against my back.

"I've never commanded so many before. I feel wrung out."

"It was an impossible task."

I huffed an exhausted laugh, then disturbed us by shuffling around to face him. "If you thought that, why did you let me do it?"

"To see if you could." He inhaled, looking over me to the distance. "So that you would know you could." He settled his onyx eyes back on me.

Cored to the bone, I couldn't muster much of a response. "Thanks. But I don't get this place. Why we're here."

"It's in your, soul, Larnie. There's a purpose here for you. It's the way the skull works."

"It's just a seeker. Isn't it? Shows you whatever you want."

"So popular lore would have everyone believe. But popular lore got one thing wrong. The skull shows you what you need." He moved away from me, stood, and then offered his hand to me.

My legs were jelly as I stood. Jarro went to head back to the skull, still laying where we'd left it, with only the top of its cranium visible after all the dust disturbance. I tugged on his hand, making him turn back to me. "What do you need?"

He turned his face from me.

"If there's nothing, you wouldn't have taken the skull."

He moved his body around to face me. "To know a person's needs is to know their weakness."

"And no one must know yours or you risk letting them in."

"No one could handle my needs." He dropped my hand and walked away.

I inhaled, leaning back to stare at the gloomy sky, feeling like something was leaving me, some small, important thing I had yet to realize was even there, or understand its meaning.

Jarro crouched in front of the skull. He cleared around it, removing the dust from the cranium. I copied him.

"Will it take us back?"

"It's what you need right now, isn't it?"

"More than anything."

"Touch it with me." He lowered his hands, palms flat.

"Wait."

His hands stilled, his eyes shifted to mine.

"At a witch's initiation into her coven, she is given a substance that sets her on her dakeu—her soul's journey. Like this trip we're on now." I glanced around me. "It was really confusing. The weirdest thing was, I'm sure I came here. Like I actually came here, even though the dakeu is supposed to only be a mental journey. And there was...a bright light and..." I sucked in the next word, then breathed it out. "You."

"I know."

"How do you know?"

"Because as you say, I was there."

"But how could you be? That was my dakeu. It was all in my head. But when I came out of it, your smell was on my clothes."

Jarro's eyes would not let mine go.

"One day our fates will collide, Larnie. When they do, I will not be so merciful."

CHAPTER 25

Shouts rushed down the stairs the moment we landed back in the dungeons of doom. Jarro was halfway up by the time someone met him on the stairs, but in the dark I could not see who it was.

"An incursion," the male voice said.

"They dared," snarled Jarro.

I was still on the dirt floor, my hand on the skull. The Cantonia. It could only mean a Cantonia attack, as I doubted nothing else would put a stick of dynamite under the Vehan.

"I want Valree down here."

"She's already left for the breach."

"Miriam, I want her secured in her room."

The *her* was me. And lucky for me, the Cantonia had created such a frenzy, Jarro disappeared up the stairs along with the other male vamp who came to deliver the news.

Wasting no time, I scooped the skull under my sweatshirt, moving it around to my back, surprising myself by not dropping it, given I felt all thumbs, no fingers. While navigating the stairs, I tucked the back of my sweatshirt into my jeans to act as a cradle for the skull. It was amazing how self-preservation could pick you out of a physical or emotional slump.

The corridor of despair was clear, but I had to reach my room before Miriam caught up with me. Given the speed of vampires, I had little time. I raced down the corridor, one hand to my back, holding the skull in place, and made it into the entrance of insanity when a lean, female vampire appeared from the corridor of the condemned. I skidded to a halt and faced her, conscious of the bulge at my back.

Her hair was pixie short and dyed brilliant red, lightening to orange at the roots.

"I was on my way upstairs." *Dark mother, you insane fool.* This wasn't going to work. A great big lump at my back. How would I explain that?

"Be swift, little lamb, before I eat you." She smirked. Like every other vampire in this place, she did not look warm or welcoming, despite being lithe and small.

I stayed where I was, because I couldn't move, couldn't walk past her and head up the stairs with the skull at my back.

"Are you stupid?" she paced toward me.

I shook my head, for once words deserting me, washed away on the current of my pulse. I wasn't afraid of her; I was afraid of her finding out.

"All witches are stupid. That's why you won't win this war."

"The war you're meaning is?"

"Jarro said you weren't from around here."

Standing directly in front of me, she was my height. In contrast to Valree, she wore low-heeled boots. Mean ass looking boots suitable for kicking in heads. "The war between us and the Cantonia. Everyone will pick sides. The only way to the survive is to make sure you're on the right side."

"The Vehan."

She smiled without a trace of warmth. "Not so stupid."

Auntie Bea and I needed to be out of here before anything like this happened. "I gather it's not starting today, else you won't be here."

"The Cantonia scum risk incursions all the time. We will deal it with swift enough."

I didn't have time.

"Then you'd better take me to my room before Jarro returns. He hates disobedience."

She got right in my face, and I swear the skull was about to fall out the back of my sweatshirt cradle.

"Listen, bitch. For some inexplicable reason, he hasn't killed you yet, but the moment he lifts his protection, you're mine. It takes a long time to die because I savor my food."

"Understood." She was wasting my time, but I couldn't go in front of her.

After cementing her threat with a solid eyeballing, she turned and stomped across the stone floor, leaving me to scuttle after her. While she wasn't looking, I kept a hand at my back, paranoid the weight of the skull would unravel the tuck of my sweatshirt.

Miriam didn't mess around climbing the stairs, and while she did it with poise and grace, I was panting halfway up and ready to walk. I just wanted to hide out in my room, so I kept myself going, for once grateful for a vamp's speed.

At my room, she turned on me. "If you come out before Jarro has returned, I may mistake you for a rat."

"Don't worry. I won't budge."

She glared down her nose at me, not moving herself, so I backed around her and fumbled with my doorknob. Hopefully she thought I acted weird because I was afraid of her and not because I had something to hide. Her eyes followed me like a cat on a mouse. I stumbled backward inside, flashing an innocent smile as I closed my door. She'd hear my galloping heartbeat and put it down to climbing the stairs at an uncomfortable rate or being in the presence of a lethal killer, not the fear of losing the one thing I'd been hunting since we arrived in Davenport after finally acquiring it.

I closed the door as gently and calmly as my nerves would allow and rested back against the door, listening for her footsteps to walk away, which I didn't hear, and probably wouldn't since vamps could move with stealth like no other. She was likely already downstairs in the blood banquet hall, gnawing on a slice of raw meat.

At my bed, I pulled the sweatshirt from my back and allowed the skull to plop out onto the covers. Sliding to the floor, I kneeled beside my bed and stared at the treasure.

This had to work. Not just work but work right. I didn't want to end up back in whatever realm that was. How had Jarro invaded my dakeu? How had I ended up there myself? Agatha, my ex coven's high priestess, had said the dakeu was all in a witch's head, not a physical journey somewhere. It had certainly felt real while I experienced it, and Jarro had been there with me. What had he said to me? That he would burn me in hell if I took what was his.

I sat back, making distance from the skull. Did he mean the skull? Would he burn me in hell because I took this from him? I rose and paced in front of my bed. If I didn't take the skull, Auntie Bea would continue to suffer, and I'd be stuck here. Jarro didn't seem any closer to letting me go, nor was he willing to tell me why he kept me. Maybe he hoped to prevent whatever future clash he prophesied between us, something he perhaps learned from being pulled into my dakeu. If that was the case, I could be a bag of bones before I saw the outside of this place.

Save myself from Jarro's revenge, or save Auntie Bea from the Apostles. I settled back on the floor beside my bed. There was only one choice. Besides, between now and the future, I may have thought of a plan to keep myself alive and unharmed.

"Okay. Do your thing."

I rubbed my hands together, then placed them on the top of the skull. "I need to get to Auntie Bea. I need to save her from the Apostles."

I closed my eyes and thought about my aunt and how much she meant to me, and the pain it gave me to think of her suffering. "Please. Do this right and send me to Auntie Bea."

At the first feeling of the tingling under my palms, my eyes flew open. The skull did its magical color swirl as it charged up. I pulled it from the bed and cradled it close to my chest, encased in my arms and curled myself into a ball, waiting for the ejection of energy that catapulted me backward last time.

When it did, I lost my grip on the skull, my arms and legs unraveling. The light blinded me. My body became a rag doll, tossed through the air.

I landed on solid ground, rolling painfully over and over, banging my knees and scraping my hands on the hard surface.

Resting on my side, I lifted my head and looked around. Judging by how high the sun sat in the sky, I would say it was midday or thereabouts. I was lying on the paving in a park. The skull sat right side up, staring at me from where it rested on the grass.

"Are you all right, my dear?" came a croaky, fragile voice from behind me.

I sat up and swiveled to look at her. "Yeah. I'm fine."

"Did you trip, or something? I was sitting over there." She slowly turned to point at the park bench a couple of meters away before turning back to me. Watching her move was like watching grass grow. "And suddenly I heard this funny grunting sound. And there you were rolling over on the pavement."

"I must've tripped on some uneven ground."

"The council really ought to do something about the poor quality of the grounds. It's a danger to anyone using the park. I find myself becoming more and more hesitant to walk here these days, with all the fallen twigs and leaves across the path."

I nodded because I had nothing else to add, and got to my feet. "I best be going. Thanks for your concern."

"I wanted to make sure you weren't hurt. Otherwise you would have to take it up with the council."

I pulled my sleeves low over my hands and scooped the skull up, cradling it in the crook of my bent elbow.

"It's not broken, is it?"

"No. It's fine. Thanks, once again." I gave her a small wave and headed down the path. There were a few more people in the park busy enjoying the weak sun, but none seemed to have noticed me dropping in from out of nowhere.

Which district was I in? If the skull had done its job, I should be in Lower Boddock. What was the street name for the Apostles church? I couldn't remember. Damn Jarro for taking my phone when he absconded with me from Lunaris. How long would it take for Jarro and his vampires to deal with the Cantonia incursion?

I stopped and spun back to see the old lady pushing her walker along in front of her as she headed back to the bench seat. I doubled back to catch up with her.

"Hey, sorry, I just wanted to ask you what district we're in. I'm not from here and have been wandering around aimlessly for a while now."

"Oh dear, you're in Sparrow Swift. I live one street back from this park. Any further, and I wouldn't be able to come here as often as I like to do."

Sparrow Swift. But I should've been in Lower Boddock. And I couldn't remember where Sparrow Swift was on the map. "How far away is Lower Boddock?"

"The next district over."

"Which way do I head from here?"

"North. That way."

"Thanks. Enjoy your sun."

"Oh, I will, dear. When you're my age, every day is a blessing, sun, rain or snow."

"Dammit," I muttered once I was out of hearing range of the old lady. I had hoped the skull would take me to Lower Boddock, to the Apostles of Eternal Night, not a whole district over. Unless... I slowed. Were they keeping Auntie Bea somewhere in Sparrow Swift? I spun as I walked, taking in my surroundings. Seeing nothing but open parkland and a playground, I stopped, my hope falling flat to the paving. I wouldn't find her like this. The skull hadn't bought me close enough.

"Dammit," I said aloud. I was closer to her, but not close enough. My only option was to head back to Dim Bazaar, let Hyun-woo know I was all right, and see if he could help me unravel the mystery of this skull. I couldn't believe it didn't work.

At the edge of the parkland, I stood on the curb, glancing both ways. If I headed north to Lower Boddock, I could ask someone if they knew of a church nearby. Munsib wouldn't know it by Church of Eternal Night, but they would know of any iconic buildings in the district. And the Apostles built big, especially back in the beginning. Many, many centuries ago, our churches were built, with a continual line of inheritance from those early days until now. This meant the Apostles had existed in that very church for hundreds of years, as had the Daughters in our own churches, the Brothers of the Redentore, the witches of the Living Light, and the Order of the Sotiria.

I couldn't spare any time heading back to Dim Bazar. Surely Jarro's distraction wouldn't be for too long. Miriam certainly didn't seem to think it was a major event. I didn't want to think what he'd do if he caught me. Likely remove his protection and throw me to the hive.

I waited for a truck to lumber past, then raced across the street, dodging a few more cars. On the other side, I chose left, as good a direction as any, walking blind without my phone to direct me to the nearest bus stop.

Lost to my next turn, I stood at the corner of the street with a horrible weight in my gut because of my predicament and twitchy itchy feelings that made me want to run. The clock was ticking. I'd made it out of Wrathridge Manor, and I was hopelessly lost in my freedom.

About ready to cry in frustration, I saw the church. It was a huge, architecturally archaic monster of stone and gargoyles, which could be nothing else but a church of a paranormal faction. I knew what districts every other paranormal faction had staked as theirs, except the Living Light. This had to be it. The dark side's only claim to a virtuous existence.

The witches of Living Light worshiped Hestia and conformed to her devout purity, swearing an oath of chastity and shunning all sinful pursuits. Though no brethren of mine, seeing the church lightened my soul a smidge. It was like I'd come out of the wilds and found a bread crumb leading me home.

I would pass it heading north, but there was no need to cross the street and get away closer. While there was no guardian to shred me to pieces should I choose to enter, I doubted their welcome would be warm. The Daughters and the Living Light weren't on the best of terms.

A third of the way down the street, I got a tingling warning that something was off, that I was being watched. Keeping my pace, I glanced over my shoulder at an empty street. No way would Jarro hang in the shadows. Could the Apostles really have found me that fast?

The street was deserted, except for a few passing cars. I scanned the driveways of the houses, the shadowy areas, the shrubs—anywhere someone could hide. Not seeing anything, I nursed the skull closer and quickened my pace when a guy moved out from behind the parked truck in front of me to stand menacingly across the path.

He was mean-looking enough to be an Apostle, dressed in the typical garb, including the heavy-duty steel-capped boots. His shiny scalp glistened in the sunlight, but it was the scar on the left side of his face that had me sucking in a breath.

"Let me lighten your burden," he said with an attempt at a seductive swagger as he moved toward me.

"It's a burden I am happy to carry, demon."

It was the scar that gave him away. Their master branded his demons in hell as proof of their loyalty, an ugly mark in the messy shape of a handprint, because it was Lucifer's hand that gave the burn. Those with scars on their left were Lucifer's tightest, his most loyal, his right-hand men.

He stopped, legs wide in that classic alpha male stance. "Then we have ourselves a problem."

"There's no problem my end, which means it's yours and has nothing to do with me." I collapsed the binds and flung my mind free, seeking every creature in the area. A mass onslaught should buy me time.

"Where's your friends, sister?" He made a show of looking around him.

"Biding their time."

The skull lured him. Whatever curse he'd used to follow its movement was no doubt triggered the moment I crossed over the hive boundary.

My search snagged on many recruits. Thanks to my time in that abandoned realm, and Jarro's encouragement, I knew I could harness a flock. What better than a murder of crows. They were intelligent birds and fast carnivores, with a wicked point on their beaks for peeking. After the hard fight with the lizard-bird creatures in the abandoned realm, I slipped right into each of their minds with a mass invasion.

The demon chuckled to himself. "You witches are all the same." Dropping the false humor in seconds, he said, "I hate a lippy bitch. They get right under my skin."

"Bad for you, but it makes no difference to me." Then I toppled to the side as the murder took flight and vertigoed my brain, tripped on the lip between the grass and paving and hit the ground elbow first.

The demon laughed until the skull rolled from my grasp. I heard the smacking of his boots as he pounded toward me along the paving, intent on snatching the skull. I rolled toward it, scooped it in, enfolded it close and curled into a fetal position just as he landed on top of me.

A kick to my back and I cried, spasmed out of my hold enough for the skull to fall free. The demon lunged for the skull. At the same time, I snatched it up, and we ended up in a tug of war.

"Back off," came the harsh cry from behind us both.

The demon's hold lessened. He recoiled.

"You're gonna wish you weren't on this street," the demon said.

I twisted, looking up at the munsib facing off with the demon. Unfortunately for the munsib, he had no idea who he'd just picked a fight with. He held a crowbar in his hand, raised to shoulder height, and was edging away from the demon.

"I need a warmup before I deal with bitch."

"I've called the cops. If you don't want trouble with them, I suggest you leave."

"If you don't want trouble with them," the demon mimicked in a childish voice. "You don't know what trouble means."

I went to sit up, but the flight of the crows as they skimmed the treeline at high speed wavered my head once more. Steeling my determination, I pushed to my feet. "You know what? I think you should just go back to hell. That's the only place you're welcome."

The demon spun to face me, his lips pulling back in a snarl.

"Get out of here," I yelled to the guy who'd been nice enough to stop for me.

"Do as the bitch says." The demon spoke over his shoulder, while keeping his attention on me. "If you have any self-preservation, that is."

Seemingly out of nowhere, the murder descended in a chaotic jumble, screeching and flapping. I steered their focus to the bald scalp of the demon. Also his eyes.

Behind the black mass the munsib backed up, eyes bulging wide enough they'd pop out of his head at any moment. And I wasn't waiting around for him to get moving, nor was I waiting for the demon to extract himself from the feathered frenzy.

Clutching the skull close, I erupted out onto the street, heading for the church. My legs were a spastic mess with my mind all fuzzed up with swooping birds. The ground swayed beneath me as I twisted and turned, dived and climbed and yet my feet were pounding the road. My stomach felt like it was being inverted. Good thing I'd missed breakfast in favor of hunting down the skull, but that didn't stop the bile from burning up my throat. I staggered forward, bent double and hit the asphalt the moment the meagre contents of my stomach dribbled to the ground.

Adrenaline, blessed savior. It gave me the strength to pull myself up to my wobbly feet and keep going. It wasn't the adrenaline alone. My balance returned. The frenetic noise behind me had lessened. *Sorry crows, but you were my only hope.* The demon was winning, through.

A singe of hot lava swiped me across the left shoulder and sent me airborne for seconds until I crashed stomach first onto the road. The impact snapped my head back, and the skull punched into my stomach. I cried in agony. I was almost to the other side of the road. Not much further, and I would've made it.

I panted through the throb of the burn on my shoulder as hard-soled shoes smacked their way across the asphalt. I gritted my teeth, ignoring the spasms in my side, and rolled to face the demon.

"Looks like it's just you and me, bitch."

With no smart words left in me, I pushed up to sit, not wanting to face him on my back. I could try again and harness the plethora of animals in the vicinity, but I'd be throwing innocent creatures to their slaughter, and none could reach me in time. I'd rescued myself from one catastrophic situation, only to fall into another.

"You wanna play some more games? 'Cause I'm just getting started."

I ducked my head, about to close my eyes in defeat, wanting to wipe this moment out, but instead I stared at the skull. The useless, stupid skull that wasn't shimmering or turning galactic in my bare hands, my bare hands that had sent Jarro and me to the abandoned realm and brought me here. At my greatest time of need it remained devoid of magic.

"I have a message for your master."

I straightened at the sound of that voice.

Jarro stood on the other side of the road, looking like he was out for an afternoon stroll, smart in black from neck to shoe, not a scratch or smear of blood to show he'd hurried over from a fight with the Cantonia. Maybe he'd stopped to shower before chasing me down.

The demon turned to stone, stayed facing me. His face went neutral as he wove his hands in circles around each other, gathering power for a strike. The warning was on the tip of my tongue, but the demon beat me to it, spinning as he raised his left arm to strike.

I rolled to my front, powered up from the ground and ran. Feeling the heat behind me, hearing the cracks and fizzles, understanding the awesome fight, I pounded my limbs so hard they felt ready to jackhammer into the ground. The agony in my side from the burn, the knee bangs, hip bumps and the scraps. My might, adrenaline and instinct to survive gave me the gift to ignore all the aches. I ran with lungs burning, breaths only wheezes. I ran with one arm machining along beside me, legs pistoning up and down.

I leaped for the steps, missed my timing, staggered, stayed partway on my feet to the top. I flew off the top step and smashed into the front door of the Church of Living Light because it wouldn't open. Bastards.

I banged on the wood so hard, I practically dislocated my wrist. "Open up," I screeched. "Please." I begged. My wrist ached. The vibration moved up my arm. Soon it would be in my head. I banged and pleaded, and the door stayed closed.

I looked over my shoulder to see Jarro at the bottom of the steps, standing there like he was waiting for a date. His hair wasn't even ruffled. No sign of the remains of the demon.

"How is this to play out, Larnie?" His voice was calm, sultry low, sharp and lethal as an icepick.

I turned, back pressed flat to the door. "You know why I did this."

"Of course. Family is important."

"Glad you understand."

"I warned you I would show no mercy."

"Our fates haven't collided. They're sliding alongside each other. Just give me this, please. This one moment to save my aunt. You'll get the stupid thing back. You know you will."

"That's not the point."

"What is?"

"I don't like being betrayed."

"How can a prisoner betray someone? I made no deal. You forced me into the hive." My voice had risen, anger giving it a depth I never thought I'd find in a moment like this.

As a response, he gave me one of his death stares, an eyeball lock that was impossible to break from. Statued like marble, the twitch in his left jaw muscle was the giveaway of his fury.

In a blur, he struck. He was nothing but a vision of black, and I was falling backward. In an instant, I crashed onto my back and slid across the floor, the skull clattering noisily beside me.

I looked between my legs to see Jarro standing just outside the entrance to the church door while I lay on the patterned marble floor of the narthex. I scrambled backward as I gathered myself, but he remained where he was, barred entrance by the wards of purity. No person with evil intent could cross.

It was like he'd turned to stone. Nothing about him moved, except his rage, a palpable torrent scorching in his eyes, emanating as a burn so great I felt sure it would cinder me to ash if the ward didn't hold in place.

"You've made me your enemy." A harsh tone said with finality. There was no going back from this moment. For Auntie Bea it was a decision I had to make.

"Wasn't I already your enemy?"

"Not the way you are now." He crouched down to be at my level, since I was still sitting on my ass. "Remember what I said to you during your dakeu?"

"Barely. I can't believe you remember."

"You remember, Larnie. Tell me what I said."

"That you would see me burn in hell for eternity if I took what was yours. The skull was up for grabs. You stole it off of Preston. And now I've stolen it off of you. The way I see it, whoever has it in their hands owns it."

He rose slowly to stand. We ended up in a frozen moment full of silence, pulsing with a deafening chorus of lethal menace. Jarro's death stares were a weapon all of their own, and I remained on the floor like a wounded moth suffering the feel of it, along with the throbs and stings of all my other injuries.

"I'm coming for you, Larnie. Nothing you do will stop me." Threat delivered, he vanished, taking with him the clamp on my lungs, allowing me to finally suck in a breath.

CHAPTER 26

Blue, red, and yellow light glistened across the pews and along the patterned marble floor of the church, like jewels. On both sides of the aisle, the ornate stained glass windows rose like colored crystals in the morning light. The imagery stamped into the glass wove a story of sacrifice and worship to the goddess Hestia in all her pious glory.

Auntie Bea would often scoff at the sufferers of Hestia, as she called them. In her eyes, they were a milder form of crazy than the nephilim, with all their obsessive punishment for the vices they desired. Despite rarely caving to their vices, the sufferers of Hestia still saw fit to punish themselves for their unrighteous thoughts, because a pure soul came not from action alone but stemmed from deep within. I was a sinner, tainting their aisles with my tarnished blood dripping from the hem of my sweatshirt onto the stone floor where I sat.

One thing I would have to say about the Church of Living Light, the interior looked more welcoming than the Dark Mother's church—lighter—and the smells were different too. The incense and herbs they burned were unfamiliar to me.

On hearing a heavy thunk, like a door closing in the direction of the west transept, I grabbed the skull and staggered to my feet. My limbs were cooling and stiffening, not to mention the wound on my shoulder would need some attention. I hobbled forward into the nave, slid down to the closest pew and waited for whoever had arrived to find me.

The young woman was dressed in white. Not unusual. The initiates were often made to dress in the same garb as the nuns of the christian faith to remind them of the necessity for purity. Once fully accepted into the church and their apprentice years served, did they get the choice to dress in more causal modern clothes, nothing too alluring though, not as the dutiful daughters of the goddess Hestia.

The Church of Living Light allowed its followers two choices. They could deepen their worship to goddess Hestia and transcend to the Order of Sanakara, a devout, puritanical order within the church, which required austerity in its strictest measure, or they could marry and produce Living Light progeny. The former didn't sound so crash hot, but the Order of Sanakara tapped into the essence of the goddess Hestia and manifested some nifty powers, with no blood sacrifices.

The young woman glided down the aisle toward me in her white robes, and I shoved the skull up under my sweatshirt for safe keeping. She had a beautiful heart-shaped face framed by all the restrictive starched white material that kept her hair and neck hidden. I bet she ripped that off the moment she was out of sight.

I had little to do with the coven that worshiped Hestia or its Church, so I knew little of their practices. I had rarely run into these ghost women in their all white.

There was more noise from the transept, more footsteps, many of them, smacking their boots on the marble as they rushed toward where I sat.

Six of them, wearing black pants, a polo neck sweatshirt, and black garb over their heads to cover everything but their faces. By the way they pounded toward us, jogging in formation, I could only imagine these were women from the order.

Three continued on past, heading for the nave, the other three sliding to a halt in front of me, barreling the ghost woman out the way.

"You are not welcome here," barked a stern-faced woman with pencil eyebrows and super thin lips. She was slight but charged with energy. You only needed to glance at her bunched fists to know she was tipped to a fight.

"I'm seeking sanctuary."

"Not in our church, daughter of darkness."

"You have brought a great evil to our church. You must leave now," said another member of the remaining three. She was wide hipped with powerful looking legs, which would likely keep her jogging long after everyone else collapsed in exhaustion.

"But she's injured," said the ghost woman, in a soft pious voice. She knew her place amongst the Order.

"That is not our problem," replied the strong-looking woman.

"Please, just let me get cleaned up, then I'll go."

"I can't see anything," yelled one of the Order who'd skipped past us and headed for the entrance, no doubt to see what evil still lurked. "Neither can I sense any filth lingering outside."

Good to know. I had thought Jarro would hang around until the church ejected me, which they would do, eventually. No way would the Living Light allow such a heathen as me to sully their halls.

"There is no reason for her to stay. She can seek refuge with her own kind," the stern one replied.

"But the mother permitted her entry," said the ghost woman.

Thank the dark mother for that; although I was best not even thinking her name in a house of light. I'd feared the church would shut me out. Rushing here had been a desperate plan. Thankfully, one that worked.

Jarro had said the skull gave you want you needed, not wanted. Was that why it had brought me here? Because there was no way I would've got this far without the sanctuary of goodness to counter the evil. Our own church was not so fortified against those that peddled in dark deeds. Light countered dark so much easier than any factions that peddled in dark deeds. Lucky for me, their light mother did not see me as a threat. Understandably, given few saw me as a threat.

"Please, let me tend to her wounds first before she leaves."

"You know we do not involve ourselves in faction rivalries," the stern one of the three said.

The ghost woman bowed her head. "You're right, sister, but cleaning her up is the righteous thing to do."

The three order exchanged looks full of conversation neither myself nor the ghost woman understood. Knowing little about the order except the fact they existed meant they could actually be talking to each other telepathically, for all I knew.

"Since the danger has passed, and the mother bid her entrance, we shall let you tend her wounds. But once you have done so, she is to leave before she brings a greater force down on our heads," said the strong looking one.

"Have no fear of that. I'm not that exciting to the rest of the factions."

The strong woman stepped forth. "Then why is a vampire hunting you?"

"Not just any vampire," said the third of the group standing in front of me. The plain Jane of the three. She wore her head coverings tight, so it bunched her cheeks. Was that a form of punishment to help keep her thoughts pure? "The King."

"How do you know?"

He'd not lingered, so how did they know it was him? But the three of them acted like I wasn't there.

"Tend to her wounds, Lottie, then she must go," the stern woman who had spoken first said to the initiate.

Two of the three who'd raced past us for the entrance returned, the third perhaps keeping further watch.

"We must remain vigilante. I fear the king of vampires has not given up so lightly," said the plain Jane.

The five left Lottie and me alone, marching back toward the transept and into their church warren to convene, no doubt, with further order members and perhaps the high priestess herself. Though why she did not come in person I couldn't say.

"Thanks for that. I don't like my chances out there at the moment." I grimaced, shifting myself to get more comfortable. Sitting here, listening to the order determine my fate had seized my muscles.

"We need to get these clothes off of you so I may have a better look."

She offered me her hand, which I gratefully took. Cradling the skull under my sweatshirt with one hand like a pregnant lady, I slipped my other arm over her shoulder as she directed. Despite being slight, she seemed willing to shoulder most of the burden of my weight. I didn't want to appear an invalid, but my hip was throbbing out of sync with the rest of me.

"Why is the vampire king after you?"

"He's foul-tempered and can't take a joke."

"I don't understand. You know him?"

"Little, thank the dark mother...oh sorry."

"That's all right. I accept your faith."

"Actually, it's not so much a faith as being stuck with it."

She did a small intake of breath. "You shouldn't say such things."

"I'm grateful to our Dark Mother for the boons she gives upon those willing to offer a blood sacrifice, but she's not done a heck of a lot for me."

"But she protects you, provides for you, as does your coven."

"My Auntie Bea and I have been providing for ourselves a long time with no of the coven, or blessed be to our Dark Mother, her either."

"But this is terrible. You are adrift from your coven."

"Kicked out."

She stopped, and since she propped me up, stopped me as well. "What did you do?"

"Nothing." Hopefully she wasn't regretting offering her help. "We did nothing, but we also couldn't give them anything."

"You are a rummy?"

"Not me."

"It is honorable of you to stand by your aunt."

"She's more important than some coven or church."

"How have you survived all this time without their protection?"

"It's not so hard, once you know how. As long as you keep your business to yourself and keep out of everyone's way. Coming to Davenport was our biggest mistake."

"Oh, you're not from here?"

"Been here less than two weeks. And look at me." I shook my head. Four years, we'd been doing just fine. Two weeks in this hell-hole and Auntie Bea's a prisoner, and I had just made an enemy out of a lethal predator.

"How can you have made such a powerful enemy in under two weeks?"

"I'm talented."

She huffed. "Or not talented enough."

By now we'd made it to the transept door. Lottie eased out from under my arm to open the door.

"I think I can take it from here. Things are warming up again."

"Come this way," she said, ducking in behind me and steering me off to the left. "The order occupy that area." She waved her hand down the creepy dim passage to the right. "The initiates are down this way."

"How long have you been an initiate?"

"Seven months."

"So you're eighteen?"

"Coming on nineteen in two months."

"I don't know a lot about the Living Light, for obvious reasons." I shrugged as a pseudo-apology for my ignorance. "But what will be your choice when the time comes?"

"The order for sure."

She walked slowly beside me as I tried my best to keep a good pace.

"You'd give up all vices." Why did I think of Jarro when I asked that question? And why did my traitorous thoughts flash to the party night, his lips on mine, even if for the briefest moment and for the merest touch? If only my body wasn't feeling weakened at the thought of him. He stated we were now enemies, he wasn't interested in women outside the hive and yet if he appeared before me right now and kissed me, I wouldn't push him away.

"I'd give up my life to serve."

It took me moments to digest that. I had never believed in many things, not enough to give up such an important part of living. "Good on you. I envy your conviction."

"You as well. I know few witches who would abandon it all to stand by a rummy. I admire you for that. One of our initiates, Heidi—her sister was a rummy. Her mom and dad abandoned her. Everyone did, the coven included. Last Heidi heard, the Apostles picked her up, and she's not been heard from since. Heidi won't speak about it. She's ashamed. I think she should be sad. It wasn't her sister's fault. Even her parents have not tried to rescue her or ensure she's all right, which I doubt. If it had been my sister, I would have done something to help her. No one deserves a fate as a prisoner of the Apostles. In here."

She led me into a stale smelling dark room. Lottie flicked a switch, and a dim glow from a single bulb overhead cast a gentle light on the room. "This is your room?" It was small and austere. She'd pushed the single bed against the cold stone wall. A small metal table beside the bed was the only other sign someone occupied the room. Resting on that an ancient-looking grimoire.

"It's our family heritage," Lottie said, following my gaze. "I bought you here as I thought you'd be more comfortable. You know, since you need to remove your shirt."

"Thanks, but it doesn't bother me."

"I'll go get supplies. You can wait here. And we should probably be quick. I somehow don't feel the order will tolerate your presence for long."

"Whatever you can do would be great."

She departed on her slippered feet. The moment I was alone, I eased over to the grimoire, slid it off her side table and ran my hands over the carvings on the surface. It had been a long time since I'd handled a proper grimoire, a witch's bible and survival guide. I missed the feeling, missed the connection with something that reminded me of my heritage, what my mother had passed down to me, which was not a lot.

Agatha assured me there was more within in that had yet to manifest. That the gift of goddess Diana did not appear to a rummy. The Dark Mother blessed only a chosen few with such a gift. She made out like the gift was special. I was special. But nothing else happened. I had tried to excel at my studies, but in the end, I hid the fact I was useless at remembering any of the incantations or spell words to enact any magic. And even with a grimoire to read verbatim during casting work, I couldn't get much to work beyond parlor tricks. Maybe that mysterious man, my father, had been a munsib, diluting my power to insignificance. But if so, why would mom hide Elka and me? Why would she be afraid of him?

Hearing Lottie's return, I slipped the book back on her side table. In my haste made a mess of it and dropped the thing on the floor. A witch's personal grimoire, a family heirloom, was a private matter not to be shared.

Lottie entered as the grimoire ended up face down, pages bent on the stone floor.

"I'm sorry," I dived for it. "It's..." I turned it over to see two pages had folded back on themselves. At the same time, the skull, tucked under my sweatshirt all this time, rolled out onto the stone floor. Forgetting the grimoire, I dived for the skull and swept it close.

"What is that?" The book forgotten in the new discovery.

"Um... just something." Did she not know about the skull? Perhaps not, if she was an initiate of eight months. I'd been a witch for four years and hadn't known about the skull.

"Does it belong to the vampires?"

"No, it doesn't. It belongs to no one, but everyone wants it."

"Then it must be powerful. Is this the cause of your troubles?" She replaced her grimoire on her night table.

She set the bowl of water she had returned with on the bed beside me, pulling bandages and whatnot out of the pockets at the front of her formless white outfit and spilling them on the bed as well.

"It's the biggest headache of my life and also the only thing that will save my aunt."

"What is wrong with your aunt?"

"The Apostles have her."

She came around to the other side of me to avoid the bowl of water and sat. "That is terrible. You are a truly wonderful person."

I had to search her wide blue eyes for sarcasm since it had been so long since I had met anyone sincere in their praise. "Stupid maybe."

"No, you faced the vampire king to save your aunt."

"I wouldn't say faced him exactly. It's not like we went head-to-head. I snuck this out of his keeping while he was distracted."

Her eyes widened further. "But that would mean you were at their hive. How did you survive?"

"Dumb luck, the skull, and you guys. But I don't like my chances, once your order kick me out."

"I will speak to them. They will surely be lenient once they know the truth."

"Forget it. I know how these church hierarchies work. There's nothing soft about them."

I could see in the way she slumped and dropped her gaze from me, that she knew I spoke the truth. She stood and came around to the bowl of water. "Let me tend to your wounds."

I would say she was resigned to my fate, but there was something about her expression that made me think otherwise. The hard crease of her brow, the press of her lips—she was thinking hard.

I slid the sweatshirt over my head and then my t-shirt, so I sat in my bra. Lottie made every effort to keep her eyes averted from my semi-nakedness as she turned with her wet cloth. "This is nasty."

"Demon."

"Blessed mother, you faced a demon."

"I would be a puddle of burned flesh if Jarro had not arrived in time."

"Who is Jarro?"

I hesitated. Telling her about Jarro, even if it was to say his name in reference to what he was, made me feel awkward with her being so pious and virginal and all my scandalous thoughts. And the party. "The king of vampires."

"You call him by name?"

"I could've said asshole, but the paranormal world is so full of those you'd get confused." I winced, sucking in a breath as Lottie dabbed at my wound. "He turned up and dealt with the demon before the demon could finish me. And then, well, I ended up on your door."

"All of this for that skull."

I winced again.

"Sorry, but if you want it clean."

"I've suffered worse." I hadn't, but it helped to pretend.

I bit my bottom lip but stayed silent as she worked on my wound. Finally she'd finished cleaning and wrapped me in bandages.

"Thanks."

She didn't respond, instead placed the bowl of bloody water on the floor and sat next to me, resting her hands in her lap, staring at the floor. "I have an idea. It may not work, but I'm willing to try."

"Is this idea going to get you in trouble with your order?"

"I'm not sure they would care." She pulled her grimoire into her lap. "There is something in here that may be of help. It's not fool-proof, and I can't guarantee the longevity of it, but it may be enough to protect you from the vampires for a while, possibly, once you're outside our wards. It's a concealment spell."

"Okay." It didn't sound like much, but if I could slip away from under their noses, that would be something, at least until I rescued Auntie Bea. From there, I wasn't sure what I would do. "Sure. Anything is better than nothing."

"I'm just an initiate, so don't expect much. And I think to ensure it works we will need to use the altar chalice and call upon our splendid mother for divine guidance."

"Whatever, sounds good."

Lottie flicked through the pages of her grimoire until she landed on what she was after. "Here." She patted the page she wanted. "I'll take you back to the transept entrance. You best wait at the altar, and I'll get the other things we'll need. But we must hurry. The order will come looking for you soon."

I put my clothes back on, scooped the skull up under my sweat-shirt and tucked it in at the front to create another cradle for it. Standing hurt, but with the possibility of escaping Jarro's notice, I'd found the will to overcome the pain, and move.

Lottie returned me to the door of the transept, bid me farewell, and disappeared off toward the direction of the order's quarters. I slipped back into the church and walked stiffly toward the altar at the front of the church. Behind the stone altar, risen on its dais, loomed the statue of the rather plain looking Hestia, in her flowing robes with her head demurely covered.

I headed for the dais and the chalice, not sure what part the chalice played in their rituals, since they didn't do blood offerings. But given its position, it meant something important.

I spun at the sound of the door opening, half expecting some of the order to reappear, but it was Lottie. She hurried on her quiet slippered feet toward the altar, carrying a thin flask tucked to her chest.

"What is that?" I asked once she reached me.

"Something Manuela mixed up for another purpose, but we'll use a bit now. It won't take much, so I'm sure she won't notice." She stepped up onto the dais and stood beside me, placing the flask down on the alter, her hands flat either side of it. "The chalice is the mortal womb of our goddess, her fertility, that comes to us in the form of her power. When we evoke sacred spells, or anything that requires more magic than a witch can call, we use the chalice. You are to drink the herbal mix in the flask from the chalice, then recite the words I give you. But I warn you, this may not work. Hestia doesn't bestow her favor always. And I am not worthy of evoking her will. That's something only the order can do. All we can do is try."

"Anything's better than the chance I have at the moment."

She gave me a small smile that held little hope. "Are you ready?"

"I've got nothing to lose."

Lottie poured a small amount of the contents of the flask into the chalice. I waited, expecting a hiss or some other evidence there was magic at work, but the liquid sat on the bottom like pea soup. "Swirl it around and then drink it down. Once drunk, you must recite these words. You see me not, for I am but a shadow."

"That's it?"

"I think so. At least that's all I've seen the order do. They do have more magic than me."

"We'll work with what we have." I put the skull down on the alter, took the chalice from Lottie and swirled the liquid around at the bottom. I gave it a sniff, but it was neutral in smell, making it more tolerable to drink. The outer rim was rough on my lips from the fine detail etched into the gold cup. The liquid had a thick consistency, coating the top of my tongue and the inside of my mouth like syrup, and sludged down my throat. Much like its smell, I tasted nothing. I tipped the chalice up to ensure I took every drop, since Lottie wasn't overly confident about the results. Once done, I set the chalice down. "You see me not, for I am but a shadow."

I turned to Lottie, still standing beside me.

"Maybe you should say it again. Perhaps you could true enthusing it with greater intention."

I nodded, breathed in. "You see me not, for I am but a shadow."

"Okay. Close your eyes this time and meditate on the words as you say them."

"You see me not, I am the shadows."

"No. You said it wrong. For I am but a shadow."

"Do you think it matters?"

"Spell-casting needs to be exact. You can't just change what you say randomly as you see fit." She spoke with emotion, balling her fists. Bizarrely, this seemed to mean something to her. Or maybe she was a perfectionist in her magick work.

"Should I say it again?"

"It wouldn't hurt, but make sure you say it proper this time."

I opened my mouth, about to begin, when the door to the transept burst open. Both Lottie and I spun to see the order spilling out like ants. At that exact moment, a loud boom sounded outside, making the stained glass windows rattle and the church's foundations shake.

CHAPTER 27

The order scattered throughout the church, down the nave, and into the aisles, taking up positions all around.

"What's happening?" Why did I ask, when I knew? The battle-ready way the order moved themselves into position? The church of Living Light was under attack. No two guesses from who.

In the order's wake, a short, broad woman strode through the door transept to the crossing. She wore the same outfit of the order, but around her neckline, her face, and on her cuffs, a gold band in the hems denoted her ranking amongst them as the high priestess, I would guess. Her face was a mask of solemnity and power. "Double the wards." Her voice echoed through the church and off the pillars lining the nave.

Another mighty noise slammed into the invisible wards on the left side of the church, following a colorful display of light works from the clash of energies.

"We need extra support on the left flank," the high priestess yelled, waving her hand to three order woman to join their sisters bearing the brunt of the attack. While coordinating the effort, she spied Lottie and I still standing at the altar, her hand slowing its motion as her eyes settled on me.

"You," she barked.

She had every right to be angry. This was because of me.

The next attack felt more brutal than the last, rattling the windows with such violence I expected them to break. Jarro, with whatever magical ability he possessed, that a vampire should not possess—at least no vampire I'd heard of—tested the might of the order. With so many of them holding the wards, he would surely not break through.

The high priestess marched toward us, her face a knot of fury. "Look what you have brought upon us," she yelled before she reached us.

"I'm sorry. I didn't think it would be so special to him."

"It? What are you talking about?"

The skull rested on the alter behind me. If I showed her, she would insist on handing it over to save her church, and I'd be out the door as well. It was wrong to expect them to do anything else. I was not one of them. In fact, it was common knowledge within my ex-coven that the Living Light hated us, believed we had spawned from the darkest reaches of the realms beyond; along with every other paranormal, so we never took it personally.

A blistering noise stole the first word out of my mouth, blew the left-hand-side windows of the church inward, raining blue, red, and yellow like a lethal shower onto the order standing below. Outside, a wave of colored energy warped and rippled trough the air as a residual of the mighty energetic clash. Four of the order collapsed to their hands and knees. Others rushed to their aid.

"To the breach," the high priestess boomed.

As she did, streaks of black pierced through the shattered windows, forking down like lightning onto the patterned marble of the church nave. No longer moving, they revealed themselves as people. It was their speed that had turned them into a blur.

The Vehan. Jarro had returned with his hive.

The order attacked, casting spells which sent the pews into the air like a tornado wind. But the hive was fast, impossibly fast, moving from the spot before the order had released the spell from their hold. The spells spiraled uselessly into the pews, sending them skyward, bursting them to flames or petrifying them where they sat.

Chaos tore through the church. A cacophony of shouts, yells of pain, grunts of exertion, the clashing and splintering of everything that was not welded to the church floor.

"We will not suffer because of you." The high priestess grabbed my arm, but I shook free and reached for the skull. After everything, no point in abandoning it.

I hugged it close and turned back to the high priestess. "I'm sorry for everything."

Behind the high priestess, the front doors to the church blew open with such violence they ripped from their hinges and cartwheeled up the aisle to crash into the already splintered rubble of pews.

Jarro stood in the entrance, a dark silhouette backlit by the miserable day outside. His entrance stilled the room. Everyone turned as he strode forward, taking his time through the narthex and up the nave, walking around or over the mess created by the fight. "I want what is mine."

"You dare enter our sacred house," the high priestess boomed.

"By harboring her here, you bought this upon yourselves."

My stomach sunk through to my feet. All of this devastation because of what I had done.

"Attacking us is a violation, an act of war. The ripple effect through the city will have devastating consequences."

"Do you think I care?"

As sexy as the vamp was, he was such an arrogant ass. Did he really think his hive could withstand all the paranormal factions? Did he even care what would be left of the city and the people in it?

"You know as well as I do, the city has been heading for disaster for some time now," he said.

"And you would hasten its end."

"All I ask is the return of what is mine."

I wanted to speak out and say I was not his, but he was likely meaning the skull, and I was the added bonus for some hive like fun.

"Take her. We don't want her."

Jarro continued to stare at the high priestess, ignoring me. He'd not glanced at me the whole time. Then he gestured with his hands as if to say well and looked around at his fellow hive members. What was he doing?

The high priestess frowned, seeming as confused as me. "I said she's yours."

"I know she's here somewhere. I can smell her scent. Bring her out."

Oh, my dark mother. I looked to Lottie. She mouthed something back at me, but I sucked at lip reading. The spell had worked, sort of. Jarro could not see me, only the order could.

"What do you mean? She's—"

"Please." Lottie rushed forth. "I will get her."

"Lottie, what are you talking about?"

"Let me, Mistress of Light." She bowed to the high priestess. "I will bring her here."

She hurried toward me, begging with her eyes for the high priestess to stay quiet about the fact I stood to the side of her.

A soft hissing from behind me interrupted us all. I turned my head to see the chalice glowing golden.

Forgetting everything, the high priestess walked toward it. She splayed her hands wide as if in readiness to receive some divine help. "Oh mother, deliver your daughters from this scourge of evil," she begged, bowing herself forward in humble obedience.

The chalice's glow intensified, so surreally bright I was sure the thing would melt to liquid gold. "Our mother hears our cries. She has come to our aid," the high priestess breathed, straightening. She spun, raising her arms into the air. "Feel our mother's wrath," she yelled with exaltation.

On cue, a light burst forth from the chalice, streaming up into the ribbed ceiling of the church, funneling up like a great stream of water. Lottie and I ducked and moved away at the suddenness of it, and the noise. It was like standing beside a massive waterfall.

The church fall silent, except for the noise of the light. The order went down on their knees, bowing their heads in reverence to their goddess.

The light continued to spill forth, turning the ceiling into a glowing ball, the light penetrating through and out, up into the sky.

From the light burst a shield of flames, billowing out of the chalice, crackling and sparking with a rush of hot wind that blew outward to sweep us all backward. The high priestess staggered, threatening to topple, her face a glow of dancing light. Lottie stumbled into me, pushing us both onto the marbled floor. I lost the skull on impact. It didn't roll far, so I leaned over and scooped it up again.

The fury of flames burned wild and bright. I shielded my eyes, my face feeling peeled of skin. The noise became deafening, like a battering of hurricane-strength wind, barreling across the land and destroying everything in its path.

Unable to bear it, I was about to turn my back on the awesome might of energy, when I saw the flames spiral into a whip, thrash like a snake, and arc up to the ceiling before funneling downward, streaming in a deadly golden burning channel straight toward me, straight into me.

I fell backward onto the marble, pummeled by the energy. The light and flames became me, the heat so intense I felt sure I was melting. I could do nothing but suffer under the weight, the fear. Was this my end? A wailing penetrated through the onslaught to fill my ears, haunting, heart wrenching, a sound drenched in agony. It was me, my voice burning the back of my throat raw.

Just when I thought I would die, it stopped. The flames, the light, the noise, ceased in an instant. I collapsed on my side, a smoldering, exhausted mess, curling into a ball, cradling my head in my elbows. My throat felt like I'd rubbed it bare with sandpaper.

How had I made it through alive?

It took me a moment to hear the noises outside my cocoon of wounds. When I felt sure I was still in one piece and not a puddle of bones and flesh on the floor, I released my head from its elbow cradle to confirm what I heard. The hustle and bustle of street noises. I got halfway upright when the wound from the demon on my shoulder intensified its reminder that I needed to go gently. A couple of deep, steadying breaths, and I slowly stood, using the brick wall behind me as an aid, favoring my wounded arm.

I was in an alley, a dirty stinking alley full of refuse. Some moldy discarded food stuck to my left arm. I flicked it off as best I could, then left the trash heap and headed to the mouth of the alley.

The place was alive with people, hawkers, carts of street food, and shoppers. Across from where I stood was Hyun-woo's Korean store and takeout restaurant. I sagged back against the wall of the shop. What the hell? Then remembering the skull, I spun back to where I'd lain to see nothing but piles of cardboard, paper, food scraps and whatever else lay underneath. The skull was gone. And I was back in Dim Bazaar.

I rubbed my face as if the act would wipe this reality away and give me back my horrible, doomed reality I had just left behind. The skull had brought me here. At my most desperate moment, it had returned me to where it all began. But where had it gone?

I pressed my palms into my stomach. I don't know what led me to do that. Nor do I know what made me peel up my sweatshirt and the shirt underneath. Some sixth sense, some weird knowing in my subconscious. Whatever it was, I did it and peered down at my exposed skin. Stamped like a smudged, faded, inky mark was the rough tattoo of a skull.

I dropped my clothes back down like they were soaked in poison, pressed back against the wall, and cupped my hands to my mouth. Oh, dark mother, what has happened? "No," I gasped, then cupped my mouth again. I've... I've become the skull. I pushed off the wall, paced, fisted the hairs on my scalp, then ran them down to cover my mouth in disbelief once more.

"I am the skull."

———

The skull is a curse
There may be one person who can save me from it
But he's branded me his greatest enemy

Deviant's Curse

Sit tight, dear readers, for this is not the end of this book.

There was so much mention of Laz's dakeu that I felt I needed to write about it. Keep flipping the pages for a novelette, Eternity Burn, set four years prior to the start of Sinner's Game.

About writing this book:

Most of my stories usually start with the vision of a scene. The auction house was that scene. But it played out differently in my head to how it ended up on the page.

I outlined the book from start to finish, then when I felt happy with what I'd done, began to write. However, from the beginning, the story did not play nice. I'd not planned for certain events to happen nor certain people to appear.

Hyun-woo was one. All of a sudden I found myself writing about a character who was never meant to be there, and I knew nothing about him. But I welcomed him onboard and went along with his story. And now I have to be honest. I don't yet know where he's going. In some respects that's a little scary as I want to do him justice.

I have the same problem with Elka. She was always meant to be

Laz's sister, but from the moment she walked into that bathroom she was someone entirely different from the Elka I had planned.

I now have two characters whose arcs I'm in the dark about. Will they both stay good, or will one or both turn bad?

BONUS CONTENT

Those on my newsletter will receive two maps of places integral to Sinner's Game: Wrathridge Manor and Davenport. If you'd love to get your hands on those, then click this link to join my newsletter. There are also plenty more goodies waiting, such as free novels and novellas and my monthly serial.

Signup on my website at: www.terinaadams.com

TERINA ADAMS

ETERNITY
BURN

He was cute, in that preppy school boy kind of way, except he had to be at least twenty-five, pacing up and down the rows between our desks in his tan vans, snug stretch chinos and linen shirt as he explained something about some ratios being negative and some positive. His hair needed a good comb through with some fingers, preferably mine, and that promise of a beard worked well. Whoever said math was a boring subject had never taken classes with Mr G, short for Giannopoulos, which was impossible to pronounce drunk or sober. He was Greek. Maybe I'd take a vacation in Greece once I graduated.

I was failing this class miserably, but it probably had more to do with my lack of concentration rather than me being an idiot. Although Milly called me that all the time. She thought Mr G was old because he had a whisper of premature grey at his temples. It made him look distinguished, what with his black-rimmed square glasses and all. A math teacher in glasses, so cliched and yet so perfect on him.

"Miss Jennings."

"Ah...yes."

Mr G's faded blue eyes were like crystal pools. "Your answer."

"Yes."

"Don't you mean 126 degrees."

"Yes."

The rest of the classroom laughed. They were used to my dizzy responses. I always answered questions fielded my way like I'd just landed from outer space.

"How many questions have you answered on your assignment so far?"

My hand involuntarily slid my unopened math book down over my blank assignment. "I'm steadily making my way through it."

"Good to hear. If you have any problems, be sure to let me know before the due date, which is Monday."

"Monday?" Good thing there was the weekend. "I was having difficulty with question ten." Hopefully the assignment went up to question ten.

"That's halfway through. Good progress. You can see me after class."

I flicked a glance to Milly sitting at the desk over from me to see her eyes roll. Once done, she frowned at me and mouthed something I couldn't read because she exaggerated every word, making it look like she was doing mouth stretching exercises. It would have something to do with wanting to grab the seats closest to the fish tank in the cafeteria because that's where Leon always sat. Everyone grabbed the fish tank seats, making it a sprint if you were out of class late. I winked at her then focused on Mr G who was lapping the classroom again.

At the sound of the bell, the room exploded with the noise of chairs scraping on the floor. Slapping her books together, Milly glared at me. "Thanks for nothing."

"I want a good mark on this assignment."

"Have you even started the assignment?"

"I will once Mr G gives me a helping hand."

"I'm smashing this class."

"I know, but you've got chem, english lit and physics assignments as well. I didn't want to bother you."

She gave me one of her impatient sideways looks that said she was humoring my BS.

"Save me a seat," I called after her as she marched toward the door. She didn't respond, but she would.

I gathered my things and headed to Mr G's desk. He was talking to Mathews, a pale, scrawny English kid whose dad, a geneticist, so he kept telling the class at every opportunity, transferred from Oxford university to work on some research project to do with stem cells. Mathews had the hots for Milly. She laughed in my face when I told her that, but he couldn't stop staring at her every time she answered one of Mr G's questions, which was multiple times throughout each lesson.

I leaned against the closest desk and waited for Mathews to stop wasting Mr G's time with some math problem that had nothing to do with the class work or assignment. At least I don't think it did. None of it sounded familiar, but I had no clue what was in the assignment.

From here, I could smell the faint strains of sandalwood and patchouli mixed with a dash of vanilla. Whenever Mr G walked past my desk, I always swayed slightly into the aisle as my nose followed the delicate intoxication of his cologne. When Simon overheard me gushing to Milly and Francis about the trail of his scent, he turned up at school smothered in enough cologne to burn a hole through your nose if you stood too close.

Mr G's gaze shifted to mine as he patiently listened to Mathews. He must've felt my eyes lingering on his face. I darted my gaze to look out the window, a guilty tick, which was even more embarrassing than being caught staring. I didn't want him to think I had some stupid girlie crush.

The sky was overcast, the day cold. Everyone would be in the cafeteria, which meant Milly was going to have a hard time getting fish tank seats. A pigeon landed on the windowsill, bobbed its head a few times, then awkwardly turned to walk along the sill. The boring grey feathers around its neck tinged green at certain angles.

An image flashed into my head so fast I wasn't sure what it was. My head fuzzed up, and I slapped my right hand down on the desk to stop me from swaying any farther.

"Are you all right, Miss Jennings?"

I shielded my eyes with a hand as I blinked myself back into the classroom. Seconds later, my head stopped spinning. "Yeah, I'm fine."

I emerged from behind my palm to see how well a frown suited Mr G's face. Mathews spared me one look, an expression that said he thought me weird, then resumed his rapid-fire question.

The pigeon remained perched on the windowsill, facing outward into the garden. I craned my neck a little higher to see the view from where it sat. *Totally bizarre.* It was like I'd seen... Nah, I imagined it. Like a lot of the other stuff I made up in my head. Mathews's voice became a drone humming in the background as I fixated on the pigeon. This was not... It didn't feel like it was. *Nothing's going to happen, Laz.* Not believing me, my pulse hammered a tune through my ears.

It slammed into me like a thrown chair. My head felt viced, stretched, torn apart, and another vision flashed into my mind. This time it lingered long enough for me to be sure of what I saw. The garden, the staff carpark, to the left of the building, inside the classroom, me, a panoramic view and not a montage. It blinked out as quick as it came, leaving me to swim through a tornado in my head. I had the vague thought I needed to catch myself, before my hip crashed into the wood floor. A chair scraped across the floor, then someone grabbed my arm.

"Larnie?"

I wanted to latch on to Mr G's soothing voice, but it felt like my head was mimicking the exorcist. I closed my eyes because it was like being stuck in a carnival ride.

"Mathews, get Ms Draper."

"I'm fine." My voice seemed to spin with my head, I tried to stand, but my legs felt like they didn't belong to me. In the end, I had to lean on Mr G. Any other circumstance and I'd be blushing scarlet while my stomach did a fairy dance, but not when things got freaky.

"Don't try and get up."

"I'm fine."

But he wouldn't listen to me, instead Mr. G pressed gently on my right shoulder, encouraging me to obey. Fighting to gather the pieces of my scattered brain, I caved to his gentle command and folded to the floor, surrendering only because everything was subtly shifting back to normal. I knew because the vice on my chest eased, and my eyes worked in sync once more, as in I now focused straight in front like a predator and not in a three sixty degree arc like the prey. Was this the next level of decay on my shredded sanity?

Mr G's concerned eyes peered down at me, crystalline blue like diamonds reflecting the corn blue sky. It was straight out of a romance novel, and the accumulation of a year worth of swooning and crafting the perfect romance for the two of us. Now it was ruined by the embarrassing fact I wore a short flare skirt, which had probably ridden high when I crash landed to the floor.

I swear I'd had a flash vision of me leaning against the desk in the classroom like I was standing at the window looking in, but with eyes at the back of my head so I also saw the garden and the carpark simultaneously. The moment had been brief. I could be making it up. Knowing me, I wasn't.

"I had a head spin. I think it's past," I mumbled.

"Is this common?"

"Not really." *Yep.* "I'm fine. I don't need Ms Draper." I tried to rise, but Mr G soothed me back down.

"I think its safest if we let the nurse give you a once over. Here she comes now, by the sounds of it."

His mentioning it, I heard the click of high heels rushing down the corridor. Next minute she burst through the door, Mathews close behind. The school nurse crouched beside us, surrounding me with a cloud of jasmine perfume.

"Oh, my dear," Ms Draper gasped.

"She felt light-headed," Mr G said.

"And looks very pale."

"But I'm fine now." I pushed up from the floor, aided by Mr G and Ms Draper.

Once I was siting, Ms Draper cupped my chin in her hand and turned my face toward her, giving me an extra shot of perfume. She leaned forward, peering into my eyes while I stared at her eyelash extensions. "Do you think you can stand?"

"I'm sure I can. Like I said, I feel fine."

"We'll take it easy heading back to my office." Her office was a fancy word for sick bay.

"I don't need to go there." Milly and Francis would wonder where I was. Hopefully they scored fish tank seats. And Milly got to talk with Leon about Marco's party tonight. Milly was hoping for invites. She fancied him. Rumors said he fancied Mabel, who was half as smart but way sexier.

My head had stopped spinning by now, and I was feeling better, so I got to my feet mostly on my own. Once standing, I glanced to the window, not sure why, to see the pigeon sitting where it had been before I went down. In my periphery, I caught Mr G turn toward the window, following my gaze. I shook my head in hope it would shake the weird from my brain.

"Let's go, shall we?" Ms Draper said from beside me.

The pigeon was like a magnet, my eyeballs the iron drawn by an invisible force. This was not on my usual list of freaky visions, but since freaky visions were part of my life, my body wouldn't brush off what just happened. Not when experience told me it was all going to slide to creepy weird about now, and my heart shot a round of adrenaline through my veins to give me the junkie shakes.

Turning away from the pigeon to follow Ms Draper, my head did that strange vicing, stretching thing again, like it was some kid's play dough being rolled and squished. On instinct, I splayed my arms for balance, gripped the first thing I felt.

Beside me, Mr G made a garbled groan as he buckled, his hand springing to his crotch and peeling my fisted fingers away. I'd flame red if my mind wasn't slicing into twenty pieces.

Ms Draper said something, but her words didn't make it through my kaleidoscoped mind.

"Huh?" I mumbled, or did I speak it in my head.

The magnetic tug stretched like an elastic band about to snap. I gave in, glancing over my shoulder to see the pigeon take flight. My stomach lurched, and my head felt like a basketball bouncing down the court. Strong arms gripped me. I fell into a soft, warm, yet solid wall. "Larnie?" It was Mr G's voice.

The ground receded from me, cars shrunk, the school roof as well, clouds drew near. The road spread below me. I squeezed my eyes closed, my stomach flipping somersaults. I couldn't handle the sight. But even with my eyes closed, the vision continued. I was soaring away. Everything was in view, the town ahead, the streets below, even the school way behind.

"I don't want this," I groaned, then slammed my lips closed when a lump welled up from my restless stomach.

"Good god. Lower her down again," Ms Draper said.

I palmed my mouth, fighting against the two of them as they lowered me to the floor.

"I gotta go..." It was all I could say before palming my mouth again. The lump wedged thick at the base of my throat. I shook my head, but with the vision blanking out, my head missing the hoop and bouncing off the backboard, I was going to vomit. "Really, I gotta—" And that was it. Chunks of orange gushed out in a thick soupy mess all over Mr G's shirt. I couldn't stop, my stomach spasming another hurl, which rushed up and splattered half on Mr G and half on the floor because by now he'd stepped away.

"Yuck." I'd forgotten Mathews was still here.

"Right, young lady. The sick bay for you, and I'll have to call your aunt."

My head swam through a hazy fog, and I felt too weak from my violent vomiting to fight her.

Yep, another weight had been slung onto the worst of my life.

CHAPTER 2

"Yar fucking idiot," Auntie Bea kindly informed me from my bedroom doorway.

"It was nothing."

"That Ms Draper chick didn't think so."

"Adults always exaggerate things."

"Kids don't just faint."

"I didn't faint."

"Then what ya doing rolling on the classroom floor?"

I looked at Auntie Bea through my mirror. She leaned against my doorjamb, thin, scraggly hair pulled back off her face in a tight bun that did nothing to soften her features, especially not while they were hijacked by such a stern look. Auntie Bea wasn't much of a rule enforcer. She'd let me know what she thought of my decision with colorful adjectives, but she never said no, so I knew she wouldn't stop me from going to the party.

After glaring at me for what she thought a suitable amount of time, her belly started jiggling under her maxi dress, her expression softening as a smile pricked the corners of her lips. She slapped a hand to her mouth, but the raucous laugh slipped between the gaps in her fingers. "What I would've given to be there." The words broken around the laughter. "Chucking up all over ya teacher."

"Yeah, laugh a minute, Auntie Bea. It was a total blast."

"Mr Ganniullppoollusss...He's the one ya think's shaggable."

"He's good looking, not shaggable. It was all over his shirt. Dripped down to the floor. In front of Mathews who spread it around the school quicker than VD. I've brushed my teeth four times already, and I can still taste it."

It seemed hearing the story from my mouth was even funnier than from Ms Draper's because she disintegrated into another round of hard laughing until she couldn't get a breath in and turned red in the face. Finally she calmed, wheezily sucking in air and shaking her head.

"Glad someone's enjoying my humiliation. He'll remember me as the girl who chucked up all over his expensive shirt and shoes."

"At least he'll remember ya."

It took her a while longer to ease out of the last few chuckles, rubbing at her belly like she'd developed an ache, the tension lines on her face smoothed after the rejuvenating laugh. She leaned back against the doorjamb, hugging her elbows. "Seriously, ya right to go out tonight?"

"I'm totally fine. It's like it never happened."

I hadn't told Auntie Bea everything about today, not the entire truth, like how I swore I had the vision of a pigeon. The sudden, warping movement of flying when I could still feel my feet on the ground spun me into vertigo. How could I be honest about that? Auntie Bea would think I'd stolen some of her drugs.

"Don't be late home. Ya think ya may be alright, but ya just don't know. And don't go drinking or drugging neither. Not after something like that."

"I don't drink or take drugs."

"It may cure you of some of ya problems," she huffed.

I lacked zest for life, according to Auntie Bea. At my age she'd seen the inside of a lock up multiple times, knew her dealer's son's nickname and had a string of men she juggled nightly. I doubted most of the stories, but I guess she wasn't always this old.

"Have a little fun. If ya still know how." She did a little jig, which made the skin at the back of her arms wobble.

"Don't worry about me. I'll be all right. If I feel funny at the party, I'll come home, or crash at Milly's."

"That Simon kid going to be there?"

I dropped my lipstick back on the dresser. "I think so, but nothing's going to happen."

"Ya eighteen, Laz. Act like an eighteen-year-old. Do something illegal, be reckless. Ya lifeless. Sometimes I think I'm gonna have to do that mouth to mouth shit on ya. Ya can't leave high school a virgin."

"Have you just made up your first house rule?" I asked as I rummaged through my makeup supply, heaped in a mess in front of the mirror.

"Yeah, but ya not going to listen, are ya?"

"Can I at least have a relationship first?"

"Fuck that. Since when have ya been in a relationship? Ya be fifty before ya do either."

"Thanks."

"Friendly advice."

"It's weird getting sex tips from my Aunt." I threw the eyeliner back amongst the pile.

"Ya wanna be a nun, it's none of my business." She backed up out the door, hands raised in surrender.

I watched her disappear down the hall, still wearing her slippers from this morning, and I couldn't help but bled a little at the sight. Mothering wasn't easy for Auntie Bea. She wasn't the type. I asked her once if she'd wanted kids, and she'd replied with some crude joke, her most common response, and her barricade. But she didn't hesitate to take me on board when Mom died. And she'd done the best she could. Sure, she wasn't perfect, but there's no such thing these days. A lot of kids at school seem to have one problem or another at home.

I'm not one of them. Auntie Bea and I rarely fight, and she trusts me to do the right thing, which is easy given her idea of doing the right thing covered a broad range of vices. Every family has its dark secrets, its hidden skeletons. We're nothing unusual.

I heard Milly's car swing into the driveway first, but she honked to make sure so I would meet her at the door. Rarely did she come inside because she thought Auntie Bea was a gambler and a drug pusher. She was partially right. Auntie Bea had a gambling habit, and she took drugs, but didn't promote either lifestyle. She drank more than she did drugs, so I'd say her problem was more drinking than drugging.

I grabbed my mid waist jacket in case it got cold and rushed out of my room before Auntie Bea answered the door. I caught her halfway across the lounge room.

"When's that girl gonna come inside?" She yelled over the blaring TV.

"When you stop answering the door drunk."

"I'm not drunk now."

"Night, Auntie Bea." I leaned over and kissed her on the cheek and inhaled old tobacco that clung to her like mold.

I paused at the door, watching her head back to the sofa where she'd likely spend the night. Around this time, I always got the guilts. It was her foul mouth, caustic personality and distrust of most people that kept her alone on the couch, but I sometimes wondered if I was responsible. How much of her life had she surrendered to care for me? She laughed a lot in rare moments when she crumbled that barricade and shared a special memory. Any stories told after I arrived in her life no longer held the same luster.

Milly was already across the lawn, her face brightening into a big smile when she saw me coming out the door. I reached her when Auntie Bea bellowed from behind. I spun around to see her standing on the doorstep, waving a bottle of gin in her hand. "Come in quiet, will ya, I'll be entertaining. If ya know what I mean." Then she hacked her smoker's laugh and headed back inside.

I rolled my eyes at Milly.

"Your aunt's scary."

"She does that on purpose. She's harmless really."

"Harmless," she snorted in disagreement.

The first and only time Milly had turned up at my house, Auntie Bea was elbow deep in her ashtray, face buried in her poker cards, sharing the table with a group of men who looked like they'd sell you into the sex trade for some easy cash. The place smelt like a pool hall, tobacco, stale alcohol and sweat.

"You look nice," I said to her as I opened the passenger door. She wore an emerald green mini dress with a dramatic V line over black leggings and a large silver pendant that drew the eye to her cleavage. She'd finished the look with a loose herring bone plait. Maybe I shouldn't have worn my ripped skinnys and done something with my hair.

"I've got someone to impress."

"What about Mabel?"

"He's not interested in her. He told me at lunch when he invited us to come along tonight."

"That's a quick turnaround." *Damn, why did I say that?* It reeked of envy.

"He wasn't much into her. It was just people spreading rumors."

Leon was hoping for a scholarship, and Milly was the top of every class. And I definitely wouldn't say that. I seemed to pick up Auntie Bea's cynicism on love by osmosis. According to her, men were only good for shagging, and even then only some made it worth the time.

"Make him sweat for it then."

She laughed. "Oh my god, Laz, that's something your aunt would say."

I pressed my lips together and looked out the window. Yep, it was hard not to live with her attitude when you breathed it in every day.

"What you going to do about Simon?"

"Why do I need to do anything about him?"

"You're a thick head, sometimes. He's majorly into you."

"I like him..."

"But?"

"I'm not into him."

"He's kind of cute."

"A little."

"Thoughtful, kind, smart—"

"Do I need to be into him?"

"There are far worse out there."

"Doesn't mean I have to catch him."

Milly gave me a sideways glance. If she wore glasses, she'd be peering over them right now. I pulled a weird face, then looked out my passenger window. End of conversation, please.

So far my boyfriend score was two. Two short painful relationships that lasted a couple of weeks for the first and a few months longer on the second. Milly had dated seven times, one lasting a whole year. In fact, she'd practically spent her high school years in some phase of relationship. My other good friend, Francis, was hitched to Parker. They'd been dating so long they were practically married. This left me the virgin in our trio, something I was painfully aware of.

"You sure you're all right after today?"

"It was some weird thing that came and went. I wish I could forget about it." Dig it in deep like the other freaky things that were a part of my life, gave me sleepless nights and buried me deep under the bedclothes in the dark of night while I Googled what was wrong with me.

"No kidding. After tonight, everyone will have other things to gossip about."

———

By the time we reached the party, Milly had me promise I wouldn't shut Simon out until I gave him a chance. But we were so close to graduating I didn't see the point in attempting to start something now.

The music was so loud I swear the walls of Marco's house were expanding outward with every base beat. We'd arrived two hours late because every Friday Milly had to go visit her nan in care. Two hours into the party and already people had spilled out onto the lawn playing some crazy party game half naked.

"Looks like we're missing out," Milly said as she maneuvered her small car into a tight space between a hedge and a Cherokee.

When Francis saw us she screamed, disengaged herself from Parker and staggered across the paving to wrap us both in a trio hug. "I didn't think you were going to make it."

"I had to see my nan."

"Oh yeah, of course you did. Laz, are you all right? I thought after today..."

I resisted rolling my eyes, instead took a deep breath. "Yep."

"She wants to forget about it."

"Oh, yeah. Understandable," Francis said, nodding her head. "You're two hours behind. Go, get yourselves some drinks." She waved us toward the house.

Squished together, we did the party shuffle forward into the living room, not knowing where we were heading but shuffling on while a base beat pounded through my ribcage. We pushed through a funnel of backs until Milly was swept sideways and into a close huddle of guys. Leon spun her around and playfully kissed her cheek. She gushed up pink with flirtatious excitement, and I had to look away, swallowing real envy this time. She deserved a good guy to adore her. Didn't everyone? Including me?

And because she was such a good friend, Milly broke from Leon and pushed her way toward me, taking my hand and pulling me over to join their huddle.

I placed a hand on hers. "I'm going to get a drink."

"You sure?" She gave me one of her level eyed I-know-what's-going-on-here looks.

"You have a good time."

"Don't leave without telling me."

"I should be saying that to you."

She gave me a peck on the lips, then surrendered herself to Leon's attention.

I continued on through the funnel of backs until I broke out of the knot of people and spied a spare bit of floor space in the kitchen. By the time I got there a fat bulldog had beat me to the space, snuffling his nose along the ground, looking for dropped morsels. I'd always wanted a dog, but Auntie Bea claimed to be allergic to them, and our place was too small for anything bigger than a miniature chihuahua. He paused his search long enough to lean into my tickles at his ear, then coming unpaused continued on his way like the pleasure had never happened.

Black denimed legs appeared at the side of me while I was still in my crouch. I glanced up to see Simon holding two drinks in white plastic cups.

"I'm s'pose to keep an eye on y," he yelled down at me.

"Says who?" I smiled, straightening and accepting the cup he handed.

He leaned over, sloshing some of his drink onto his hand and not noticing the cold, wet sensation.

"Maybe I'll be keeping an eye on you."

"I'dlikethat."

He was slur yelling despite standing right next to me, partly because the music was so loud and partially because I don't think he had good vocal control at the moment. And that was not meant to be a cheesy pickup line on my behalf. But he'd never remember by morning. I took a sip to fill the impending awkward silence, only to choke on the burn. "It tastes like battery acid."

"Yeah." He chuckled. "I coon't read the lablesh."

Drink mixes, lethal stuff. "How many of these have you had?"

He held up his hand. "One, two." He demonstrated, mucking up the amount of fingers he showed me. "Deadly, init? Me fee', carn feel 'em. I carn feel mush of nothin'. But I won puke. Don't worry." Suddenly realizing what he said, he added, "Shorry, no puke talk."

It could be worse. I could be standing alone at a party. Auntie Bea was right. I rarely had fun. And that was because I could never let go, couldn't trust myself to not flip a loopy and embarrass myself so much worse than puking on a teacher.

I was waiting for something. That's how I felt, always, from my earliest memories, like there was some pivotal moment approaching, and I had to be ready for the impending doom. There were times it got so bad it was like taking a big breath under water or a compression on my chest squeezing my lungs. I woke some nights suffocating on air. I had grown up believing something terrible was about to happen but had no words to explain it, in fear of sharing it aloud in case it turned nightmares to reality.

It got worse as I got older. The suffocating feeling of some dark dread played tricks with my mind. I saw things that weren't real. Macabre images stamped on my vision, so convincing sometimes I struggled to work out reality from fabrication.

A few years ago, I found the courage to tell Auntie Bea a muted version of the truth. She looked at me for the longest moment, her brow creasing up into heaps of ridges like an aerial view of sand dunes, the silence hovering long enough it grew eerie. Auntie Bea didn't do silences when there were plenty of foul words to say. This only added to my sense of doom. That and the fact she pressed her lips pencil thin and walked away like she couldn't deal with a cracked kid. We never talked about it again, both of us scared for different reasons. I didn't want to re-experience the silence that accompanied the expression she'd worn. I didn't want to be rejected. She probably didn't want to face the fact she may have made too many terrible mistakes in my upbringing.

Dammit. Why did I let myself think of that? It often flared one of my freaky moments. Today's episode left me feeling peeled like rotten fruit, so all my soft squidgy inside bits were exposed and vulnerable to attack. Long ago I had tried meditation to hone my focus and mental control, only to find the practice was a perfect conduit to all the nightmares festering in my subconscious.

"Looks like the entire school's come." Not the best conversation line to use, but anything would do, for right now my heart thumped the bongo beat.

"Rippos's startin' a skullin' game." He got right into my face, raising his eyebrows as his question to whether or not I wanted to join in and breathing alcohol over my face.

Alcohol might make me forget. Either that or it would open the gates and let the horde of nightmares through. I plugged my nose and gulped, arched my head and inhaled the burn sliding down my throat.

"Is it a yesh?" Simon clumsily grabbed my hand, knocking my cup to the floor, spraying the dark brown battery acid concoction all over the bulldog's head. His sloppy tongue darted out and licked the wet off his nose.

"Shorry."

"Simon, don't worry. I wasn't going to drink it anyway." I grabbed his arm before he bent all the way to pick up my cup.

"Y leave it to me." He glanced over his shoulder in his half bent position, and I stared into hollow eyes.

I jerked my hand away, jumped back into the kitchen bench behind me. Simon had enough alcohol free brain cells to notice my strange reaction and straightened himself as he turned to face me, bearing down on me with his flaming black eyes, lips curling into a sneer.

"Simon." I lashed out, gripping his wrists. *Not real, Laz, not real.* I closed my eyes at the feel of his warm, soft human skin punished under my manacle grip. *This is real.*

"Y right?"

I'm fine, I'm fine, I'm fine. "Can you get me a drink?"

"Shame?"

"Yeah...sure, whatever." I shook my head, spinning, spinning, spinning. *Not now, please.*

"Y look pale."

I wanted to crouch in the corner and hug myself while I rocked in time to the music. Behind Simon the room montaged into some hideous apocalyptic movie, exploding into a ball of crimson light with flaming arms lashing at the walls, eating the furniture, cindering the carpet. Flames reached, raged, chased the rushing fire storm, stripping flesh, leaving bones.

The kitchen bench bit into my back as I fell into it, smothered by the heat of the blast wave bathing my face, licking my skin, threatening with its fiery tongue to burn me dry. Simon loomed toward me, stenciled on the gruesome backdrop like a harbinger of doom, arms slowly rising as if to embrace me. A blaze forked through his eyes, sparked from his sneer as the tips of his fingers elongated to blades.

Stop it, stop it, stop it. I buried my head between my elbows, eyes squeezed closed. Slowly my knees buckled and slid me to the tiles where I went fetal.

"Laz, y right?" Hands clumsily pressed on my head, forcing it downward and cracking my neck as Simon fell into me while trying to lower himself to the floor. He head butted the cupboards behind us, then lost his footing and went down on his stomach like a skater taking a tumble, mashing his face into my calves.

He saved me. In his drunken fumbles, Simon broke me free. Feeling his very human, warm hands and hearing his grunts and groans smacked me back into reality. I surfaced from my cocoon to see people still wore their skin and the room had returned to normal.

"Simon, you fool." I wanted to hug him.

"Yeah, yeah...I'm fine. Jush give me a moment," he mumbled against my calves, sounding sleepy.

I pressed a palm to my cheek to find it hot—left from a lapping flame. I sprung it away, as a feverish chill shimmered up my spine. A sharp pain shot through my brain, hammering my head down into my neck. In reverse, it soon felt stretched on a rack, elongated to a strip. I clenched my teeth, fisted my hands, popping my knuckles white. When I blinked again, I was staring at myself, seeing my wide eyes, gaping mouth, flushed face, Simon flat on his stomach at my feet. There was a weirdly combined detachment in the way I looked at myself and flurried panic like a bird bashing at a window trying to escape.

I ducked my head, shook it vigorously. "Stop it," I growled.

When I looked back I saw the bulldog, tongue lolling a pant as it placidly looked at me.

I threw back my covers, blinked at the sun streaming in through my window and pulled them back over my head with a groan. The light was like annoying perennially cheerful people resistant to the drain of life. I was hungover from all the mental strain of fighting my visions. Thank god it had been Simon with me when I freaked. Double thank god he'd been too drunk to notice much and would likely remember nothing today.

The swim coach had phoned a paramedic once when she found me backed in a corner swatting air with a noodle floaty, and I'd taken out a waiter at Chescos Barbecue House when he supposedly came at me with a skewer of seared beef. Those two incidences aside, I'd been lucky in time and location when it came to my wacky trips. There were always public conveniences nearby or empty aisles.

I was so screwed up. And getting worse. At the moment hijacking an animal's mind freaked me out more than my dark visions and lurking shadow of doom, probably because I'd lived with them all my life, but the former was something new. Did this mean the longer I lived, the more mental problems I would gain? I hadn't just looked through the eyes of those hijacked animals, I had slipped into their skin. And that was too crazy to even think about. Was this the foreboding darkness I'd lived with all my life?

I lurched up, the covers falling to my waist. If I allowed my mental health to deteriorate any further, I'd be institutionalized by twenty, which meant I needed to share my problem with someone, preferably a professional someone, before I started communicating with dead people. Who? My friends weren't equipped to deal with the depth of my insanity. They would never spill what I said to anyone, but gossip was like a virus. It could easily escape confinement, spread with invisibility and was impossible to stop once free.

I swung my legs out of bed when Auntie Bea gave a brief knock, then flung my door wide. "Ya don't look hungover?"

"That's not a knock."

"What ya got to hide?"

"My privacy."

She leaned against the doorjamb and folded her arms across her chest. "You slunk in early last night. I was expecting ya home in the early hours shit faced with no bra. At least I was hoping for it."

I couldn't find enough strength to act like everything was all right, so I slumped backward onto my bed and flopped my arm over my face with a groan.

"I've got a pick me up if ya needing it."

"Really, Auntie Bea."

"I wasn't meaning drugs. Got a prescription for 'em."

"A talk would work just as well and it's cheaper."

"Ya wanna talk? Shit, I can listen." The bed dipped as she settled herself beside me with a huff. "Shoot."

Where do I start? We didn't talk, not the proper talk that I'm sure parents and their children are supposed to do. We had the sex talk, but it was more crude than explanatory and pockmarked with examples of her own exploits, not in graphic detail mind. Then there was the drug talk she gave while toking on a joint as she threatened me with a convent if I ever took any of her stash without telling her so she could make sure she didn't run low. She gave the alcohol talk over a bottle of gin when I was thirteen. She offered me a shot more than once while hacking her smoker's laugh and reminiscing on her alcoholic exploits.

We'd never had a heart to heart, no history of being honest about our feelings. She mentioned Mom only a handful of times, but not in great detail. Anyone could see the subject gouged at unhealed wounds, and so I didn't press further. I knew very little of her private life before I came, not the tragic parts at least. But there had to be a lot lurking else why was she such a mess. Her broken words, sudden silences and lightning swift subject changes told me losing her sister had a lot to do with it. This was going to be awkward, yet if I said nothing, I would go insane.

"Right. Conversation over." Auntie Bea slapped my thigh, then heaved herself up.

"Wait." I sat up.

"For how long? I've gotta prepare some shit before the boys come over."

"Have you got any money left to gamble?"

"This is the night, Laz."

Said like she said every night she had the boys around for a poker night. She rubbed her hands together as she waddled to the door.

"I'm having out-of-body experiences."

Auntie Bea morphed into stone.

It was out. Time to vomit it all since I've been vomiting a lot lately. "It's happened twice now. Yesterday with Mr G. I chucked up all over his shirt because I ended up in a pigeon's head and flew over the city. Last night I stared at myself from the eyes of a fat bulldog."

She inched around to face me.

"I know it sounds crazy. It's just...I don't know what's going on. And please be adult about this. None of your innuendo." The last few words came muffled through my hands. I closed my eyes and preyed she wasn't shifting through mental health experts in her head.

She eased herself back down beside me. "Don't be so dramatic. You'll get used to it."

I peeled my hand away. "Is this you being an adult?" I heaved myself up. "You did hear what I said?"

"Look, I may not be of any use to you in your normal, mundane human existence, but in this I know a few things."

"Human existence as opposed to animal existence? What are the comparisons here, Auntie Bea?"

Poor Auntie Bea. She smoked too much weed, popped too many pills and downed too much gin. It was hard to know if half of what she said was induced by a marinade of all her vices.

"Is it just with animals?"

"Were you expecting it to be with something else?"

"A manifestation of goddess Diana. Yep, that's a surprise."

"You're scaring me, Auntie Bea." She had to be lost in her tarot cards with that comment.

"Not something ya mom displayed. Me either." She sighed, staring across my room with a distant expression. "And I don't know ya father, so that leaves it a mystery. It doesn't matter none, I guess, since ya've got it."

"I know what I've told you is insane. I need you to be the sane one in this conversation."

"Ya mom didn't want this for ya. She made me promise to keep ya out of it. And I did as best I could. But there's nothing I can do if ya channeling abilities."

She was serious. I had this horrible spine snapping, gut rupturing understanding she was deadly serious. Auntie Bea had gone gaga. She was lost in this fantasy world of her making. Her mind had twisted all the programs she watched on TV and all the bloody tarot card readings she gave to desperate women who came around looking for solace out of the holes of their lives and mixed everything up with the slurry in her brain and fabricated her own reality. One that was no doubt less painful than the world she existed in.

"Maybe we don't have to talk about this now."

"We ain't gonna get a better time. But I need me smokes and a gin to get through this conversation. See ya on the porch." She heaved herself up, flashed me a solemn smile, then left me dizzy and my heart sinking to my feet like the biggest lead sinker on any fishing line.

As hard as it would be for me to hear what she had to say, I couldn't abandon her. Things were going to change between us. This day forward, I needed to be the adult and take care of her. Her life had always been a hopeless mess. It was amazing we'd got this far without being evicted from our home. Somehow she'd always pulled us through the rough times, but now it smacked me in the face so hard I was surprised I didn't have a blood nose. I wasn't the only one with a warped mind, but at least I had enough clarity to realize our predicament, which meant our lives were now my responsibility.

Walking outside was like walking to the gallows, but there Auntie Bea sat on the rickety swing chair someone had dumped on the roadside with her feet up on the railing, sucking away on a cigarette while nursing a good dash of gin. I slid down beside her.

"Just gotta think what to say and what to leave for later."

Francis's parents sent her to a counselor once because she developed an anxious tick during stressful situations. According to her, he asked a few questions, scribbled on a pad but mostly listened a lot, so I stayed quiet, allowing Auntie Bea to ramble wherever she wanted to go. It was all I could think to do. Maybe later I could ask my friends about referring her to a psychologist or something. And then I would refer myself.

"Ya mom was a witch. I'm a witch. So that means yar one too."

"Okay." I measured out my words.

She jerked her head around to face me. "What's that supposed to mean?"

"I was responding to what you said."

"Don't give me that bullshit. *Okay*. What do ya fucking mean *okay*? This is ya fucking heritage, Laz."

"I get it."

"Nah, ya don't. I know ya, girl. Ya think I'm full of shit. Ya think I've gone fucking loopy." She twirled her finger, holding the cigarette jammed between her pointer and thumb around her temple, drawing a small smoke swirl in her finger's wake. "I ain't loopy, Laz. Sometimes I wish I were, but in this I'm dead fucking sane.

Ya think ya know the world. Ya think it's safe. That's because of me, girlie. I've kept ya safe. Ya mom wanted it that way." She took a long drag on her cigarette, then blew the smoke from the corner of her mouth, away from me. Smoke exhaled, she stared into her glass of gin. "I was happy to do it. Ya don't want any of them shit heads in ya life."

Holy crap, what do I say? I didn't just get the tingles. An entire army of ants were dancing all over my body. Her words hit a hidden place inside of me and sparked it alive, dredging out the darkness and doom of my entire life. It felt like someone had stuck paddles on my happily beating heart and zapped it with a hundred volts.

"People think magic would be fun to have. They think being a witch is like bewitched and charmed, fighting demons that don't bleed, fucking cute guys and then making pie. There's a whole metric fuck ton of shit out there ya don't wanna know about, that I've shielded ya from. But I can't do it anymore, Laz. Not now that ya manifesting some abilities. I hoped it wouldn't happen, thought maybe if I kept ya away it would just miss ya." She looked to the sky as she took another drag. "Stupid fucking me. The coven will know."

The more she said, the more I listened, the more I believed. Her words sunk through the emerging gloom into a place inside my head and heart that understood and knew this as the truth.

"Why haven't you told me?"

"I told ya, Laz. Ya mom wanted ya out." When she said all this, she waved her arm around like she was encompassing the world. Perhaps she was.

"So I'm a witch?"

"Yep," she said, her gin glass balanced on her lips for a gulp.

"I've been living with a witch all this time. How did you manage to keep this from me? I mean... All those guys that belong to your gambling club. Are they part of....this new world?"

"Low lifes. The rejects of the paranormal world." Her tone ground on a hard edge of bitterness.

"But harmless, right?"

"Ain't nothing harmless about them. Ya know how to deal with them and ya safe...ish."

For the tenth time today, I buried my head in my hands. "I don't know how to deal with this. It's..."

"A mind fuck Yeah, it sure is. I'm kind of relieved ya know. It's been hard hiding things. But it ain't gonna be pretty. Everyone on the dark side of the fence are as greedy and power hungry as those on the light, problem is they're more dangerous."

"That's why you stayed silent all those years ago when I told you about the dark feelings and visions I was experiencing."

"Honestly, kiddo, I didn't know what to make of it. Never heard of that before. But it had to be linked to ya heritage. I saw it coming. This day. It was a matter of time. It's also a matter of time before we receive a message from the coven. They won't leave ya alone. No active witch may remain a stray."

"We have a coven?"

"Every witch does. Ya don't think we're allowed to be free."

"You make it sound like a jail term."

"Depends on ya point of view, I guess. And how much ya can give 'em. And they'll want ya initiated into the church."

"Witches go to church?" More incredible was the fact *Auntie Bea* went to church.

"Our blessed mother watches over us. She's the only one that does." Bowing her head, Auntie Bea put down her glass, clasped her hands and closed her eyes like she was praying, which couldn't be the case. Her cigarette, almost a stump now, swirled smoke up into her eyes. She broke out of her reverence as suddenly as she slipped into it. "Do as I say when we get to church and everything should be all right...I hope."

CHAPTER 4

Everything was different now. I walked between Milly and Francis, feeling like an alien. 'Humans aren't to know' Auntie Bea had warned me. Then added 'on pain of death', but I'm sure she was being dramatic with that part. 'The coven will know if you reveal the secret' she had said. I knew nothing about witchcraft and covens to call her bluff.

"We face-timed for most of the night," Milly gushed. She and Leon had hit it off at the party. They thoroughly explored first base but had yet to get all the way around for a home run. She was hanging out to jump into bed with him, but guys that get what they want straight away rarely hang around for afters. If he had to wait, he'd fall in love. So the plan went.

I hadn't seen or spoken to Simon since Friday night. I wanted to ensure he remembered little if any of my freak out, but he was a good guy, so I doubted he'd make a deal out of it or think it worth spreading as gossip.

"He's hooked. And you haven't even held his dick," Francis said, and they both laughed.

It was going to take time, Auntie Bea said, for me to get a handle on my connection with animals. A gift from goddess Diana, thanks very much. A significant gift, according to Auntie Bea. So significant it mushed my head, then stretched it like chewing gum and made me hurl. Familiarity would subside the sickness, faster if I practiced. No thanks. I was in no hurry to experiment with my *significant* gift. When I'd asked her what she could do, she clammed up and left the swing chair, which left me wondering if the coven had forbid her from practicing magic, if something bad had happened while she was doing it, or if she had little to show me.

"So how about you?" Milly nudged my shoulder. "I can't believe you kept your phone off for the whole of the weekend. Why didn't you facetime me the moment you saw my million messages?"

"I had stuff to do."

"So what's the deal. You've been silent about Simon this morning. I know you two were getting sweet in the kitchen. Johnathon saw you."

"Oh my god, she's blushing," Francis chimed in.

"I'm not blushing. Not about what you think, 'cause what you're thinking didn't happen."

"You and Simon left early," Francis said.

"Separately."

"Why did Angel say she saw you both getting into the same cab?"

"He was drunk. He couldn't drive."

"So where did you end up?" Francis demanded.

I shook my head.

"We're your BFFs, Laz," Milly said.

I stopped in the hall and they left me behind, but soon doubled back to surround me with eager glares. "I had another one of those weird moments, like when I threw up on Mr G. I didn't throw up this time, but I couldn't stay. And Simon could barely walk, so I thought he was better off at home."

"Boring," Milly sighed.

Francis wrapped her arm around mine. "You're too much a virgin for your own good. But it's good to take it one step at a time. Simon will be good for you."

Normality came back into my world when talking to these two. It was like Auntie Bea had never dropped the bomb. But I couldn't shut out my new life for long. Just thinking about the other night reminded me of the fat bulldog and my mind leap—my *significant* ability—and the fact I descended from a line of witches and belonged to a coven. Paranormals shared the air we breathed. Anyone here could be one of them, a non-human, deadly.

"Look, there's Simon. You should talk to him." Milly pushed me forward and the two of them disintegrated into the background as Simon moved through the crowded corridor toward me. What if Simon was one of the many different paranormal species? This was bad. Everyone was a suspect now because according to Auntie Bea there was no way of knowing until they revealed themselves.

"Hi." I gave a timid brief wave and found my eyes scouring his face for obvious signs of non-humanness.

"Hey, Laz. I phoned you over the weekend. A few times."

"I saw. Sorry, I was busy with my aunt. How did you feel Saturday?"

"Wished I was dead. I don't remember much of Friday. Did I totally embarrass myself?"

"Yeah, totally. But you were sweet about it. Was your nose sore?"

He quirked an eyebrow. A perfectly natural human facial tick. "Should it've been?"

"You tripped and face planted onto the kitchen tiles."

He smacked his forehead and arched his head back. "What an idiot."

"In a cute sort of way." Why was I talking like this?

He looked lost for words, but with a glowing face. And the bell saved me.

"I'll see you at lunch," he said.

"Sure. I'll save you a seat by the fish tank."

He leaned in and gave me a soft kiss on the cheek, and a few blossoming flutters below pleasantly surprised me. Simon was one of the good guys, and I had been so stupid to not consider him boyfriend material for all this time. One year he'd been sweet on me, so Milly reckons. All that time and I'd avoided him, dismissing him for the hope of someone sexier. And if those few flutters were anything to go by, I'd been really, really stupid.

Oh boy were my new feelings towards him bad timing. Humans weren't to know. The rules were strict, apparently. No human boys. What about paranormal ones? We'd not got that far in the conversation. I doubted relationships and sex would be a big concern for me anytime soon now that I had to juggle learning my *significant* ability, the laws governing the coven and every detail I could find regarding the paranormal world.

I turned to watch him disappear into his classroom. He was actually kind of cute. And I was a witch, bound by a strict set of laws regarding human and non-human interaction. The truth slammed home like a ball into the catcher's mitt. My luck sucked.

A new door had opened into my life. All these years I'd been fearing the darkness, suffering through the compression of suffocation and believing a terrible bad was heading my way, and it turned out to be something miraculous. Not that I thought it such when Auntie Bea first told me. Twenty-four hours later and I'd done a one eighty. Why did I even need to bother with this school anymore? Witches learned their craft through mentorship and practice, with a handy little companion recipe book on the side. And I was failing practically every class. Then I thought of Milly and Francis and now Simon. I couldn't leave without saying goodbye and graduation was the perfect time. They'd be heading off to college, and I could silently disappear into my new life.

I had so many questions about my mom. Not knowing how to broach the subject without upsetting Auntie Bea, I now had the perfect opportunity to get answers. This had been mom's coven. Someone there could tell me what I craved to know.

I'd remained standing on the spot, thinking all those thoughts for long enough the hall had emptied by the time I snapped out of it. I spun to head for bio but tripped over my first step at the sight of a guy filling the hall. Dressed head to toe in leathers, calf high black leather biker boots, he didn't look like he belonged here. He'd tied his thick dreadlocks, knotted with colorful scraps of material, into a ponytail.

"Here little witch, witch, witch." The smile he shared with his sarcastic song freaked my pulse to thrash speed.

I wasn't used to dealing with the sorts of men Auntie Bea had at her gambling table, and this guy sure was one of those sorts.

"I've got a game for you." He paced one foot in front of the other like a slow lethal dance.

"I have school. Maybe later."

"Did you think I was asking? Poor little witch, doesn't know what to do."

Move, Laz.

"I'd better get to class."

"No powers to protect her. No coven to comfort her. It's almost too easy. And where's the fun in that, ah?"

It took all my strength to turn my back on the freak and walk away, quick step actually. And I did glance over my shoulder twice to see he'd not bothered to increase his steps in line with my pace, which creeped a queasy twist into my gut. What did he know I didn't? Everything, given I knew nothing.

"Aren't you curious about my game?"

"I don't talk to strangers," I semi yelled over my shoulder, my heart choking up my throat.

"Hey, witch girl. Wait a moment."

"I don't think so." I was gaining distance, a bit more and I'd be around the corner. Then I could do a flat out sprint to somewhere. I had yet to think that part through.

"Wait, wait, wait," he crooned. And my legs grew heavy, turning to weights I was forced to drag along like wading through a pool of rapidly setting cement.

"A good little witch always does what she's told." His voice was closer, his big boots treading whisper soft on the tiled floor, but I couldn't turn around to gauge the distance he'd gained because my neck had seized up too.

"You've made a mistake. I'm not a witch." My voice bordered on whimpering, I was that freaking scared. Who the hell was this guy? What the hell was this guy? Maybe that was more important.

"Not yet, bitch. But you will be."

Hair fisted, he yanked my head back hard enough I heard a crack in my neck. The threatening whimper finally escaped, and I bite my lip to force any more traitorous sounds back inside. If only I could plug my nose to stem the foul odor of rotting eggs.

He leaned down, pressing our cheeks together while one hand roamed the side of my body. Luckily, whatever he'd done to me had not reached my arms, leaving me free to slap him away as best I could. Fat lot of good it did when I was pinned to the spot and the hulk was on my back.

He laughed while dancing his hands around my slaps, treating it like a game. "Feisty, eh." He pulled my hair harder, extending my head back further. "I'm getting a hard on with all your struggling," he hissed in my ear through clenched teeth. His hand snaked around my stomach, forcing my body flush against him, thrusting his crotch forward into my ass like he hoped to spear me through my jeans. *Don't you dare make a sound.* He may not be human, but he was male, and males like him got off on the same things, control and fear. They sniffed it out like bloodhounds. My ears were full of my thrashing pulse but I would not make a sound. He was not getting any satisfaction from me.

"Bet you'd scream, huh? Are you a screamer?" He panted his warm breath into my ear. "I bet you are, little witch. I bet you like it dirty. Real dirty," he said, stringing out the words. Then he nipped my ear.

"I think that's enough." A clipped female voice drowned my budding cry.

The guy spun, and because he'd wrapped me tight against him, he spun me with him. A smartly dressed woman stood meters away, one hip flared, arms folded across her chest. Either she worked out her upper body or she wore shoulder pads in her tailored jacket, clinging to her narrow waste and tapering out over a pencil skirt. Both jacket and skirt were a pale lilac, to match her high-heeled sandals. Her sandy colored hair swam in a long wave over her left shoulder, the right side swept back and held in place by a slim gold clip.

"Finders keepers. And lookie here, my hands are all over her. So it looks like you're too late, witch."

The woman smiled. The sort of smile that came with a good dose of acid. "So I see. Yes, your hands are all over her." The acid smile continued. The woman stayed as marble, her expression like liquid nitrogen.

"Friendly advice, witch. Fuck off back to your coven if you don't want me to snap her neck right now." There was an edge to his voice, the slightest hesitancy as he spoke. He was cautious of her, maybe even a little afraid of her. Thank whoever took care of witch souls for that mercy.

"You won't do that."

"Don't fuck with me. You push me and you watch her die."

"You won't kill her." She unfolded her arms slowly like people do when there's a gun in their face and they don't want to excite the trigger finger. "You know who I am, don't you?" She spoke like a school teacher dealing with a small child.

"You're a fucking witch? That's all I need to know. I'll kill the lot of you."

Her calm yet firm voice, exuding an air of authority, maxed the tension in his body. Still plastered to the front of him, it waved into me, sliding my panic a notch up the scale. Desperate people acted on reflex, no logic involved. She'd better do something or stop taunting him, else he may decide he didn't want me after all.

"You want her head on your doorstep? Is that what you want? 'Cause I'm thinking you don't care about this one. You left her unprotected when she's vulnerable. You were hoping someone would clean your scraps." His voice rose on the last sentence, like he'd come up with a puzzle's solution.

"You're right. I don't like leaving scraps behind. I like things ordered and tidy."

"Yeah, see, huh... Now you need to make sure everything's been taken care off. The messy shit's tidied."

"Very astute of you." She pouted, which had the effect of popping her sharp cheekbones. "I'll mention that quality of yours when I next see your master."

He didn't reply. Being tucked up under his chin, I couldn't see his face. A terrible smell wafted across my face. A hint that soon thickened to a suffocating cloud. The guy eased his hold from my waist. "What the fuck?"

Feeling my sudden freedom, I stumbled forward toward the woman and spun to see him smoking, all of him, a thin plume oozing out of every pour.

"What did you do, fucking witch?"

The woman casually strode up beside me. In her heels, she was a foot taller than me. "Did you really think we would leave one of our own unprotected?"

"Fucking bitch. What's going on?" He raised his hands, watched as the black smoke thickened and cracks, bursting with a red glow, appeared between his fingers, running like veins across his hands, then disappearing down the sleeves of his jacket.

I palmed my mouth, horrified but morbidly fascinated by the way the cracks slithered like tiny agitated snakes from his collar, up his neck, then writhed across his face. He staggered backward, mouth wide, screaming in silence as they sliced his cheeks and forehead open. Out poured a crimson glow of syrup like lava down his face. His eye sockets melted onto his cheeks, releasing his eyeballs to droop forward and hang by the optic nerve like a wilting flower. As the man crumbled to his knees, the hall filled with the dying smell of him, burning flesh and putrid decay.

All this should gross me out. Why was I still looking? If he'd not done the things he'd done to me, been someone other than the sick, twisted whatever paranormal he was and this world was still the same sane human world I had grown up in, I would be screaming down the hall about now. Instead, I watched until the guy melted into a crimson glowing gloop, which fizzled and spat and shrunk until there was nothing left but a dark stain on the floor.

"Fun's over, time to go," said the power dressed woman, not a hair out of place or a smudge in her makeup. She used the sort of voice pretentious, class centric, snooty people liked to use on those they deemed of lower rank. Any minute icicles would form around the breath of her words.

"Who are you?"

"Agatha." I accepted her handshake, noting her frosty pink manicured talon like nails. She had a warm hand, not the marble cold feel I'd been expecting.

"And you're part of the coven?"

"Not *the* coven. Your coven. Remember that. A witch never forgets who she belongs to."

Right. This didn't sound good. I now understood Auntie Bea's statement about not being free.

"I have class."

A pencil drawn eyebrow quirked in an artful arch. "You're schooling in this..."—She swept her hand abstractly to encompass the hall—"institution is no longer of any use to you. Now come." She turned and strode away, expecting me to heel like an obedient dog.

"I need more than that if you want me to come with you."

She spun, darting me through the eyes with her glare, then inhaled for composure. "I can only pray your aunt's influence has not ruined you overly. I will reprimand her, of course."

"For what?"

"She failed to alert us of your ascension, which exposed you to danger."

"By ascension you mean..."

She rolled her eyes, pressed her palms together in front of her, fingertips arrowing to the floor. "I hope you will not be a problem, Larnie. There is no patience for problems in our coven."

Agatha was all barbs and prickles, no soft spongy bits to be seen in her personality or slim figure. I'm sure if she stripped right now I'd see nothing but geometric angles.

"What do you mean by reprimand?"

"That's too many questions for a novice. This is wasting time."

"I deserve some answers. You can't just expect me to follow you. A man just—"

"He wasn't a man," she sighed.

"A thing looking like a man just threatened to rape me, then kill me and—"

"I see you share your aunt's flare for dramatics."

The man...paranormal thing was right. She was a bitch.

"What did you do to...him?" I stared down at the stain. How many students would walk over it, not realizing how close they brushed with the other side of reality?

"It was a simple protection enchantment placed upon all witchlings as infants. It lasts for a short while after your ascension. By then a witch should be initiated and accepted within her coven."

"So you kept him talking until the enchantment could take effect."

"The enchantment is triggered by a witch's ascension and activated by the touch of a dark paranormal. I was particularly pleased when I discovered they had sent him to collect you."

"You knew this was going to happen?"

She sighed, wandered her eyes along the lockers against the wall, taking it slow like she was waiting for my hissy fit to pass.

"You knew and you let it happen. You could've collected me early, before he turned up. But you wanted him out the way, so you used me as the bait to ensure your *scraps were cleaned up*."

She slowly shook her head, displaying her inpatients and displeasure rather than to dismiss what I'd said.

"I'm not coming with you."

The sighs of inpatients, head shakes and eye rolling were over. Agatha morphed into a blade of steel, striding toward me, nail guns for eyes. "I can make this painful for you. Very painful."

"I thought my coven was supposed to protect me."

"We don't protect the stupid."

Our eyes locked in a battle I was going to lose because glaring wasn't as effective when you were a head shorter than your opponent. Also, I didn't have any nifty magic like I'm sure she had. I read nothing in her eyes that suggested she was bluffing. Agatha would make it hurt and likely enjoy the pain she inflicted.

I walked around her and headed for the exit. There was no choice, but I sure as hell would not walk behind her.

CHAPTER 5

I don't know what I had been expecting, but it wasn't this. Agatha's harsh exterior and frosted interior, her threats and lethal magic had me believing she would drive me to the gates of hell, not a doll's house on the outskirts of town. It was a square like a house built from Lego with window box planters at every window, blooming bright with rainbow colors. A creeper twisted its way up the face of the building to reach the top story, some of it escaping the lattice to strangle the down-pipe with its green grip. Squeezed between boxed hedges and golf green perfect lawn was a neat row of miniature clumped shrubs speckled with white flowers.

I kept my pace beside her as she clopped along white pavings laid diamond shaped along the lawn. Before we reached the steps, Auntie Bea slipped out of the large entrance doors. Her eyes skimmed Agatha, then settled on me. Never had I seen her act so reserved as she demurely averted her gaze from me to her feet. A sudden injection of heat blanketed my heart and swelled up my throat into my head. Not even the tough sorts that gathered at Auntie Bea's poker table could dim her bluster. But this ice berg beside me had her cowering.

"So this is the coven's hideout," I said to Auntie Bea once Agatha and I had climbed the steps.

Auntie Bea frowned and gave one shake of her head, while Agatha strode past toward the doors. Hand settled on the huge brass hanger, she turned her head to glare at Auntie Bea. "I want you in my office in an hour." Threat delivered, she disappeared inside without another word.

"In you go, kiddo."

"I'd rather stay out here with you. She's one scary witch."

"Just do as she says, Laz, and yall be all right."

"I'm not convinced they're not the enemy."

"Don't fight this, Laz."

"Some paranormal asshole turned up at school threatening me and they knew about it, only they decided not to do anything about it until he'd already had a little fun."

"Yar not hurt, are ya?" Her eyes darted over my body.

"Just my nerves."

She looked down onto the lawn. I knew my Auntie Bea, knew the guilts that haunted her, knew what the emotion looked like on her face. "Was it meant to be a test? To scare me into joining them?"

"No, Laz. It wasn't a test. Nor was there any intention to scare ya. Ya weren't in any real danger. Sometimes Agatha makes decisions for the good of the coven rather than the good of the individual."

"Is she the leader?"

"Our high priestess."

"Then she's a shit high priestess. Number one rule of any leader, always think of the welfare of your followers."

She nodded. "I hear ya, kiddo. That fuck Kalito was a bag of shit, causing our coven a world of problems. And, well, now he ain't."

"I was bait."

"Ya ain't hurt, so don't take it so hard. It was nothing personal. I argued against it, if that's any help."

"Jesus, Auntie Bea. You knew as well."

She heaved the biggest sigh, and it practically deflated her to a shriveled prune. "I'm really sorry, Laz. Sorry for everything. I wanted to do the best by ya mom. But Agatha wanted ya in. She wanted ya here. Right from the start, she wanted ya within the coven walls. But I fought her on that. First time I ever stood up to her, and she's never forgiven me for it. The rest of the elders sided with me 'cause it was Hannah's choice. They wanted to honor her memory."

"Thank Christ for that."

"Ya woulda done good here. Agatha may be a hard bitch, but she's a powerful witch. Ya woulda learned a lot growing up here. So that once ya ascended ya'd already be practicing."

"I don't care about that. I'm even wondering if I want to be a part of this."

"Ya can't turn away, Laz. Ya announced to the paranormal world now. The gift of goddess Diana ain't a simple thing. It's good power."

"Agatha said he wanted me."

"Goblins are greedy little shits."

"That was a goblin?"

"In its glamoured form. Ya wouldn't want to see the real thing. But power of the goddess Diana is particularly attractive to a goblin."

The entrance doors flew wide open and bashed into the interior walls either side, making me jump.

"Ya wanted."

"*That* was my welcome?"

"She's trying to be patient."

"Are you coming?"

"Later, kiddo. Don't wanna push that thin thread of patience too far."

I gave Auntie Bea a long, pleading save me look. As comfort she patted me on the shoulder, then nudged me forward. "I'll sit in the sun awhile. Have a smoke."

I stepped onto high polished wooden floors, in the center an intricately carved inlay in the pattern of a large dog or wolf. Its eyes were embedded with onyx stone. Bloated overhead, a chandelier arrangement of diamond shaped crystals and candles with stalactite wax appeared on the verge of crashing to the floor under the burden of its weight.

A sudden draft of wind swept out of nowhere, pushing at my back before whipping my hair into a spiral as it tornadeoed into a frenzy and twisted off across the floor toward the far room. The portraits on the wall either side of the door tremored in its wake. I guess that was the way I was supposed to head.

I walked into a cavernous room lush with thick carpets, fluffed cushions on plump couches, bookcases instead of walls and palms with dinner plate sized leaves in glossy ceramic pots. Open bay doors extended the room into a greenhouse.

The doors closed by themselves once I stepped farther into the empty room. Behind the large charcoal colored desk sat an empty high backed leather chair. The wind had led me to a vacant room.

I turned toward the door but heard a noise coming from the greenhouse, so headed that way. The place was a palette of green, jungling up the glass walls with creepers and suckers and every other sort of plant and alive with a loamy smell. Peeking inside, I spied the back of the ice berg queen. Was she gardening?

Not wanting to catch her attention, I tip-toed into the greenhouse.

"You may wait for me inside," came her crisp voice.

"This place is amazing."

"Inside, Miss Jennings."

Don't try her patience. I backed out and headed for one of the plump couches. Might as well be comfortable while she finished potting her plants or feeding her earthworms. Although the couches looked comfortable, the cushion was hard, balancing me on its surface rather than swallowing me up into a cradle. No surprises there given the woman who owned them.

She came back into the room carrying a pot full of greenery. At the same moment, a small woman wearing a rainbow kaftan entered the room.

"You know what to do," Agatha said as she came over to take the pot Agatha offered her.

She darted a look at me, then scurried from the door, hugging the pot of greenery to her chest.

Agatha eased herself down into her high-backed chair, placed her elbows on the armrests and steepled her fingers. "This will be your new home until you are proficient in your abilities."

"Um... I don't think so."

Before she could reply with something to match the sharp twist in her expression, I hurried on. "I'm happy where I am. This place isn't so far. I can come here when I need to."

She glided forward, palms placed flat on the desk. "You are a witch."

"Mom wanted me out. Forcing me to become a part of this coven is dishonoring her wishes."

Her eyes slitted.

"But I'm willing to explore my heritage. I don't know why Mom wanted me out. Auntie Bea can't say"—*maybe you could*—"and while I'd love to respect her choice for me, I think I'm old enough to make my own. So I'm willing to learn. I'm willing to join. But I want to have a say in what I do and don't have to do. The first being I want to stay with Auntie Bea. She's done the best for me so far."

She made a derisive snort. I sucked in a breath and continued before my confidence waned. "I'll learn the stuff you want me to learn, but I won't stay here. And I want answers to the questions I ask. I don't want to be fobbed off with some lame excuse about not being ready."

"You'll find no shelter from the truth here. As much as you may beg."

"Good." Things were going well. Perhaps the ice berg queen wasn't as hard-nosed as she first appeared.

"You're to give up your old life."

"But I'm so close to graduating." And failing. "What about my friends?"

"A proficient witch can juggle both, but as a novice you will need to cut all ties."

"It's too sudden. People just don't disappear. They'll think someone's murdered me."

"And will forget you in time."

"Geez, thanks."

"There are reasons for our rules. It keeps both worlds separate and safe."

She needed to give me a good compromise for giving up my friends. "When will I be able to do magic?"

"You have the gift of goddess Diana."

"Does that include magic?"

"Is that not enough?"

"It's stomach churning. It would be good to do some real magic, like spells."

"If our mother permits."

That was a weird statement. Before I could ask anymore, the woman in the kaftan reappeared, this time carrying a tray with a china pot and one cup, which was rude considering there were two of us in the room. Not that I drank tea. She set the tray on the table, then dipped her head at Agatha before leaving the room again. Her timidity said a lot about the high priestess.

Agatha leaned forward, reaching for the teapot. "You're bold. A good trait to have. Presumptuous, which is easily remedied. It's your ignorance I find appalling. Again that's remedied, but it will take a great deal of effort on your behalf."

"I'm willing to put in the work." It was the goblin that did it for me, his masochistic behavior, and my choking fear. I had never been a victim of anything, not even rumors, unless you wanted to include vomiting on Mr G. Nor had I experienced that sort of fear. And I was damn well going to make sure I would never experience either again.

"You better be, Miss Jennings." She finished pouring the tea, which came out an interesting poo color brown and sludgy like pureed soup. Not something I'd be willing to drink. Thank god for the one tea cup.

Tea poured, she rose out of her seat and came around to lean on the desk, teacup in hand. "Our path is difficult, Miss Jennings. You must be firm in your resolve to learn and achieve."

"Oh, I am. Believe me."

"The world you are about to enter is not for the weak. You must take this." She handed me the cup of poo colored tea.

"What is this?"

"Your dakeu."

"Is this like a celebratory, glad-you're-one-of-us drinks." I delicately sniffed the rim of the cup to smell sodden clothes left in the gutter.

"It will send you on your hidden path."

"Do I really need to drink this? How about if I just meditate?"

"You must draw on the animae to follow the path. But this is not something the living can do."

"This is going to *kill* me?"

"Mors Viventium. The living death, Miss Jennings. Not a true death. It is a journey you must take if you wish to move through your ascension and manifest your true powers and your true path."

"But I thought you were going to teach me all that."

"But your soul must learn. It must recognize that which it truly is. No text books, teachings or spells will assist with that."

"What will I see on this path?"

"It's an individual path, so I can't say. For some there is nothing at all."

"So I risk seeing nothing by drinking this...slurry"—it was the politest word I could think of at short notice.

"You have the gift of the goddess Diana. I doubt you are a rummy." She said the last word with a distasteful twang in her tone.

"A what?"

"A witch with insignificant ability." She rose from her position leaning against the desk. "You needn't worry, yours will not be such a disastrous fate. I will leave you. The dakeu is a private affair. I suggest you find a comfortable place to lie down before you begin. It could be a rough ride."

I halted her before she disappeared out the door. "Go easy on my aunt. She did the best she could."

She gave me that snooty what-would-you-know look, after the how-dare-you-speak-to-me-like-that look. I diverted my gaze to my cup of pureed poo as she left. This was going to make me vomit.

Before I chickened out, I headed for the couches and was about to toss the fluffed cushions onto the floor when an image of Agatha pinch lipped and severe browed at seeing her expensive cushions carelessly discarded had me hurl them onto the next couch over. I sat heavily but made barely a dent in the resistant foam and gave the cup one more look. *Just do it.* Nose pinched between my fingers, I sculled a good half a cup before I had to come up for air. Amazingly, it had a neutral flavor. I finished it in case half wasn't enough, then placed the cup on the floor and laid down. *Rough ride, huh?*

Ages later I was still lying on the couch staring at the ceiling rose, not feeling much at all, not even an upset stomach. Perhaps it didn't work. I sprung up. *Did this mean I wasn't really a witch?* That I was the other kind. What was the name she used? I rolled to the side and looked down at the cup. Yep, it was empty. So where was my dakeu?

I straightened out on the couch again and closed my eyes. I sucked at meditation. Right now was the worst time to try. Would they kick me out if I turned out to be a...what was it again? Why should I care? Agatha's a bitch, and who wants to be caught up in such a horrible world? Just when I'd met a nice guy, too. And poor Milly and Francis. It hadn't taken me long to trade them in for some spells.

I sat and swung my legs over the edge. It wasn't working. I'd go find Agatha and tell her she was wasting her time. I stood, but the blood in my veins didn't follow, instead pooled at my feet. Thinking I took a step forward, I actually found myself on my knees, head spinning like a Yo-Yo. To make it stop, I sandwiched it between my elbows and groaned with the vertigo feeling, Yo-Yoing my stomach as well. That pureed poo was lethal.

After a while, the dizziness subsided, as did my stomach flips. At least I didn't vomit. I gave the room one quick scan to make sure no nearby animal had been the reason for my dizzy queasiness. Nope, this was definitely the fault of the pureed poo. Once I felt sure I could stand without going down again, I got to my feet and made it to the door, about to open it when a funny sucking sound came from behind.

It was something about the plants. The green on the leaves was changing color to a dark brown. Not just changing color, being sucked out of the leaves from the tips to the stem. It spared no plant. With the color gone, the leaf withered and crinkled, the infection spreading down the stem and into the soil, which smoked green. This was aging full speed. And also likely my dakeu. It had worked.

I left the door closed and inched toward the greenhouse. Agatha had warned of a rough ride. Maybe I should go lay on the couch and ride this one out in my head. Fascination kept me walking.

All the plants had died. Died so bad there was nothing left in the pots. I bent to touch the green smoking soil when it hissed and glooped a puddle of greenish brown onto the rim of the pot. The hissing sound turned to stereo. All the pots were making the noise. I was turning a circle looking at them all when the glass wall at the back of the greenhouse imploded, vacuumed outward into the garden, only the garden was no longer there, just a black cavity. The suction intensified, ripping up the soil, pots and the band in my hair so that it whipped free, sucked horizontally around my face. Then my feet went. But I didn't land on my ass. Instead, I disappeared into the void like everything else in the greenhouse.

I felt the wind whip my skin. Over the roar I heard the rip of my jacket seams, then my sleeves disappeared into the nothingness. One by one, I lost my shoes. And just when I thought I'd lose my jeans as well, the wind died, and I landed on my ass onto burned ground, billowing soot as a cloud up to my chest. The greenhouse was gone, the doll's house too.

If there was a sun, a dense gloom had shrouded it, tinging every-thing a rich brown so nothing grew. I'd landed in the realm of the dead. This was my soul's purpose? Just great.

"Help." A man's voice echoed through the still air.

"Hello." It was like my voice reverberated the air around me, oscillating every molecule until the air itself became my voice, forcing me to shield my ears.

"Are you still there?" His voice came again.

I was nervous about answering, not wanting my words to assault me again. I climbed to my feet and moved toward his call, slowly as there was little here to distinguish up from down, everything varying shades of dead brown, making the uneven ground hard to define.

"Where are you?"

"I'm here?" I replied, then clamped my hands over my ears as my words turned to a storm that tore down onto me.

"Come find me," he called, his voice the plea of a child.

A shape emerged in my periphery. Like bricks stacked by invis-ible hands, it grew out of the murky brown, pillars spearing into the gloom, walls soaring high above me. A temple without a ceiling, an ancient place of worship with no door to bar my entrance. The soft edges of a light reached out from somewhere deep inside like a welcoming hand.

"Please find me." No longer somewhere out there, the male voice was now in my head, tickling at my conscious. Was this a trap? Agatha had said nothing about this being a test, only that I needed to follow the path, learn my soul's journey. I stood at the entrance, the soft rays of the light dancing across my torso. It was the only light in this dead place, and I, like a moth, felt compelled to follow it inside. Maybe it was the voice invading my head.

"I need you," the voice said, shifting an octave lower to bedroom sensual—or it could've been my wicked imagination.

I wove around a labyrinth of walls, etched with intricate designs.

So ensnared by the light, I didn't bother to stop to understand the patterns. They could be significant to my dakeu, but the light, the voice crooned me on.

"You are the only one that can help me." The voice was a purr through my body.

Then it was there in front of me, an intense brightness, like the sun. I shielded my eyes with my forearm.

"Take it."

"I can't see." My voice savaged me from all sides. I turned away from the light to protect my ears.

"You must...touch it. You are the only one."

I can't. I stretched my hand toward the light, felt the furnace resist me like a shield. I dared press farther, caught in some mesmeric spell of curiosity. The bright halo warbled and swayed bending away from my palm. The temperature cooled a fraction. Perhaps I could do this. For what? The male voice in my head abandoned me. Still, I felt a tightening in my gut, an excitement notching my breath, an inexplicable need to plunge inside the glow of light. Something waited in there for me, called to me, beyond the voice. Something, something that was in the light but also deeper, deeper...inside of me.

A hard force propelled me backward, so swiftly I'd left my breath where I'd been standing. No warning, no flash of movement. One minute I was standing there, driven by the mysterious voice inside my head before being consumed by my own desire to touch, take whatever lay concealed below the intense light. The next a violence swept me away, crushed me against the pillar, pressed hard into the front of my body, so I was sandwiched in a suffocating hold, my arms strapped beside me.

Finally, my breath caught up with me, but the pressure at my chest made it impossible to take more than shallow breaths. The force had contours, the mold of a man, one thigh pressed between my legs, chest heaved up against my own. The intense light turned him into an imposing silhouette looming over me. I squinted up at him, my head half turned, but could make out none of his features.

My breath hitched with every inch he lowered his head until his breath was on my cheek. The lower he dipped, the higher my pulse fled. Lower and lower to my neck. I wriggled, testing the binds he created with his body, only to feel him tighten the pressure by pressing himself harder against me, his leg inching higher between my thighs. Did I just gasp? I dared not utter a squeak after being assaulted by my punishing voice every time I uttered a sound. He inhaled deep, his nose teasing feather soft along my skin. "I will not forget your scent."

A deep voice. A dreamy, romantic bedroom voice if it didn't have the timbre of a threat. Bad, bad girl. I shouldn't think this was sexy. Nothing about the way he'd forced me backward, pinioned me in place like I was a life-sized doll and not a human with fragile bits, spoke of a man looking to be friendly. This was my dakeu, not real at all. Then why did I feel the cold, hard pillar at my back, the firm pressure of his body flush along mine and, geez, I didn't want to focus on it, the anchor of his thigh...down there? *Dampen the hell down, pussy cat.* Was I this desperate for a shag? Was that all my soul could think about?

My heart went thump-dee-dump in rapid timing, then bang bang bang when I felt a soft, wet warmth on my neck like a...tongue. Did he have his tongue on my neck? Not licking, just holding it there like he was savoring the spot. Holy crap, this could be dangerous, possibly lethal, weirdly erotic. There weren't just sparks in my nether region, more like a ton of dynamite thrown into a shipping container worth of fireworks going off.

"You won't win. I'll make sure of that." He whispered into my neck, his lips brushing my skin. *Focus, Laz.* And not on those lips, not on him. What did I need to learn? What was my soul telling me beyond the obvious?

I went to speak, but clammed my mouth shut again as my ears still pricked and smarted from the last time I said something. Why did he get to say everything and not suffer the same effect?

His fingers gripped my chin, tilted my face up to his, but his features were all shadows and darkness thanks to the intense light behind us. "I'll see you burn for eternity if you dare take what's mine. Remember that." Looming mere inches from me. "Witch." The tickle of his breath skimmed my lips. Said like he'd already stripped my flesh and was feasting on my vitals.

"Who are you?" I whispered, unable to stay quiet any longer after all the threats he got to share.

"I'm the predator you need to fear."

"Miss Jennings."

My dakeu blinked out in a second. Agatha's office warbled back into view. First the ceiling rose and then her face, peering down at me with its usual frosty expression. She folded her arms, impatience bleeding from her every pore. I rose halfway from the couch, then had to slow and allow my blood pressure time to catch up. I was on the couch. At what point had I returned to the couch? Had I even left the couch?

"Wow, that was...intense." I sniffed at my jacket sleeve and smelt charcoal. I lifted the front of my shirt and sniffed that as well, smelling something very different, something very male. "How real is the dakeu supposed to be?"

"It's a journey within your mind, tapping into your imagination."

I liked my imagination very much.

"I hope you learned something valuable, Miss Jennings. It will guide you on your path." She turned and strode back toward her desk with short steps to accommodate her pencil skirt. I learned a lot, like I needed some fun. But the dark, threatening stranger was a puzzle as was my draw to the intense light and what lay within. And who belonged to the voice?

"Your journey must begin." Agatha glided into her seat and glared at me, still slouched on her couch. "Whether you're ready or not."

When I wasn't riding a camel through the Rajasthani desert, white water rafting the rapids on the Zambezi, bungee jumping off the Victoria Falls bridge or hiking the peeks in Pakistan, I was piloting a twin prop into remote aboriginal communities in northern Western Australia or staring down a microscope in a laboratory.

Now somewhat tamed, the microscope has morphed into a computer and I spend more time plotting dire situations for my protagonists than being in them myself.

I am the author of books that won't stay normal.

facebook.com/terinaadamsbooks

instagram.com/terinaadamsauthor

amazon.com/~/e/B088NQVG7L

bookbub.com/profile/2890827497

goodreads.com/terinaadams